To my good friend,
Alex Bussell

You are a very bright young man,

thank you for your kindness to a "Yank" far across the oc

Hope you lex.

Kind re

Joe B

July 14, 2003

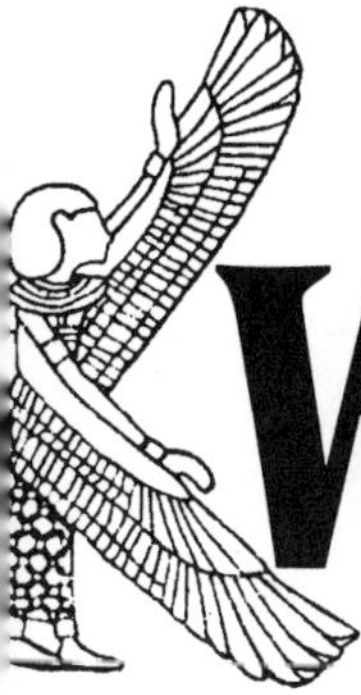

WAITING FOR AGNES

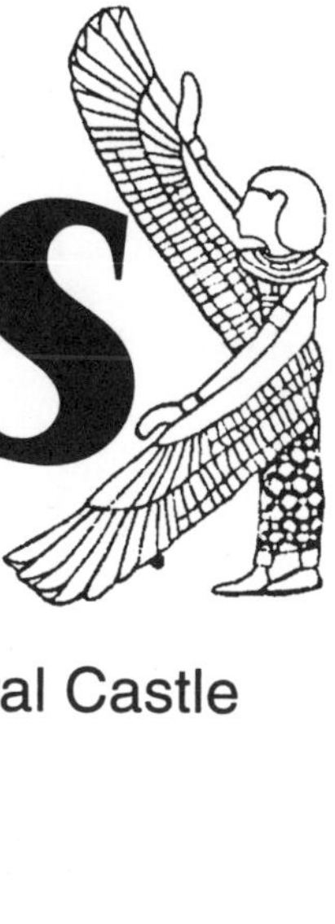

Inspired by the true story of Coral Castle

Written by:

Joe Bullard

Paris • Honduras • Argentina

This book is dedicated to the memory of Ed Leedskalnin, a genius. He displayed the knowledge of a secret lost science in the massive stones of Coral Castle. With his stubby little hands, he recorded his devotion to the one love of his life, Agnes Scuffs, his "Sweet Sixteen" at Coral Castle, a stone masterpiece. He is the only person in recorded history who understood the secret of the Great Pyramid.

Mayan Swastika.

This is a type of Swastika that can be found on the Mayan Ruins in Honduras and Mexico.

Where was Atlantis?

Edgar Cayce gave the position in a reading done in 1932. In reading #364-3, the "sleeping prophet" said: "The continent of Atlantis existed between the Gulf of Mexico on the one hand and the Mediterranean upon the other.

"Evidences of this lost civilization are to be found in the Pyrenees and Morocco, British Honduras, Yucatan and America. There are some protruding portions... that must have at one time or another been a portion of this great continent.

"The British West Indies, or the Bahamas, are a portion of same (Atlantis) that may be seen in the present. If the geological survey would be made in some of these especially, or notably in Bimini and in the Gulf Stream through this vicinity, these may be even yet determined."

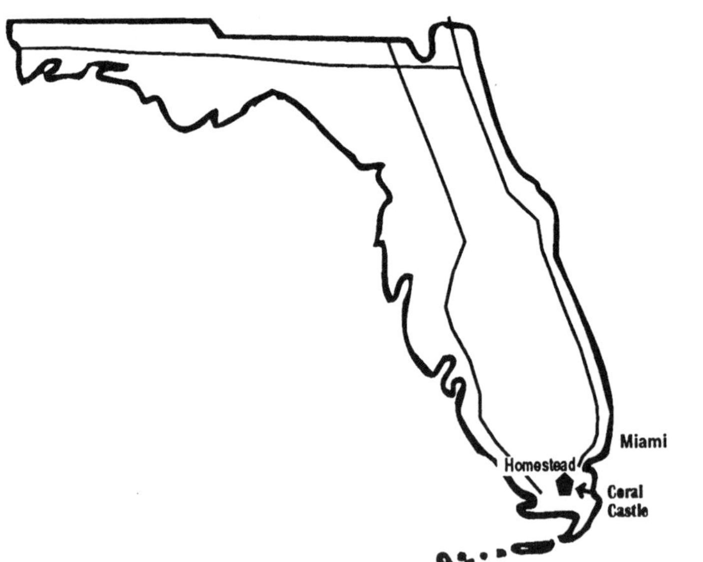

Preface

This book is based on the true story of Coral Castle, in Homestead, Florida. It's about the man who built this castle, Ed Leedskalnin. The mysterious part is, how did a 5 foot tall man, weighing 100 pounds, cut, smooth and lift, huge coral stones weighing tons? And, why? Ed claimed his only tools were a shovel, a wheel barrow with no body, a small block and tackle, and truck springs he sharpened into wedges. These tools can still be seen in Ed's tool room at the castle.

Florida sits on a base of "Oolitic limestone." The tiny spheres making up this limestone are named ooliths, which are tiny grains of sand formed around the secretions of animals named "corals." The oolitic limestone is extremely porous, fragile, and hard to work with. If you try to cut it, it tends to break off easily. I'm explaining this, because understanding the difficulty, makes what Ed did here seem even more impossible.

In the east wall of Coral Castle, Ed put up a 9 ton (18,000 lbs.) swinging gate. Somehow, Ed found the stone's center of gravity, then drilled a perfect, finger-sized hole, straight down the center; then he ran a rod down the hole and connected it to the wheel bearings of a 1920 Ford Model A truck. The gate is so perfectly balanced on this gear box, that, using one finger, the gate swings around itself easily, like a revolving door.

Scientists and engineers, who X-rayed this gate, said that to duplicate this engineering feat today, would require the use of laser technology. And yet, Ed always claimed that he made all his tools from a junkyard (it's known that he had no heavy equipment; and besides, tests have proven that most of today's heavy equipment cannot move Ed's stones).

The average weight of Coral Castle's stones is greater than those used in the Great Pyramid. Several of Ed's stones are taller than those of Stonehenge. A study of the immense size and weight of the coral Ed cut and moved here, establishes Coral Castle as an authentic wonder of the world. Ed used over 1,100 tons of coral to build the castle and the objects in it.

Ed's castle has been compared to Stonehenge and the Great Pyramid because of Ed's precise stone cutting, fitting, and the size and weight of the stones. Ed only worked late at night, so no one ever saw him moving the great stones. Ed had a sixth sense that alerted him when people tried to catch him working. It's debatable whether or not Ed allowed the photographs (showing him at work) in this book to be taken.

If this story interests you, I gave more information in the "About this book" section. If you decide to join me on this journey, you'll be seeing Ed at work; for my money, Coral Castle should be the 8th wonder of the world. But sadly, it's been forgotten.

Joe Bullard

ABOUT THIS BOOK

Dear Reader, since you've laid down your hard earned money for this book, and decided to spend your valuable time reading it, I thought I'd tell you something about it.

As you listen to these words in your head, I hope it sounds like Ed Leedskalnin is talking to you. I spent 15 years, studying his books, trying to find the formula for how he would speak to us today. If someone takes the time to write about their life in books, they weave a pattern, leaving behind a trail for us to follow. Like a sidewinder snake, moving on the desert sand, you can follow the S marks and see where it's going.

The tricky part to following Ed's S marks, is that sometimes, he was like the wily coon, who, when chased by the dog pack, he crosses many streams, and runs up trees, to throw the dogs off his scent. Ed is a very private person; I say is, because for me, his spirit still lives in the house of huge stones he created at Coral Castle. Ed loved to keep people guessing about how he cut and moved the huge, jagged, delicate coral stones.

As a child, I was fascinated by the Great Pyramid and I read many books on it's construction. I believe there once existed a lost science for the raising of great stones.

In the fall of 1984, at Coral Castle, I found the greatest voice for the existence of this lost science. While watching television one night, I saw an episode of the series "In Search Of" narrated by Leonard Nimoy. The show featured Coral Castle. At the time, I was the Director of Communications for Lake City Community College in Lake City, Florida.

I was off the next day, and so I jumped into my 1984 Datsun 280 ZX, and literally flew down the Florida Turnpike to Homestead, Florida. Here began my addiction and fascination with Coral Castle. If you are curious about ancient stone cultures, then I think this story will fascinate you.

If you don't like these kinds of things, then don't waste your money on this book. (This is how Ed talked in his books; he was always polite, but he did speak his mind). But, if you're mainly drawn to odd love stories, and you're too cheap to spend your money, you might borrow this book from a romance friend, (if you have any romance friends, or friends at all); it's not a bad love story, just skip the parts about moving big rocks and you'll get along fine.

The difficulty with this story is that most of the people who were close to Ed have been dead for many years. However, I was fortunate, on one of my many trips to Homestead, to meet a man who owned a gas station and fruit business, on Key West Highway. Oddly, his last name was Bullard.

Mr. Bullard said that, sometimes, Ed would ride his bicycle from Coral Castle to his gas station and pick up milk, soda crackers and sardines.

When I met Mr. Bullard, he was quite elderly and got around with the aid of a walking cane. The old gas station was closed, but it was an interesting looking building, so I pulled off Key West Highway for a closer look. I was peering into the dusty front window, when a long red Buick pulled up. Mr. Bullard got out slowly with his cane and walked over to me.

I explained my mission and was surprised to find that Mr. Bullard had owned the gas station for the entire time that Ed had lived in Florida City, and later, Homestead. Mr. Bullard took out his key, opened the door, and invited me in. He put his cane down and took a seat in a green, cracked leather easy chair behind an old oak desk. Behind him, were dusty green books, containing the records of his many years in business.

There were only a few people that Ed trusted to confide in, and Mr. Bullard was one of them. (The other person was the farmer who found Ed on the side of the road). To ease the story telling process, I combined the character of Mr. Bullard, and the farmer, together. His name is Herman Harmless in the book.

I was unable to interview the farmer and relied on the historical writings in Coral Castle's museum to tell parts of the story. Sometimes, when we talked, Mr. Bullard would drift off from the story, asking me questions like: "Where'd you say your family was from? Georgia? Yeah, well, you know, originally, there were three Bullard boys; they came over here from Ireland–probably horse thieves or womanizers, running from the law I'd guess."

I would then have to steer him back to Ed's story. For this story, I chose to use some of the material that I got from conversations with Mr. Bullard. Maybe I chose it because of the feeling of a remote family connection; or maybe I chose it because he's dead now, and he can't come back and sue me, or call me a liar for what I'm saying in this book.

So, here's what I did. I took all the known facts of what happened here at Coral Castle, and I blended them with the things Mr. Bullard told me.

I changed the names of the supporting characters in this story because I was unable to interview them. As I said, most of these people were dead. I didn't want any living relatives to sue me because maybe I misquoted something somebody said. This story is a blend of possible fiction (I qualify this because I don't know, it could've happened this way; since I'm not sure, I figure it has a chance of being true) and the real events.

I did ten years of research and reading Ed's books. I began writing the story in February of 1994 and finished in February of 1999, so it took me a good five years to get it from my head on to paper. I continued reading Ed's books even as I wrote the story, to keep in touch with his voice spirit.

During the writing process, I kept Ed's photo by my bedside; I took a long look at it before I went to sleep; I tried to program my mind to dream about Ed's life. If you're thinking about writing something, be prepared to live with it 24 hours a day until you finish it.

Writing is a lonely project, and sometimes, I found myself living his life and not mine. But if you want to do something, and do it well, like Ed, or Ghandi, you should get obsessed with it, and so I did. The romance of this story, and that it has never been told, is what inspired me the most.

Ed wrote and published his own books. I like what he said on the first page of the first book. Ed wrote:

AUTHOR'S PREFACE

Dear Reader, if for any reason, you do not like the things I say in this little book, I left just as much space as I used, so you can write your own opinion opposite it, and see if you can do any better.

The Author
COPYRIGHT,1936,
By Edward Leedskalnin

Ed left every other page blank. This book is available in the museum and gift shop at Coral Castle. I hope you like this book; if you do, please write or call me and ask any questions you might have. If you don't like it, you can come down here, research it, and like Ed said, write your own opinion.

P.S. I like to read newspapers, so I wrote this book using a newspaper format, with short choppy paragraphs. It's been proven that long, unbroken paragraphs are hard to read and bad for your eyes. Maybe Mark Twain or Proust can get away with it, but I wanted to make this book easy to read. This way, if you don't like it, at least you can't say it was "hard to read."

If you don't like newspapers, you better skim through the book, and read a few sections, before you take out that wallet; as of yet, there's no law requiring refunds for badly written books, so, you were warned.

In 1984 Coral Castle was listed as a genuine National Historical Monument. I'm going to give some further details of Ed's life at the end of the book. If you're moved by this story, and are thinking of visiting Coral Castle, come on down, you'll never regret it.

As Ed's story unfolds in these pages, you'll meet a man who displayed his deep love for one woman, Agnes Scuffs, in the giant stones of Coral Castle.

CAUTION: There is some violence in this book, but no sex or cursing; Ed loved children and I wanted them to be able to read it.

Sincerely,
Joe Bullard

WAITING FOR AGNES

First Printing

ISBN 0-9673133-0-9

CORAL CASTLE SURVIVES HURRICANE ANDREW

HOMESTEAD, FL. 1992 (Press release): Herman Harmless, an old man, sat at his favorite table near the window in the Myna Bird diner. Herman liked it here because he could watch the traffic go by on Key West Highway.

It was August 1992. Herman was reading the Miami Herald newspaper. The headline story was about the devastation of Hurricane Andrew, one of Florida's worst in history. Andrew's 200 mph winds had leveled most of South Florida. The Myna Bird was one of the few places that had restored it's power. Herman was having lunch with his best friend Lamar McClung.

"Well, I'll be," Herman said.

"What is it?" Lamar asked. He was reading a paperback book titled "Space Invaders."

"Coral Castle didn't get hurt by the storm," Herman said. "Listen to this headline: America's Stonehenge stands through Andrew. HOMESTEAD, FL. (AP): After Ed Leedskalnin built Coral Castle, he said he'd never need fire or hurricane insurance. Hurricane Andrew did it's best to make him a liar, but Ed's coral walls were loyal to him until the end.

"Ed's 1,100 ton Coral Castle still stands, suffering only a few gashes here and there from fallen trees downed by the storm's severe winds. Barbara Agramonte, manager at Coral Castle, the strange tourist attraction whose owners call it 'America's Stonehenge' said: 'Probably the safest place you could've been in the storm was right here inside Coral Castle."

"Isn't that something," Lamar said. "Ed's been dead over forty years and still making the news."

"Yep, seems like yesterday," Herman said.

Someone put a quarter in the old Wurlitzer juke box and played three Glenn Miller songs and one of them was Ed's favorite, "At Last." As the song played, Herman thought back to the old days, when he was selling fruit and souvenirs to the tourists passing by Key West Highway.

The Myna Bird hadn't changed much over the years, except the owner, Imogene Conley, who everyone called "Imo," had retired and passed it on to her two daughters. Herman Harmless could come in here and feel the past like no other place, except his store.

Imo had named the place "Imo's Diner," when she first opened. But one day, a lady brought her a sick baby Myna bird because she knew Imo loved animals.

And Imo nursed him and fed him from behind the counter. People started coming by for lunch and to see how the baby bird was doing. Tourists passing through liked the food and would go home and tell their friends about it. But they'd say: "Oh, I can't remember the name of the place, but just ask around for the place where the myna bird is."

The tourists would come in and tell Imo how they had hunted for the myna bird place. That gave Imo the idea to change the name to make it easier for the tourists.

Imo had an artist draw a myna bird on the glass front door, and he drew words coming out of the bird's mouth reading: "Good food, cheap prices. All my friends eat here."

Herman drank the last part of his sweet tea. Groaning, he stretched his arms back: "Oh, I ate too much, but that corn bread was good. Well, I'm going over to the old store and put this newspaper article on Coral Castle in my scrapbook. You getting lunch today?"

"Yeah, it's my turn."

"Okay, I'll see ya' later," Herman said, and he got up to leave. Herman put on his thin, green-tinted, aviator-style sun glasses, and he stepped out into the bright south Florida sun. He got in his long, four door, 1923 Ford touring car. It was burgundy with a painted black top and wire-spoke wheels, with wide white sidewalls and a spare tire fixed to the back.

Herman pulled out onto Key West Highway, headed south, and he drove a couple of hundred yards and stopped at a red light. Glancing off to his right, he saw Coral Castle, standing just off the highway.

It's walls were partly covered with thick vegetation, where it stands at 28655 Key West Highway, amid tall, skinny palm trees. A coral block sign with black plastic letters out front read: "Coral Castle, America's Stonehenge."

Herman was glad now, as he looked at the sign and he thought about Ed, that he'd never sold this car; it had too many memories in it. He had just bought the car, he remembered, the night he almost ran over Ed Leedskalnin, lying on the side of a dirt road—back, when was it? 1920? Yeah, somewhere around there.

Herman remembered how everyone had wondered why Ed had built Coral Castle, at the edge of the Florida Everglades, in the small farming town of Homestead, located seventeen miles southwest of Miami.

The light changed and Herman drove a couple of blocks and then turned right and pulled into his old gas station and souvenir shop where he used to sell Indian River fruit. The painted sign over the tin roofed porch read: "The Paradise Fruit Co."

And painted below that, was a lovely, blonde haired girl in a red bathing suit, sunning herself on the beach, surrounded by mangos and watermelons.

Herman liked antiques and old houses. He had gone to college in Gainesville at the University of Florida. He studied public relations, with a minor in archaeology. He got his degree but he wasn't worried about finding a job; he always knew he'd come back to Homestead and go into business in something dealing with plants and sales.

Sometimes on Sundays, after lunch at the Myna Bird, Herman liked to go over to his old business. He'd sit behind his oak, roll-top desk, and look over his old papers, photos and mementos from the old days.

People in Homestead wondered how Ed might've cut the huge stones. But nobody ever saw Ed working because he only worked late at night. Some folks tried to sneak up on him and watch him work.

But Ed had a sharp sixth sense and it was amazing how he could know when people were trying to catch him at work. The only time his sixth sense might not be working was if he was real tired or he'd been drinking—then he was like Sampson without his hair.

"Most tourists," Herman said, "who come down here and tour the castle, and most of the local folks who drive by Coral Castle every day, don't realize what it really is. People have come to expect strange things in Florida, everything here is geared towards fantasy and entertainment."

Most people, Herman said, want to know how Ed built the castle and why he built it. They're also curious about a strange looking face, imbedded in a mound of coral, and surrounded by large and small sea shells, that Ed sculpted near his laboratory.

The face is made of smoothed coral. Some people say it looks like a monkey and some say it looks like an alien. The small, fish-looking mouth, with thin lips, is half-open. The nose is blank, except for two breathing holes.

The eyes were once only blank sockets, but now there are two yellow marbles staring out. A playful little boy on one of the castle tour years ago, stuck them into the eye sockets and nobody could get them out, so they just left them in there.

Usually, every couple of years or so, Herman said, I'll get a call from a newspaper reporter from the

Miami Herald, who wants to interview me about Coral Castle. One time, a reporter asked Ed if he levitated the stones out of the ground.

Ed said, "Well, sir, I'm sure there's a reasonable amount of truth in that—just like a reasonable amount of fleas is good for a dog—it keeps him from brooding about being a dog."

Ed could be real vague when it came to avoiding questions he didn't want to answer.

There were some things about Ed that Herman had never told anyone about; things Ed said he could tell one day if he wanted to, but Ed would prefer they remain untold. But Herman was getting old now, and it seemed to him that his beloved friend Ed Leedskalnin, had been forgotten by the world.

Herman figured Ed was the only man who had come along and disproved the theory, claimed by most Egyptologists, that it took a hundred thousand slaves, dragging stones weighing tons on a sled, a hundred years to build The Great Pyramid.

But here, Herman said, in the massive stones of Coral Castle, jagged coral stones that have been smoothed into comfortable chairs and beds, is the living proof that Ed had expertly displayed a lost science used in pyramid building.

A few days had passed now, since Hurricane Andrew had left nearly everything in Homestead, except for Coral Castle, in a big mess.

Carl Swisher had been assigned to cover the hurricane for the Enterprise, a Homestead newspaper. Carl was finishing his report after having breakfast at the Myna Bird Diner. Carl overheard some locals in the diner talking about how the Coral Castle had survived the storm. Carl was new to the area and hadn't heard of Coral Castle. Carl got interested in the story and the people told him to contact Herman Harmless because Herman knew the story better than anybody. And, they told him, most of the people who were around in Ed's day had moved or were dead now.

Herman Harmless, Lamar McClung, and "Lucky" Mizell were about the only people still alive that were close to Ed. So Carl called Herman and Herman agreed to be interviewed at Coral Castle the next morning at nine o'clock.

The castle was closed to the public on this humid August day in 1992, to clean up the downed trees. But Herman told Barbara Agramonte, the castle manager, about the interview and she let them do it inside the castle. Herman told her he wanted to get the feel of the old place as he was telling the story.

Herman pulled up in the castle parking lot in his 1923 Ford touring car. Carl Swisher saw him and he walked over and introduced himself. Herman was wearing a Stetson "Gambler" style straw hat, and carrying an old worn leather travel bag that held some of the things that Ed had left him when he died.

Carl and Herman walked up to the front entrance. They stopped to look at some old newspapers encased in a clear glass window unit attached to the stone wall. The old newspapers and photos showed Ed at the various stages of when he was working on Coral Castle.

And in the middle of these other newspaper articles, Carl Swisher saw a picture of the rock singer Billy Idol. Idol, dressed in black leather, was shown reclining with his guitar in the large crescent, moon-shaped stone that Ed had put up on top of the east castle wall.

The newspaper article headline underneath Idol's picture read: "IDOL PUTS CASTLE INTO HIGH GEAR." And the caption under the picture read: "Punk rocker Billy Idol records music video for "Sweet Sixteen" his latest release, at Coral Castle."

"Billy Idol made a video here?" Carl asked.

"Oh, yeah," Herman said. "He went crazy when he saw this place. He wrote the song "Sweet Sixteen" because that's what Ed used to call his girlfriend. I don't remember what year it was now. I'll ask Barbara when we get in."

When they got inside, Carl was looking around, and, up on the wall, he saw color pictures of Billy Idol, dressed in black leather, with his shock of bleach-blonde spiked hair, walking around inside the castle, posing for various pictures on the stone objects inside. Up over the pictures, written on white poster paper with a black, felt tip pen, was: "Billy Idol sings of Coral Castle."

"Barbara," Herman asked, "what year did Billy Idol come down here and make that video?"

"Oh, gosh, Herman, I'm not sure. I think it was around 1986 or '87."

"That is wild," Carl said, looking at Idol's photos. "Billy Idol—I bet he got some stares around here with that hair-do, didn't he?"

"Oh yeah," Herman said. "But I met him and talked to him; he was a nice guy. He said his hair and the way he dressed was just his stage act. He asked me a lot of questions about Ed and this place. He was fascinated by it.

"He said being in here felt like you were on the moon or something. A lot of people say that when they're here. Well, let's go into the castle," Herman said. They went through the glass side door of the gift shop and out into the castle grounds.

"Carl, come on, I'm going to show you one of the most significant things that Ed put here."

Herman headed for the north end of the castle and stopped in front of a large block of stone with three smaller stones on top of it.

"You'll notice," Herman said, "on top of this stone, Ed placed two small stones, and then, on top of that, he put the inverted V-shaped stone. That configuration of three stones was a mystery to me for a long time. Now, when he was giving a tour, Ed would explain about this thirty ton block of stone being the heaviest he ever moved.

"Then, he'd point to the stones on top and say, 'So I put these stones on top as a king's crown because it's the "king" stone of the castle.'

"But he wasn't telling the whole story behind it. Come on, and I'll show you another thing." But, as Herman started to walk back in, he thought of something, and stopped and turned around: "Wait a minute—Carl, let me ask you something—do you believe in UFO's?"

"Yes sir, I do. I've always believed in them."

"Do you know about Roswell?"

"Oh sure. I've read all the documents about it."

"Did it happen, or was it a government cover up?"

"I think it was a blatant cover up."

"Smart man; Roswell was a cover up Carl. Since Ed died, I've made it my hobby to study a lot of things he talked about."

Herman walked over near Ed's tool room and stopped at a blob-shaped, triangular configuration of coral, that looked something like an altar.

Embedded in the coral altar, was a bunch of sea shells. Embedded down near the bottom, right above a big conch shell, was the smooth coral, strange looking alien face, with yellow-marble eyes, that everyone was curious about.

Herman kneeled down on one knee for a better view and Carl knelt with him. Herman ran his fingers over the face, then moved his hand.

"Run your fingers over the face Carl," Herman told him, and Carl did it. "Can you believe that Ed smoothed this jagged coral stone until if feels like glass?"

"Amazing," Carl answered.

"Carl, what does that face look like to you?"

Carl paused a moment, studying the face: "It looks like an alien. What does it mean?"

Herman smiled: "I better not say—it won't make sense until I tell you the whole story. Come on, let's go over to the easy reading chairs."

They walked over to the west side of the castle,

about twenty yards from the castle's iron front door, and stopped in front of the two reading chairs. The chairs were cut in the exact contoured shape of the same reclining chairs we have today, Herman said. But this form was unknown in Ed's day—except to Ed.

Ed quit work everyday at four o'clock, Herman explained, and then he'd come over here and read for awhile. Then Herman and Carl sat down in the stone easy chairs.

"Isn't that comfortable Carl?"

"Yes, perfect fit. Ed was a genius. I appreciate you taking the time to talk with me Herman."

"Well, I'm getting old now, Carl. I could go at any time. If I die without telling these things, then they'll be lost forever.

"You see," Herman said, "some people won't believe what I'm going to tell you Carl, no more than they can accept UFO's and government cover-ups. They'll say, 'ol man Harmless was crazy as a sprayed roach.'"

Herman was drinking a mango soda, in a yellow plastic mug, imprinted with a red pig's face and the word's "Big Rascal Bar-B-Que, Ocala, Florida," in bold red letters.

Herman sipped his mango soda and explained to Carl that Ed was from Latvia, one of the small Baltic States bordering Russia. Ed was born on March 26, 1887, in Stramereens Pogosta, a small village not far from Latvia's capital city named Riga.

Ed said his father, Gustov, was a husky-built farmer, and Corina, his mother, was small, around 5 feet tall, and shapely, with dark hair and eyes, giving her a Spanish look.

"I looked like my grandfather, Nick Krone," Ed said. "Nick was small-framed like me." Ed said Nick had lived with Gustov and Corina since his wife Alma had died of pneumonia years ago.

We lived in a large castle, Ed said, that "Gus,"

as they called my father, and Nick had built with defective granite tombstones. The tombstones were discarded because of spelling errors or they had been badly chipped during the engraving process, making then unfit to sell.

So Nick picked them up for nothing and piled them up on a piece of hilltop land he owned overlooking the town of Pogosta. Nick also collected some cast-off stones from the granite quarry near Bear mountain, where he sometimes worked as a stone cutter. The mountain was named for the bear population that lived there and foraged around for blueberries and they fished in Lake Koza, near the mountain top.

Nick was a merchant marine and he traveled all over the world hauling various types of freight. During his travels, he'd learned to speak English so well that he'd lost most of his Latvian accent.

Nick loved to read books and he liked to cut stone the way that timber men like to cut trees. When Nick was a young boy, he had a job after school working for a tombstone company.

That was where he learned to cut stone. Nick designed the castle we lived in from the books he'd read and from some of the castles he'd seen on his trips to England.

Our castle in Latvia had a moat and a drawbridge that could be raised and lowered. But mainly, it was for "ancient castle" looking effects, so it usually stayed in the lowered position.

Nick had found the castle's wooden front door in a junkyard; it was once the door off a pirate ship, or so the junk man claimed. Nick put a big, fancy, round brass door knocker on the door; he said all the castles in England had them so he wanted the door to look like authentic England.

After supper, my grandfather Nick liked to go up on the third story open balcony and watch the sun go down and read his books. He read the Bible and books on The Great Pyramid, but "Atlantis" a book by Ignatius

J. Donnelly was his favorite.

Nick sat there in his red suspenders and faded blue carpenter pants, frozen looking, as he read until it got dark, and then he read by the light of a kerosene lamp on the table by his rocking chair.

Some salesmen and relatives refused to go to the castle because it was made of cast-off tombstones. They didn't feel it was proper for the living to build a home from something intended for the dead. They were afraid the ghost of the dead might come in one night and drag off their children for disrespecting the dead.

And besides, they declared, it would be disgusting to be in there eating a meal and glance over at the wall and see someone's birthday and departure day carved right next to it. That place would be awful at night—like sleeping in someone else's tomb. Nick never gave those things much thought; after all, he said, "I chiseled out most of the tombstone writing."

One saturday, Ed wrote later in his diary, in February, 1887, in Latvia, my mother Corina was seven months pregnant with me. She needed fabric for a new dress so she went into Riga, where the fabric store was, to buy it.

She told me a light snow was falling that day, in the gray, overcast sky, around five o'clock, as she walked along a cobblestone sidewalk. She stopped when she came by the psychic Madame Drusa's place, facing Duval street.

A black, wrought-iron gate at the entrance had a red lettered sign reading: "Madame Drusa's. See the past, know the future." The overlapping boards of the wooden house were painted red, and faded now from the sun. The silver tin roof, pyramid shaped, had a large, life-like image of Anubis, the jackal-headed Egyptian god of death, painted on it in black and gold.

In the front yard, Corina saw six standing figures of Anubis with outstretched arms, on either side of the cobblestone path leading up to the front door. Their jackal heads were done in a brilliant gold, gleaming bright against their dull black bodies, adorned with golden waistcloths and golden sandals on their feet.

Corina said she had always wanted to have a reading done with Madame Drusa. A reading is where a psychic gives the details of past, present and future lives of reincarnated spirits.

Corina walked up to the front gate, pushed it open and then closed it behind her. She walked slowly and carefully down the cobblestone path because she was pregnant and she didn't want to slip and fall on the slippery stone path.

She got to the porch and walked up the creaky wooden steps and stepped onto the porch. A large, black, bob-tailed cat with amber eyes, lay sleeping on a black rocking chair. Seeing Corina, he picked his head up, and then he stretched out, yawned, and gave a polite greeting cry.

"Hi kitty," Corina said, knocking on the front door. A fat, grey-haired, pleasant looking woman, in a fancy blue dress, wearing heavy make up, came to the door.

"Welcome to Madame Drusa's dear—I'm Sylvia, the Madame's secretary. Come on in out of the cold, child."

Corina introduced herself as they stepped inside.

"I was passing by," Corina said, "and I'd always heard how Madame Drusa could tell you about things—"

"And," Sylvia says, pointing to Corina's bulging stomach, "the curiosity about your coming child overcame your fears and made you come in."

"Yes. How did you know?"

"Oh, child, reading minds gets to be a habit around here. I imagine we've done hundreds of new arrivals. Later, you'll be so glad you came. We just finished a fascinating case about a boy who was afraid to go fishing.

"So Madame Drusa took the boy back in his past

life, and discovered he had lived in France over two hundred years ago. He'd drowned while playing around a lake. Isn't that something?"

"Oh yes. Nick, my father, he's fascinated with past lives."

"Well, come on and I'll introduce you. We were just about to have some hot tea."

The floor was made of imported, tongue-in-groove mahogany, polished to a high shine. Thick wool, hand-embroidered rugs, showing Egyptian hieroglyphics in rich colors, covered the slick hall floor.

Sylvia pulled back two large, inset, mahogany doors and they entered the parlor. A thin layer of hazy smoke hung in the air above their heads. Corina smelled the sweet scent of wild gardenia from a burning cone of incense in a tiny silver bowl.

At both ends of two, long, red leather couches, there were two, tall, gold-painted angels, with outstretched arms, wearing soft blue dresses and matching blue sandals on their feet.

Madame Drusa was thirty years old. She said these angels were exact copies of the ones the Egyptians used to protect the bodies of the entombed pharaohs; it was their duty to protect him from tomb robbers and evil spirits.

Madame Drusa sat on one of the red couches and she was pouring tea. Madame Drusa was slim and beautiful in an exotic way, with full pouting lips and big, round, deep green eyes and long red, curly hair down to her shoulders.

She had on a silk green dress and she was covered in magnificent gold and turquoise Egyptian jewelry. She had a necklace around her neck, showing a pharaoh's head emerging from a lotus flower.

She said the lotus flower grows wild around the edges of the Nile in Egypt and that the Egyptians believed the pharaoh created himself and emerged at the edge of the Nile from the petals of the lotus flower.

The Egyptians believed that when the pharaoh died, he entered the underworld, where Anubis, the god of death, weighed his heart to see if he was pure enough to continue on the spiritual journey, or, if he must be born again.

Sylvia got another cup for Corina and Corina sat down on the other red leather couch, facing Madame Drusa, and Sylvia poured her some tea. Sylvia put two sugars and a slice of lemon in hers and took a sip to warm her up.

Madame Drusa told Corina that she believed she had inherited her talents as a psychic from her grandmother, who was a psychic.

"Later on," Madame Drusa explained, "I read some books and I learned to hypnotize myself. I developed the ability to call up visions in the hypnotic state. Corina, when I do a reading for someone, I disconnect myself from my body, and I travel through, to another realm of time; when I get there, I see and feel everything—I am there. It's a time when the spirit travels and mingles with others of that time.

"In the hypnotic state, you leave this dimension, and relive the things of former lives, stored for recall in our unconscious memories. Can you accept this Corina?"

"Yes," Corina answered. Being in Madame Drusa's presence reminded her of talking with Nick, her father, when he expressed his ideas of possible former lives. Corina thought Madame Drusa could be some wise, ancient former mystic who had returned to speak of other times to those who would listen.

Then, they got to talking about books and Corina told Madame Drusa that Nick liked to read the story of Atlantis.

Madame Drusa said she had done extensive research on Atlantis. She had read Ignatius Donnelly's book on Atlantis and Madame Drusa said she believed that Plato's Atlantis story was true.

"Listen Corina," Madame Drusa explained, "Plato had never written any fictional stories before—now why would he make up a wild story like Atlantis? It doesn't fit his pattern of writing.

"We know that Plato got the Atlantis story from some Egyptian priests, who were the keepers of historical documents, when Plato had visited Egypt.

"The priests told Plato that the original documents describing Atlantis and it's destruction had been placed in a secret chamber inside the Sphinx by those escaping Atlantis before the final destruction. I've done a few readings for people who had former lives in Atlantis, and in Atlantis, there existed the greatest scientific advancements the world has ever known.

"Well, Corina, let's get started; I know you're anxious to hear about this child. Relax, take your shoes off and sit back on the couch while I go to work," and Corina did.

Madame Drusa took off her black, soft leather boots and laid back on the red couch with a soft purple pillow behind her neck. She crossed her arms across her chest in the same way the Egyptian pharaohs did when they were buried.

On the table next to Madame Drusa's head, there was a crystal pyramid, about the size of a lamp shade, attached to a flexible wooden arm on a stand. Sylvia swung the pyramid over until it was over Madame Drusa's face.

Sylvia brought out a compass and lined up the pyramid corners so that one corner faced the exact true north. Sylvia explained that this alignment creates a magnetic spiral energy field inside the pyramid; it surrounds the body and helps the spirit to escape the body. And it aids in the out-of-body experience. Sylvia said Madame Drusa discovered this knowledge from past readings.

Sylvia took some vanilla oil from a small brown bottle and rubbed it between Madame Drusa's eyes. Corina smelled the sweet oil and Sylvia told her that the aroma helped the Madame to relax and concentrate. Sylvia got a pencil and a pad of paper and pulled her chair up close to the Madame. Madame Drusa closed her eyes, took a deep breath and held it momentarily, then she slowly exhaled. Sylvia began:

"Madame Drusa, you will tune in telepathically on the mind and body of Corina Leedskalnin. You will go over this body carefully and focus on the present and past conditions of this child. Please speak clearly. You understand that you will not lose consciousness, but you will enter the unconscious realm, where all recorded events are stored. Here, you will experience a former bodily realm.

"You are the guide, taking us into a previous experience of this child. I am now speaking to your spirit: Please detach from the body. You are now in the altered state, a brief sense of escape from ordinary time and space."

Corina noticed that Madame Drusa's body made a twitching motion now, as though she were in a dream state. Then, her face and body got calm.

"Do you have the child?" Sylvia asked.

"Yes, I see the body," Madame Drusa answered. "A son will be born to her in late March, near the 25th. He will be thirty days premature; a restless spirit, he couldn't wait to get into the world—he'll never be able to wait for anything. This body is strange to other bodies in it's ideas."

"What was the most significant former life of this body?"

"He existed in Atlantis, where great inventions were created. He was a sculptor named Rozano; inhabiting the same body then, but a different name in the year of 10,000 B.C."

"Why was Atlantis destroyed?"

"This information is not available at this time. A prophet will come later who sees this time clearly."

"Please tell me about the child."

"He shall astound the world, bringing back an ancient lost science, used in The Great Pyramid, and known in the former Atlantic existence. Each person and all invented things have been before—nothing new is discovered, only re-discovered. All spirits choose the time, place, and people, for re-entry to attain advancement of self.

"Many exist in the same body, different name. He is one of the first spirits to re-enter from Atlantis; many will follow in this present time period. This time, the world now repeats the Atlantic pattern of great knowledge and great destruction."

"Go back now," Sylvia urged the Madame, "to Atlantis and find Rozano. Please describe."

The Madame was silent for a moment, breathing regularly. Then she smiled: "Yes, I'm here, in the middle of a beautiful flower garden. It's warm here in the bright sunshine."

Each time was different for Madame Drusa, Sylvia said, as she traveled in the spirit realm. The Madame said it was like crossing a bridge from one life into another.

Madame Drusa then described seeing a lagoon, filled with dark brown water. The still water reflected the image of a lovely blonde-haired girl, wearing a ruffled yellow dress and carrying a yellow parasol. The girl took some bread crumbs and tossed them into the lagoon and Madame Drusa saw some small fish surface and snatch the crumbs.

Madame Drusa walked along a winding brick pathway, bordered on both sides by a closely-cropped green lawn. In front of her, she described seeing a large waterfall, surrounded by colorful flowers. Madame Drusa saw a wrought iron bench, painted red with yellow slat boards, near the waterfall and she went over and sat down. There were people mingling around in what seemed to be a park, she said.

Nobody seemed to be in a hurry and some people ate picnic lunches on the grass, while others, men, women and children, strolled past her on the brick pathway. She had been sitting there about five minutes, she said, when a tall black man, dressed in a red silk tuxedo, and red felt top hat, walked up to her. He was pushing a cart with a piece of odd-looking equipment on it that she didn't recognize.

He tipped his hat politely: "Good afternoon, pretty lady," he said, "do you recognize me?"

"Oh, I'm afraid not. I'm new in town."

"New in town? But madam, I'm known all over Atlantis. Well, it's been awhile since I've had a hit song. But you might remember my name—Paradise Hunter?"

"Gosh, I'm sorry. You see, I just got out of the hospital. I had an accident and bumped my head and I've got a form of temporary amnesia."

"Oh, I see. I'm sorry. I hope you get better soon. Well, I'm in the park all the time. Maybe next time I see you, you'll be better and ready to buy my music. Well, I'm sorry to have bothered you. As I leave, I'll give you a sample of my music," he said. Then he took out a shiny, flat silver disc, about the size of a saucer cup, and he put it into the machine on his cart.

"Well," he says, tipping his hat again, "I'll see you later." And as he walked off, Madame Drusa said, "I heard a beautiful song coming out of the machine, and Paradise Hunter was humming along with the tune as he walked along." And Madame Drusa marveled at how clear the song sounded.

Then, about the time Paradise Hunter got out of sight, a man carrying a leather briefcase came up and said: "Hello, do you mind if I sit down beside you for a moment?"

"Oh, no, please do."

"Thank you. My name is Brizz Bane. Are you taking a late lunch break?"

She wanted to know about this place and she told him her invented story about the amnesia. "You know," she told him, "I think I've wandered from the hospital. I don't know what day it is; I don't even remember what city this is."

"Oh, that's terrible. This city is called Zolameta and we're in Atlantic Gardens—it's a city park. Listen, there's an aid station not far from here. Would you like me to take you there?"

"Thank you. But I'm tired. I'd just like to sit here and talk with you, if you don't mind."

"Sure. But first, I have to make a call. I'm in the futures business," he said, opening his briefcase and pulling out a gray, hand-sized object with buttons on it, and a short piece of wire coming out of the top.

"In the futures business—you're a medium?"

"Oh, no. I mean, I deal in the stock market—we buy and sell the futures of grain, animals and vegetables. That's my office over there," he said, pointing to a row of odd-looking, glass pyramid buildings.

The bottom half of the buildings was an upside down pyramid, with it's point touching the ground, and a second regular upright pyramid was fixed to the flat, base part of the upside down pyramid. The pyramid buildings were attached to each other at the side, giving it a "honeycomb" effect.

They looked like someone had taken two diamonds and forged them together at the base, so now you saw two, sharp-pointed ends at the bottom and top, Madame Drusa said. Brizz explained they were built that way to capture the sun's energy to power the city.

Madame Drusa said she saw what Brizz called "air ships" shaped like stingrays, darting around in the sky like bees. Sometimes, they hovered and then landed on a flat topped building.

The city had all kind of wonderful things Brizz told her. "But out in the country," he said mournfully, "there's great poverty. Some people live in shacks without power. And they have to grow everything they eat."

Some of the buildings had large signs with flashing lights. One of them read: "Quigley's root beer" and showed a little boy wearing a white sailor's cap and raising his arm to drink a bottle of it.

Madame Drusa heard a curious ringing sound, and she saw Brizz punch a button on the little gray machine he was holding, and he held it up to his ear: "Hello," he spoke into it.

Madame Drusa looked around to see who he was talking to but she didn't see anybody.

"I see," he said. "Okay, listen, sell the corn and wheat shares. We'll take the money and buy hogs, they're plentiful and cheap now—yeah, we'll buy them cheap and then see if we can find a way to kill'em off and drive up the price. Do you know a good veterinarian?

"You're right, we better not talk like that on this thing. She called? Yes, tell Doreen I'll meet her at The Constellation Club for dinner at seven. Thanks, bye." Brizz pushed a button on the machine and he put it back in his case.

Puzzled looking, Madame Drusa stared at him: "Who were you talking to?"

"My secretary. She gave me the latest weather reports, that's how we chart the grain market."

"Your secretary? I don't understand—I'm the only one here."

"What? She's in my office. I was talking to her on the phone. Do you mean you've forgotten what a phone is?"

"She's in your office?" Madame Drusa said, trying to clear her head, "and you talked to her on that machine?"

"Well, yes of course—"

"You mean people can hear your voice on that thing?"

"Yes," he said, and, reaching back into his case he brought the machine back out. He punched some buttons on the machine again and held it up to his ear. After a pause, he said: "Erica, I've got a friend here, she wants to say hello," then he handed Madame Drusa the machine. At first she was afraid to take it, but he urged her and she put it up to her ear.

"What do I say?" she asked him nervously.

"Just say, 'Hello Erica' and tell her your name."

"But I don't remember my name—"

"Oh, please, just say hello."

Madame Drusa did and she was surprised when she heard the lady's voice come back and she quickly handed the machine back to Brizz. He thanked Erica and pushed a button and put it back in the case.

"How does it work?" she asked him.

"I'm not sure. There's some wires inside the machine and the vibrations of your voice travels on the wires through the air. And the sound gets trapped in the machine and it comes out. Something like that, I guess."

Brizz looked at his watch and got excited: "Oh, the monkey-man show is coming up. Come on, I want you to see this," he said, taking her hand and pulling her off the bench. And as they were leaving, Madame Drusa heard some beautiful music playing and Brizz explained that there was a band that always played in the park.

She was so shocked with this place (in her Atlantis vision) that she almost forgot to look for Rozano. But they came to a bridge over a pool of water and she saw Rozano, leaning against a wooden railing, looking over the pool of water. Next to him was a pretty girl, with long, black curly hair; it was fastened with a black hair pin at the back of her head and pulled over so it fell way down over her left shoulder.

She had smooth skin, the color of olive oil, and big, oriental, almond-shaped eyes, set in her face at a tilted angle, giving her face an exotic, oriental look. "She looked like a cross of Spanish and Asian mix and she had a look of distinctive beauty—like Nefertiti. She looked younger than him and he looked to be about twenty," Madame Drusa said.

Rozano tossed some bread crumbs into the pool of water below and Madame Drusa was close enough now to see a large herd of turtles go rushing at the bread. They snatched them quickly from the surface and then took off to eat them before another turtle could take it from them. The lovely girl pointed down to the turtles:

"Oh look Rozano, that baby turtle didn't get any. Darling, please throw him some," and he did. The baby turtle grabbed it and took off for the bottom.

"Oh, he got it!" she squealed, "the little baby got it."

They looked so happy, Madame Drusa thought. She wanted to stay near them but Brizz said they had to go and see the show. She wanted to see more of this place and Brizz could be her guide. Maybe she would catch up with Rozano later.

"We came to an outdoor theater," Madame Drusa said, "with stone benches like the old Roman theaters. A crowd was starting to gather but we got front row seats. A man walked out wearing a white tuxedo and top hat."

"Ladies and gentlemen," he said, "welcome to Atlantic Gardens. Today, we have a man who wanders the world with his beloved monkeys. His name is Rah-moon, but he's better known as the "Monkey-man." Please give him a warm welcome," he said, and everyone clapped.

Rah-moon, an indian, walked out with two monkeys trailing him. He was thin, dark skinned, and looked to be in his sixties. He wore a bright red turban and a yellow silk robe and pants, with red leather sandals on his feet. There was a medium sized male and a female monkey, with a small baby riding on her back.

The female had on a yellow lace, low-cut dress, stuffed with tissue to simulate breasts. She wore a small red hat and dangling, carved wood, yellow parrot earrings and bright red lipstick. The baby wore a blue sailors outfit with a white cap.

The male wore a black leather vest with no shirt and a shiny black turban. The monkeys had smooth, pink flesh faces with an intelligent, curious, child-like appearance.

They had yellow eyes, sitting back under a bony, protruding forehead and soft brown eyebrows. With their humanly pink hands and feet and quick intelligence they were easy to love, Rah-moon said. Their coats were clean and shiny and they smelled of jasmine perfume that Rah-moon sprayed on them before each show.

The monkeys stopped politely now, behind Rah-moon. He set a leather travel bag down beside him and put his hands together in prayer form and he bowed to the crowd.

"Thank you," he began. "I'm known as the monkey-man because I've always lived with monkeys. My father had monkeys when I was a child and when they got old and died, my father and I buried them. Then my father got more monkeys. When I grew up, I got some monkeys too and I've kept them ever since.

"We sleep on the ground under the stars; we eat the same food: rice, fruit and vegetables. We bathe in the rivers and we go where like; no man tells us when to get up or where to lay down. We go where we like.

"The monkeys have their own money from these shows and they always pick out the shiniest coins from the pot that's passed around after every show. Then, we go into town and the monkeys themselves hand over the coins to the merchant and they point to a piece of fruit or cake. They're smart too, they know how much change they should get back. I think they'd make good bankers."

Then Rah-moon turned and led the female with the baby off to one side of him. He sat down cross-legged between the monkeys. Beside him was a wide copper pot and two long, thin, bamboo poles. He put the pot and the poles near him and looked out at the audience: "My monkeys are married; a gorilla priest performed the ceremony. The male's name is Tasha; the female is Pasha, and Sasha, the baby, is four months old.

"I hate to bring out our family problems, but after the last show, the male, Tasha, took his money, bought beer and got drunk. Well, sometimes, he gets mean when he's drinking; he comes home late and his wife Pasha fusses at him; he gets mad and beats her. He did this in front of his baby, Sasha, and I told him if he ever did that again, I'd have to whip him.

"But, he didn't listen to me. So, today, I'm going to have to whip him in front of you. I told him I was going to, so he knows what's coming and why. Look at him," Rah-moon said, pointing to Tasha, "see how he's dressed?—like a gangster. He threw away his good suit and traded it for black leather."

Then, Rah-moon pointed his finger menacingly at Tasha: "Tasha, you're a bad boy," and Tasha put his hands over his face in fake shame.

"Oh, it's too late to be sorry now—you must take your whipping like a man—I mean a monkey." Pasha, the female, sat still, holding her baby Sasha in her arms. Rah-moon was holding Tasha's long rope leash in one hand, and with the other, he reached over and picked up one of the long bamboo poles.

And when he picked it up, Tasha acted nervous, like he knew what was coming. When Pasha saw Rah-moon pick up the pole, she put her hands together, like she was pleading for Rah-moon not to whip Tasha.

"No, Pasha," Rah-moon told her, "don't beg for Tasha—do you want him to beat you up again?" Pasha shook her head no. "Okay then, let me whip him," and now, Pasha nodded her head yes.

But as Rah-moon raised the pole to whip Tasha, Tasha quickly grabbed the other pole, just in time to block the blow from Rah-moon's pole—WHACK! Tasha quickly pulled his pole back and he took a baseball bat swing at Rah-moon's head—WHACK! The sound of the hollow poles hitting each other vibrated all through the stands. Rah-moon, like a veteran swordsman, expertly blocked Tasha's big swing. Excited, Rah-moon shouted:

"Look at this insolent monkey! I feed you and you want to fight me—okay, let's fight!"

Madame Drusa said there was some wild swinging going on; they must've dueled a good three minutes. The blows were hard and well placed, but neither one ever got hit. Rah-moon kept holding Tasha's leash with one hand, and he would swing at the jumping monkey with the other.

Every now and then, Tasha would get excited, and he'd circle Rah-moon, like a boxer, looking for a chance to strike, then suddenly, he'd leap straight up in the air, like a wild chicken, and he'd come crashing down with a smashing blow, aimed at Rah-moon's head. But, with a flick of the wrist, Rah-moon would block the blow, as if he could do it while shaving. Then, he'd taunt the monkey:

"Oh, my big, bad Tasha—you're so weak—your woman could beat you." And the crowd loved it and they laughed and clapped. But they groaned each time the two poles would come close to the opponent's head, making that loud cracking noise, barely missing it's target.

Later, after the show, Rah-moon explained that he and Tasha practice the duel every day and the monkey loves the mock fight. Rah-moon said he was sure the monkey understood it was only play-acting for the crowd. Tasha knew exactly how to place his blows for Rah-moon to block them.

Suddenly, in the middle of a blow, Rah-moon blew a whistle hanging around his neck, and he yelled: "That's enough Tasha! You've shamed me in front of all these nice people. Next thing I know, you'll be wanting an old trashy-looking tattoo—now you go out there and walk through the crowd and apologize."

Tasha hung his head down and put his hands

over his face in shame again: "That's right," Rah-moon told him, "I know you're sorry; now you go on out there and face these people who paid to come in here and watch you act like a juvenile—go on, hurry up! Take your leash off so you don't get tangled up."

Tasha reached up and undid his leash and he walked over and picked up the copper pot with his little pink monkey hands. As he did this, and started walking out into the crowd, Rahmoon put his hands to his head in fake surprise: "Oh, no. Tasha, have you no shame? Don't go out there begging for tips."

But Tasha put on a beggars face as he walked out into the crowd, holding the pot out as he went. And the people laughed and started digging in their pockets for change.

They put it in the pot, and laughed when, sometimes after somebody put a coin in the pot, Tasha would look scornfully at the pot, and then he'd look back at the person, and he'd shake his head and motion with his free hand for them to put more in—and most of them did. And the people said amongst themselves: "I can't believe he's so smart."

When Rah-moon saw this, he put his hands up in mock surprise:

"Oh, the shame of it," he muttered. "Oh, please friends, remember, you're feeding a drunk and a wife beater. I promise you, not one penny of this money will go to Tasha's beer."

Then, he blew the whistle again: "That's enough Tasha," he said, and the monkey came back and handed him the pot. Rah-moon took Tasha by the hand and Tasha held hands with his "wife" and child and they all bowed before the crowd.

Rah-moon thanked them and he walked off the stone platform. The man in the silk suit came back out: "Wasn't he great? Please give the monkey-man another hand," and everybody clapped hard.

"As we got up to leave," (Madame Drusa

described, in her Atlantis vision, as she lay on the red leather couch) Brizz said, "They have a wonderful boat tour through the park; come on, I'll show you."

Madame Drusa said they walked down the street brick pathway for about forty yards and they came to a wide canal with a wooden boat house and dock. Madame Drusa saw people stepping into some little white boats. The people handed a ticket to a man near the boat, dressed in a safari outfit, and he directed them into the boats.

When the boats were full, they moved silently down the canal, guided at the back by another man in a safari outfit. The guide spoke to them through a meg-a-phone device that amplified his voice, giving it a strong nasal twang.

As they got in line for a ticket, Madame Drusa suddenly noticed the couple in front of them was Rozano and his girlfriend. They were holding hands. Then, she heard him say to his girl:

"Jami, have you got our tickets?"

"I kept thinking," Madame Drusa said later, of her Atlantis vision, "I"m seeing this man as an adult in this time, before he's a child in my time."

Madame Drusa and Brizz stepped off the dock into the boat and sat at the rear, near the guide, directly behind Rozano and Jami. After everyone was seated, the guide, who looked about twenty-five, with brown hair and green eyes, spoke through the megaphone, in that heavy nasal twang:

"Good afternoon, my name is Carl Van Hoose. I'm your guide today. They call me "careful Carl" because I haven't lost any passengers yet, well there was that one little boy—I told him to quit leaning over the edge of the boat, but he kept on. It was horrible, a big crocodile came up, grabbed him by the head, and dragged him overboard.

"So, I'll have to ask you not to dangle any arms, legs or children, overboard, on our dangerous jungle cruise. These whiskey-brown waters are infested by huge, wild crocodiles. I hope we don't meet "Bonecrusher" he's the largest known living crocodile. He lives in this little canal. He's over fifteen feet long and weighs around thirteen hundred pounds—that's what he weighed before he ate that little boy.

"Okay, I'm going to get serious now, as we leave, and tell you about some of the exotic plant life you'll see on both sides of the canal. Don't worry, there are no crocodiles here—I don't think."

As the boat began to move slowly in the water, a man on the dock, unseen by the boat passengers, pushed a button and suddenly, about a paddle length away from the moving boat, a gigantic crocodile came up quickly and fiercely; his big mouth open, showing long rows of curled-down, white-daggered teeth.

He blew out a tremendous hissing noise; his huge head came up, lunging at the boat. One lady screamed out, stumbled over a man, and jumped to the other side; the guide cried out: "Oh no—it's Bonecrusher!"

Other people tried to scramble away too; the little boat rocked violently from the shifting weight, as everyone on the dock, realizing the trick, started laughing as the crocodile went back down in the water.

The guide quickly calmed everyone, assuring them the crocodile was mechanical and part of the tour. "Does anyone need to use the bathroom before we continue?" he asked. Then he drove the boat forward, and, in that nasal twang, he said:

"Along the walls here, you'll see some large Asparagus Ferns. They're easily maintained here in Atlantic Gardens, and they're a common houseplant."

Rozano, amused by the guide's nasal twang, turned to Jami, and in a low, mocking nasal tone, he said: "And they are a common houseplant." She smiled but got embarrassed and whispered back to him: "Hush Rozano, he'll hear you."

"Coming up on our left," the guide said, "before the bridge, we have our split-leaf philodendron."

Rozano imitated him again, and as Jami quietly scolded him, they looked and saw a chimpanzee, dressed in blue overalls and a white baseball cap, come walking out on the railing of a crossing wooden bridge, just up ahead.

He sat down overhead, looking down on them, and dangled his bare feet over the water, where the boat would have to pass under, up near the middle of the bridge.

Seeing him, the guide quickly stopped his quiet little boat engine, and put his hands over his face:

"Oh, no—I'm sorry, we'll have to turn back—I forgot, this is a toll bridge," he said, then pointed to the monkey, "there's the toll-taker, and I haven't got any money.

"Anyone got a spare banana?" Then quickly, he reached down in the boat and picked up a hidden banana. "Oh look," he says, "we're saved—I hope one is enough."

He tossed the banana high in the air, over the monkey's head. The monkey quickly stuck his arm up, caught the flying banana, and lazily sat down, peeling it as the boat passed under the bridge and everyone clapped for the monkey.

The boat wound around a corner, to the right, and Madame Drusa said she saw a huge, seated golden Buddha in the middle of a tropical garden; he was big as a house, and lit by the sun. It was odd, she thought, seeing the golden Buddha here; she wondered if it was the only religion here, or if all the religions of the world were maybe founded in Atlantis.

The boat stopped again; the guide pointed to an opening through some trees, where you could see, on a distant hill, a large, white-domed gazebo with fluted columns. A crowd of people stood around the gazebo. Then, the crowd parted back as a happy wedding couple, smiling, walked past them and got into a waiting, silver and blue, horse drawn carriage.

"We have a lot of marriages performed here every year," the guide told them. "People rent the wedding outfits and have the ceremony performed all for one price. Some people come in, book the wedding for the afternoon, and spend the morning in leisure here at the park."

After the boat tour was over, Madame Drusa lost sight of Rozano and Jami in the crowd. She and Brizz walked along the brick path, heading back to the bench area where she had met Brizz. As they came to the bridge over the pond, where she had seen Rozano and Jami feeding the turtles, she looked and saw Rozano leaning on the bridge railing by himself. He looked dazed and he had a white muslin bandage wrapped around his head, covering his forehead.

Curious, Madame Drusa walked up to him: "Excuse me young man, but are you okay? I saw you here earlier, with the pretty girl—where is she?"

He stared absently at her: "She's gone—I'm sorry, but I'd like to be alone," he said, and he turned from her and stared down into the pond.

"Yes, of course. I'm sorry I bothered you," she said, and walked on over the bridge to where Brizz was waiting for her.

"Did you know him?" Brizz asked her.

"He looked familiar, but I can't seem to remember him," she explained, because she didn't want Brizz to know that she knew him from another time. They walked along the path in silence, each lost in their thoughts. Madame Drusa heard the beautiful music from the band in the park and it relaxed her: "Brizz, I love that music."

"Really? A lot of people come to the park just to listen to the music." He looked at his watch: "Say, I've got some time before I meet my wife at the Constellation Club; we'll go over and listen to the band until I have to go. And I want to take you to the aid station so someone can help you."

"I like that name—where's the Constellation Club?"

"It's at 901 Stardust road, in the middle of downtown. It's a beautiful club—it's pyramid-shaped and the top part is all done in glass. And at night, you can look up at the sky and see the moon and stars. All the buildings and street names in this section of town have a cosmic theme and name. Even the street lamps have a curving shape, like a crescent moon."

"Oh, it sounds lovely. I wish I could go with you—"

And suddenly, as Brizz turned to answer her, to his amazement, Madame Drusa's body began to slowly fade, turning misty, like when a rainbow begins to lose it's colors.

Madame Drusa felt it; she knew was leaving this space. It was always this way in a reading, you never knew how long you'd stay. But suddenly, she explained later, there's a tingling sensation in the body, like jarring your funny-bone, then the vanishing begins.

She saw the surprised look on Brizz's face, staring, but he couldn't speak. She wished for more time to explain things but the time was out. She had lost the ability to speak, so she smiled at him now and raised her hand to wave goodbye. Then, she vanished from his sight.

She came back into her body on the red couch in Latvia. Later, Madame Drusa recorded her Atlantic vision in a book of her readings. The last part of her journal read: "And so it happened, that on a sunny day, in the garden of Atlantis, in a time long since passed, I, Madame Drusa, had glimpsed a former adult life of a male child, while he was still in the womb of his mother Corina, in my home in Riga, the capital of Latvia."

As I grew up in Latvia, Ed wrote, I was fascinated by this reading about me that Madame Drusa had given to my mother Corina. I read it a lot as a boy. In the beginning of the reading, Madame Drusa was asked to give specific details about Atlantis.

But she refused, saying: "A prophet who sees Atlantis clearly will come later with specific details of this time." I believe this "prophet" she was talking about, came in the form of an American from Virginia, named Edgar Cayce, famously known as "The Sleeping Prophet."

Edgar Cayce's readings were similar to Madame Drusa's. Cayce would lie down on a couch, and, placing himself under self - hypnosis, he'd be given the name of a person, and then he'd focus his mind telepathically on the person's mind and body.

Edgar Cayce once explained that in the hypnotic state, his mind traveled in a "higher plane of existence" to a great library where the recordings of the lives of former souls, called "The Akashic records" were kept. All he had to do, Cayce said, was to look up the person's name and then read about his former appearances on the earth.

Cayce said that each returning soul or "entity" as he called them, as it re-enters the earth in the human form, has unconscious access to the characteristics, mental abilities, and skills that it has developed in previous lives. But, Cayce added, the soul must fight the negative influences of hate, fear, cruelty, and impatience, that can delay it's necessary progress.

Cayce gave his first reading where he mentioned Atlantis in 1924. And he continued to give readings for hundreds of people with former Atlantic lives. Cayce gave his last reading for a person with a former life in Atlantis in the year 1944.

In his trance state on the couch, when asked the following questions by his secretary about Atlantis, Cayce gave this account:

Q: "Why was Atlantis destroyed?"

A: "Greed and ethnic hatred among the races. The races began in Atlantis and, at first, they loved each other and gave no thought to money. But later, they loved gold and material things; pleasure became their god. No civilization yet has acquired their knowledge. They traveled through the air and water in fast machines.

"In their homes, they were entertained in the manner of projected pictures on the wall that included sound and movement. They talked with each other from far away by machines that allowed voices to travel through the air by the magnetic forces. They rejuvenated their bodies through the magnetic forces created inside the pyramid that control the body."

Q: "What caused the destruction?"

A: "Atlantis was destroyed by the powerful red cosmic rays emitted from the mighty, horrible crystal. The crystal drew it's destructive powers from the sun's energy that was captured and magnified by large inverted crystal pyramids scattered around Atlantis. These forces were put into machines and used for evil purposes.

"Man turned them on his brother in three different wars; the last being the worst in the year 10,000 B.C. The explosive forces of cosmic rays caused tidal waves and volcanic eruptions that separated the land—Atlantis sank into the sea."

Q: "Give the location of Atlantis."

A: "Atlantis existed off the coast of Florida, in America, near what is known as Bimini."

And so, Ed later wrote in his diary: "I re-entered the earth's plane, March 26, 1887, thirty days premature, just as Madame Drusa predicted. According to her, it was the first time I'd been in a human body since my former existence in Atlantis."

When I was a growing up, I used to sit in Nick's lap, on the open balcony after supper, and he'd read to me in English, from books about Atlantis, The Great Pyramid, and the Bible.

That's where I learned to speak English. I had a good ear for languages and various accents. I could easily mimic Irish, English and Spanish speaking people. Nick thought it was because I'd had former lives there, but he tended to explain a lot of things by linking them to reincarnation.

As I got older, I watched Nick, carving stone on the balcony at dusk, after supper, and well into the night by the light of a kerosene lamp. I was fascinated watching Nick (I've called him Nick since I was a child) take a cold piece of stone and give it life.

"I'm going to cut stone like Nick one day," I said to myself. I badgered Nick to get me some tools that would fit my small hands and Nick did it.

Nick had brought back an eight inch high, expertly carved, stone statue of a Mayan Chief, sitting crosslegged, from one of his banana hauling trips to Honduras.

The statue was carved by an old Mayan indian who had copied it from a scene off of one of the pyramids of Copan, near the famous ball court. The statue, with bulging eyes and heavy eyelids, was made of almost the same kind of gritty, yellow field stones littering the farmsides of Latvia.

Well, I got some field stone and tried to copy the chief as Nick instructed me on the carving. Nick said I couldn't use expensive granite until I'd proven myself on the cheaper field stone. I messed up a field of field stone before I got good.

And, I began to feel a connection with the stone, like Nick said. After practicing a lot, I got to where I could copy that statue so good, only Nick could tell the original from the copies.

I took some of the statues to school and sold them. Well, I stretched the truth some, so they'd fetch a higher price. I told the kids that Nick had brought them back from the South American jungle, where the head-hunters live. I explained that a retired head-hunter, who lived in a house made out of human skulls, had carved them.

The story went over good. Then I had a brilliant idea; I pulled the ticks off my dog, popped them, and smeared the blood on some of statues, and I got more for them.

I told the kids it was genuine head-hunter's blood. I was selling them as fast as I could carve them—I smiled every time I found a tick. But it was too good to be true.

Rumors got to flying around town that Nick had fought off and killed a head-hunter to get the statues, and a local Latvian newspaper reporter came to interview Nick about it. Nick had no idea what the reporter was talking about, but the trail led back to me. Nick tore my butt up with his belt for lying, and made me refund all the children's money.

I told Nick I was sorry; I claimed I was saving up for a rifle, and that was true, but I reckoned I better figure another way. Later, after I'd gone to bed that night, Nick laughed about it and told Gus it sure did hurt him to spank me; he admired my fine imagination, but he couldn't allow me to prosper off of lies.

Nick had gone to the American west several times on the cargo hauling ship. He used to bring me back arrowheads and other indian artifacts when I was a kid. And I loved the feel of the chipped flint arrowheads as I ran my fingers over them. Nick brought me some books back that told the stories of the cowboy and indian wars. I don't know why, but I always wanted the indians to win. Nick said I must've been an indian in a previous life.

When I was four years old, I told mama I wanted a bow and arrow. But she said I was too young to have one. I had a bow and arrow set with arrows that had soft rubber tips on the end, but now I wanted the arrows that had the sharp metal tips on the end. You could hurt somebody with one of them.

But I begged and begged and finally, she thought she'd figure a way to shut me up. She said: "Okay Ed, I'll make a deal with you; if you can quit sucking your thumb, I'll buy you the sharp tipped arrows." She just knew that I couldn't do that because I loved to suck my thumb—I mean I sucked it so hard, sometimes the flesh got pink and sore.

And my heart sank when she said that; I thought, Oh, no, I can't do that—ask me anything but that. Well, she was standing there waiting for an answer. And I took my thumb out of my mouth and I looked down at it, and I studied about that thing for awhile. And finally, I figured I wanted that bow and arrow more than anything in the world.

I looked at my thumb, and I stuck it in my mouth one more time, and I took me a good suck on it, for old time's sake.

I knew I was saying goodbye to an old friend. And I didn't say it out loud to mama, but I said to myself, "Okay, I'm gonna quit sucking my thumb so I can have a bow and arrow set, like the real American indians have."

I said, "Now mama, do you mean that?"

"Son, have I ever lied to you?—you do it and it's yours. But now Ed, I'm warning you, you've always been the most honest boy I know. So I'm putting you on the honor system.

"I can't follow you around all the time to see if you're sneaking around behind my back and sucking your thumb. But I'm going to check your thumb every now and then, and see if it's looks sore or not, so I want you not to lie to me—if you suck it just one time—the deal is off, fair enough?"

"Okay, mama, I'm gonna do it—you have just seen me suck my thumb for the last time," and we shook on it to make it official.

I didn't remember much about this story, mama told me about it later, when I got older. I've got that stubborn spirit that most Aries people have; if I make up my mind to do something, I'll do it or die.

Mama said it was so funny; she said I wouldn't see her watching me, sometimes when I'd be playing, and without thinking about it, I'd start to put my thumb in my mouth and suck it; well, that came from years of diligent sucking.

So anyway, mama said, all of sudden I'd realize that I was about to stick it in my mouth, and I'd jerk it away quickly. I wasn't about to risk losing those sharp tip arrows, there wasn't a thumb suck in the world that was worth a good arrow.

Mama said I used to get on my knees and lean on my bed to pray before I went to bed at night. And sometimes, she'd stop in the doorway and listen to what I was praying. She told me sometimes I'd say: "And God, please give me strength not to suck my thumb, so I can have those arrows."

Then, she said I'd climb in bed and go to sleep. And it was strange, she said, I had so much will power that I wouldn't dare touch my thumb in the day time; but at night, she'd go back and check on me later, and I'd be sound asleep with my thumb in my mouth, just sucking away. Mama never told me I was sucking it in the night, because I didn't know I was doing it.

Mama said, "And I didn't believe you could do it, but after two months, you proved it to me, and I went down to the store, bought you the arrows and brought them home to you. You were so happy. You grinned and said, "Mama, I'm a real American indian now."

I was proud of you, mama said, because you were very careful where you shot those arrows.

One time, Nick brought a Mayan indian book back from Honduras named "The Rattlesnake Pattern." He got it from a Mayan indian friend of his in Copan. I was eight years old at the time. Nick and I would sit on that balcony and he'd read to me. We'd look at the pictures from this book and he'd explain how the Mayans thought.

One of the pictures, taken from the side of a pyramid in Copan, showed a round disc object coming down from the sky and landing on the earth. Then it showed a small creature, with a large diamond-shaped head, big eyes and a small mouth, coming out of the disc. The little creature then handed a Mayan priest a rolled up scroll of paper.

The Mayan hieroglyphics, written beside the stone drawing, explained that, thousands of years ago, "men from the sky" as the Mayans described these creatures in the disc, came down from the sky and gave the Mayan culture the mathematical secrets of the universe.

Nick had great respect for the incredible pyramid buildings that the Mayans had built. And Nick never, even for a minute, believed that The Great Pyramid was built by slaves dragging stones up an embankment of dirt.

Nick had read books proving that The Great Pyramid used advanced mathematics not rediscovered in our time until the seventeenth century. The stone drawing of the sky creatures coming down in the disc; and the Mayans, saying they were given knowledge of a secret universal math from these "sky gods" convinced Nick that the earth had been visited by a race of intelligent beings.

Nick had a little book he'd picked up in his travels titled "Strange occurrences." The book gave all kinds of different examples from various cultures who had reported numerous sightings of disc-shaped objects in the sky dating way back in history. Some of the examples the book noted read:

An Egyptian papyrus in the year 1649 B.C. mentioned "circles of fire in the sky, bright like the sun. Over twenty were counted flying at great speed through the sky."

In 330 B.C., Alexander The Great's army was frightened and chased by "shiny disc-shaped objects flying closely overhead" causing the horses to panic and run wild."

In 1492, just before he sighted land, Christopher Columbus reported seeing a "glimmering light" moving up and down in the sky. It made several appearances during the night, Columbus said.

In 1209, some monks in England reported in

their records seeing a large, round, metallic disc-shaped object, flying slowly at a low altitude as it passed directly overhead.

"So you see, Ed, I think," Nick said, "the Mayans recorded the visits of the "men from the sky" as they called them, by carving the stories into the stone pyramids."

"Nick, what Solomon said, about everything here has been done in some other time, that nothing is new, do you think we've been here before and done these things? Like reincarnation?"

"I can't say for sure Ed, that's dealing with the spiritual world, but I think it's possible."

That night, Ed wrote, I had trouble sleeping, after Nick and I had talked on the balcony about reincarnation and life on other planets. I was looking at the wooden hoop "dream weaver" Nick gave me, hanging over my bed. It had a bird feather tied to it and it was wrapped with leather. It was made by an American indian and was supposed to keep the evil spirits away so you'll only have pleasant dreams. The bird feather helped your spirit to fly in the night.

Then I got sleepy. That night, I had a strange dream. In the dream, I found myself in what seemed like the bottom of a rocky canyon, with high walls, surrounded in the distance by mountains, with valleys in between.

I was an indian boy, with long black hair and dressed in deerskin clothes. I sat around a campfire at night, on the top of a tall cliff, among a group of indian boys. Behind us were long wooden ladders, leaning up against the canyon walls, and we climbed up the ladders at night to reach our homes that were carved into the high cliff walls.

We were watching an old indian man, with long gray hair hanging loosely on his shoulders, as he chipped away at a long flint spearhead. He was making it for the buffalo hunts, he explained to us. The sky overhead was clear that night, the moon in it's quarter phase, and I could see the stars shining brightly.

Suddenly, a bright round light appeared in the sky, moving in a wobbly motion, at a downward angle toward the earth.

The object slowed down before it hit the earth, and I saw it better now; it was a shiny disc-shaped object, with a row of small blinking lights around it. The ship hit the earth at an angle in a sandy area of the valley below, and it skipped over the sandy surface a couple of times and then it smashed into a towering rocky cliff. For a moment, we sat there stunned, not knowing what to think of this. Then, curiosity overcame our fear and we moved quickly down the cliff face, and reaching the flat valley, we ran over to where the object had landed. When we got there, there was a small creature, (about 4 feet tall) dressed in a one-piece, shiny blue suit. His silver helmet was off and he was sitting on the ground, with a dazed look on his face. He had pinkish gray skin, and he was hairless. There was a cut on his forehead that oozed out something resembling blood, only it was blue.

The creature extended his hand to the old indian man; his fingers were thin and resembled string beans. The old indian man told one of the boys to run back and fetch the medicine man and the boy did. When the medicine man got there, he gave the creature an herbal mixture to drink to strengthen him.

And he smeared a small blob of turpentine on his forehead cut. The creature didn't flinch when the turpentine hit the cut and I know it had to have stung him, but he didn't show it. He only nodded his head. I was standing near the creature now. He had large black eyes, angled like an oriental person, a small pug nose, a small mouth with almost no lips, and he had dull white teeth. The herbal drink must've helped him because later, he got up and motioned us to follow him into the crashed ship, and so we went in.

There were eight other creatures lying dead, scattered around inside the ship. There were four small metallic chairs with cushions, in the middle of the ship, and other chairs around the ship's edges. And directly in front of the chairs, at the edges, there was some kind of black screen with blinking lights on it.

The creature went over and sat down on one of the chairs at the edge. In front of him was a black screen with green colored lights moving around on it, making all kinds of shapes; like ocean waves, and then it would change into a green line that moved like a sidewinder snake across the sand.

The creature punched some white buttons on a black box and then he got up and went over to the corner and opened a metallic door. He reached in and started pulling out loaves of bread, wrapped in a silver sticky paper, and he handed them to us and we took them. He opened the silver paper and tore off a corner of the bread and he ate it. He smiled at us and motioned for us to eat the bread too, and we did. It was the best tasting bread I'd ever had—it had a honey sweet taste to it, and it was crispy brown on the outside and chewy in the middle. Then he opened another metal door and pulled out some small, shiny metal cans and he opened one and drank from it. He handed us some cans and showed us how to open them and we did and we drank from them. The drink was sweet too and it bubbled in your mouth.

Then, he motioned us to follow him as he walked back outside, and we did. We stood around the crashed ship and ate our sweet bread and drank from the shiny can. The creature pointed to his chest and then he looked up and pointed to the sky, and then he pointed to the ground.

He said something to us, but we couldn't understand him. His voice had a gurgling sound to it, like fast water in a stream rushing over rocks. We shrugged our shoulders and shook our heads and he just nodded his head and grinned.

Suddenly, in the blink of an eye, another ship,

like the crashed one, appeared in the sky above us. It hovered a moment in midair, like a humming bird, and it made no sound. Then, it descended slowly and touched down on the earth.

We were frightened by it, and started to run, but the creature started wildly waving his arms at us, and he motioned for us to come back; he stooped down and picked up a loaf of the sweet bread and pointed to it and we came back.

As we stood there, looking at the ship, the creature pointed again to his chest and then he pointed at the ship. A shiny metal door opened out of the ship. Metal stairs came out of the door and rested on the ground. Then we saw a group of about six creatures coming out of the door, dressed in shiny blue suits; they looked similar to the creature we helped, but each one had different facial features.

The hurt creature went over to one of the creatures, who seemed to be the chief because he had colored shoulder patches on his suit, and they hugged each other. Then the hurt creature turned around and pointed at us, then he pointed to the cut on his head, and he spoke to the chief in that gurgling language.

The chief creature smiled and nodded his head, then he turned and said something to the other creatures and they nodded their heads in approval at us.

After they had removed the dead creatures bodies from the crashed ship into the new ship, the hurt creature then came over to us and motioned us to follow him and we did.

He backed us up away from the crashed ship, and then he looked at the chief and he nodded his head. The chief looked over to the pane of red windows on his ship; I looked and saw the form of a creature standing in the window.

The chief waved his hand in the air, and the creature in the window waved back. And suddenly, a bright red light came out of the ship, completely covering the crashed ship. And as we watched, the crashed ship slowly faded away, like a dying rainbow. And when the old indian, who had been shaping the spearhead, saw this, he fell to his knees and bowed to the chief creature.

But when the chief creature saw him do this, he walked over to the old indian and, shaking his head, he reached out his hand and brought the old man up to his feet. Then the chief creature patted the old indian's shoulder and he turned and walked back toward the ship; and the other creatures followed him as he walked back up the metal steps.

And then the hurt creature collected the shiny metal cans he'd given us and he put them in a clear bag. He patted the old indian man's shoulder and then he turned around and headed back towards the ship. But as he went, the old indian called out to him and the creature turned and looked at him. The old indian smiled and held up a loaf of the sweet bread and he pointed to it.

The creature turned and disappeared into the ship. He came out a few moments later, carrying two armloads of the sweet bread, and came over and handed them to us. Then he stepped back and gave us a half-bow, and we all bowed back.

The creature turned and went back up the steps, and when he got to the last step, he turned and waved to us, and we waved back.

The ship's door closed behind him, and then the ship rose quietly up in the air. It paused a second, and through the red glass panes, we could see the creatures forms inside, and all of them stood side by side, waving at us, and as we waved back, the ship took off fast, swinging off into the night sky, like a hummingbird.

We walked back up to our campfire, carrying the loaves of sweet bread. Then, the old man picked four of us boys to go with him, me included, and he gathered up his paint brush and some paints. And he led us to a hidden cave, about a ten minute walk down off the canyon floor.

We took turns holding up the torches so he could see, and the old indian began painting and re-creating on the cave wall, the scenes of the crashed ship, and the creatures that we had seen. And when he was done, we were amazed at how well he had drawn out what we had seen. And that night, we set out a plate of food with candles lit around it, to give thanks to the "Star Gods" as the old indian called them, for their gift of sweet bread.

And suddenly, as we were walking along the rocky trail, leading back up to where we slept, I woke up in my warm bed in Latvia, to the ticking sound of the small grandfather clock I had next to my bed.

I looked at the clock, and in the moonlight coming through the window, I saw that it was three o'clock in the morning. For some reason I was not groggy, but I woke up feeling refreshed, with the dream clearly in my mind. I must wake up Nick and tell him, I thought. Excited by the dream, I threw the covers back and hurriedly put on my leather slippers so my feet didn't get cold from the stone floor. I got up and tried to be quiet, but the door gave out a loud squeaking noise.

Nick's room was three doors down and across the long hallway from my room. I got to his door and tried to quietly open it but it squeaked and squealed too, like a caught pig.

Nick woke up when he heard the door squeak, and he saw me standing there.

"What's the matter boy?" Nick said, groggy. "What time is it?"

"It's three o'clock Nick," I whispered, and sat down on his bed beside him. "Nick, I just saw 'the men from the sky.'"

"Who?" he asked, not yet fully awake. "Men? What men?"

"The men from the sky—remember? The men you told me about from the Rattlesnake book—the men the Mayans saw and wrote it in the pyramid stone."

"Oh, yeah, those men—they were here Eddie?"

he asked me, puzzled.

"No, Nick, I saw them in a dream I just had."

"Oh, a dream—well, that's just as good. Okay," he said, getting out of bed, "now we've got to write it down. Remember how I've always told you to write down your dreams and visions? I don't care how crazy they seem.

"You know the Bible prophets always wrote down their dreams and visions. I think the dreams are messages from the past or the future. And one day, you'll see them again.

"You see Ed, a dream from your past life doesn't go away, oh, it sleeps sometimes, but it always comes back to help you—but how can it help you if you forget the details of it? Now, I'm a better writer than you right now, so you tell me the dream and I'll write it down for you. But later on, when you get older, you remember to write them down."

So Nick lit the kerosene lamp on the bedside table and he took out a new tablet of paper with a black cover. He took his pencil out and wrote: "Dreams and visions of Ed Leedskalnin. Beginning on the night of April 29, 1893. Ed woke his Grandfather Nick up at three o'clock in the morning, to tell him of the dream, and Nick wrote it down for him."

Then, as I was describing the dream to Nick, the door opened and mama appeared: "What are you two doing? Having a party?"

I explained to her about the dream and that Nick said I should write it down, so that's what we're doing.

"All right," she said, "but be quiet, Ed, going back to your room so you don't wake Gus—you know how ornery he can get when he doesn't get his sleep."

I was so proud of the dream book when Nick got it all written down; I liked to see my dream written out in words. Somehow, just seeing the gray penciled words on the white paper seemed to give the dream a certain sense of reality—like the stories I read in the Bible or something, I don't know; I just liked it. And when I got older, I loved the feel of the pencil in my hand as the words took life on the paper.

And I don't know why, but I loved the feel of newspaper—I liked the crinkling sound it made when you rolled it in your fingers.

Another thing I loved, was when my pencil got dull, and I had to take out my pocket knife Nick had given me, and sharpen it—I loved the smell of the fresh-cut pencil wood, mingled with the fresh-cut lead. And when I got done sharpening it, I'd hold the sharpened end up to my nostrils, and I'd take a deep inhale—it was a clean, woodsy, intoxicating smell to me.

And then, I'd take the pencil and roll it in my fingers, looking closely at the newly exposed wood grains that I'd created on the sharpened end. And I always sharpened it over an open match box, to catch the little wood and lead shavings that fell off. And sometimes, before I'd write in my tablet, I'd open the match box and I'd inhale the smell of the lead and wood shavings. It was just a little writing ritual that I had cultivated, because for some reason, it seemed to put me in the mood for putting words on paper.

One of my favorite books when I was growing up was "The Time Traveler" by H.G. Wells. I remember Nick bought me a copy of it, because I about wore the library's copy out. The copy he bought me had a red leather cover, with the title and the author's name printed in gold letters.

I got bored with school and quit in the fourth grade. I knew what I wanted to do. I wanted to be a stone cutter. I'd been practicing at it for a long time now, and I'm not bragging, but Nick said I had a natural talent for it.

I went up into the quarry mines near Bear mountain and bought my own pieces of granite. Then, I'd carve them into fancy tombstones and sell them to the wealthier class. I set my own office up in an empty room in the castle. And it wasn't long before I was doing a good business just by word of mouth.

I think a lot of people enjoyed coming to the castle and driving in over the draw bridge. They seemed to enjoy the personal attention I gave them, and they left satisfied.

When I was eighteen, Nick came home from one of his sea-going trips and he thought we ought to expand my business and build a building for the tombstone company. Nick wanted me to manage it—he didn't want to be tied down to it. Ever since his wife Alma had died, he said the sea became his best mistress. And every now and then, he had to get on a boat and feel the wind and smell the ocean.

Nick got a bank loan and we bought a half-acre lot in downtown Riga, on Herzog street, straight across from the Karl Landrum hospital. Maybe it was morbid thinking, Nick said, but why not build a tombstone business across the street from a hospital? Sometimes it's a short trip from the womb to the tomb, Nick said.

Nick had the idea to build a small scale version of The Great Pyramid for our tombstone office. We built it with field stone, covered over inside and out with polished limestone blocks and marble.

Nick finished the top of the pyramid with glass so the building needed very few lights on sunny days. Nick put a limestone balcony on the top floor so he could gaze at the stars at night through his telescope. The pyramid stood as tall and wide as a courthouse. The carved mahogany door had flying angels playing harps on it.

Nick named the place "The Pharaoh Monument Company." The place was lit up at night with soft blue neon lights skirting the bottom and running all the way up the corner pyramid sides.

A six foot wide pathway, made of smooth gray cobblestones, led up to the front door. Six large carved, limestone sphinxes, sat facing each other on both sides of the path. Sometimes at night, people liked to walk by and they'd stop and stare at the place.

We were making good money in the tombstone business, Ed wrote in his diary, in the year 1912. I was twenty six years old. We drove a brand new, black, Ford Model T car, imported from America. We would've bought a different color than black if we could have (we saw enough black at funerals in the tombstone business) but they only made them in black.

We always wondered why Mr. Ford was so fond of black. 1912 was the year the Titanic sank. And it was the year I met Agnes Scuffs.

"I'll never forget the day;" Ed wrote in his diary, "I wrote it down; it was a sunny monday, April 25, 1912, at exactly 1:30 P.M. I'd just returned from a wonderful lunch at the Tamariz, a little indoor, outdoor cafe on Estoril street in downtown Riga. I had smoked salmon with thin-sliced, deep fried potatoes and green peas with mushrooms."

I was sitting at my desk, doing some paperwork, when I heard the front door bell ring as the door opened. I stepped out into the display area and saw two, well dressed women, that at first glance, appeared to be a mother and her young daughter. The older attractive lady had on a long navy blue dress with a matching hat and the daughter had on a shiny red, lacy dress that went almost to the floor; she had a matching red hat and she carried a red parasol bordered with red lace.

Years later, Ed wrote, people always asked me what was so special about Agnes, and what did she have that so affected me. Love at first sight is a hard thing to describe, but I guess if I had to put it in one word, it would be exotic. Agnes had the most unusual combination of facial features I'd ever seen.

Agnes had big, dark black oriental eyes. They were almond shaped, sitting at a slightly tilted angle in her small face. She was shorter than me, about 4 feet 9 inches tall, with a pug nose that ended with slightly flaring nostrils. Her mouth, with thick full lips, stood out with a prominent "M" shape in the middle of her top lip. Her ears were small and laid flat against her head. I never did like girls with ears that stuck out too far from their head.

Her thick, wavy, shiny black hair, hung down almost to her waist. She had it all combed over to one side, so that it hung over her left shoulder.

And it was held up at the top of her head with a tortoise shell comb. Her dark hair was a lovely contrast to her creamy, olive oil colored skin.

Her eyebrows were wide and thick, with black hair crowded close together, like a feather, and they went all the way over the sides of her eyes, ending just short of the point where the sides of her eyes ended.

I had always loved the pictures of the Polynesian girls that Nick had brought back from his trips to Tahiti. If you put Agnes in a grass skirt, and darken her skin some, you've got that polynesian look. I used to always tell Nick that when I decided to get married, I was going to Tahiti and get me an island girl. I was thinking of this as I watched them come closer to me; and I'm thinking, miss Tahiti has just walked into my door.

I didn't realize it until later, when I went back and read Madame Drusa's description of the girl she saw with me in the park, in her dream before I was born, how much Agnes fit Madame Drusa's description of the girl in her dream. Agnes even had her hair fixed in the same manner as Madame Drusa had described.

I got nervous just looking at Agnes; my hands shook and got sweaty. I swallowed hard and nervously cleared my throat. The mother looked distressed, and I had learned to react to the mood of the people who came in. I kept a somber, professional expression and introduced myself.

"I'm Marina Scuffs," the older lady said, looking dazed, "and this is my daughter Agnes."

Then she explained that her nephew, who was sixteen, "the same age as my daughter" she added, had been killed. Her sister, the boy's mother, was too shocked to come and pick out a tombstone so she was coming to do it for her.

Marina explained her sister's family had gone to Spain on holidays during the time of the annual running of the bulls. They were watching them run through the street from the balcony of their hotel. One minute, their son was standing by them, and the next minute, he was gone.

He got carried away in the excitement and ran down into the crowd near the street as the bulls came in front of the hotel. He got knocked down as the bulls suddenly veered toward the section of people he was standing with, and he got trampled to death by the people and the bulls.

As she talked, looking away from me sometimes, I was able to make eye contact with Agnes. She eyed me shyly, giving me a slight smile as our eyes met. I wondered if she could see, or feel, from the look in my eyes, what I was thinking. When Marina Scuffs had finished her story, I briefly expressed my sympathy and asked her if she'd like to look at some models of tombstones.

"Yes, I'm ready now," she said, and I led them down the hallway and into another display area room. She looked around for a moment at the various styles and she asked me: "Could you engrave a stone with a horse's head on it? Victor, my nephew, was fond of horses, like my late husband."

"Oh, yes, I could do that. Why don't we use a square granite block and that way I could do several horses with their manes flying in the breeze?"

"Yes, I'd like that. What do you think Agnes?"

"That sounds nice. Victor would like it."

"I'll begin at once. If you'll follow me back to my office, we'll write it up."

Sitting behind my desk, I was trying to think of a way to get Agnes' address and phone number, if she had one. Then it hit me: "Mrs. Scuffs, why don't I bill this to you? That will save your sister from seeing the bill in the mail and having to remember this all over again. Your sister can pay you back later."

"That's a wonderful idea. I'm so glad I came here now. Everybody speaks so well of your place Mr. Leedskalnin—"

"Oh please, call me Ed. You can give me your address if you'd like and I'll write it here on the bill." And she did, and they also had a phone number. There weren't too many phones in Riga at this time so I was happy to know they had one.

I knew Agnes was young, only sixteen, but she seemed to be very mature. That's only ten years difference between us. I wonder if that would matter to her?

I've never had the sight of any other girl affect me like this. I've always been a very careful, practical person; I'd never believed in love at first sight, but I do now.

When they had left and walked out the door, I moved from the door over to the front window so I could watch them walk away. Agnes had opened her red parasol and was carrying it over her shoulder. We had some lovely flowers growing along the walkway and Marina Scuffs stopped and bent down to look closer at them. Agnes stood there a moment, watching her mother. Then, to my surprise, Agnes turned around and looked back towards the front door. She saw me staring at them out of the window and she waved at me. I smiled and waved back. I was ruined for the rest of the day, except for thinking about Agnes. I just sat at my desk, hoping nobody would come in.

I was daydreaming about Agnes and I, on a beach somewhere, feeding each other fresh coconut and mango, and then taking a stroll on the beach at sunset. It was those Tahitian eyes that made me crazy. As soon as five o'clock came, I closed the shop and headed for The Blue Moon to have a beer. I left my car parked out behind the shop and walked; I needed to walk off some of this nervous energy.

The Blue Moon was only a few blocks from our

shop, in downtown Riga, at the corner of Kosco and Ruskin street. It was owned by Bruno Kravco, my best friend. The entire building, inside and out, was made of black slate rock. The Blue Moon was dome shaped, like an Arabian mosque.

It had a square porch, roofed with thin sheets of black slate layered close against each other. Lined up in a single file across the top of the porch were twenty six, black slate replicas of a crescent moon. The name, "The Blue Moon" was done in blue neon letters, and fixed to the row of crescent moons positioned over the front, heavy-slate door. The Blue Moon name, done in fancy silver letters, was also bolted to the front door's face.

Bruno Kravco, like my grandfather Nick, was fascinated by the moon and he looked at it often through his telescope. When he went into the bar business, he wanted something different, so he built The Blue Moon out of black slate, and being inside it, gave you the feeling of the nighttime sky.

The floor was done in a rough finished black slate. Lined up against the walls were cozy booths of black slate fitted with comfortable blue cloth cushions. All the lights in the place were done in a moon theme.

There was a large slate fireplace in the middle of the bar room. Near the fireplace, was a full-sized shiny suit of knight's armor. The right arm of the armor was raised up towards the knight's face, with the metal fingers of it's hand close to the mouth. The hand held an empty liquor bottle instead of a jousting pole. Bruno said some drunk had put it in the knight's hand one night and he had just left it there.

I walked up the black slate steps and stepped into the half light of the cavernous Blue Moon. People were just coming in for a beer before they went home. Bruno was leaning with his elbows on the bar, talking to some elderly man I didn't know.

I walked to the middle of the slate bar top and

pulled out a brass stool and sat down. I wanted to get Bruno away from his customer so I could talk to him.

Bruno excused himself from the man and walked over to me.

He wasn't very tall but he was built like a gorilla, with an enormously wide chest and huge arms; but he wasn't fat, he had good tight muscles. But even though he was a big man, he didn't push people around, he was friendly and everybody loved him. His personality was perfect for the bar business.

"Hey Bru," I said, "have a beer with me, I'm celebrating."

"Celebrating what?—some rich person die and need a tombstone?"

"Nope. Pour the beer first, then I'll tell you."

Bruno turned around, filled two mugs, and then sat one down in front of me. I picked up the mug and raised in the air towards him and our mugs clinked together. I took a sip and set it down on the counter.

"So, what's the big secret?—you strike gold?"

"Better than that—I'm getting married."

"Getting married? I thought you broke up with Helena—"

"It's not Helena. I just met her, today. A couple of hours ago. Bru, you know how I've always told you I wanted one of those Tahitian looking girls, like the ones in the photos Nick brought back?"

"Yeah, I remember."

"Well, she walked in the shop this afternoon, right after lunch. Bru, I've never seen anything like this one—I mean I could hear the Tahitian music and the ocean waves breaking on the warm sand."

"What has got into you? I've never heard you talk like this. It took you two years to decide on the color of a car, and they only come in black. Who is this girl? Do I know her?"

"I don't know, her name is Agnes Scuffs." Bruno looked surprised when I said her name. He said:

"Agnes Scuffs?—she's still in diapers."

"Diapers? Oh come on, she's sixteen years old—and she's very mature for her age—I think. How do you know her?"

"I don't. I've seen her around, but it's been awhile. I knew her daddy. He used to come in here sometimes and have a cognac."

"What happened to him?"

"Nobody knows for sure. He was some big time race horse trainer. He was a small guy, built about like you. He started off as a jockey until he had a bad fall and hurt his leg. After he got better, he decided to quit jockeying and go into training.

"They said he had a wonderful way with horses, and before long, he was working with the best bred horses in the world. All the big money people fought over him to train their horses.

"His name was Kovak. He was returning from a big race in Ireland, heading back to Latvia on a ship at night. He'd caught a virus or something in Ireland, a couple of hours before the ship left. They pulled out of Ireland at dusk and they said Kovak ate a light supper and then went back and laid down in his cabin.

"Well, he was sweating like a whore in church, they said, his stomach started cramping, and then he'd get dizzy spells. Kovak went to sleep about ten o'clock, they said. The cabin boy said when he went to Kovak's room, around eleven o'clock, Kovak was gone.

"The cabin boy said he noticed vomit on the floor near the bed. They searched the entire ship and figured that Kovak must've started vomiting, and he got up and went outside and maybe hung onto the rail to vomit; then at some point, maybe the ship lurched in the sea or something, and Kovak fell over the rail and into the sea. Anyway, his body was never found.

"Agnes looks just like her daddy—he had those same oriental eyes and olive skin. He was a nice guy too. He could've been a ladies man if he'd wanted, but he was crazy about Marina and Agnes, and he was strictly a family man. Agnes was crazy about her daddy too. She was an only child, like you. Kovak was teaching her how to train horses; she loved horses and the track. Her mama was against it, you know, a girl hanging around a race track, but Agnes is a highly spirited girl, and Marina gave in and let her go with her daddy a lot."

"Was Agnes on the trip with him when he died?"

"No, she didn't go on that trip. Kovak came in for a drink right before he left for Ireland. We got to talking and he told me that Agnes had fallen madly in love with a boy at the track six months before, but the boy dropped her; Agnes was still heartbroken so she couldn't think of setting foot in Ireland again so soon."

"Well, when did Kovak die?"

"It hasn't been that long ago—about a year ago. Agnes had just turned fifteen and I think Kovak said the boy was eighteen. Kovak said he thought it was puppy love and that Agnes would get over it in time, but she was still shook up about it. You know how that first love can mess you up when it goes wrong. Do you think Agnes is interested in you?"

"I'm not sure Bru—you really think I'm too old for her?"

"No, I was just giving you a hard time. Hey, my grandfather was twelve years older than my grandmother and they got along great."

"Did they really?"

"Sure—ten years is nothing. Well, come to think of it, they did have a problem one time—"

"What happened?"

"Well, it seems grandaddy had an impotent spell, the doctor said it was from the strain of trying to keep up with a younger woman—and grandmother got to messing around with a younger man—"

"Now Bru, don't tell me that—you're lying—aren't you?"

"Yeah, I'm lying. They got along fine. Hey, if anything, grandma, when she got older, she told mama she had a hard time keeping up with my grandfather—he was a stud, she used to say."

"Really? Your folks talked about stuff like that?"

"Oh yeah, all my family on both sides were always talking and joking about that kind of stuff. It was just part of life they always said, nothing to be ashamed of."

Three days later, on a rainy wednesday afternoon, I went to the funeral for Agnes' cousin. I stood around in the crowd behind the casket at the burial site, but I didn't go under the tent, and give my condolences because there were so many people.

All I wanted was for Agnes to see me there and we made a brief eye contact. I didn't go by her cousin's house after the funeral because it was for family only.

After lunch, on friday, two days after the funeral, Ed wrote, I drove out to Agnes' house. It was just inside the city limits, on a dirt road named Elba. Mama had baked a fresh blueberry pie, and I figured I'd carry it over to Agnes and talk to her awhile.

Her house was made of nicely finished field stone, with a long front porch and a shingled tin roof, imprinted with a fancy, fish-scale design. Agnes was sitting on the front porch in a rocking chair, peeling potatoes over a tin wash pan, when I pulled up. She was dressed in a plain white, linen work dress, with an apron embroidered with fabric cut outs of black and white cows. Her long, curly black hair was pulled over and hanging down on her left shoulder, like the first time I saw her.

An old speckled, brown and white hound, wearing a frayed leather collar, stood up on the porch and barked like he'd seen a burglar. "Hush Ozlo!" Agnes yelled at him, and he lowered his head, but he kept his eyes on me, and woofed as I came up the stone steps.

"Hi Ed. I do wish you'd called before you came out—I look like a mess."

"What? Oh, you look fine to me. I brought you a blueberry pie, mama just baked it."

"Oh, that was sweet of her. I'll take it inside and

put it in the pie safe. Have a seat. Mama isn't here, she's over visiting the relatives. Excuse me for working while we talk but I need to finish these potatoes before supper."

I handed her the pie and sat down in a rocking chair. "Oh, that's fine. Bring me a knife back and I'll help you—"

"Oh no, you don't have to do that. You like potatoes?"

"I love'em; fried, boiled, run over, shot at—any way you make'em, I'll eat'em."

She took the pie in and came back out and started on the potatoes. She had small delicate hands, hands that looked like they were meant for a piano or a doctor's hands.

"Listen, Ed," she said, "you hear that?" In the distance I heard a bird shrieking and then a woodpecker banging on a tree.

"That's one of those giant woodpeckers; they're big as a crow. I love that loud banging noise he makes. He's hunting his insect lunch in some old tree."

"Yeah. I looked at one of those birds through some binoculars one day—their bill looks as big as a pick-axe. Can you imagine what he'd do to your head if he ever got hold of you? I like your apron."

"Thank you. Mama made it for me. She's good at sewing."

I couldn't believe I was sitting so close to this beautiful woman. I got nervous when she looked at me with those slanted eyes; my throat got dry and my palms sweaty. She had on a soft red lipstick and her lips shined in the reflected sun light. As as I watched her mouth her words, I couldn't help but stare at her full lips, as the light off her lips moved up and down.

For me she possessed every appealing virtue necessary to please a man in every way. She was slim, lovely to look at; innocent, and she had a childlike, giggling laugh.

She brought life to a chore as boring as peeling potatoes. With a knife in her delicate hands, she went quickly, around a potato, smiling at me now and then, as her hands continued the work unconsciously. I got nervous as I thought of how to ask her out—would she think I'm too old for her? Only one way to find out, Bruno had said. "Agnes, have you ever been to the Tamiriz?"

"Oh, yeah, but it's been awhile. I went with mama and daddy a few times. It's a wonderful place. I love the band there. Do you like to dance?"

"Yeah. I love music and dancing. They have great crab legs, too. Do you like sea food? I'm thinking of going there tomorrow night, would you like to go with me?"

"Oh Ed, I'd love to—but I don't think mama will let me go alone. I mean she likes you a lot, it's just that, well, me being sixteen—"

"Oh, I completely agree, I'd love to have her come along. It'd do her good to get out of the house. Will she be okay at the Tamiriz?—you know, dealing with the past memories there?"

"Oh sure, she's been back there since we lost daddy. You wouldn't mind her going along?"

"No, of course not. Agnes, I'm twenty six—does that bother you?"

"No. If it had bothered me, I would've told you."

Oh, the way she talked! She made me feel like I could tell her anything. Encouraged by her words, I asked her if I could tell her things that I normally wouldn't tell someone until I knew them better. She was curious and told me to go ahead.

I asked her if she believed in reincarnation, and she said she wasn't sure but she thought that it was possible. And then I told her about mama getting the reading from Madame Drusa before I was born. I told her about the girl Madame Drusa described seeing me with in her dream of my former life in Atlantis.

"Madame Drusa's description of that girl fits you Agnes, even your oriental eyes, even the way you wear your hair."

"Really? Isn't that strange? But what a wonderful story. And isn't that something?—that she predicted when you would be born. I think it's possible that certain people are chosen and given prophecies of things to come—like the Bible prophets used to do."

"Agnes, can I tell you something even deeper?" She looked at me and grinned when I said this. "What is it?" I said, "why are you laughing? Are you making fun of me?"

"Oh no!" she assured me, "please continue, I like they way you talk, it's just your face, the way you express yourself; I can tell you're sincere, there's nothing fake in what you say. Now what is it? Please tell me."

"All right, I'll tell you, but I'm telling you something I shouldn't tell you—don't get swell-headed when I tell you, promise me?"

"Yes captain," she mocked, "your words are safe with me."

"You'll think I'm crazy, but Agnes, you're going to be my love—I knew it the first time I saw you when you walked into my shop. I've never known anything like this. Does it bother you for me to talk like this?"

"Oh, no. I like your honesty and courage to say it. But Ed, it is crazy—you don't even know me."

Maybe Agnes was right, but all I knew was that what I felt for her was something new and wonderful, and I wanted to see where it went.

Then, a voice from below the porch said: "Excuse me Aggie." We looked down and there stood a midget-looking man, less than four feet tall. He was dressed in a green silk, jockey's outfit with a matching green riding cap, and knee-length, black riding boots.

He had a handsome boyish face and appeared to be about twenty five years old. And I was thinking, now what is this boy doing dressed like he's getting ready to ride in a horse race?

"I'm sorry to bother you," he says, "but I wanted

you to listen out for me—I finished chopping the fire wood, so I'm going out back and try to cut Monster's tusks—"

"Eldar, please don't do that—mama told you to leave that crazy hog alone. The circus man said he's too wild to tame—"

"Yeah, but that circus man don't know how good I am with animals. Don't worry Aggie, when I get his tusks off, all he can do is gum me to death—or run over me—and I reckon I'm used to that."

"Ed," Agnes said, "this is my cousin Eldar. Eldar this is Ed—"

"You know anything about hogs?" he asked me.

"Well, I know they go good with eggs. Yeah, my father has hogs—"

"I bet he don't have any as big as Monster. I got him from the Russian circus when they was passing through. The circus man told me he was listed as the biggest African boar hog ever caught."

Then Eldar, using his hands to explain, said: "And Ed, he's got pink balls as big as grapefruits—"

"Eldar!" Agnes yelled indignantly, "watch your mouth around company."

But Eldar ignored her and continued: "Now when I cut his tusks off, I'm gonna cross-breed him with my other hogs, then I'll have the biggest slaughter hogs in the entire world; they might even put my picture in the paper."

"That's a good idea Eldar," I told him, "but have you got some big sows?"

"No, they're just regular size—why?"

"Well, see, if you take that big hog and cross him on a regular hog, then the babies may be too big for the smaller sow to handle and she may die trying to have them—"

"Oh—I hadn't thought of that."

"What you need to do is find the biggest sows in Latvia and buy some of them to cross on Monster. There's a man my daddy knows, his name is Viktor Alla.

"He's got some big sows—he imported them from a farming area of Ukraine. Hey, what you might work out, is to make a deal with him to use his sows and then split the babies later on, and you wouldn't have to buy a sow. He's a good man, you can trust him—"

"Oh, great. Would you ask him for me?"

"Sure, be glad to."

"Thanks. Well, goodbye, I got some surgery to do," Eldar said, and he walked off.

"Oh Ed, I'm sorry for the way he talked," Agnes said, when Eldar was out of sight. "Eldar isn't right in the head. He was one of the best jockeys in the country until his horse went down in a race in Ireland and he got kicked in the head. The doctors said he has a mild form of brain damage—he's not dangerous, but he'll always be like a child.

"He wanted to come live with us after daddy died, to help us out, and his parents let him come. He and daddy were real close—daddy taught him how to ride.

"Eldar is unpredictable. Not long ago, he went into town, dressed in nothing but his bath robe, riding hat and boots. And he still thinks he's a jockey—I believe he'd try and ride a kangaroo if he could find one."

"That's a shame." Then, as I was leaving, I said: "Agnes, ask your mama about dinner tomorrow night—I'll call you later and see what she says."

When I got home, I walked into the kitchen and mama was making dinner. I said, "Mama, what would you say if I told you I was in love?"

"I'd say it's about time—you're twenty six years old. Who is it?"

"Agnes Scuffs."

"Oh, the girl you met in the shop? She's young isn't she?"

"Yep. Sweet Sixteen—do you think I'm too old for her? Bruno gave me a hard time about it, but he thinks it's okay."

"Well, I think it depends on Agnes. If she's mature for her age, I don't think ten years would matter."

"Really? Oh, mama, she's real mature. She said she had to grow up when her daddy died. You think it's okay?"

"Yes. But how does she feel about you?"

"I think she likes me. I mean, she agreed to go out with me. She's beautiful mama—I've had girlfriends, but I've never had anybody hit me like Agnes. It's her eyes mama, she's got the most incredible eyes—and real long, curly eyelashes. I tell you, when she looks at me with those big slanted eyes, and she bats those long eyelashes—I can feel my heart start pounding. I'm telling you, now I see why some people can go crazy over love affairs."

Mama said: "Boy, I believe you've got it bad."

Then I told mama about maybe taking Agnes and her mother out to dinner at the Tamiriz tomorrow night. She thought it was smart, asking Agnes' mother to go along, and mama said, "I sure hope it works out for you son, you've waited a long time to fall in love."

I called Agnes the next day, around noon, and she made me feel good because she sounded happy and excited to talk to me. She said, "Oh Ed, mama was delighted that you're interested in me—I told her about how you were so honest on the porch, when you told me how you liked me the first day you saw me.

"And she thought it was sweet of you to think of asking her to go with us—I don't know why but she trusts you; I think she might've let us go alone, but it's better this way, now she knows you're sincere."

I had a favorite shirt that I liked to dress up in. It was a white, Egyptian cotton shirt with a banded collar that Nick had picked up for me on one of his travels to England. Egyptian cotton is world famous for it's strength and softness; it's weave is so tight that there's only a slight wrinkle in it after it's washed, so it doesn't need much ironing. But mama ironed it for me anyway; she didn't want me leaving the house in even a slightly wrinkled shirt.

That saturday night, I picked Agnes and her mother up at six and we went to the Tamariz. It was a warm August night and we sat outside and had dinner under the open sky. They had a band set up at the end of the place and a slab of smooth concrete to dance on. The band was good and I danced with Agnes one dance and her mother the next.

I got nervous when I held Agnes' hand in mine as we danced. Her hand was so tiny and dainty and it fit perfectly in my small hand. As we danced, she would get a serious look on her face and she would stare deeply into my eyes. She said, "I like the way you dance." And it drove me crazy to have her this close to me. Her waist was tiny, and my arms fell perfectly around her small hips. But it was looking into those Tahitian eyes that got to me; I had simply never seen anything like her.

Agnes was sweet and shy for someone so beautiful. I couldn't believe I had this beautiful thing in my arms. I knew then I had to have her. I knew I loved her. I had never loved anyone in my life until now. My heart felt like it was going to beat itself out of my chest.

Later on, a man who knew Agnes' mother came by our table and joined us. He was a nice man and Agnes' mother seemed to like him and they danced a lot. I was surprised when later, Agnes' mother told me to go ahead and take Agnes home, she said she trusted me and it was all right. I was a happy man. When Agnes and I got in the car, she slid right over so close that her knee was touching mine.

Before I could put the car in gear, she was looking serious at me, and I stared back at her. I put my arms around her neck, and we looked at each other for a minute. I said, "I'm crazy about you."

And she said, "I'm crazy about you too."

"You told me on the porch I was crazy for saying you were going to be my love."

"I know. That means I'm just as crazy as you are. Ed, please don't hurt me."

"Hurt you? Baby, I would never do that to you."

And then she kissed me deeply and she pulled back: "I hope you don't think bad of me, but I've been wanting to do that all night. I've been thinking of you and how sweet you talked to me on the porch."

"No, I don't think bad of you at all. And what I said was true." I put the car in gear and headed out for Agnes' house. On the way over she laid her head on my shoulder and I could feel the warmth of her body. I knew it was all over for me. She was my girl now.

When we got to her house, I pulled into the dirt driveway and shut the car off.

I turned and looked at her and she lifted her head off my shoulder and kissed me deeply again. After a moment of deep kissing, I pulled back and cupped both of my hands around her face, I stared into her eyes without saying anything. She stared back a moment, then she said: "What are you thinking about?"

"When is your birthday?"

"April 10, when is yours?"

"April 10? I should've known—I don't believe this—mine is March 26, we're both Aries. No wonder we're so much alike; you're the first Aries woman I've known."

"I take it that's a good sign? I don't know much about that kind of stuff."

"Well, I don't get up and read horoscopes every day to figure out what to do, but I believe that people do have certain personality traits that are caused by the position of the planets at the birth time. Remember, when Jesus was born, the wise men were guided by a star."

"Oh yes, that's right. I'm glad you like to read. Some men don't like reading. What are Aries people supposed to be like?"

"Well, mainly, they have an obsessive type of personality, so I have to be careful not to smoke, or I'll smoke all day; and if I drink, sometimes I don't know when to quit. I like to control things, and I don't want to be a drunk, so I have to tell myself that I can quit when I want to."

"I'm glad you're an honest man; how do you feel when you're with me?"

"Why don't you tell me something about you? I'm the one doing all the talking—"

"I'll talk later, you first. I want to hear it—every detail, from the moment you first saw me in your shop—I saw the way you looked at me. I liked it very much."

"Okay, I'm twenty six and I've never been in love. I've had some close calls but never had anybody that got to me. Mama said love isn't practical—it's a thing of mystery. When you have the right person it's beautiful; when you have the wrong person, it's ugly. I don't know why Agnes, but I was shocked when I first saw you in my shop—"

"Okay, tell me the exact thought that popped into your head; do you remember it?"

"Yes. I thought, 'Oh my God—there's miss Tahiti.' You've got those exotic eyes—they did me in. Is there some oriental blood in your family somewhere?"

"Yes, my great grandmother on my Father's side, is chinese; she was from the mountains in Mongolia. That's where I got my black hair, olive skin and slanted eyes. Ed, don't be afraid to talk to me—I like what you're saying—but I've got to know you mean it. Some men tell you things to get what they want and then they're gone. I've got to know that you're not like that.

"Listen, if you feel something, anything, I don't care what it is—don't drive out of here tonight without telling me. I need to know you're serious about what you're saying; it's very important to me. Think about it and be sure that you mean what you say."

"I don't need to think about it—I told you the

truth. One trait about Aries is loyalty—when they find the right person that is. Aries men have a lot of the qualities of a child, they like to play. And, they may play the field for a long time, but when they decide to settle down, they give all they've got."

It was strange to me that we could have such a deep conversation this quickly. But things with Agnes always seemed to move fast. It flashed through my mind that Agnes might be a bit insecure. I thought about Bruno telling me about her boyfriend in Ireland who had rejected her. Is she maybe thinking that I'm like him?

I now had the feeling that she might be in love with me, but she was afraid to say it, for fear that I might reject her, like the guy in Ireland. This made me feel better because now I wasn't so intimidated by her beauty. Even beautiful women get insecure when they get jilted. I don't mean I was happy about her suffering, not at all, it's just that now I felt I could trust her to tell her that I loved her and she wasn't going to run off when I said the word love.

I had the feeling that maybe what she needed the most right now was for someone to reassure her that there was nothing wrong with her; to tell her that she was still desirable. I decided to let the hair go with the hide and tell her what I felt; if I lose, I lose.

"Look, you're the girl for me. I've never known anybody that I wanted to give everything I had to; when we danced tonight, and I held you in my arms—what I'm feeling is warm and strange to me. I'm going to enjoy this time with you—I can't believe I'm talking like this to you. Have I said too much Agnes?"

"No Ed, it was what I needed to hear; I'm not afraid now."

Then we both agreed that it felt like we'd known each other for a long time. Maybe she had been the girl in the park, in Madame Drusa's Atlantic vision.

Agnes and I both loved the ocean. During the next month, every friday night, we would go for dinner and dancing at the Tamariz. Then, saturday afternoon, about three o'clock, we'd get in my car and drive over to the port of Riga, to a little town named Jurmala (about an hour away).

We'd have dinner at our favorite seafood restaurant there called "Chef Lubana's." Agnes loved to walk along the beach at sunset and collect seashells. There were mostly only small shells scattered along the sand.

But sometimes, after a big storm at sea, Agnes would find the larger conch shells that had blown in from a little island named "Ruhun" that sat in the middle of the Gulf of Riga. Agnes would squeal with delight when she found one of the larger shells and she would carry it home and put it in her room.

One day, I found a large clam shell, complete with both sides. I slipped it into my pocket without Agnes noticing. I drilled two small holes at the base of the clam shell and put Agnes' diamond engagement ring in it and then I filled the small holes with cement so the ring wouldn't slip out. The next saturday night, at the beach, Agnes and I built a fire from driftwood and sat around watching the fire and drinking wine.

The moon was full tonight so it was good for hunting shells. Agnes said, "Ed, let's go looking for shells," so we got up and took a small wicker basket to put the shells in and we went walking along the beach. Agnes spotted a small shell sticking up in the sand and she bent down to pick it up. As she did, I slipped the clam shell out of my pocket and tossed it a few yards away so she wouldn't see it.

Agnes brushed the sand off the shell and put it in the basket and we continued walking. As Agnes was looking on her side, I said, "Hey, there's one!" And I hurried over and picked up the clam shell with her ring in it. "Oh, it's beautiful Ed," Agnes said, admiring the perfect shape and brown and white striped color.

"I can't believe this," I said.

"What—that's it's a complete shell and not a half?"

"Well, yes but even more, it's a brown and white stripe. My grandfather said that this type of shell is common on the African coastline. And years ago, when the slaves were being carried away, sometimes they'd slip diamonds into clam shells and wear them as jewelry, and nobody suspected there were diamonds in them. Then, when the slaves got to America, or wherever they were going, they'd buy their freedom with the diamonds."

"Really? I never heard of that."

I was studying the clam shell closely as Agnes talked. "I don't believe this," I said, running my fingers over the shell's base.

"What? What is it?"

"Well, grandfather said that sometimes the slaves would drill two tiny holes at the shell's base, put the diamonds in and then seal the holes so it was hard to see the hole marks. The only way you could tell was to run your fingers along the back and feel for a small rough edge. I can feel a small rough edge, here run your fingers along here." I handed her the shell and she did it.

"Can you feel it?" I asked her.

"Yes! I feel it! Oh, Ed, do you really think there could be diamonds in here?"

"Well, baby, think about it—we've got a brown and white stripe clam shell, just like they used; and, we've got a rough-edged base—oh, I just thought of something!"

"What?"

"Well, if there's diamonds in here, then they're going to rattle if we shake the shell, right?"

"Oh, yes of course! I didn't even think of that! Shake it up darling—we may be rich!"

I started to shake it, then I said, "Wait—I better say a little incantation to bring forth the diamond spirits: 'Oh, God of silence, God of sound, let there be a diamond, when I shake this shell around.' Oh, honey, I'm too nervous—here you do it," I said, and handed her the shell. She took it in her hand and held it up to her right ear and she shook it gently; the diamond ring made a muffled rattling sound as it bounced around in the shell. Agnes got excited:

"Oh baby! There's something in there, here listen," she said, holding the shell up near my ear and shaking it.

"You're right!—I hear it! Let's go back to the camp fire and we'll open it by the light of the fire." So we hurried back to the fire and sat down. I took out a small pocket knife and began prying open the shell. When I had loosened it, I handed it to her: "Here baby, you open it; you seem to have good luck."

Agnes took it and held it close to the firelight. Her hands trembled as she slowly lifted the top off. Her eyes got big when she saw the ring: "It's a diamond ring!" she exclaimed, staring at it. Then she looked at me: "But if slaves had put it in here, wouldn't it be a raw diamond?"

"Well, you never know—it's possible it was their ring. Let me look at it closer." Agnes handed me the ring and I held it close to the firelight and I was looking closely at the inside of the gold band. On the inside band, I had the jeweler inscribe in tiny letters the name "Agnes."

I said: "I don't believe this, baby, look closely at the inside of the band," and I handed her the ring and she looked at it.

Surprised, she said: "Oh, Ed! You rat! I ought to know better than to believe you! You planted this here—I don't believe this!"

"Baby, do you like it?"

"Yes," she said, and she flung her arms around me and kissed me.

I took her hands in mine and I looked into her eyes. I said:

"Agnes Scuffs, will you marry me?"

"Yes, my darling rat," she said, and she kissed me and then she put her arms around me and she gave me a tight hug.

We set the wedding date for December 21,

1912. I chose that day, I told Agnes, because it's the shortest day of the year, and I wanted the marriage ceremony over quickly so we could get to the honeymoon. I realized later that I still hadn't learned the lesson of patience that Madame Drusa had mentioned in my reading before I was born. Patience was hard for me—when I wanted something, I wanted it now, not later.

It was now almost four months until our wedding and it seemed like it would never come. Agnes wanted to go to Florida on our honeymoon, which was fine with me. Nick had been there numerous times and told me it was beautiful. I loved the idea of spending Christmas in a place where it was warm and there was no snow to shovel.

One night, when we were going out to dinner at the Tamariz, Agnes gave me a bottle of bay rum cologne. She said it was her father's and she wanted me to have it, if I liked the smell. And after that, if I was out somewhere, or in a store and smelled some bay rum, it made me think of Agnes.

I loved it's clean fresh smell, and it reminded me of some far off, exotic island. The bay rum she gave me was called "Royal Spyce," and the brown bottle had a bay leaf imprinted on the front, and "Made in England," stamped on the bottom. The top was made of lead, molded in the shape of a king's crown.

I thought it must have been expensive to come in such a classy looking bottle; I kept the bottle in my room long after the cologne was gone. I kept it because it had been in Agnes' house and in her hands, and that made it special for me. Sometimes, when I smelled the bay rum, I liked to think that Agnes and I were living on some lush tropical island.

It had always been my dream to live on an island one day. Sometimes, when I was daydreaming about living in the tropics, I wondered if my tropical desires were maybe inspired by my former life in Atlantis. I'd always thought there had to be a reason or an explanation behind everything we do or want to do on earth. And the idea that I had been here before appealed to me greatly and I saw no harm in indulging my fantasies of a former life in Plato's and Edgar Cayce's Atlantis.

One thursday after work, about six o'clock, Agnes and I were walking down the street, going to see a movie, and we came by a little photography shop. It was one of those places where they had all kinds of costumes that you could put on and have your picture taken in. A couple of popular American western movies were a big hit in Latvia at the time, and there was a cowboy outfit and a red saloon girl's costume featured in the front window.

My eyes lit up when I saw the saloon girl mannequin, wearing a skimpy, red sequin, low-cut, tight-fitting body suit with red, fish-net stockings, and glossy red, high heel dress shoes.

"Oh baby," I said, "look at those red high heels and—oo! fish-net stockings. Baby, I've got to have a picture of you in that—let's have one made."

"No, no, I don't think so. What would mama say?"

"Nothing, if we don't tell her. Come on baby, do it for me, you know how I love red."

She finally gave in, but she made me promise not to let anyone else see the picture. Later, I went back and bought the saloon girl's outfit and I had it cleaned and I gave it to Agnes one night as a surprise. I would've bought her a new one but it was impossible to find such an outfit in Latvia.

Agnes had to keep it hidden from her mother. And one night I asked her to wear it under her dress, and when the evening was over, I wanted her to take it off and give it to me. The reason I did that is because I wanted the smell of Agnes' body to be left in the clothes. I don't know the right words for what you call a person who is greatly influenced by the sense of smell, but whatever the proper term is, I am one of those people.

And I was surprised, because Agnes didn't seem

to mind my request. I locked the red saloon outfit and Agnes' picture of her dressed up in it, in a large wooden trunk in my room. I carried that picture of Agnes with me everywhere I went, even into the trenches of WWI.

About a month before we got married, I had a strange dream one night. In the dream, the sun was shining brightly. Agnes and I were in the back seat of a red convertible with tan leather seats and a chauffeur was driving. We turned off to the right onto a curving paved highway lined on both sides with palm trees. A big wooden sign, painted pink and grey read: "Welcome to the Chalet Simone. Restaurant and Country Inn."

Then the car stopped in front of the restaurant. The whole place was made of pink and grey plastered concrete. It was designed to resemble a Swiss village, with grey wooden shutters on each window. There was a water fountain in the middle of the driveway with a white wrought iron bench in front of it.

The office was next to the restaurant and the two-story, pink guest houses were located behind the office. The office had a wood shingled roof where there was a small outdoor restaurant with a concrete dance floor, leading up to a swimming pool.

There were white wrought iron tables and chairs in the outdoor restaurant, and some were placed near the pool, in case you wanted to eat near the pool.

I saw mostly young couples dressed in brightly colored bathing suits, splashing around in the pool and some of them floated on rubber rafts. The chauffeur got out and opened the car door for us and told us to have a good meal.

An indoor restaurant was next to the outdoor restaurant. Inside, the wood floor was done in highly polished oak with thick luxurious persian rugs scattered around. There were oak bookcases, with hundreds of books in them, lining the parlor walls, done in pink plaster. All of the tables and chairs were done in a rich, dark-stained Victorian mahogany, with brass lamps covered in a dark green glass shade.

On the reception desk, I saw a book titled, "India Love Lyrics," by Lawrence Hope. The brightly colored cover showed a dark-skinned couple sitting under a skinny palm tree gazing intently at each other under a starry sky. A camel caravan, loaded down with spices, passed in the background behind them.

A lovely slim girl with long blonde hair and wearing a long, shiny blue dress, stood up from the reception desk: "Good afternoon and welcome to Chalet Simone. I'm sorry, but all the front tables are taken. But we have a room in the back with a long table, if you don't mind sharing it with others."

"That's fine," I said, and she led us off to the back through an open door. We entered a large dining room, with a vaulted ceiling and a long table in the middle, covered with a white cotton table cloth with crocheted hearts. Colored sunlight flooded the room from a large stained glass window on the south side.

On a second story, to the right of the food table, embedded into the wall, was a carved wooden replica of an ancient sailing ship. Emerging from the ship's bow was a life-like, painted wooden figure of a beautiful smiling woman, with long blonde hair; she was carved from the waist up. She wore a white, low cut dress, displaying the deep cleavage of her large breasts. Her arms were pulled back to her sides, as though she were flying.

Then, suddenly, the scene (in my Atlantis dream) changed. Agnes and I were sitting next to the pool at the outdoor restaurant, located near the indoor restaurant where the ship on the wall was. I remember that the tables had yellow tile tops, with hand painted scenes showing ancient oriental warriors in a battle, riding horses and firing arrows at their enemies.

I don't know why this scene stuck in my memory for so long, but I'll never forget it. There was a soft, glowing amber spotlight shining across the opposite end of the pool, and when the light reached our table, it bathed us in a golden glow; the same kind of glow that the setting sun makes at my favorite time of day.

I stared at Agnes' face in the amber glow. The whole scene seemed like a mirage. Then the band played a slow song that Agnes liked and we got up and danced. And that's where the dream ended. But when I woke up in the morning, it all came back to me, even the name of the book that I saw on the reception desk, and I wrote it all down.

Nick had always told me how important it was to write dreams down, because usually, if you studied your dreams, he said, somewhere later in life they might mean something to you.

It seemed like it took forever for December to come, but it finally did. I'll never forget December 20, 1912, the night before our wedding—I was so excited, I knew it was going to be hard to sleep tonight. About nine o'clock that night, Nick and I had gone up to the third story balcony for one last good drink of apricot brandy and a good cigar—my last as a single man. My father Gus had gone to bed and mama was downstairs ironing my wedding clothes.

Nick and I were looking over a map of Florida at some of the places Agnes and I might go on our honeymoon. Nick told me to be sure and stop at Florida City on the way to the Keys.

Nick said it was just a farming town but the soil there was rich and produced some of Florida's finest fruits and vegetables. Nick said the watermelons there were especially sweet because of the soil.

Nick had just finished saying, "Well, son, Agnes is a wonderful girl—I think you'll like being married. Twenty-six is a good age—" when mama appeared at the door.

"Ed," she said, "Agnes is on the phone, she wants to talk to you."

"Uh-oh, I hope she hasn't got cold feet," I joked, and I got up and went downstairs.

I picked up the phone, "Hi baby, Nick and I

were looking at a map of Florida; he said we should stop at Florida City—"

"Ed," she interrupted, "I can't marry you."

"What? Baby, what's wrong?"

She started crying, and in between the sobs, she said, "Ed, darling, please forgive me—I'm so confused, I don't know what to do—"

"Agnes don't do this to me—you're my life. Don't you love me?"

"Darling, I can't say I don't love you—but I'm saying that I can't marry you—"

"Agnes that doesn't make sense; now please, it's important for me to know why. What's going on?"

"Ed, I've got to go now—goodbye—"

"Agnes, wait, if you need time, I'll wait for you, I'll give you all the time you need—"

"No, Ed, don't wait for me—go on with your life. I'm telling you now, I can't marry you—"

"Aggie look, let me come over and talk to you—at least look me in the eyes and tell me you can't marry me—"

"No, Ed, don't come over," she said, her voice firm and somewhat colder. "Goodbye darling, please try and forgive me—" and she hung up.

Mama came into the kitchen as I hung up. She saw the pale and painful expression on my face.

"What's wrong Ed?" she asked.

"Agnes jilted me—she said she can't marry me."

"What? Oh God, no—she waits until the night before the wedding to tell you? But why? What did she say?"

"She wouldn't tell me why, just said she's confused. She said she loves me but couldn't marry me—"

"Oh, that's nonsense! What is she talking about?"

"I don't know mama—I don't know."

"Oh, Ed, she's panicked—that's what it is; she's young and maybe she's afraid of leaving her mama alone now that her daddy's dead. That's got to be it. Give her a few days and she'll be over it—"

"I don't know," I said, dazed.

"Oh, Ed I'm so sorry. But Ed, maybe it's better you found out now, instead of later."

I knew she was just trying to make me feel better, but I didn't want to hear it. I had lost the only thing in life that mattered to me. I wasn't in the mood for the practical side of it.

I had to move, I couldn't look at mama's painful expression. I knew she was hurting for me—she knew this was my first love and I was older when it happened, so maybe it hurt more. I don't know—pain is pain for me, no matter when it comes.

"Well, I guess I better go up and tell Nick," I said, and turned toward the upstairs.

"Ed," she called out to me, "honey, don't let this destroy you—there'll be others."

Mama meant well, but if there was anything I didn't want to hear it was "there'll be others." I didn't want "others," I wanted Agnes. I didn't turn around, I just mumbled, "Oh, I'll be fine mama, don't worry about me." And as I was saying this my legs felt wobbly and I felt weak in my stomach as I made my way slowly up the stairs. And I broke out into a cold sweat as I reached the balcony where Nick sat.

Nick took one look at me and said, "What's wrong? Is Aggie okay?"

"She jilted me Nick—said she can't marry me." Then I had to go into the whole story again. I'd only given it twice now and I was already sick of saying it, and hearing myself say it. Nick didn't give me any lectures of how it was good it happened now, which I was grateful for. He did better than that, he told me how he had handled the death of my grandmother. Here was something I could use.

"I tell you," he began, "when I lost your grandmother, I went crazy as a head-shot bat."

"What did you do Nick?"

"Well, right after the funeral—I mean, as soon as I could pack my bags, I jumped on a cargo ship headed for Tahiti. I couldn't stand the thought of going back to that empty house without your grandmother in it. No sir, I knew I had to get on the sea—I believe I'd of shot myself if I'd stayed on land.

"I knew it'd be awhile before we landed in Tahiti, and working on that ship and smelling the sea was the only medicine I could think of. Well, when we got to Tahiti, the first thing I did after we docked was to hit a little bar there, and I took me a good dose of drunk.

"Well, anyway, we'd been there for two days, when one day, I was at the market place, picking up some fresh fruit and vegetables, when I saw the most beautiful girl I've ever seen—shiny black hair, hanging down to her waist and straight as an ironing board.

"She saw me staring at her and she grinned at me—oh, she had beautiful white teeth. Well, that did it. I walked over to her and tried to introduce myself to her but she couldn't understand me.

"I noticed she was barefoot. And I had seen some nice leather sandals hanging there in the market for sale. So I bought her the sandals. And when she understood what I was doing, she got tears in her eyes. I went back over to the food place and bought all of her groceries and we went back to her house.

"The ship left three days later and I left three months later."

"Why didn't you stay and marry her Nick?"

"Oh, she wanted me too—she was crazy about me. But, I just didn't love her the same way I did your grandmother. I guess I'm just a one woman man; I never did find anyone else that made me feel like your grandmother."

Then Nick reached into his back pocket and pulled out his worn leather wallet. He opened it and took out a tattered slip of paper, yellowed with age. He handed it to me: "I found that in a book I was reading when your grandmother died—I don't even remember who wrote it. If you get depressed, just pull it out and read it."

The words read: The grand essentials of happiness are: "Something to do, Something to love and Something to hope for." Nick said the most important of the three was hope; he said nothing is possible without hope. As I finished reading the note, I heard the mournful sound of the evening train horn blowing, announcing it's departure. The train was leaving Latvia. I wondered where it was going tonight—I wish I could get on it—I don't care where it's going.

Why does the lonesome sound of that horn always make me sad, like nothing else can? Nick and I had talked about the train horn before, but we never could figure out why it was a sad sound; it was just one of those things. It sounded even sadder now for me—the train is leaving Latvia and Agnes has left me.

I went back downstairs and packed the rest of my personal things; all my books and the Mayan statue Nick had given me when I was a boy. I had decided to go on to Florida alone.

Mama said: "Son, you are coming back aren't you?"

"I don't know mama, I don't really know anything right now. But I don't think I could live here now—the Tamariz will never be the same. I could never eat or dance there again—I just couldn't."

Then mama handed me a book with my baby picture on the front cover of it and the date of my birth March 26, 1887. It was the reading that Madame Drusa had given her before I was born.

"I was gonna give it to you for your birthday," she told me, "but I guess I better give it to you now."

"It's beautiful mama," I told her and I hugged her.

She whispered to me: "You got to be strong now son—don't let this beat you; just try to hang on until tomorrow—tomorrow is another day."

I had decided to go into Riga and get a room at the hotel. I could go over and have a drink with Bruno and get up in the morning and catch the boat for Florida.

Agnes and I had planned a quick marriage ceremony and then we were going on and catch the eleven o'clock boat for Florida because it was the only one for another month.

Nick and mama were going to drive me into town now and drop me off and then come back the next day and see me off at the dock.

I didn't wake my father because he liked to get his sleep and it would just upset him anyway. I got in the car and we drove away. I looked back one last time at the castle where I grew up; it was illuminated now in the dim outside lamps. I wondered if I would ever see my home or my family again.

We stood beside the car now, parked in front of Bruno's. It had rained earlier in town and the curb and the grey cobblestone street were illuminated in a soft blue haze from the "Blue Moon" sign of Bruno's place.

Mama said: "Son, are you sure you're gonna be okay? Promise me you won't do something foolish, like jumping off the ship—"

"Oh, mama, now don't worry about me. I'll be fine." Then she hugged me.

Nick put his arm around my shoulder and said, "Now son, if you don't find anything in Florida to your liking, remember what I told you about Tahiti. You just go on down there and see if you can't find something to make you happy—even if it's only a short time. And remember what the French poet Paul Geraldy said: 'It is well to love; not to love anymore is well also.'"

Nick hugged me tightly and then they said they'd see me tomorrow at the dock. They got to the car and mama paused at the door and she looked back at me and smiled. She got in the car and they drove off.

The car disappeared out of the soft blue neon light and into the dark and I watched it go until the tail lights disappeared. I felt alone, confused and for the first time in my life, I felt fear—fear of the unknown. I'd always welcomed the challenge of the unknown but I didn't like it too much now.

There was a smoky haze inside Bruno's, but it wasn't very crowded when I stepped in carrying my bags. Bruno had on some snappy, brassy dance music, I guess he was trying to liven up the place.

Bruno was mixing a drink and had his back to me, but just as I walked up to the bar, he turned around and saw me and grinned.

I put my bags on the floor near a stool and sat down. "Bru, I need a tequila—and I wish you'd join me." He didn't say anything but he handed a man his drink, excused himself and turned around and poured us both a tequila.

"Is everything all right?" he asked, as we squeezed some lime juice into the fold of skin at the thumb. "You and Aggie have a fight?"

I didn't say anything, I just nodded my head as we took a pinch of salt, spread it on the lime juice, and before we turned up the jigger of tequila, Bruno said: "What're we drinking to?"

"I don't know—let's just drink to drinking," and we turned it up, then quickly sucked on the spot of lime juice and melted salt. The strong tequila blended nicely with the lime and salt, leaving a clean salty taste in my mouth.

"How bad is it?—just a little fight I hope," Bruno asked.

"No, Bru—she jilted me, just called me up and said it was off."

Then I told him the story. Bruno just listened, he didn't offer much advice which I appreciated. Bruno had heard enough sad bar tales to know that a person like me didn't want advice, just someone to listen.

On my third tequila, I lost it. I knew if I stayed on this bar stool and looked at Bruno, I wasn't going to be able to hold back the tears. I felt my lips quivering and tears coming to my eyes—I tried to speak but the words choked down in my throat. All I could do was shake my head and I moved quickly from the stool and went to the bathroom.

Bruno came from behind the bar and followed me. When he got to the bathroom, I was leaning up against the wall with my forehead pressed against the cool concrete stucco. I was sobbing uncontrollably, slapping the wall with my open palm. Bruno was standing in the doorway. He leaned on it and said gruffly:

"What're you doing! Why are you crying? Why do you cry for this girl? Where is she? Is she crying for you? No! You don't even know what she's doing now!"

I knew he was frustrated and upset at seeing me upset, and there was nothing he could do.

"Oh, you don't understand!" I moaned. "Haven't you ever cried for a woman?"

"Of course I've cried for a woman—but not anymore! I got smart—I don't cry for any woman that doesn't cry for me. Okay, get it out of your system. Your drink is waiting on you—now don't take too long," he said, and left.

After awhile, I blew my nose, washed my face and I went back out to the bar and sat down. Bruno smiled at me and slid my drink over to me.

Just then, a tall man walked through the front door. He was dressed in a blue work shirt and jeans; a navy blue wool jacket, double-breasted, with slick brass buttons; a wool, navy blue, captains cap with a leather brim dyed blue, and decorated with little brass anchors.

He was an American, named Captain John Finegan, but everybody called him "Captain Fin" for short. He was about fifty years old, with thick gray hair. He was a big man, about six feet four, with thin legs and wide broad shoulders. He had a handsome face with a square jaw.

Fin owned his own cargo ship. He ferried everything; Nordic sardines, boat parts, American made goods, caviar, for just about anything you needed ferrying anywhere, Captain Fin was the man to know.

Captain Fin spotted Bruno and came over to us. He sat down on the stool beside me and said:

"Friend, don't believe a word he says, this man would skin a flea for his hide—"

"Oh my God, Captain Fin! It's been awhile," Bruno said, sticking out his hand. "Captain Fin, this is my best friend Ed Leedskalnin."

Bruno had learned to speak good broken English from all the sailor business he got when they came through picking up goods from the nearby Port of Jurmala.

Bruno poured Fin a glass of rum. Bruno and the Captain started talking about old times. Captain Fin liked to talk and I was glad, because I didn't feel much like talking. I mainly drank while they talked. At one point, Bruno told Fin what had happened to me and that I was going to Florida tomorrow.

Fin said, "Well, I can't think of a better place to look for women than Florida—if you don't find one there, then you don't want one."

About one thirty in the morning, Captain Fin looked at his watch: "Well, I better go, I'm leaving for Canada tomorrow—I mean today—"

"Oh, hell, Fin," Bruno said, "stay and drink with us, Ed's got to get up early too—"

"No, I'm too drunk now Bruno," Fin told him. Then Captain Fin pulled a business card out of his wallet and gave it to me. He said to call him if I ever needed anything. Then he shook hands with us and he told me not to worry, there were plenty of good-looking women in Florida.

"But if you don't mind ugly ones," he says, "I'll set you up with the ones I go out with when I'm down there. Good night gentleman, it's been a pleasure," he told us, and he staggered out the door.

"Now there goes one classy man Ed," Bruno told

me, watching Fin go out.

"And modest too; he's never had to take an ugly woman, unless he just wanted to experiment with one, you know, see if they feel the same and all."

That was the last thing I remember. The next thing I knew, I heard a loud banging on Bruno's front door. I had passed out on the floor and Bruno was laying on the floor behind the bar. I got up and went to the door. It was Mama, and Nick and Gus.

"What happened son?" Mama asked me. "We went to the dock to see you off and you weren't there."

"What time is it?" I asked her.

"It's twelve o'clock," she said.

I couldn't believe I'd overslept. I woke Bruno up and he made us a pot of coffee and I felt better after my third cup. I decided to go down the dock anyway; I thought I could check the schedule and maybe some other ship would be going out soon. And when we got to the dock, we saw Captain Fin having lunch in the dock cafe.

"I wondered what happened to you," Fin said. "I looked for you getting on the boat to Florida, but I just figured I'd missed you—"

"What happened to you?" I asked him. "I thought you were going to Canada?"

"I was but we blew a head cylinder. We should be ready to pull out in about an hour."

I was thinking about how much I wanted to get away from Latvia when I thought of something.

"Captain Fin," I asked, "do you think you could get me a job cutting timber in Canada? Didn't you say last night they were always hiring?"

"Well, yeah, Ed," he said, "but even if I could, how would you get there?"

"Couldn't I go with you?"

"Well, normally, sure—but the boat's full of sardines, there's no place for you to sleep—"

"Oh please Captain Fin—I'll throw a blanket over

the sardine barrels—I can sleep anywhere; please, I need to get out of here."

I guess Fin must've realized how bad I was hurting, because he let me go. When the boat was ready, I said goodbye to Bruno and my family and we headed out over the ocean, bound for Canada.

Fin told me the journey would take about a week if the weather stayed good. We were out at a sea three days now and the weather had only been rough one night.

I woke up at four o'clock one night, and couldn't go back to sleep, so I got up and went out to the deck area. The ocean was slightly rough from a light wind but the sky was clear with a half-full moon. Being on the Atlantic ocean made me think of Atlantis.

I was leaning on the rail of the boat, watching the moonlight playing off the ocean swells, when I noticed a small funnel of wind near the boat. The wind funnel had created a swirling funnel of water.

As I watched the moonlight reflecting off the swirling water, I lost track of time, and I had a vision of Atlantis. While the boat rose and fell, with the rhythm of the waves slapping against the boat, I had a strange feeling of slowly drifting away from my body.

I don't know how long I stayed in this dark suspended time, but gradually, from someplace, a fraction of time and twilight slipped in and I was formed again. I found myself floating in the darkness above a large city. There was an immediate presence of knowledge that entered my thoughts. Almost as though it was acquired common knowledge coming in from a previous life. I knew this was Atlantis.

Even the buildings that I saw below were built in the same diamond-shaped pyramid form as Madame Drusa had described them in my mother's reading.

It was a beautiful city, all lit up by a dazzling array of neon lights. The section I floated above had a long, wide paved street, lit up by small blue lights down the middle and on both sides, like an airfield runway. The paved street was lined on both sides by pyramid buildings made of glass and shiny steel and lit by beautiful fluorescent colored lights of many colors.

The street dead-ended in a paved square that was surrounded by more pyramid buildings. The paved street ran in front of a huge pyramid; as tall and as wide as The Great Pyramid and it sat just behind the section of pyramid buildings lining the street.

The pyramid was covered in white marble with a series of marble steps leading up to it's squared-off top; it was lit all the way around with soft colored lights.

I saw the dark shapes of mountains behind the pyramid. Each one of these pyramid buildings along the street were musical clubs, having different styles of music and some of them had entertainment shows in them. They had any kind of music there you could imagine and some that I couldn't have imagined. And some of the wildest dancing I'd ever seen. All the races were here, mingling in the clubs; there were Africans, Whites, Asians, and Indians of brown and red skin and Hispanics.

I also saw the odd-looking race with enlarged heads and gray skin; it was the same race of people that I had seen in my earlier dream when I was a child. It was the race the early Mayan and American Indians had called "men from the sky." The "sky people" were all very short and had mongolian features with large slanted eyes.

Some of the buildings along the street of the entertainment section had small individual crystal pyramids that glowed red; people who were tired from dancing or just needing an energy boost would come in and lie down in the pyramid for thirty minutes and get rejuvenated.

Quite suddenly, the scene changed and I was no longer floating but I found myself walking along the street with Agnes.

We came to the Constellation Club and went in.

There was a band playing soft music and the lead singer was the same black man that Madame Drusa had described seeing in the park in her vision, his name was Paradise Hunter. Agnes (her name was Jami in Atlantis; she was in the same body, different name) and I slow danced to the music, and as we were dancing, the scene (in my vision) changed.

The next thing I knew, I found myself driving a car on a steep mountain road. Then the vision was over and I was back on Fin's boat, looking out over the water. I looked for the water funnel but it was gone now.

And as I stood there, wondering about the vision, I remembered the other vision I'd had where Agnes and I went into the restaurant where the books and the boat in the wall with the carved girl on the front, was. And we had danced at night around the pool. And now, I have an Atlantic vision where we're dancing in the Constellation Club.

It seemed obvious to me that parts of my former life were being shown to me in dreams and visions, just as Madame Drusa had predicted would happen. I was sure now that Agnes was the girl Madame Drusa had seen me with in her Atlantic vision before I was born. But I couldn't put the pieces together. I was trying to figure out why Agnes and I had seemed to be so happy in this former time, and yet it had been a recent disaster in this time when she jilted me.

I wished now that I had thought to go by and talk to Madame Drusa, and maybe have a reading, to see if it could tell me anything. But I'd just been too shook up to think straight.

Three days later, when we got to Canada, Fin took me to a big lumber yard managed by a French-Canadian man named Maurice LeBlanc. He took one look at me and told Fin I was too small to be cutting timber. But Fin told him that I'd worked in the stone quarries of Latvia, and that if I could cut stone, surely I could cut wood, so Mr. LeBlanc agreed to let me try.

Mr. LeBlanc paired me up with a big American, half-indian man named Beaver Twist. Beaver was half-cherokee indian and he was from Santa Fe New Mexico. Beaver said he was raised in the Jemez Mountains, not far from Chaco Canyon. My grandfather Nick told me about Chaco Canyon. He said he'd always wanted to see it but he never made it.

Beaver promised me that one day he would take me and show me Chaco Canyon. He said the indians still perform ancient religious rites there, and that he would take me there if I ever came to America.

The barracks of the lumber mill were set up like an army post. They were two story and housed a total of fifty men each. When I first met Beaver, it was a rainy Sunday afternoon. Beaver was sitting next to a bunk bed sharpening an axe. I noticed a ring-shaped object, made of wood and covered with colored yarn and feathers, hanging about two feet above his pillow.

Pointing to the object, I smiled and said, "I know what that is—a dream weaver." And I reached into my bag and dug around until I found the one Nick had given me when I was a kid. Beaver took it and looked at it.

"It's a little bit worn with age," I said, as he admired it.

"This is original—where'd you get it?"

"My grandfather," I told him. And then I explained about how I'd loved indian things since I was a boy; I told Beaver about some of the strange dreams I'd had as a child. And Beaver looked surprised when I told him about the dream where I was an indian boy and I saw "the men from the sky."

"Nick said the indians told him when you hang the dream weaver over your head at night, it's supposed to keep the evil spirits away so you'll only have pleasant dreams. Is that true Beaver?"

"Yes," Beaver said, "that's what the indians believed in."

Beaver Twist was a good man and I was glad that I'd decided to come to Canada now, it was worth it just to meet Beaver.

Well, Ed wrote, it took me a few days to get used to sawing with those big, two-man saws they were using. But after awhile, I got stronger and hard as a nail. I got to where I could keep up with Beaver and he was surprised that he couldn't tire me out as quickly as he had when I first got there. Even Mr. LeBlanc was impressed and he told me I was doing a good job.

We were always so busy that two years went by fast. Beaver took me out trout fishing on Sundays, and I got to where I loved it. The fresh water rainbow trout were beautiful and tasty when battered and fried up crispy.

I got a little sad one day though, when beaver showed me something strange about the trout's eye. The iris part was shaped just like a watermelon seed, and the sharp point of the iris always faced forward when the fish was alive.

But after he was dead, about an hour, you could see the pointed part of the eye moving from the three o'clock position back up to the twelve o'clock position or straight up to the sky. Beaver said, "It's like the fish is telling God he's coming home." So Beaver always said a little thank you prayer to God over the fish we caught.

I was hoping that by going to Canada and doing hard labor, maybe I could forget about Agnes. But nothing had changed—I still loved her just as much.

But in the year 1914, when the First World War broke out, I got a letter from my cousin, on mama's side, Karl Bietak. Mama's sister Karin had married a German man, named Mannfred Bietak, she met him when he was working in Latvia. Later, he moved the family to his home in Berlin where he was an engineer.

In the letter, Karl told me he wanted me to come to Germany and fight for Germany in the war. Karl said that France and England wanted to take over Europe and make slaves out of us, like England had done to America.

Well, this war business sounded exciting to me. I'd gotten bored with lumber camp stuff and I needed a new challenge. And when I looked back at this time later, I was miserable and I think I had a death wish. As hard as I tried, I couldn't shake Agnes out of my system. I had this crazy notion that maybe I'd be a war hero and she'd read about me in the paper and want me back. I was young and foolish and I didn't care about anything.

So, I thanked Mr. LeBlanc for giving me the job and he told me I had a job whenever I wanted it. I didn't tell him that I was going to fight for Germany, because some of the pure French men were leaving to fight for France. I hoped I wouldn't have to meet them in battle one day. They had all treated me very good while I was here.

I took the next boat out and passed through the Norwegian Sea, and landed at the port of Cuxhaven, which isn't far from Hamburg Germany. I met some German soldiers at the port and caught a ride with them to Hamburg and then we caught another truck to Berlin. I got a book in Hamburg and started learning German.

Karl and I went through boot camp with Adolf Hitler. To most people, Adolf Hitler was moody and aloof, but he was different with me. For one thing, he greatly admired me for not being German, (he was Austrian) and for coming to help fight this war.

I think Hitler liked me because of our shared interest in Atlantis. Hitler was surprised when he found out that he and I had read Donnelly's book on Atlantis. Hitler then told me he was absolutely convinced the German people were direct descendants from Atlantis.

Hitler said that it was in their former Atlantean lives that the Germans had developed their superior engineering talents. Hitler said no one else in the world could develop complex machinery items like the Germans produced.

Hitler was also convinced that perhaps he and I

had some kind of former acquaintance in Atlantis. Destiny had now, Hitler told me with a somber look, brought us back together in this time of great struggle.

I was older than Hitler, and even though we'd been through boot camp together, Hitler was given the job of messenger runner. He was not issued a rifle, for which he sulked for a long time. Sometimes, when he found me in the trench, he would stop and and ask me to hold my rifle. He would take it in his hands and admire it; and he would point it at an imagined target.

Hitler told me then that he had found his passion for life in this war. Hitler loved the mud, the smell of gunpowder and the danger of dodging artillery shells.

Hitler opened up to me and told me how much he loved his mother but that his father was cold and distant to him. He said his father would often get drunk and beat him with his belt, a stick, or anything he could lay his hands on. I've always believed that is why Hitler never drank—only a little champagne on occasions, he was afraid of being like his father.

I think that through the whole war, part of Hitler's bravery under fire—he was a brave man, was that he was seeking his father's approval, which he never got; even when he was awarded the Iron Cross for single-handedly capturing four French soldiers.

Adolf liked to draw sketches, and I thought he was rather good at it. He was good at depicting the battlefield, with it's mud, broken trees, a constant, eerie smoky mist, crater holes from artillery shells; dead horses and mangled bodies strewn everywhere. I think he had a certain fascination with death.

One day, Hitler showed me a drawing he had done depicting a crude form of the swastika he would later make famous. Hitler told me that he'd first seen the symbol in church, when he was twelve years old. He was singing in the choir, he told me, when one day, he looked up on the wall and saw a version of the swastika on a religious painting.

Hitler was surprised when I drew out for him the various forms of swastikas that I remembered seeing on the photographs of the Mayan pyramids in the Mayan book that Nick had given me. We talked about Atlantis. Hitler then told me that he believed he had once been a great leader in Atlantis—something like a Caesar.

He also told me that he'd had a vision, that one day, he'd lead Germany through a great crisis. At the time, I dismissed this as only the dreams of a young enthusiastic soldier.

Years later, after the war, a man named M.A. Blackwell, wrote a book called "The Swastika and Atlantis." He had done extensive research on the Mayan pyramids and concluded that it was highly possible that the swastika was a symbol used in Atlantis.

Hitler was fascinated when I told him about the dream I had about the "men from the sky." I quoted him the scripture from Genesis, where it said the spirits came down and mated with the earth women. Hitler agreed with me that life on other planets was highly possible.

One day, we were catching hell from the French artillery and English machine guns. Then, through a clearing in the smoke, we looked up and here came the first tanks we'd ever seen, lumbering slowly and methodically across the cratered field. We panicked. We thought: "What in the hell have they unleashed on us now?" In desperation, our artillery unleashed poison gas shells; hoping to delay the advancing French and English foot soldiers until we could get back to our lines. I had just finished talking with Hitler, and he was making his way back with news of the tank, when one of our poison shells went off, falling short of it's target, and landing not far from our front line.

I had put on my gas mask when I looked and saw Hitler go down in the trench, overcome by poison gas. I rushed over to him, where he was flopping around in the trench like a fish. It was a good thing the trench was there, the gas was heavier than air so it didn't go in the trench but stayed along the top.

His eyes were burning up and he was coughing and gasping for air. I quickly got my water canteen, splashed his face, and then I tore his gas mask from his belt and put it over his head.

About that time, some medics came by, wearing gas masks and they grabbed Hitler and hauled him back to our lines. We turned and fired some hopeless volleys at the oncoming tanks and enemy troops, and then we got out of there. When we got back, I went over to the field hospital to check on Hitler. He was lucky.

He'd only gotten a small amount of gas in his lungs—much more and the medics said he would've died. Hitler was sitting up in bed and he was glad to see me. He thanked me profusely for saving his life. After that, Hitler was assigned to another company, so that was the last time I saw Adolf Hitler—until I saw him later in the newsreels, showing him as chancellor of Germany.

The war dragged on. After three years of dodging bullets and artillery shells and seeing mangled bodies, the romantic notions I'd had of war were long gone. Day and night, my ears rang with the sound of gunfire. Karl and I had gone through many a battle without a scratch. Karl still believed that Germany could win the war—I didn't care who won, all I wanted was out. I was soon to get my wish.

Our company was situated on a hilltop, overlooking the battlefield. We felt secure because of our position and we had machine gun nests everywhere. One day at dawn, we were attacked by American and British divisions. They opened up with artillery, then the troops poured across the field.

Karl and I were standing side by side in a hilltop trench, firing our rifles as we watched the American and British soldiers being blown into the sky from our artillery; and they folded up and dropped in their tracks from the murderous fire of our machine guns.

But suddenly, I noticed the men on our left side were quickly falling down, like dominos. I nervously glanced to my left, and through the hazy smoke of the battlefield, I saw the helmets of some American soldiers, popping up now and then, from one of our machine gun nests. They had an angle on our flank side; the German soldiers were dropping like flies from the rifle fire.

When our sergeant saw there was nothing to do but surrender, he grabbed a dirty white undershirt, stuck it on his bayonet, and started waving it wildly at the American soldiers. I was glad he did this—Karl and I were only three men away from being shot down. They signaled for us to lay down our arms and we did. To my delight, they marched us back to the American lines.

Karl and I spent the last year of the war in a French prison camp. The French weren't as hard on me when they found out that I was from Latvia and not Germany. I didn't speak much French but I'd learned a little from when I worked at the Canadian lumber camp; and the French words I did know, I made sure to pronounce them correctly and that helped me out.

About six months before the war was over, I got sick in the French prison camp. And when the war was over, in November of 1918, Karl asked me to go back to Germany with him, but I said no. I got weak spells sometimes and I coughed a lot. I thought maybe it was an infection from those poison gas shells. I was thankful to have survived the war and I decided now to go to America and see Beaver Twist, my indian friend I'd met in Canada before the war.

I said goodbye to Karl and I wrote my family that I was okay and told them about my plans to visit Beaver and then move to Florida. I wanted to go somewhere where the sun was always shining and it didn't get cold.

Our prison camp was located about five miles out of the town of Bordeaux, which was only twenty five miles from the coast. I caught a ride with some French soldiers to the port town of Gironde, where I found a cargo ship bound for Brownsville Texas. Texas was the closest I could get to New Mexico and I was just happy to be going anywhere.

I wrote to Beaver and told him that I was coming and if he could, to please meet me in Brownsville. And when the ship docked, Beaver was there to meet me.

Beaver hugged me and said, "Boy, I never thought I'd see you again. I'd heard you'd gone to fight in the war. I reckon the only thing that saved you was you were so small, them machine guns couldn't get a shot at you."

"It was a stupid thing to do Beaver—I want to forget about it."

Beaver was driving a flat bed Ford truck, with a wood rail body. Beaver had gone into the saddle repair business and he also did some blacksmith work when the saddle business was slow.

It was a twelve hour drive to Santa Fe where Beaver lived. I was exhausted and I napped and listened to him on the way up as he told me about his business and that he hadn't married yet. He wanted to put some money in the bank first, he said. I asked him when we could go to Chaco Canyon.

Beaver said, "Well, it's a six hour ride by horseback—that's the only way to go, the roads aren't too good. You rest up a day and then we'll go."

So, two days later, Ed wrote, we saddled up the horses and started off for Chaco Canyon. After only an hour in the saddle, my tail got so sore I had to make Beaver stop and let me stretch my legs out.

Our route took us up past Los Alamos, past the Valles Caldera, a large meadow with herds of wild horses and antelope. It's the only thing that remains of the worn out Jemez volcanos. Chaco Canyon lies sunk down in the dusty dry earth on the other side of the Continental Divide.

We rode through lush mountain forests, past towering waterfalls, and then we'd go through a barren desert, where I saw tumbleweeds roll by us in the dusty wind, on their way to nowhere. It took us an extra hour to get there, because of my stops to stretch, so it was around one o'clock when Beaver signaled me with his hand to stop.

We got off our horses and tied them to some scrub trees. Beaver told me he wanted me to see the view from the Zuni mountain top before we went down into the sunken valley of Chaco Canyon. It was a cool, crisp fall day, as we stood there, looking down on the Chaco Canyon cliff dwellings they call "great houses." The stone cliffside apartments stand four or five stories high against the sheer north walls of the canyon.

Beaver said that some people say these massive structures were built around nine hundred years ago by the Anasazi indians. But Beaver said the indians believed they could've been built thousands of years ago. As we looked down on the canyon, there were indians moving around everywhere amid campfires, barking dogs and kids playing kickball in the narrow dusty streets. I saw connecting stone stairways and wooden ladders leaning against the walls of the houses. This place seemed familiar to me now. It reminded me of the dream I'd had when I was a small indian boy and I saw the crash of the shiny disc in the sky. Then we mounted our horses and headed down the mountain towards Chaco Canyon.

That evening, as the sun went down, the indians were dressing up in their magnificent feather and leather costumes for a religious ceremony that only a few white men had ever been allowed to see. Beaver had told the chief about the dream I had where I was an indian boy and the chief had great respect for me and he let me see this ceremony.

Beaver and I and the chief of the tribe, named Johnny Montoya, sat around a fire and ate roasted rabbit and potatoes. Then, the chief took out a long wooden pipe and he put some finely ground tobacco in the bowl. I thought he was going to light it and smoke it, but he didn't; instead, he lifted the bowl to his nose, put one finger over his nostril, and then he snorted the tobacco up his nose. Then he started filling the bowl again. I was quite surprised as I had never seen this done before.

"What's he doing?" I asked Beaver.

"He's using tobacco; it's part of the religious ceremony. It will be an insult if you refuse," Beaver was saying, as the old chief handed him the pipe. Beaver took it and snorted the dark brown tobacco and handed the pipe back to the chief to be refilled. I was nervous because I didn't know what to expect.

Beaver put the pipe in my hands and said, "Don't worry, it'll make you a little relaxed and light-headed, but it won't hurt you." I raised the pipe to my nose and smelled the tobacco—it had a strong ammonia smell to it. The old chief smiled at me and gestured with his hands for me to go ahead and snort it, which I did quickly without thinking.

My face flushed red and I immediately felt a burning sensation in my nostrils and lungs; I tried to hold back my cough but I couldn't do it. Beaver quickly handed me a gourd full of cool spring water which I gulped down between coughing spells. After a few minutes, the coughing spells died down and I felt somewhat lightheaded.

We sat cross-legged on indian blankets and watched as a procession of indians, covered in feathered garments, came out in a long line and began dancing to a drum and flute arrangement. The indian dancers held a live rattlesnake by his head in their right hand, and they held his tail gently in their mouth as their feet stayed with the beating drum rhythm.

Beaver leaned over and whispered to me that this was the most secret part of the ceremony. He explained that the rattlesnake was one of the gods of an ancient indian tribe. As he spoke, I remembered how the ancient Mayan cult had believed in the mythical creation powers of the rattlesnake, because when he shed his skin, they believed he had been born again.

As the line of snake-holding indian dancers disappeared behind an adobe building, the music continued and another indian man appeared directly in front of me. He had rubbed the ashes from a fire on his skin until his skin was completely gray. He wore a gray clay mask with large oversized eyes, a small fish mouth and tiny ears.

In his hands he carried a saucer shaped object, made of glazed gray clay, with small portholes around it's edges. The entire saucer shaped object was covered in silver beadwork. The masked indian pointed to the sky, then he raised the saucer object up skyward, then he brought it slowly down and he pushed it in the sand. The masked indian then picked up the saucer object, held it up to the sky, and he walked away, holding the object high in the air.

And suddenly, it came into my mind that the masked indian was playing out the scene that I'd had in my boyhood dream, where I saw the shiny disc crash. As I was thinking of this, Beaver said: "When we were in the lumber camp, and you told me of the dream you had, I knew you were a special person—maybe even a reborn "Shaman" (ancient name for holy man). That is why my people have performed this ancient ceremony for you. They believe that you have returned to your ancestral home."

As darkness fell, Beaver got a lantern and said, "Come on, I want to show you something," and Beaver, along with the chief, led me over to a hidden cave entrance about a hundred yards away. We stopped at the cave's entrance and Beaver held the lantern up to a flat spot on the rocks to the side of the cave's narrow entrance.

Beaver pointed to an engraved inscription of characters on the rock and said, "Do you recognize this?" I leaned forward for a better look. There inscribed on the rock, was a scene showing a round disc object, coming down from the sky; the next scene showed the disc sitting on a line representing the earth; the next frame showed the "men from the sky" emerging from the craft.

The last scene showed the sky men handing a group of indians what appeared to be a loaf of bread.

"Just like my dream," I muttered. I wanted to touch this ancient manuscript, and I put out my hand and delicately ran my fingers over the chiseled inscription, feeling the aged smoothness of the stone.

Beaver then led us into the mouth of the cave. After we'd gone about twenty yards, Beaver stopped. He lifted the lantern up to a section of the flat smooth wall.

And as I stared, there painted in vibrant colors, was the scene of the crashed silver disc I had seen in my boyhood dream. The drawing showed a "men from the sky" creature, standing outside the crashed ship, raising his hand to a group of indians who stood staring at the strange looking being.

"Beaver, why didn't you tell me about this when I told you about my dream?"

"It's forbidden for us to tell the white man about this place," Beaver said. "It's only because you are a Shaman that you're allowed to see it."

Seeing this, I became more convinced that I had been here before; I was also convinced that it was natural that these "men from the sky" people, had once lived on this earth as a result of the "spirit beings" who came down and mated with the earth women. Perhaps over time, something like a plague had destroyed them, maybe the same way the dinosaurs had walked on the earth and then disappeared. The only thing left of these people now were these stone etchings.

The next morning, Beaver drove me back to Brownsville Texas. Beaver had a friend there, named Pozie Williams, who drove to Homestead Florida and picked up fresh vegetables and brought them back to sell in Texas.

Homestead was near Florida City. Nick said land was cheap around this area because in some places in South Florida, there is a solid bed of coral stone that goes down four thousand feet. There's not much top soil, Nick said, so most people say the land is no good, unless you want to farm a bunch of rocks.

I shook Beaver's hand as we said goodbye and I thanked him for showing me the secret cave; I promised him I would never reveal it's location. Truth was, I was so messed up from snorting that tobacco, I don't think I could ever find that cave again anyway. Beaver told me he was going to visit me one day.

But that was the last time I ever saw my friend Beaver Twist. Two years later, I got a letter from his mama telling me that Beaver had got involved with a married woman who was getting a divorce. Beaver's mama said the woman's husband came up on them one night as they were in Beaver's truck, parked beside a lover's lake site. Her husband pulled out a .38 caliber revolver and shot them both in the head, and then he put the gun to his head and killed himself.

I was sad to hear of Beaver's death. I remembered he used to joke: "Oh, Ed, I reckon one day I'll get shot by some jealous husband."

I remembered a Bible verse that Nick used to quote a lot. It went: "You can have what you say, but you're saying what you have." Nick said the lesson was, watch what you say. I wondered if, out of his own mouth, Beaver Twist had declared the method of his own death.

Three days later, after we left Beaver's place in New Mexico, Pozie Williams and I pulled into the outskirts of Homestead Florida, around nine o'clock at night. We were driving along a dirt road with the windows down because it was warm and muggy here in south Florida. We had run out of small talk and we hadn't spoken a word for awhile when all of a sudden, I saw a bunch of tiny green, blinking lights, scattered around both sides of the bushes along the road.

"What're those lights doing way out here Pozie?"

"What lights?" he said.

"All those green flashing lights," I said, pointing

out the window. "They seem to be attached to the bushes."

"Oh—them ain't lights Ed—well, I mean they're lights but they're bugs; ain't you never seen lightning bugs before?"

"You mean those lights are alive—insects?"

"Yep. They're not much bigger than houseflies. That's her rear end you see lit up; it's mating season see, and the bugs fly around trying to find a lover. But it's only the female that lights up; and the male is attracted to the light, see, and he flies up there and they rub antennas and see if they like each other. If the female likes him, then they mate right there on the limb. But if she don't like him, she shuts her light off—'Get off my limb you bum' she says."

"Well," Ed said, "at least he didn't have to waste any money on a hotel room. You seem to know a lot about this stuff."

"Oh yeah, I got a book on Florida's insects—I read it when I'm on the toilet—knowledge Ed, that's what separates us from the beast. Most people just think I'm a dumb truck driver, but you ask'em if they know anything about lightning bugs—they don't I can tell you now.

"Yeah Ed," Pozie continued, "nature is a funny thing I tell you. Now here's a strange twist on the lightning bug story. There is a bug around here, the exact same size of the lightning bug, and he eats them. Well, this 'ol bad bug-eater, he got to studying the habits of the lightning bug—I reckon he went to a bug eating school or something—anyway, he figured out a way to make his butt light up a flashing green, just like the female lightning bug.

"So, during mating season, when the male lighting bug's mind is consumed with femalin', this bug-eater, he lights on a branch and flashes his green butt, to signal a male bug that he is ready for romance.

"And the male comes swooping in there, expecting a big 'ol antenna foreplay kiss, and this 'ol bug-eater—he's got a long sharp needle sword antenna on the front of his head—well, he just sticks that thin sword right into the male's head; then he flies off the branch, carrying off his bug shish-ka-bob.

"My daddy was talking about the poor 'ol lightning bug getting killed, and daddy said: 'Well, I reckon that's the screwing he gets for the screwing he thought he was gonna get.'"

"Is that a true story Pozie?"

"Oh yeah. I've got a buddy who studies bugs—oh, what do they call it—I remember it rhymes with enema—"

"Entomology?"

"Yeah, that's it; anyway I asked him about it and he said it's true."

"Pozie would you stop so I can get a better look at them?"

"Ed, I'd like to oblige you but I need to get on in to Homestead—I'm gone start loading vegetables when we get there."

"Oh, I see. How far is it from here to Homestead Pozie?"

"It's not far—I'd say about a mile."

I asked Pozie to stop the truck and he asked me if I had to pee and I said no, but I wanted to walk the rest of the way into town. I wanted to get a closer look at these lightning bugs. And besides, I wasn't in any hurry. So Pozie stopped the truck and I got my bags and stepped out of the truck. I tried to pay Pozie but he refused, he said he enjoyed the company.

Then I heard a strange bird call echoing through the still night air: "Pozie, what kind of bird is that?"

"That's a Whippoorwill. He only comes out at night, hunting insects. He got his name from the cry he makes—listen," Pozie said, and the bird called out again. "See, don't it sound just like he's saying, "Whip-poor-will?"

"Yeah, it sure does."

"Ed, you sure you want to walk? Heck, I'll wait here a minute if you want me to. I didn't know you were a bird and insect lover like me—"

"No, thank you Pozie, I'd rather walk. I like to walk and I'm in no hurry."

Pozie told me the Blanche Hotel was on main street which was straight down this road; he said to follow this road and I couldn't miss it. Just then, I got another bad coughing spell and Pozie said I ought to see a doctor, but I told him it wasn't serious and besides, I didn't like to go to doctors. And he said if I changed my mind, I ought to see Dr. Spooner in Homestead.

"Doc Spooner is good," Pozie said. "Well, he cured me of the clap one time—I got it from an 'ol gal out there at the Lake Lona whorehouse."

I thanked Pozie again, said goodbye, and watched him go until the truck lights disappeared. I moved my bags to the side of the road and immediately set out to see if I could catch a lightning bug. But every time I got close to one he'd fly off. I finally gave up and just sat there about twenty minutes and I watched the light show. And darned if one didn't land on my pants leg and I got to see him close up. It was getting late so I picked up my bags and started walking towards Homestead.

I was amazed at how all the bushes and trees around me were a brilliant tropical green. And I was surrounded by the sound of all kinds of frogs, barking their heads off as I walked along.

It sure was peaceful walking along there, watching the fireflies (that was another name they used for lightning bugs) and listening to the haunting call of the Whippoorwill. I had gone about fifty yards when I got another coughing attack.

This was a bad one. As I set my bags down, I got weak-legged and I went down on my knees, coughing so hard that I lost my breath and I passed out; I fell over onto the ground and part of my right arm was sticking out in the road.

"Well," Herman Harmless told Carl Swisher, the newspaper man, as they sat inside Coral Castle, "the night I found Ed, on Key West Highway, my wife Opal and Novia Lilly, one of her good friends—she worked over at the DeSoto drug store. We were coming back from having dinner at "Sasso's" a little Italian place."

We had the radio on, Herman continued, and Novia's favorite song came on, and she told me to turn it up. Well, I was aggravating her and I turned it down, and I made out like I couldn't hear her, and I turned to her and said, "What'd you say?" She popped me on the shoulder and told me to turn it up.

And about this time, Herman said, Opal sees Ed lying on the side of the road, and she screams: "Herman look out!"

And I whirled around, and looked back at the road, just in time to see him, and I swerved hard to the left—my right tire got so close to his arm and head that it threw dirt all over him.

I stopped the car and we got out and went to see about him. Novia had some medical knowledge from working in the drug store so she checked his pulse and said it was somewhat low but he wasn't in any danger. She leaned down close to his mouth, to see if she could smell any liquor and she said she didn't smell any.

We wondered if he could've been hit by a car, but it was dark and we couldn't see too good, so we decided to take him back to my house and call Dr. Spooner, Herman said. So, we loaded him in the back seat, which was easy because Ed was so small. On the way over, Ed never opened his eyes, but he did seem to have trouble with his breathing.

Five minutes later, we pulled into the brick driveway of my house on Key West Highway, Herman said. It's a victorian house, made of heart pine, done in the clapboard fashion on the outside, and inside, Opal had decorated it with fancy victorian antiques.

It used to be a boarding house—it has twenty five rooms and was built, the Homestead Historical lady said, around 1890. It has a long porch that wraps all the way around the front. We put white wicker couches and chairs, fitted with soft cushions, all along the porch.

It's got a steep pyramid style roof, like was popular in that time. But anyway, Herman went on, we called Dr. Spooner and he came right over.

He was about fifty, with thick grey hair and silver, wire rimmed glasses; he was a snappy dresser, he had on a white, short sleeve dress shirt, and pleated, gray wool trousers, black dress loafers, highly polished, and a deep blue neck tie. He was powerful built too, you could see the veins popping out on his arms; he was a fullback in football, until he tore his knee up, that's when he went into medicine. Anyway, he got there and checked Ed over.

Ed had remained unconscious during the physical. "His pulse does seem weak," Dr. Spooner said. "He seems dehydrated and anemic more than anything else. He needs some good rest, Herman. I'm concerned about that cough. I want to see him as soon as he's strong enough. Give him some orange juice in the morning and call me if you notice any changes in his breathing. Well, that's all I can do now. Good night, y'all."

"Thank you for coming at such an odd time, Doc." Herman said.

"No trouble at all," Dr. Spooner said, "see y'all later," and he turned to leave.

But, just then, Herman said, Ed opened his eyes and weakly, he said: "Dr. Spooner?—I believe you know a friend of mine, Pozie Williams."

We were all surprised that Ed had talked, and we thought it was awful strange that here he had been passed out and yet somehow, he had heard Dr. Spooner's name being called. Dr. Spooner stopped, turned around and came back over to the bed.

"How do you know Pozie?" Spooner asked Ed.

"Pozie knows a friend of mine in New Mexico and he gave me a ride here. Pozie said you're a good Doctor; I bet he's a character isn't he Doc?"

"Pozie? Oh, he's a rare bird," Spooner said.

Ed introduced himself but he was so weak he couldn't keep his eyes open; he kept opening them and closing them as he tried to talk. Ed said: "How did I get here? What happened to me?"

I explained to him what had happened, Herman said, but Doc Spooner interrupted me and told Ed to rest, we could talk tomorrow.

We left Ed to rest and we stepped out on the porch, Herman said, and stood there talking for a moment as Dr. Spooner drove off. Novia said:

"I had a good time tonight. I'd forgotten how to have fun; I guess Jimmy Roy is having fun in the Keys with his little college girl. I should've listened to y'all when you told me about him. I just couldn't see it."

"Well, Novia," Opal said, "I know it hurts, but it's best you found out about him now."

"Hey, Novia," Herman said, "this guy didn't have on a wedding ring—"

"Herman," Opal said, "leave her alone—"

"I don't care if he's a millionaire," Novia said. "I'm going back to school and get my degree. I do hope he's okay though; call me at the drug store tomorrow if you need anything for him. Well, thanks again, good night."

"Do you want Herman to follow you home?" Opal asked her.

"No, thanks, I'll be fine," Novia said, and she left.

Well, the next morning, Herman said, Ed felt strong enough to get out of bed and sit at the breakfast table. Ed and I were drinking coffee and eating bacon and eggs while Opal was at the stove finishing up some pancakes. Ed told us he was from Latvia. And he said he had come to Homestead because his grandaddy said it was a nice little town.

But Ed said he wanted to look for some land in Florida City because it might be cheaper. Ed thanked us again for getting him off the road.

"Well Ed, I'll tell you," Herman said, "if Opal hadn't screamed out last night, you might be wearing tire tracks on your face today."

"Thank you Opal," Ed said, sipping his coffee. "I got sick in jail in France—I fought on the losing side. I had a cousin who was German and he talked me into leaving Latvia and going to Germany. I don't think I'll listen to my cousin next time.

"I'd appreciate it if you didn't mention I fought for Germany—I want to live in America and I don't want people holding that against me—but you folks have been good to me, and I want to be honest with you."

"Oh forget it," Opal said. "Young men make mistakes. But this is a good lesson for you Ed, when you ride with Herman, keep your eyes on the road, because he will be everywhere but there—he thinks he can steer with his mouth. And another thing, if you want something to get around town, tell Herman—if you don't, don't tell him. "Now Herman, you heard what Ed asked you—please don't run down to the Blanche and blurt it out—"

"Yes Captain hen," Herman replied, giving Opal a mock salute. "It's nice to have your wife behind you. Ed, have you seen a doctor?"

"Oh yeah, I see them all the time—sometimes I see them on the street or in the grocery store—"

"Okay wise guy, I meant about your fainting condition."

"Herman, I don't like going to doctors. My grandaddy studied herbs all his life and he always took care of my doctoring needs."

"Well, what did he say about this?"

"I don't know, I didn't bother him about it. It'll pass. Say, Pozie told me that a man named Farnell Ferguson had some land for sale in Florida City—it's about ten miles from here?"

"Yeah that's right. I know Farnell; he's got an acre for sale—but it's no good, nothing but solid coral underneath the top soil—"

"Yes, I think the coral bed goes down about four

thousand feet—is that right?"

"Yeah—how'd you know that?"

"Nick told me. How much does he want for it?"

"Twelve dollars."

"Well, that sounds reasonable. If it's the right location, I'd like to buy it. I think I'll walk over there this afternoon and look at it. Do you mind if I leave my bags here? I'll be happy to pay you—"

"No, I'll be glad to drive you over there—"

"Oh, no Herman, I've put you out enough—"

"Now listen Ed, if you walk up to Farnell's place alone, he's liable to fill you full of buckshot. He's an old man. He doesn't see good, or hear good, and he doesn't take to yankees or anybody who's not from Florida City. You follow me? Now, you're still weak from last night, and that walk won't be good for you in this humidity. You savvy?"

Well, Herman said, I guess I got through to Ed because he stuck out his hand and thanked me. So, after lunch, we got in my car and drove out to Farnell's place.

Ed was still feeling weak, so I made him eat two tablespoons of honey and drink a glass of fresh-squeezed orange juice—that put some sugar in his bloodstream real quick you see, and he perked right back up.

It was a beautiful sunny day when we got to Florida City, Herman said. We slowed down as we entered the outskirts of the little town. I turned left off the main road and went down a ways, and pulled into Farnell Ferguson's place. I had called him, Herman said, before we left so he'd know we were coming.

There wasn't much to Florida City, aside from it's natural beauty. Most of the houses were styled in the "shotgun" fashion, and made with heart pine in the clapboard style. They sat raised up off the ground about two feet, with the supporting underneath beams, resting on pyramid-shaped blocks of stone.

The roof was done in a wavy tin, with most of them badly rusted and needing paint. You'd usually see chickens scratching around in the patches of bare dirt where the shade trees (mainly large memosas) kept the hot south Florida sun out.

And there was usually some worn out easy chairs and couches, with torn patches of fabric where the stuffing is sticking out, sitting on the porch. And at least four, dirty-diapered young'uns, running around the yard, chasing an old worn out bird dog.

Later on, most of the front porches were screened in to keep out the swarms of mosquitoes that could descend on you at dusk. They called them "shotgun houses" because the houses were so long and narrow, they said you could open the front door and fire a shotgun blast and kill everybody in there.

The screen wire invention didn't help the working people, it mainly helped the screen wire company; because most of the time, you could drive through here, and the screen wire was busted out, and it looked like a body had gone through there from domestic squabbles. Usually, on a friday night, the man would come home drunk and go to beating the wife and kids.

Or, sometimes the wife and kids, they'd get tired of explaining to the neighbors why their faces always looked like screen wire. So, they'd wait on the 'ol drunk, and jump him when he got on the porch, and pitch him through the screen. Then they'd take off and spend the night with relatives.

Now if a man had very many kids, and especially when he got up in age where he had young-uns big enough to pitch him off the porch, well, in that area, generally speaking, you would see the rate of "screen porch pitchings," as they called them, on the decline. You see, Herman explained, the old man had outgrown his drinkin' and femalin' ways.

"Many a sorry man," Herman told Ed, "died of a broken neck from being pitched out of those homes. That's why the women liked to build the house as high off the ground as they'd allow; hoping, you see, her goodness would save her if she went off the porch first."

Anyway, Herman said, we pulled into Farnell's yard—he lived in one of the shotgun kind of houses we'd just seen.

"Now don't let the looks of this place fool you," Herman told Ed, as they pulled up and stopped the car, "Farnell's got money, he just doesn't like spending it."

Farnell was in his seventies, and he was a big man, with greasy black hair, combed straight back. He was sitting on the porch steps, dressed in overalls with no shirt and no shoes. Farnell had his pocket knife in his right hand, and it looked like he was scraping something off of his dirty left foot when we walked up, Herman said. There was a brown bottle with a cork top, and a lit candle sitting next to him.

"I didn't know you did foot surgery Farnell," Herman said. "What in the world are you doing?"

"Oh, I got the dang biggest boil I ever had on the side of my foot. I got to lance it," Farnell said, moving the knife blade over the candle flame. "I'm sorry—I'll be right with you."

Then, Farnell set the knife down on the porch, and he reached over got the brown bottle with the cork in it, and he pulled the cork out and poured what looked like water on the boil.

"What's that?" Herman asked him.

"Carbolic acid," Farnell said, as the clear liquid started foaming up bubbles on the puss-filled boil. Then Farnell took the knife and plunged the sharp point straight into the boil, and the yellow puss gushed out. Farnell groaned but he didn't cry out. Then he took a clean white piece of gauze, and he wrapped it around his foot, covering the busted boil.

"Farnell, why didn't you go see Doc Spooner?" Herman asked him.

"What for Herman?—he'd just charge me five dollars to do the same thing."

Herman turned to Ed: "You see, I told you he was tight Ed."

"Well, hell, Herman," Farnell said, "I'm a working man—I aint' got one of them tourist traps set up like you do."

"Oh, listen to him whine—the man's got more money than Solomon. Farnell, this is my friend Ed."

"Glad to know you got one Herman," Farnell said, shaking Ed's hand. "Now see here Ed—I want you to know about this land, so we don't waste each other's time.

"It's an acre of worthless land on the back part of my place, facing the main road going into Florida City. There's only about one foot of top soil, and then it's nothing else but solid coral. I ought to be giving this land away, because you can't farm it, but I'm asking twelve dollars for it."

"Herman told me you were an honest man, Mr. Ferguson and I appreciate that. I'd sure like to look at this land."

"Okay Ed, but don't come back whining to me in six months, Herman is my witness, I told you about the land. And please call me Farnell."

Ed agreed and we got in the car and drove about two hundred yards to where the land was. It was cleared land, Farnell said, with only a few scattered pine trees.

I stopped the car, Herman said, and Ed got out without saying anything. He left us and walked over to a strip of nearby woods. He looked around the tree branches and selected a long thin oak branch, with a Y forked end. Ed took out his pocket knife and cut the branch off at the base and then he stripped all the green oak leaves off until the long stick was clean.

Then, he cut off another long branch and he cut this up into little stick-like nails, with sharpened ends and he put them in the shirt pocket of his light blue jean shirt that he wore with the sleeves rolled up about halfway up his arm.

"What in the world is he doing?" Farnell asked.

"You got me," I said.

Then we watched as Ed gently held the forked end of the stick in his hands, keeping it loose so it could move around.

Then, holding the stick at hip-level, Ed began to walk slowly out of the woods, with the sharp end of the stick pointing out straight in front of him, like he was fishing, Herman said.

"Well I'll be danged," Farnell muttered, "he's using a witchin' rod to dowse for water. You got to have a special touch to use one of them things—like 'ol Elzie Skinner—you remember how good he could do it? He was part indian you know."

"I didn't know that—what part of him was indian?"

"Hey, that's funny—I never thought about it like that—"

"You know I had forgotten about 'ol Elzie Skinner—whatever happened to him?—he was bad about cutting people with a knife wasn't he?"

"Yes sir, buddy—that boy could handle a knife now. But Verdie Lue Bryant was quicker. Elzie was courting his sister, Sally Ray, and she dumped him. Elzie got drunk and came to their house one night—she was staying at Verdie Lue's on account of she was scared of Elzie.

"Verdie Lue came to the door and told Elzie to leave and Elzie pulled a knife on him; Verdie was faster and stuck a knife in Elzie's stomach. Elzie died of E-ternal bleedin' Doc Spooner said."

"Internal bleeding?"

"Yeah, that's what Doc said—look at Ed work that witchin' rod," Farnell said, admiringly, "now he knows what he's doing. Lots of people don't believe in dowsing for water, but Ed's doing it," Farnell said.

It was beautiful to watch Ed walking carefully along, Herman said. All of a sudden, if the underground water current was strong—whap! That stick would snap towards the ground like a ten pound bass hit it. And when he found water, Ed would kneel down on the ground, and take out one of those little sticks in his shirt pocket, and he'd stick it in the ground to mark the spot.

Farnell said: "I'd have never guessed there was water on this land."

After Ed had walked over a good piece of the land, he came walking back up to us.

"The land's got good springs of water crossing it Farnell," Ed said. "It's just what I'm looking for. I'd sure like to own it Farnell."

"Okay, it's yours Ed."

"Farnell," Ed said, "I've only got five dollars American money on me—I'll go to the bank today and change it and come back—"

"Don't worry about it," Herman said, and pulling out his wallet, he handed Farnell the twelve dollars. "You can owe me Ed—"

"Oh, no, Herman please—you don't even know me—"

"I said don't worry about it Ed."

Then, Herman said, Ed paused a minute, thinking about something, and he said: "I'm gonna need to make some tools—is there a junkyard around here?"

"Yeah, Kilgore's in Homestead is the biggest," Herman told him, "we can stop by there on the way home."

Ed shook Farnell's hand and Farnell told him he'd go into town today and get the deed fixed into Ed's name. Then we left, Herman said, and headed out for Kilgore's place. When we pulled up to Kilgores, I saw Lucky (his real name was Freddy Mizell but everybody called him Lucky) standing in the driveway, fiddling with something in the back of his tow truck.

Kilgore's place was built out of thick wavy tin on the outside, attached to huge, heart-pine, inside beams, and it had a dirt floor.

Mr. Kilgore did welding, besides running the junkyard. He was a small thin man, about eighty years old, and he always had on clean, fresh-starched, blue overalls, and shiny brown brogan shoes, and he smoked a pipe when he wasn't welding. As we got out of the car, Ed heard some beautiful music coming out of the building and he looked surprised.

Ed said: "Is that Beethoven I hear?—coming out of a junkyard?"

"Yep, seems odd doesn't it. I'd never heard much Beethoven until I started coming here. I've grown to like it. Mr. Kilgore is an unusual man for these parts. He retired some years ago, he played the violin, in a band up in Pennsylvania, and he got bored when he came down here and he opened up this shop."

Ed noticed a wood sign, nailed up over the front door, painted in faded red ink. It read: "Kilgore's junkyard: You git what you pay for—no refunds to yankees."

Ed said: "How can he put that on his sign—isn't he a yankee?"

"Oh, yeah, he's just playing. The local folk around here love it. Kilgore said it's all right when a yankee makes fun of himself; but it might offend a yankee if a rebel put it up."

I wanted Ed to meet Lucky, Herman said, so we walked over to his truck. Lucky was 45 years old and he was short, about five feet five, but he was wiry-built, with a wide chest.

Lucky had bulging arm muscles, with fat blue veins popping out of his arms; he got strong from a operating a tow truck and doing mechanic work. He usually wore dirty blue jeans, greasy brown, lace up work boots, and a striped baseball shirt with Ty Cobb's name imprinted across the chest.

He had clear blue eyes and straight, thick gray hair combed straight back, with long sideburns cut at an angle on the bottom. Lucky was the nervous type, he kept his fingernails bit down to the quick, and then he'd knaw the skin around the nail until it was crater looking. Lucky was puffing on an unfiltered Lucky Strike cigarette, Herman said, (Lucky always claimed they were named after him) when

Ed and I walked up to his truck. I said:

"Lucky, what're you doing? You're supposed to be out robbing broke down tourists—"

"Well, I busted one good this morning, so I thought I'd go fishing this afternoon—"

"Lucky, I want you to meet our new citizen, this is Ed," and they shook hands. Then Herman noticed Lucky had a small black, short-haired puppy in the bed of his truck, and he was giving him some water from a little iron bucket.

"Where'd you get the dog?" Herman asked.

"From the vet," Lucky said. "They were about to put him to sleep—he had the mange real bad; I told the vet to put used motor oil and turpentine on him and he'd cure right up, but he didn't believe me, so I took him home and dipped him in it every day, and well, look at him now."

"He looks great," Herman said. "I wonder what kind of dog he is?"

"He's a target dog," Lucky said.

"A target dog? What is that?—I've never heard of it."

"A target dog—all the dogs in the neighborhood had a shot at his mama," Lucky said.

Lucky was missing his four bottom teeth from a motorcycle accident years ago, and he mumbled his words so bad it was hard to understand him.

And when he talked, he'd get excited and wave his hands around to emphasize what he was saying. If Lucky was downtown, standing on the sidewalk near the Blanche Barber Shop, where a lot of people stopped to talk, and people saw him, they'd stop what they were doing a moment just to watch Lucky talk.

"That Lucky is something else," people would say, and walk on. Lucky was easy going, Herman said,but he did have a temper too.

"Well boys," Lucky said, "I hate to leave good company, but I hear a wide-mouth bass calling me. Nice meeting you Ed," Lucky said, and he picked up the puppy and put him next to him in the driver's seat and he drove off.

Mr. Kilgore came up and spoke. I introduced Ed and explained that Ed needed some things and we were just gonna look around for awhile. So Kilgore said call him if we needed him and he went back to his welding (he said he was fixing a broke plow blade for Mr. E.V. Udell). Ed and I started plundering around in the fenced in area of the outside yard.

There was all kinds of old rusty-looking cars and trucks and wheels and rims lying around. And big 'ol coiled-up truck suspension springs; and old rusted ship engine parts, and bicycles, with and without tires and rims. Well, we messed around there about an hour, Herman said, and Ed, he piled up an odd looking bunch of junk, next to an old rusty-looking Ford truck. I went in and got Kilgore to come out and price the stuff.

"Well, let's see," Kilgore said, inventorying the junk parts in his head, "truck springs, wheel bearings, various car parts; bicycle with two flat tires and bent rims; a ball peen hammer, tool box with odd tools—and you say you want this 'ol Ford truck body?" Kilgore figured a moment and said, "I'll take five dollars for the whole lot and deliver the truck body over to Farnell's old place for you."

"That's fine," Ed said. Then Ed saw an old long iron bath tub in the corner, and asked Kilgore how much it was. Kilgore smiled, "I'll throw that in. Now Ed," Kilgore said, "you understand that truck hasn't got an engine—don't come back here next week and tell me it had an engine in it when you bought it."

Ed promised him he wouldn't and Kilgore told him he'd deliver the truck and stuff within the hour, because Ed said he'd like to have it as quick as possible. We left Kilgore's and drove back into Homestead. I took Ed over to the First National Bank and Ed opened an account. He changed over his Latvian money and he paid me back.

Next, Ed said he wanted some food supplies and a small pup tent, so I took him over to R.D. Norris' grocery store, on Poplar street. Ed picked up some bread and meat and a lot of canned goods. Then we went by Lamar McClung's Army surplus store.

Ed bought a small, army green, canvas tent with poles; an ax, a large hunting knife, a canteen, an assortment of tin plates, cups and tin knives and forks, like the army uses.

He also got a shovel, an iron cooking pot, a couple of kerosene lanterns, and a five gallon can of kerosene; a couple of green wool army blankets, two pillows without slipcovers and a broom. Ed filled up a five gallon can full of drinking water.

We left Lamar's place and headed back out to Ed's land. Kilgore had unloaded the truck body and the other stuff in the cleared part of the land, where Ed had described to him, just beyond a patch of scrub oaks, pines, and some small sweet gum trees.

We unloaded the supplies and put some of them in the old Ford truck body. Then Ed swept out the back of the truck and went to setting up the tent in back of the truck. I looked puzzled at him:

"Why are you putting up that tent in the truck?"

"This is where I'm going to sleep while I'm building my house."

"What're you talkin' about? Why don't you stay with us?—for awhile anyway. Look Ed, we've got twenty five rooms."

"I can't move in your house and interrupt your life—"

"Well, look, I didn't say forever—and it's not like I'm giving you sleeping privileges with Opal or anything." Well, Herman said, I argued with him until I saw it was no use, and I stayed and helped Ed get himself set up. And about supper time, I left. I tried to talk Ed into at least having supper with us but Ed said no, said he wanted to get started on his house. I wondered what he meant, but I didn't ask him about it.

Ed thanked me again and as I left, I told him I'd check back in a day or so and see if he needed anything.

It was just getting dusk now, Ed wrote in his diary, as I watched Herman driving off. I built me a fire and cooked a steak, medium rare, and I baked a potato in the fire coals. I was feeling weak and tired, but I felt stronger after the steak. I decided to lay down for awhile and take a short nap.

The crickets started chirping and I heard a hoot owl, hooting in the distance when I dozed off to sleep. It was midnight when I woke up. I climbed out of the tent and put some more logs on the fire and brightened it up.

I stretched my arms out and yawned, then I picked up my shovel and lantern, and walked out into the open field, not far from the fire. I could see good in the half-moon light of the clear overhead sky.

There was a cool nip in the air which surprised me, being this far down in the tropics, but it was perfect working weather. I put the lantern on the ground and started digging out a big square hole. When I'd gone down about a foot, I hit the solid bed of coral and then I started clearing the dirt off a six foot wide section of the coral. Then, when I'd just about cleared the section of coral, I suddenly sensed that something was out of balance, so I stopped digging. It was coming from behind me in a section of woods. I turned and looked in the direction of the disturbance.

I realized that somebody was out there watching me. I hadn't heard or seen them; but I felt their presence. I laid my shovel down and then I sat down on the ground near the hole I'd dug.

I cupped my hands around my mouth and I hollered out: "Hello out there! Nice evening isn't it?"

I found out later, from Herman Harmless, that it was Farnell Ferguson, Lamar McClung and Lucky; they were huddled down and watching me behind some bushes in the woods. Lucky told Herman later, they were shocked when I spoke out in their direction.

Lucky said, Lamar McClung had whispered: "How did he know we was out here?"

"Somebody must've made a noise— "Lucky whispered back.

"What'd he say?" Farnell asked, forgetting to whisper.

"Damn Farnell!" Lucky whispered, "let's get out of here!" And we went to backing out of there, Lucky said. The next day, around noon, Ed wrote, Farnell came by to check on me and he noticed the hole.

I told him I was digging the foundation. Then I said: "Yeah, I think I had some people spying on me last night."

"No foolin'?" Farnell said. "Did you get a look at'em?"

"No, I didn't see or hear them;" I said, "I felt them Farnell."

Farnell looked nervous and troubled, and his voice quivered some when he said: "You say you felt them Ed?— how's that?"

"Magnetics, Farnell; you see the whole human body is run by magnets. The body vibrates and sends out signals—to those who tune in. I was a boy when I discovered I had this gift; you see, I was behind my house one day in Latvia. I was out carving some stone, and something told me to turn around quick, and I did.

"Behind me was a man dressed in a black hooded monk's robe; he had a long knife, raised in the air, above my head, ready to stab me. I dropped my chisel and took off, and he started chasing me, but I outran him and made it to some woods. Later, we found out he was one of my grandfather's friends; he was a Druid, he had gotten drunk and was planning on sacrificing me to his gods I reckon."

"What's a Drude, Ed?"

"Oh, they're like a group of monks who wear robes and hang around Stonehenge in England; they study astronomy and metaphysics, things of the mind, you know."

"Oh yeah, well, Ed, it might've been an animal you heard. They's a lot of critters around here at night—might've just been an 'ol possum or a coon—"

"Oh, I don't think it was a possum or a coon, Farnell."

"Why's that?"

"Well," I said, and digging into my pocket, I pulled out a yellow, bone-handled, Case pocket knife, "not unless that coon was carrying around a pocket knife with the initials F.F. carved in it—see it right there?—I found it in the bushes where I thought I heard somebody last night."

"Well, I'll be dang," Farnell said nervously, "I must've dropped it sometime ago—I've been looking for it."

In the next few days, Herman said, I went out and checked on Ed every afternoon after work. Ed needed some more tools so we went by Kilgore's and picked them up. One day, Herman said, I walked into Lamar's place, Lucky was there and they were drinking bottled Cokes with peanuts in them, and standing around talking. So I got a Coke and joined them.

Lucky said: "We was just talking about Ed, your witch buddy."

"What're you talking about Lucky?"

"Farnell thinks Ed is a witch," Lucky said, "because he 'felt us' sneaking up on him the other night."

"Y'all better be careful spying on people. Ed told me about finding Farnell's knife."

"We wasn't spying," Lamar says, "we just happened by that way."

I went by Ed's place that day to see him, Herman Harmless said, and Ed got tickled at how nosy they were; and he got to laughing so hard, he got into one of those coughing spells again, and he about lost his breath. I said: "Ed, when are you gonna go back and let Doc Spooner look at you?"

But Ed shook his head: "I'll be okay," he said.

A couple of days went by, Herman said, and I got busy and didn't get out and check on Ed, but Farnell told me that he had given Ed some scrap lumber and helped him build an outhouse.

Ed said he had gotten tired of digging so many holes and sitting on a flimsy board, with a hole cut in it, to do his job, so Farnell helped him out.

"I patched up the old bicycle I got from Kilgore's," Ed wrote in his diary, "and sometimes, I'd ride over to Homestead and pick up small things like soda crackers, milk and sardines."

One day, I got a nasty cut on my finger from a sardine can, so I got on my bicycle and rode over to the DeSoto drug store in Homestead to get some iodine. I sat down at the soda fountain counter and Novia Lilly was behind the counter making up some chicken salad.

I said, "Hi Novia, where do you keep the iodine?" She turned around and noticed my bandaged finger. "Hi Ed, what did you do to your finger?"

"I'm embarrassed to tell you— I cut it on a sardine can."

"Well, let me look at it. I've got a little bottle back here we use." She put a towel down on the counter and got to looking close at my finger: "What kind of bandage is that?"

"A spider's web," I told her. "It stops the bleeding—"

"A spider's web?—are you crazy?—there's probably all kinds of bacteria in that."

"Oh, no, I only use webs with Red Cross approval—"

"I'm serious—that could be dangerous."

"Really? My grandfather did it all the time and he never had a problem—well, come to think of it, he did foam at the mouth sometimes."

"This is disgusting," she said, removing the spider's web with some tweezers.

Pat Loomis, her co-worker, walked up behind the counter and came over to watch us. Novia said: "Pat, have you ever heard of putting a spider's web on a cut?"

"Sure," Pat said, "stops the bleeding."

"Pat," Ed said, "you'd think someone working in a pharmacy would at least know the basics."

"I know y'all are crazy," Novia said.

"Honey," Pat said, "when you live out in the country and they ain't no doctors, a spider's web is mighty handy. You can use turpentine to close a bad wound too."

Novia cleaned the cut with alcohol and a cotton pad and then she dabbed some iodine on it and wrapped a fresh gauze bandage around the cut.

When she was done, she said: "Now be more careful next time when you eat sardines."

"Thanks Dr. Lilly," I said. And as I turned to go, I felt another coughing spell coming on. I tried to get out before it got too bad, and Novia said, "Ed, did you ever go back and see Dr. Spooner?"

"Yeah, I did," I said, lying.

"What did he say?"

"He told me I might have an infection of the lungs, due to using spider's webs on cuts—"

"Oh, real funny—seriously Ed, you better go and see him—"

"Oh, you and Herman—I'll be okay." Novia wouldn't let me pay for the iodine and I hurried on out before the coughing got too bad.

Later that night, about ten o'clock, Ed wrote, I was sitting around a fire I'd built when Novia pulled up at my place in Florida City. I had picked up a couple of old wood picnic chairs at Kilgore's and I was sitting in one, when she walked up. She had some pillow cases in her hand.

"Well, hi Doc," I said, standing up, "have a seat." I moved a chair closer to mine.

"Thank you," she said. "I just felt like going for a drive and I remembered you forgot your iodine."

She reached in her purse and handed me a bottle of iodine.

"Thank you very much. That's awful nice of you to come out this far."

"Herman said you were sleeping in a tent with scratchy pillows with no slipcovers, so I brought you some; I always have more of them than I need. I can't stand a scratchy pillow."

"Or a spider's web."

"I still don't believe that—I think you and Pat made that up. I see you have a wall put up," she said, pointing behind me.

"Yeah, it's coming along slowly."

"Ed, I'm going to come right to the point—Herman and I are worried about you. Everybody likes you. You're easy going and you have a crazy sense of humor. Ed, you can get mad at me if you want—I mean I know you like to keep things to yourself, well, that's the way you seem to me. You're here with no family, living in the woods—and I think you're sicker than you realize. Why won't you go to the doctor?"

I was surprised by what she was saying, but I knew she was sincere. She had driven all the way out here to check up on me. I stared into the fire a moment, collecting my thoughts, then I told Novia the story of how Agnes had jilted me. I told her how nothing mattered to me anymore; that life without Agnes had lost it's flavor. She listened to me and she seemed somewhat surprised by what I told her.

When I finished, she said: "I understand what you're saying. The same thing just happened to me, six months ago. Jimmy Roy Tyler and I were engaged, and about two months before the wedding, he stops on the side of the road, and changes some college girl's tire. She was on her way to the Keys.

"I guess they fell in love while he changed her tire and she changed his mind. I tell you—it about killed me. I'd known him since grade school."

"Do you think about him a lot?"

"Yeah, sometimes. But I got tired of crying over him. One night, I got frustrated and I took everything he ever gave me and I went out in the yard, dug a big hole, and put the stuff in it and covered it up. I put a little wooden grave marker with his name on it; I'd go out and look at it when I was feeling sad."

"Did it help you?"

"Yes, it did. Each time I looked at the marker, I tried to visualize that for me, he was dead; I made up an imaginary car wreck and had him die in it—have you told Herman about this?"

"No, I haven't told him—I've been meaning to, but I haven't."

"If you don't mind, I'll tell him—he's awfully worried about you."

I told Novia she could tell him, it didn't matter to me. She stayed awhile longer and we talked. She was easy to talk to and I was glad she'd come out. I liked her name "Novia" and she said it was a Spanish word meaning "girlfriend." Novia Lilly wasn't Spanish but her mother liked the word and so she named her daughter Novia.

One warm sunny day, around four o'clock, Herman said, I was sitting on the front porch of my fruit shop, talking to Dr. Bruce Timmons. He was a big time psychiatrist who had retired from Atlanta. Ed pulled up in the old pickup he'd bought at Kilgore's and he got out and came up and sat down.

I introduced Ed to Dr. Timmons, and I said: "Well, I see you got the old truck running," then I realized that the truck hadn't made any sound when he pulled up: "What happened Ed? You run out of gas and have to coast in here?"

"No, this truck doesn't use gas."

"What? What are you talking about?"

"Come on, I'll show you," Ed said.

Ed lifted the hood, Herman said, and there was an iron, clover-leaf shaped object, about the size of a car tire, sitting where the engine would normally be. This magnetic motor had tightly wound coils of copper wire on the inside, and was surrounded by rows of half-brick sized magnets, lined up in a circle next to each other on the outside, like teeth.

There was an iron handle on the side of the clover leaf frame. Ed put his hand on the handle: "When you spin this handle," he said, "the magnetic motor device starts whirling; it won't stop until you break the charge by removing a little copper charging wire—right here," he said, pointing.

"What kind of mess is this?" Herman said.

"This is my perpetual motion holder," Ed said. (This energy machine and the plans for building it, are still sitting in Coral Castle today, Herman explained.) "I can show it to you now because I just applied for a patent on it.

"The way it works is this: Once you put the magnets in motion, by spinning the handle, the north pole magnets chase the south end magnets, and they never stop until you break the pattern. The machine actually produces more energy than it consumes, you see, because as you travel, the magnets just keep chasing each other and producing "magneticity."

"That's what electricity should be called because it's actually nothing but magnets," Ed explained.

"This is phenomenal," Dr.Timmons said, "that defies the known laws of physics. If this is true, it would erase the combustible engine."

"I just built one of these at my house site," Ed said, "and I'm running my lights and a radio I put together from parts I got at Kilgore's. One day, I hope to provide the whole world with free energy. The truck has a system of large sprockets underneath and it's belt driven—" Suddenly, Ed started coughing hard, and he braced himself against the truck fender for support.

For a few minutes he couldn't talk but just kept coughing; he got red in the face and had trouble catching his breath. His chest started rapidly rising and falling and he went to his knees.

I got worried, Herman said, I was used to seeing him cough, but not this long. Ed had a panicky look on his face. His eyes widened, then he closed his eyes and rolled over on his side and curled up in the fetal position. His tongue came out and he was panting like a dog who's been running hard.

Doc Timmons said, "Herman, we better get him over to the Lake Shore hospital," so we loaded him in my car, Herman said, and we took off for the hospital.

Dr. L.J. Spooner was at the hospital when we got there. They loaded Ed on a stretcher table and hurriedly pushed him through the front door.

His eyes were closed, he had stopped coughing and appeared to be unconscious, as we followed along and looked down at him. Dr. Spooner left his patient and came to see about Ed. We waited around in the lobby for an hour before Dr. Spooner came out and talked to us. He told me they were going to have to run some tests on Ed before he could make any diagnosis. Spooner told me to go home and eat supper and come back around nine o'clock.

Well, my wife Opal and I went back to the hospital at nine, Herman Harmless said, and we asked the nurse to tell Dr. Spooner we were here. Spooner came out in a few minutes; he had a grim look on his face. I asked how Ed was.

"Herman, I'm afraid I've got bad news. Ed's got tuberculosis—"

"Tuberculosis?"

"Yes," Doc Spooner said, "Herman, it's the worst case I've ever seen. His lungs are eaten up with it—he'll live six months, maybe."

"Oh, God no," Opal said.

"I really don't know how he's been able to walk around," Spooner said, "much less how he's done all that work at his place."

"Oh, God—Doc, did you tell him?" Herman asked.

"Yes," Spooner said, "I told him a little while ago. I gave him some shots to relive the congestion in his lungs and one to rest him."

"Isn't there anything you can do doctor—some clinic you can send him to?" Opal asked.

"I'm afraid not. We don't have anything to fight Tuberculosis. Most people would be dead with what he's got."

"How do you reckon he's made it?" Herman asked.

"Medically speaking, I can't," Spooner said.

"How did he take it when you told him?" Herman asked.

"Very calmly," Spooner said. "Ed nodded his head and said, 'Well, that ought to give me time to finish my house.' He seems obsessed with finishing it—that may be a factor in keeping him here. I want him to stay here for a few days and rest. Then you can come get him. The best thing for him now is lots of fruits and vegetables and plenty of sunlight; that's about all you can do."

"I wanted to go in and see him," Herman said, but Dr. Spooner said he was sleeping. I went by to see Ed the next day at noon and he was sitting up having lunch. We talked and he was in good spirits; he didn't seem like a man who'd just been told he had six months to live. The hospital released Ed on the third day and I picked him up at noon, Herman Harmless said. I tried to get him to come home with me and stay for awhile, but Ed said: "No, I got to get on with my house Herman—I'll be okay."

"Listen Herman," Ed continued, "I never went to medical school but I know some things about the body that doctors don't know; the human body is a magnetic machine—now maybe I'll die and maybe I won't, but I'll go down fighting."

And then, Herman said, Ed and I sat down in the picnic chairs at his place and we talked awhile.

Ed told me about Agnes and about the dream he

had when he was a little boy and he dreamed he was an indian in the stone canyon and he saw the alien ship crashing.

Ed told me about going to see his indian friend in New Mexico after the war was over, and how Beaver had taken him to Chaco Canyon. Ed said after that visit, he was convinced that he'd been here before—he said that these same places that he was in now, had been before in another time and place.

He said that now he was revisiting them again in this life. I listened with great interest, Herman Harmless said, because the things he talked about were mysterious to me.

And I couldn't figure out why he wanted to build a house when he only had six months to live, Herman said. But before I left, Ed repeated what Nick used to say about happiness being:

"Something to do, Something to love and Something to hope for."

And I thought, "Well, Ed's trying to make the best of the time he has left, and maybe it's better if he thinks he has a chance." And I had already learned you couldn't argue with Ed—he was gonna do what he was gonna do and that was that.

"Herman, come back and check on me in three days," Ed told me, and so I left him alone at his place.

Three days later, around one o'clock in the afternoon, I pulled up to Ed's place.

When I got there, I saw Ed lying on a big round piece of coral stone. Above him was an open wooden pyramid, wrapped with copper wire, with it's base resting on the stone.

Ed had on a pair of gold, wire-framed sunglasses, with dark blue lenses. He was lying on his back, his head resting on a curving stone pillow that had been beautifully sculpted out of the huge, round coral stone.

Attached overhead to the copper pyramid, was

a dark blue glass spotlight; it was catching the sun's rays and casting a misty blue tint over Ed's upper body. There was a long, black metal box, sitting on a stand near Ed's head. It had a red light lit up on it's face, and was connected to the pyramid by a single wire.

When Ed saw me, to my amazement, he stuck his foot out and spun the large stone around, so he was facing me.

I said, "You're a long way from the beach aren't you?—what're you doing?"

"Hey, Herman. I'm sunbathing in my magnetron machine. I do this for two hours every day after lunch, from one to three, when the sun's the hottest."

Ed explained that he'd dug down in the ground and he cut and lifted this huge coral stone out of the ground. Then, he mounted it on the brake drum of a Ford truck, so he could turn it and position himself with the sun as it moved in the sky.

"How much does it weigh?"

"About three tons," he said, grinning. "I don't have a scale to weigh it on."

"Has Farnell seen this?"

"No, he hasn't been by, why?"

"He'll think you're a witch for sure now."

Ed got up and we sat down in the wooden easy chairs. Ed explained the idea of this bizarre looking machine to me.

"You remember, I said the human body is run by magnets. Well, you see Herman, due to the shape and the true north orientation of the pyramid, a magnetic field is set up inside the pyramid.

"Now, this little box you see here, causes the field inside to pulsate—it beats just like your heart does. Now this pulsating part is the key; what it does is cause the magnets in our blood to chase each other, and so it makes the blood flow and puts oxygen back into the cells.

"With a twenty minute treatment, it's just like you went out and ran two miles. Blood circulation is the secret to any healing."

"Well, I'll be. What's the blue light for?" I asked him.

"Oh, it's just for special effects I guess. I read one of Nick's books one time, that talked about using light for healing, and it said always use blue light for healing, so I thought, well, why not?"

"You see, Herman, magnets run the planets and every living thing. Gravity is nothing more than a perfect balance of the north and south pole magnets," Ed explained.

"Now when we eat," Ed said, "the food is broken down by stomach acid and the magnets from the food are released into our body, and that's where we get energy from. We're made to work just like the battery in a car—take the battery out, and you're not going anywhere."

Ed explained that this machine, he called it a magnetron, worked exactly like a battery charger for the human body. Then Ed took out a donut-sized magnet, cut in half, that he liked to play with, and he put it inside the pyramid. He told me to put my hand inside and touch the magnet, and when I did, I could feel the magnet vibrating in my hand.

"That is a strange feeling," I told him. "Can you tell any difference in how you feel?"

"Well, not a lot yet," Ed said, "it'll take some time." Ed explained that he'd checked out some books from the library about tuberculosis and cancer, and Ed said the books say that neither one of them could live in a magnetic field.

"You got to remember," he told me, "a magnet is the most powerful force in the world—remember, it's power holds the earth in the sky."

So, Herman Harmless said, everyday, from one to three, Ed got into his magnetron and exposed himself to the hot, tropical, south Florida sun. Then, from three to four, he would sit and read books about the Mexican pyramids and The Great Pyramid of Egypt and anything he could get his hands on about magnets.

He grew himself a little garden, growing turnips and mustard and collard greens. Lamar McClung introduced him to putting pepper sauce on the greens, in the traditional southern style, and Ed got to where he loved southern cooking.

Ed usually had dinner at six o'clock. Sometimes he'd get on his bike for exercise and ride over to Mrs. Viola Coota's grocery store on Hernando street in Florida City.

She and her husband Clarence Coota ran it; he'd go out and pump gas if you needed it and she handled most of the inside selling work. Most of the time Ed would pick up sardines and crackers and pickled eggs that Viola Coota made herself.

Ed also developed a taste for pickled pig's feet after watching Lamar eat them one day in his army surplus store. Lamar took an ice cold bottle of chocolate soda out of the drink box, called a "Brownie;" it was in a clear bottle with a picture of a little girl wearing a floppy brown hat. Lamar told him the best part of the pig's foot was chasing it with an ice cold Brownie.

Lamar shook the cold bottle up and then set it on the counter; Ed could see the brown chocolate foam bubbling up at the top, as Lamar opened it; a fizz sound came out as some chocolate foam rose up and out over the mouth.

Ed took a bite of pickled pig foot, then he bit into a cheese cracker, layered with peanut butter in the middle and sprinkled with salt on the top, and then he picked up the cold bottle, covered with tiny ice slivers, and took himself a good drink.

He set the bottle down and nodded his approval. Lamar said:

"Isn't that some kind of fine?"

"Lamar," Ed said, "not even the most famous French chef would've thought of this."

Now Ed would only work at night, Herman said, when it was cooler, and no one could see how he was cutting and moving all these enormous stones. Ed would start about midnight and work until sunrise.

I'd go out and check on him about every three days, and see how he was doing. I could see he was getting stronger every day. Every now and then, Lamar and Lucky would still sneak out at night and try to catch Ed at work, but they never did.

They said Ed would climb up on the wall he was working on, and look out into the woods where they were hiding and he'd say, "Hello out there—how are you tonight?" Farnell wouldn't go with them because he still thought Ed might be a witch. Farnell was a superstitious kind of man, and he didn't like to mess around with supernatural things, Lucky said.

One day, a lady newspaper reporter named Dorothy Sue Skidmore from the Homestead paper "Enterprise," came out to interview Ed. Ed decided it might be a good idea to speak to her and tell everyone his story, and maybe it would satisfy people's curiosity about him.

So he told her about Agnes. Ed said: "Well, I needed something to do, so I decided to build a castle for her. When I'm finished with it, I'll send her some pictures of it, and she'll know how much I love her, and she'll come over here and marry me. So, I'm waiting for Agnes, that's my plan anyway."

Dorothy Sue thanked Ed, Herman said, and she went back to Homestead and wrote her story.

The next day, the headlines of the paper read: "Magnet Man" staying alive to finish "Coral Castle" for his "Sweet Sixteen." And that's how the name of the place came to be.

The article described how Ed had been jilted by Agnes and how everybody was curious about why a dying man wanted to build a house at the edge of the Florida Everglades. And how did one small man, cut and lift huge stones, weighing tons, with handmade tools from Mr. Kilgore's junkyard?

Ed showed Dorothy Sue the round stone sun couch he'd made that he laid on every day. It was eight feet wide with three raised, sloping, stone head pillows. He mounted the stone on a 1920 Ford truck wheel drum so he could position it for the best angle of the sun.

The coral was smooth and comfortable to lay on. It was balanced so perfect, Ed told her, you could spin it with one finger. People in Homestead and Florida City read the article and it made Ed famous around here.

The six months Ed had to live went by, and he was still here, and working like a dog. Ed went back to let Dr. Spooner check him out, and Spooner looked astonished after he examined him:

"This is truly a miracle Ed," Spooner told him. "Your lungs are as clear as a baby's. I've never seen anything like it."

Dr. Spooner's original medical report, Herman said, describing Ed's condition, and his incredible recovery, is in a glass case, inside the little museum at Coral Castle.

Ed described his magnetron machine to Dr. Spooner, Herman said, and Spooner listened politely but with little interest. And Ed realized it, and he quit talking when he saw Spooner wasn't interested. When Ed finished talking, Spooner said, "A miracle like this can only come from God."

"I agree with you Dr. Spooner," Ed replied. "God gave me the knowledge to invent this machine and through it, he healed me."

And we got up, Herman said, and left Spooner's office before Ed said anymore, because he could see he was wasting his time with Spooner. We went over to Ed's place for lunch to celebrate his healing. Ed had carved a large table out of coral that was a perfect replicated map image of the state of Florida. The table had twelve rocking chairs placed around it.

Over a lunch of fried chicken, potato salad and baked beans, Ed explained his distrust of doctors: "Now Herman," he told me, "I don't mean they're all bad—it's just they have too much power. You see, Spooner wasn't interested in my machine, because he didn't invent it. It's all about ego—men love to glory in what their little minds can do."

Ed had almost finished his castle, Herman said, when one day, Lucky said, Ed rode his bicycle ten miles over to Lucky's garage in Homestead. It was around the first of March in the year 1923.

I was working on Melvin Udell's milk truck, Lucky said. After some small talk, Ed said:

"Herman told me you had a tractor and a flatbed trailer."

"Yeah, I sure do. You need it?"

"Yeah, I'd like to rent it, and pay you to drive it for me."

"Oh, I don't know if I'd rent it—but I might let you borrow it—"

"No, Lucky, I appreciate the offer, but I may need you for a couple of days, and I want to pay you just like you were working."

"What do you want me to do?"

"Could you meet me at my place in the morning, about seven thirty?"

"Well, yeah, I'll be through with Melvin's truck today."

"Great, I'll see you in the morning," Ed said, and he got on his bicycle. "I'll have breakfast ready," Ed said, as he left.

I showed up the next morning right on time, Lucky said. Ed was waiting outside at the iron front door. Ed greeted me and we went in. He led me straight over to the Florida table where he had fried eggs, bacon, pancakes, and grits.

"I wish I had time to give you a tour of the castle," Ed told Lucky, "but I'll give you one later."

There was all kinds of huge stone beds, rocking chairs, and on the top of one wall, I saw what appeared to be a copy of some planets, including a quarter moon. It was an overwhelming sight, Lucky said, more than the eyes could take in at one time.

When we finished eating, Ed said, "Well, are you ready to go to work?"

"Sure, what are we gonna do?"

"We're gonna move this entire castle to Homestead."

"Oh, yeah, right. No really, what did you want me to do?"

"Well, the first thing is I want you to do, is pull the tractor and trailer around behind the castle there," Ed said, pointing east. "I'll move the east wall first."

I found out Ed was not joking, Lucky said, he was dead serious, so I did what he said. When the trailer was in place, I got down off the tractor, and he told me to go back to the front of the castle and he'd call me when he was ready.

"Ed, if you don't mind me asking, how much does the east wall weigh?"

Ed said: "29 tons—give or take a pound or two."

So, Lucky said, I went back to the front door to wait. I guess about fifteen minutes went by, and I got curious and thought I'd sneak back around and see what he was doing.

I got down on my knees, and dog-walked towards the back, and when I got close, I got on my belly and started easing around the corner, crawling like a gator; sometimes I'd stop, listening to see if I could hear anything. When I got around the corner, where I could see my tractor, I stopped to look.

And suddenly, I felt something grab my leg; it was Ed, and he yells out: "Lucky! What're you doing?"

He scared me so bad I almost messed my britches up: "Oh, hi Ed, I thought you might need some help."

"No, the stone is loaded, I was just coming to get you. Now I'm going to let you drive, and I'm going to ride on the back with the stone."

And I looked up, Lucky said, and sure enough, the stone was on the trailer. "How in the world did you lift that stone?" I asked him.

But he just smiled and said, "I know the secret of The Great Pyramid, let's go."

"Wait, where are we going?" I asked.

"Oh, yeah, the address is road number 286 on

Key West Highway in Homestead. We've got to go right through the middle of town."

The trip into Homestead took about an hour, Lucky said, and we were just passing by The Blanche Barber shop, when the tractor made a sputtering noise. I hit the throttle and it kicked up strong again, but then it started chugging down. The tractor died right at the barber shop, and I hopped off and raised the side engine flap to see what was wrong.

People in the shops were looking out the windows, wondering what was going on, and they poured out on the streets like ants, to see the huge stone sitting on the trailer bed.

A man named Oval Overstreet came out of the Blanche Barber shop and he went over to look at the stone. He was smoking a pipe. He looked at Ed: "How'd you move that thang Ed?"

"Hi Oval—oh, I had to make me a wheel barrow—a real big one."

"Wheel barrow?—oh, bull."

About that time, Herman Harmless came out of the DeSoto drug store, and saw Ed, and he said: "What on earth are you and Lucky doing?"

"Hey Herman, I'm moving the castle to Homestead—"

"What? But why? Wasn't it almost finished?"

"Yep," Ed said, "but I saw ten acres for sale over here, and I checked it out—it's got a good spring of water on it and plenty of coral. I bought it from Clovis Turney. I gave Farnell his land back—he's been so good to me; helping me build that outhouse and all."

Ed never would give me a straight answer, Herman said, about why he moved the castle from from Florida City over to Homestead.

A policeman named Bobby Brewin had seen the traffic backing up, and he came up through the crowd to Lucky and said:

"What's the trouble Lucky?"

"Hey Bobby," Lucky said, "I'm not sure—I think I'll have it in a minute—"

"Well, hurry it up okay?" Brewin said. "Herman, how about you and Lamar and Shorty, see if you can get some people to move these cars parked along the street here; I'll go back and direct traffic around the tractor."

They did it and Brewin directed traffic as Lucky got back on the tractor. It fired up and they headed off for Ed's new home. It took a week to move the whole castle, Herman said. Lucky quit trying to sneak up on Ed, because every time he tried, Ed caught him.

When the castle was finished, Herman said, Ed decided to have a grand opening and invite everybody out to see his castle. I wanted to take Ed out to dinner at the Chalet Suzanne to celebrate the castle opening. Chalet Suzanne was a nice place, with good food and decorated with antiques.

It overlooked a big lake named Lake Suzanne, and that's how the place got it's name. It was well known for it's food; the walls of the place were covered with autographed pictures of famous movie stars.

Ed's diary entry, June 26, 1923: Herman says they have a good band playing at the Chalet Suzanne. Herman said Novia Lilly wanted to go because she likes to dance. At first, I said no, I didn't want him fixing me up with Novia. I've got a girl, her name is Agnes and I'm going to marry her one day.

But Herman said, "Hey, look, just go and dance with her—she's not looking for a man, she just got out of the romance ambulance, just like you. Why can't you just be friends?"

So, when he put it that way, I said, okay, I'll go. But I insisted on driving my truck and meeting them there; that way, it didn't seem like a date. Well, I was in for a big surprise when I got there.

Chalet Suzanne looked like a small replica of a Swiss village. It was a bed and breakfast place and the buildings were made of pink stucco plaster and they had tall spires rising into the blue Florida sky. The driveway was made of heavy streetbrick. The bed part was next to the restaurant and there was a pool in between.

I parked the truck, got out and walked over to the pool. It was next to the office and there was a covered patio with wrought iron tables and a place for a band. There were also wrought iron dining tables, painted pink, around the pool. What I saw on one of the dining tables is what surprised me. The table top was made of a shiny ceramic tile and it had a hand painted scene on it showing oriental warriors riding horseback into battle.

This was the same scene that was on the table in the dream I'd had before Agnes and I got married. As I stared at the scene on the table, I began to remember the dream that I'd had when Agnes and I were together in that lovely park in Atlantis. This Chalet Suzanne was the same place where we had danced together by the pool in Atlantis. Solomon said all things have been before.

I ran my fingers across the smooth cool tile, and I thought about these things that had been and were again. Then, I walked into the restaurant. Inside, it was nice and cool with a passing breeze from an overhead ceiling fan.

I stood there looking around, remembering everything I'd seen in the dream. There were books on the shelves, sitting against the walls in book cases. I thought, here was the same place, but in a different time, where Agnes and I had lunch one day.

A young petite girl with long blonde hair, wearing a long shimmering yellow gown, came up and stopped at the reception desk.

"Good evening sir," she said, "I'm Gina, welcome to the Chalet Suzanne. Would you like a table for one?"

"I'm meeting some friends here, Herman Harmless," I told her.

"Oh, yes, you must be Ed. They're waiting in the back. Just follow me," she said, and turned to go, but I said: "Excuse me Gina, I'm just curious—why does a restaurant have all these books?"

"Oh," she said, "people bring'em in and check-

'em out all the time. The owner, Mrs. Hinshaw, used to be a librarian before she opened this place, and so she brought her private collection of books in. And other book lovers came in and started swapping with her, and now some people, when they die, will their books to us."

"So, you mean I could check out a book from here if I wanted to?"

"Sure," she said. "Is there one in particular that you want? Of course remember, our selection is limited—"

"Oh yes, sure," I said, pausing a moment, trying to remember the name of the book I saw featured on the reception desk in my Atlantic dream. I told Gina I'd ask for the book later if I could remember it.

Gina led the way to the back, past the rows of books, and when we got there, a waitress came up and said they needed her back up front, a large party had just come in. She apologized to me, and pointed to Herman's table and excused herself and hurried off.

At the end of the room where Herman was sitting, on a second story, there was a long carved wooden ship. And emerging from the bow, I saw the same carved wooden figure of a woman (she was carved from the waist up) that had been in my Atlantis dream.

This was the same dining room where Agnes and I had eaten. And suddenly, I remembered the name of the book I'd seen here before; it was "Complete Love Lyrics," by Laurence Hope.

I hurried back up to the reception desk and, finding Gina, I told her the book's name. She wrote it down and told me she'd look in the card catalogue and see if they had it.

It was dark outside now, and after we'd finished dinner, we walked out the door, heading over to the outside dining and dance area. I had looked around at the reception desk for Gina to ask her about the book before we left, but I didn't see her.

We got a table, with the oriental warriors painted on it, near the lighted pool. We had a couple of drinks and the band cranked up with a good dance number and Herman said: "Oh, I love this song y'all, let's dance." So we did.

When the song was over, the band went quickly into another song. Herman and Opal kept dancing, but I told Novia I wanted to sit down, so we headed back to the table.

We exchanged some small talk about how good the band was and how nice it was to be out under the stars. Then we sipped our drinks in silence for a moment. I stared down at the warriors on the table top and I got to thinking about some things.

Agnes and I used to dance to this same song they were playing now at the Tamariz in Latvia.

"You can't forget her can you?" Novia asked me.

I didn't say anything I just shook my head. Gina, the hostess, walked up as we were talking.

"Sir, excuse me," Gina said, "but I found the book and someone said you'd walked out here. It was in Mrs. Hinshaw's office. I'd gone over to see her and I'd forgotten that she keeps some books in her office."

She handed me the book and asked me if I'd like to check it out. I was astonished and I didn't know what to say. I looked closely at the cover to make sure it was the same book, and I was sure that it was. I handed it back to her and thanked her.

"Maybe I'll check it out later," I said.

And then I remembered something Madame Drusa once told me:

"In the unconscious mind, nothing experienced is forgotten; the happening is merely transferred, and stored for later recall through dreams and visions. Mind is a transferred spirit, so past memories are available for review, from one life to another to those who believe."

Seeing that book made me uncomfortable. It was just too much, and I knew I had to get out of here.

"Novia," I said, "I hope you don't think I'm rude, but I'm going home. Would you give my apologies to Herman and Opal?"

"Yes of course," she said. "I understand—Ed, are you going to be okay?"

"Yes. Please forgive me. You're a wonderful person and a fabulous dancer—well, good night Novia."

"Good night Ed," she said, as I got up to leave.

When the song was over, Herman said, Opal and I came back to the table.

"Where's Ed?" Herman asked.

"He went home. I'm worried about him Herman—I'm going by to check on him," Novia said, and she thanked them for the dinner and she left.

When I pulled up to Ed's place, Novia said, I found him sitting in his backyard, around a fire. I walked over and saw a small wooden trunk with iron latches, near a hole he'd dug out in the ground.

Ed seemed to be in a trance state; he did not turn his head and look at me as I approached him and sat near him. His eyes were fixed on the fire and he looked straight into it when he finally spoke.

"Hi Novia. I wouldn't admit to doing this to anyone else but you," he said softly. "Do you remember when you said you'd buried Jimmy Roy and it helped you forget him?"

"Yeah."

"Well, I tried it—but it didn't work for me. I couldn't stand the thought of burying Agnes, even if it was only symbolic."

Inside the box was a pair of red, high heel shoes, and the picture of Agnes, dressed up in the red saloon girl's outfit.

"These were the shoes that Agnes wore in this photo," Ed said. "I bought them from the studio because Agnes had her feet in them. Novia, am I crazy to wait for her?"

"Who can say Ed?—one thing's for sure, you weren't ready to bury the past—and until you are, I'm afraid you're doomed to live in it."

Once Ed had carved out the chairs and beds for the castle, Herman said, he began building the massive walls for the new Coral Castle. Each section of wall is 8 feet tall, 4 feet wide, 3 foot thick and weighs around 13,000 pounds. Now that Ed had his health back, Herman said, he'd start working around eleven o'clock at night, and sometimes he'd work right on up past sunrise. Sometimes we'd meet at the Myna Bird for breakfast. After breakfast, Ed went back home and took a nap until around noon.

In the afternoon, after lunch, Ed tinkered around with his magnetic experiments, trying to improve on his perpetual motion holder. Then, at four o'clock, he'd quit working and read his books. He'd usually read his pyramid books or study the readings that Madame Drusa had given him over the years as he grew up in Lativa. Sometimes, he'd have sardines for supper at six and then get his things ready for work that night.

Ed was able to work most nights now without being bothered because people had learned that you couldn't sneak up on him. It took him about two months to finish the castle at Homestead.

One day, a couple of days after Ed had finished the castle, Herman said, Ed and I were sitting on the front porch of my fruit shop, drinking ice coffee and watching the traffic go by.

I asked him if he'd heard anything from the patent office on his perpetual motion machine.

"No, I haven't. But I guess it takes time. The patent form said it could be six months."

"Oh, before I forget to tell you, White Lightning and the Moonshiners are coming through here next saturday."

"Who's that?"

"Who's that?—boy, where you been? That is one of the finest blue grass bands in the country—they're just now starting to get famous. I met'em back a few years ago when they first got started. They didn't have money for a hotel room so I put'em up at our place. I got to thinking about it—isn't your grand opening next saturday?"

"Yeah."

"Well, I thought we'd get them to play for you at the Coral Castle—hey, son, you talk about drawing a crowd—they'll do it."

"Oh, that'd be great," Ed said. "I've always wanted to hear an American blue grass band. You think they'd do it?"

"Sure—I know Minnow Sutton, he plays the fiddle and manages the band—he'll do it for me."

"His name is Minnow?"

"Well, his real name is Dwander Primus Sutton, but he hates that name, and he's a little bitty guy, about your size, so they nicknamed him "Minnow." But don't let on I told you his real name—"

"Wait a minute though, Herman—how much will they charge?"

"How about nothing? I'm gone put them up at my place so they've got no expenses. And when I tell them about your castle, they'll know it's good exposure and be happy to do it."

Ed took out an ad in the paper, Herman said, announcing his grand opening at one o'clock on saturday, May 25, 1924, and he mentioned that White Lightning and the Moonshiners would be there.

"Well," Herman said, "there must've been five hundred people there on grand opening day; lots of folks drove on by because they could see there weren't any parking places. Everybody was dying of curiosity to see what kind of things Ed had been working on at night all that time inside the castle."

Farnell Ferguson, Mr. Kilgore, the junkyard man, Lamar McClung, Novia Lilly and Doc Spooner were all there. That saturday was a nice, bright sunny day, with a slight breeze blowing and it helped to keep things cool.

Alvin Truax and Lucky almost stole the show, Herman said, when they showed up at Ed's place that day, half-drunk and driving an old bright yellow, World

War I tank. Alvin had just gotten it from Lamar McClung, who got it for him at an army surplus auction.

Alvin said he got the idea about the tank after seeing a war film where they first used tanks over there in France. Alvin figured he could use that tank in the pulp woods (he was a pulp wood man) to snake trees out when the heavy rains sometimes kept the logging trucks out of the woods for weeks at a time.

What he could do, see, Alvin said, was cut a bunch of'em and then drag'em out to the trucks with his tank. But Alvin only had enough money to buy half the tank, so he talked Lucky into buying the other half, and they'd split the profits.

Alvin figured that Lucky, being a good mechanic, could fix the tank when it went down. Alvin was so proud of his tank and he couldn't wait to show it off to everybody.

Alvin Truax had never owned anything real nice you see, Herman said, because he threw most of his money away on keeping up old pulpwood trucks; keeping up his part-time girlfriend, Jerry Fay Swilley, and staying drunk on cheap moonshine.

Alvin loved music and dancing and when he heard that White Lightning was gonna be at Ed's place, he went out and bought himself a beige colored cowboy shirt, embroidered on the front with cactus plants done in fancy, copper-colored sequins. But Alvin didn't have enough money to buy himself some new cowboy boots, and truth was, he needed new boots a lot worse than he needed that cowboy shirt with the fake pearl snaps.

But he fell in love with the shirt when he saw it hanging in the front window at Lamar's shop, and he said he had to have it.

Alvin loved to wear his cowboy boots, but they were looking ragged; some small frayed holes were beginning to show through on the sides, where his little toes pushed out hard against the leather, on account of he was flat-footed, Herman said.

So Alvin got an idea from the shiny copper sequins on his shirt, and he went down to the paint store and got himself some shiny copper paint, and he painted his cowboy boots from top to bottom with copper paint.

And before he painted them, Alvin took some wood putty and he covered over the holes on the sides and he let the wood putty dry out; you wouldn't have ever known the holes were there, unless you looked real close.

At one o'clock sharp, Ed Leedskalnin stood on a stack of orange crates in front of the castle (he had to because he was so short he couldn't see over the crowd) and he spoke to the people. Ed wore a light blue, long sleeve, Egyptian cotton, work shirt, a cloth pith helmet, with brown metal eyelets on each side, and pleated khaki pants. One sign that he had carved in the coral stone wall behind him, near the iron front door, read: "What you will be seeing is an unusual accomplishment," and another sign, inside the castle read, "Notice, be careful. Anything you do on these premises is at your own risk."

To his left, was a large bell, with a sign next to it, reading: "Ring bell twice."

Behind him, was a large, square, rusty, scrap-iron door, with a strange drawing of the sun orbiting the earth etched into the front.

"I'd like to thank everybody for coming out today," Ed said. "I wasn't expecting so many people; y'all must've come out just to hear White Lightning. I haven't been here very long and I'm starting to pick up this southern slang.

"I'd like to put in a plug for Mr. Kilgore, who's here; all my tools came from his salvage place, and he was even kind enough to give me a bath tub—maybe he was trying to tell me something, I don't know. Maybe it was because I smelled so bad after working nights here and he felt sorry for me.

"Well, let me begin the tour by telling you about my front door bell," he said, pointing to it.

"It came from a Model T Ford truck that I found at Mr. Kilgore's place. I made it from the bell housing of the rear end from the truck.

"You'll notice the sign reads, 'ring twice,' so if visitors want to tour the castle, they can let me know they're here. Please follow these directions; don't ring it once and don't ring it three times. If I'm not too busy, I'll answer it and give you a tour; if I don't answer it, you either ignored the directions, or I'm busy working or I'm taking a bath.

"Now, anything you do here is at your own risk—I don't have accident insurance, and I don't need fire insurance because I don't have anything that will burn—except me; and I don't have hurricane insurance because I challenge any Florida hurricane to blow up against my walls—it'll lose, and you can bet on that.

"Well, before I start, I guess I should tell you why I built the Coral Castle. For those of you who don't know me, my name is Ed Leedskalnin.

"Just call me Ed—I don't expect any of you to pronounce my last name—it's even hard for me. As some of you know, Agnes Scuffs, my fiance in Latvia, changed her mind about marrying me on the night before our wedding.

"As you can imagine, it's been rough on me, and I figured I needed something to occupy my time, so I decided to build this castle as, well, a sort of monument to my love for her.

"I'm hoping that once she sees pictures of it, she'll realize how much I love her, and maybe then, she'll come over here and marry me. Well, I know it's far-fetched, but that's my plan and I'm sticking to it."

Then, Ed pointed to the strange drawing etched into the iron entrance door: "This drawing here, represents the correct path the earth travels on it's way around the sun. Our current geography books are wrong about this; I was fooled by them at first, but I built a rock telescope and sun-dial and they de-fooled me, so I drew this correct map on the door.

Ed's Bathtub is seen in the background. Ed's mirror, a piece of slate covered with water, is seen in the foreground.

Interior of "Repentance Corner." The taller of the two openings is for "Sweet Sixteen" in case she got "sassy".

Ed's living quarters (the tower in the background) made up of blocks weighing 4 to 9 tons each. Ed lived in the upper part, the lower level contained his tools.

Sixteen steps lead up to Ed's living quarters.

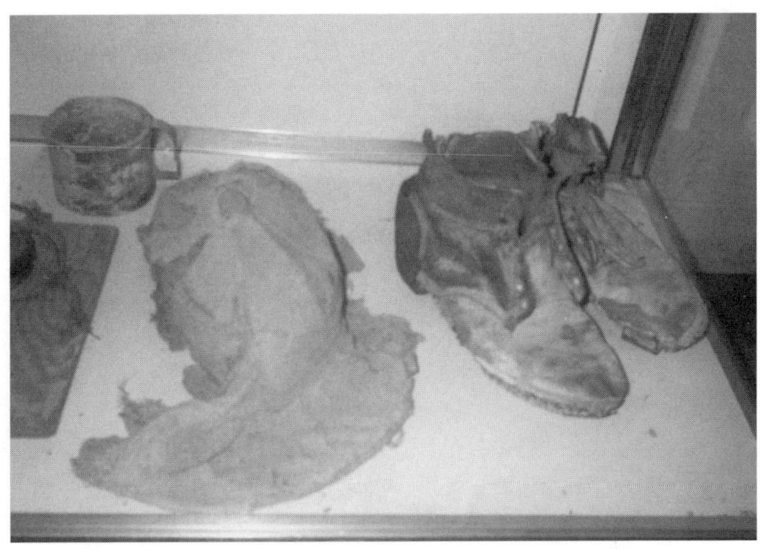

The remains of Ed's pith helmet and work shoes. Note the rusty iron heel and sole coverings.

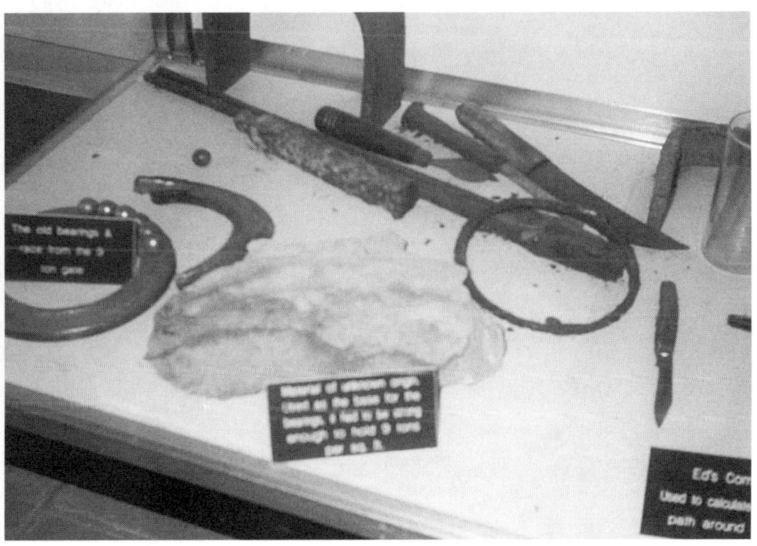

Ed used this stone as the base for the 9 ton gate. Caption under the stone reads "Material of unknown origin; it had to be strong enough to hold 9 tons per sq.ft." The stone is not found on this earth.

Ed's unique admission piece. Maybe he carved it to resemble his "Sweet Sixteen's" figure.

Entrance to Coral Castle. Note the iron door; small sign inside door way reads, "Ring Twice."

Hanging chair. The hanging chains are part of a horse harness. Ed made the chair from scrap metal and bicycle parts.

Bar-B-Que Cooker. The cooking pot is the rear end of an old Ford truck. Suspended on a pulley, it could be pulled close for food removal.

Alien Face in the altar (near the stone's bottom). A boy on one of the tours shoved two yellow marbles into the eye sockets, the staff was unable to remove them so they remain today.

Mad Rocker. Ed designed it so if he and "Sweet Sixteen" quarreled, they could sit in their chair, rock, and not have to look at each other. The planet Saturn is in the background.

Figure of the Mayan Chief Ed carved as a child.

Moon Dial. Built like the sun dial, Ed could see the time at night. It is the only known moon dial in the world.

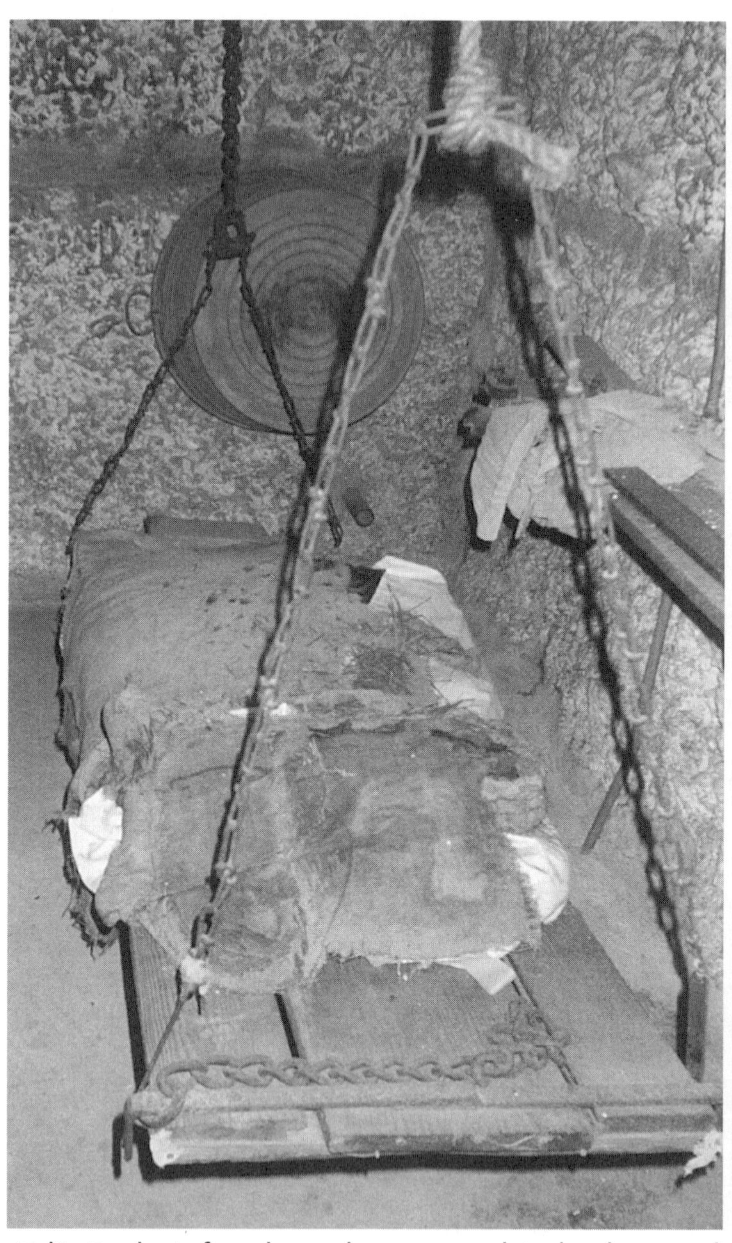

Ed's Bed. A few boards wrapped in burlap sacking; it hangs from the ceiling by chains on a pulley system so it could be moved out of the way in the day.

Stonehenge stone. Ed carved this stone to show that he understood the lost science used to move the great stones at Stonehenge.

Ed's food box and kerosene stove below it. An insect crawling down the rod drowns in the funnel of kerosene.

Ripley's Believe-It-Or-Not, lists this 5,000 lb. heart-shaped table as the world's largest valentine. Ed said now Agnes would always have a Valentine card in case he forgot to get her one.

Florida Table. Ed said the governor could come down, sit around this table, rock in the chair and figure out ways to raise taxes.

The Moon Pond, pictured here with 30 ton wall in the background, is the most photographed subject at Coral Castle. 30 ton wall has the same configuration as the stones on top of the "King's Chamber" at the Great Pyramid.

The 9 ton gate is uneven in its dimensions, but somehow Ed found it's center of gravity. The little girl shows how easy it's moved with one finger.

Ed Leedskalin was a proud man, he insisted upon being in his best attire when photographs were taken.

There are 23 tons in this Crescent Moon. The picture here is taken in the original location in Florida City.

Always pointing to the north star, the Polaris Telescope stands 25 feet high and weighs 20 tons. It helped Ed plot the earth's path around the sun and enabled him to design and construct the accurate sundial.

Perched above the sun dial, in Ed's first rocker, rocker Billy Idol warms up for "Sweet Sixteen" the song and music video he recorded at Coral Castle.

Billy Idol in a reflective mood, contemplating the many mysteries at Coral Castle.

After a break, Billy Idol heads back to the set on the filming of "Sweet Sixteen." He dedicated the song to Ed's fiance, Agnes Scuffs.

A rare picture of Coral Castle under construction. Note the three tripods fitted with the mysterious "black boxes."

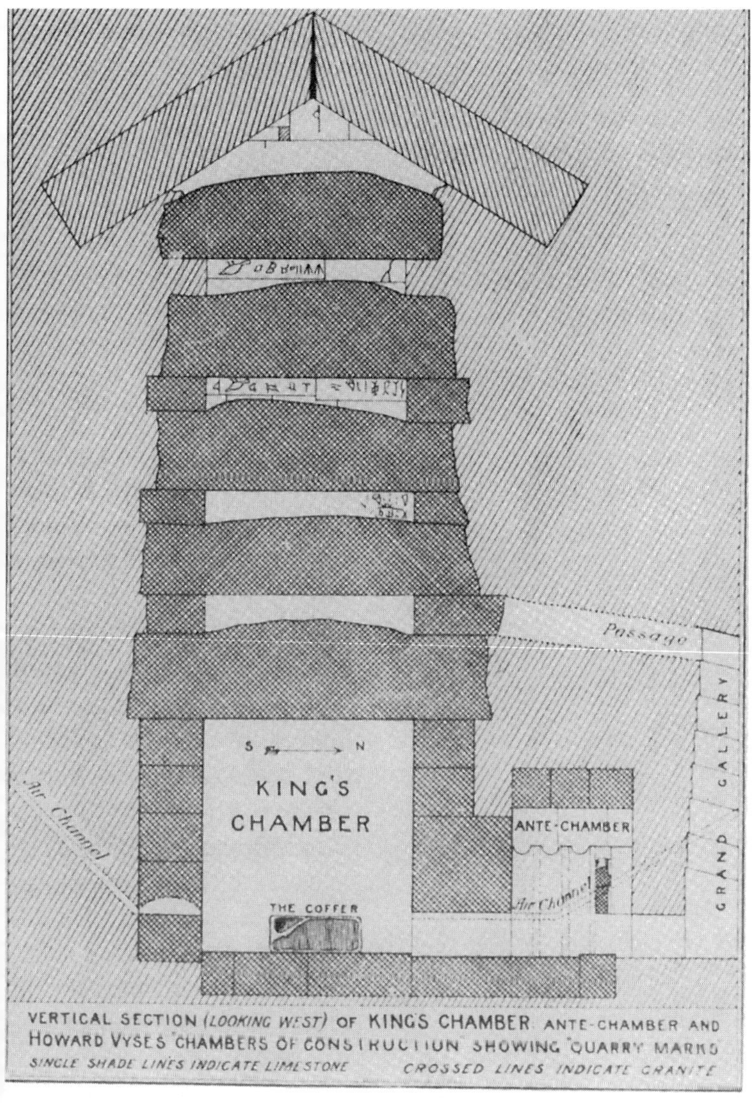

This configuration of stones above the King's Chamber, inside the Great Pyramid, matches the stones above Ed's "King's stone" the heaviest stone at Coral Castle. Did Ed leave behind this message in stone to show that he understood the secret of the Great Pyramid?

Layout of Coral Castle. The main entrance gate is in the foreground; 9 ton swinging gate is in the back, near the planet wall and throne room. To the extreme right, in the foreground, is what's left of Ed's original rock quarry bed, surrounded by black iron fence, where he excavated the coral stone for the newer stone objects after he moved the castle from Florida City. The tower, where Ed lived, can be seen to the right of the front gate.

"Now, the scientists can come down here to Homestead, and look at my drawing and see how it affects science."

Then Ed stepped off the orange crate and he opened the scrap-iron front door, and he stopped at a huge, triangular-cut coral stone, blocking the entry. It resembled a large, wedge-cut hunk of cheese.

"This coral stone entrance gate here weighs around 6,000 pounds," Ed said. "I drilled a hole down the middle of it and balanced it on the axle of a Model T Ford.

"I put a Coke bottle neck on the top axle end here," he said, pointing, "so I could lubricate it. It's a three ton stone, but the way I balanced it, you can spin it with one finger, like this."

Ed reached down and pushed the wedge-pointed stone with his index finger, and the large heavy stone spun around easily, like it was cardboard. As it spun, he led everybody past it into the courtyard.

The people were astonished at the heavy stone gate; and those walking through it, would turn around and stare, and some reached out and touched it.

The space inside the castle was huge, about one third the size of a football field. And there was all kinds of smooth carved, coral stone tables and chairs scattered around. Some of the tables had small, European fan-palm trees growing in a small patch of dirt in the table's center.

Ed had decorated the Castle's inside with all sorts of exotic palms and beautiful flowers in all varieties of shapes and vibrant colors.

Ed arranged everything on the inside like a watchface, and when as many people as could squeeze in came in, Ed walked over and stopped at the seven o'clock spot in the castle, near the front door. He stood in front of a 12 ft. tall, 4 ft. wide, T-shaped coral stone. Ed said: "I call this my 'Stonehenge' stone. It weighs about three tons. Anyone familiar with Stonehenge will immediately recognize this stone. Stonehenge was built by a culture understanding the same lost science that I've employed here at Coral Castle.

"They knew how to control the earth's magnetism; they were masters at hiding these secrets of the universe in the mathematics of their buildings. In one portion of the mathematics used in building Stonehenge in England, someone incorporated the vertical height of The Great Pyramid.

"Now, why would someone, 10,000 years ago in England—that's when I think Stonehenge was built, take the care to secrete their mathematical knowledge of The Great Pyramid in Egypt into Stonehenge?

"My theory is that they were built by the same brilliant engineers—possibly from Atlantis, the most scientific culture this earth has ever known, including our own. I remind you that the algebraic symbol of Pi is found in the mathematical structure of The Great Pyramid; and yet, our history books will tell you that Pi was not discovered until the seventeenth century; therefore, The Great Pyramid proves that Pi was understood by someone, way before the seventeenth century; and yet they don't change the history books, do they?

"Is it possible, the reason they don't change them, is that they'd have to admit that the Egyptians did not build the Pyramids? I tell you they couldn't have—they simply did not have the mathematical capability. I believe the Egyptians simply inherited the pyramids from a former, highly advanced society.

"Now if the Egyptians built The Great Pyramid as a tomb for the Pharaoh, then why didn't they put a lid on the coffin, found in the King's chamber, that was supposed to be for the pharaoh?

"I remind you, the lidless coffin was first discovered in the unplundered middle part of the pyramid called the "King's chamber." Now it was customary in those days to build an elaborate lid for the Pharaoh's coffin, showing his likeness in real life. I guarantee you, he would've chopped some heads off if he'd found out they forgot the lid on his coffin.

"Well, moving on here," he said, walking forward a few steps, and then stopping at three, reclining, contour shaped, coral stone chairs. The chairs were arranged, according to a watchface, at the ten, twelve and two o'clock positions.

"These are my reading chairs." he said. "I arranged them to take full advantage of the sunlight. In the morning, I sit in the chair on the left there," he said, pointing, "where the sun is in the east, over my shoulder. Now at noon, and the early afternoon, I sit in the middle chair, located in the noon position, so the sun is at my back. In the late afternoon, I sit in the chair on the right, in the western, two o'clock position, to catch the sun when it's setting.

"When the tour's over, come back and sit in these chairs. You'll find them extremely smooth and comfortable," he said, running his hand over the stone chair. "And another thing," he said, "you'll notice there are no chisel marks on the stones here, except for a few on some of the outer walls.

"I put those chisel marks there for the future archaeologists; they'll be forever debating whether or not I used a chisel."

Then Ed walked over to a stone rocking chair, mounted on top of a large block of coral stone. Ed carved a half-moon shaped sundial from the coral block underneath the bottom of his rocking chair. Ed said:

"The rocking chair here on top of the sundial was the first chair that I made so I put it on top here where I could look down and see what time it is. You'll notice there are no rocker arms on the chairs bottom; but notice instead, that the bottom is cut at a slight angle. I found the center of gravity of the one ton stone and I balanced it on that, so it rocks based on it's center of gravity instead of rocker arms.

"There are a total of twenty five, one ton rocking chairs inside Coral Castle, and they're all built on this same principle."

The sundial only recorded the hours from 9 a.m. to 4 p.m. Ed explained, because he thought that was the hours that people should work in the day.

Ed said: "Now before I built the sun-dial, I first

made the correct heavenly observations with my stone telescope on the north wall here;" he said, pointing, "and with that information, I was able to build the sun-dial. You'll notice it's built like the curvature of the earth in reverse, and so it keeps perpetual time. This L-shaped piece of metal, sticking out at the top of the sun-dial, casts it's shadow onto these loops," he said, fingering the loops, "giving you the correct time.

"The numbered loops are the hour and the unnumbered loops give you the half hour;" he said, looking at his watch, "my watch shows 1:40 p.m. and you'll see, my sun-dial shows exactly the same time," he said, pointing out the sun's shadow sitting on the 1:40 position. There is no other stone telescope and sun-dial like mine in the world.

"Okay, next, inside Coral Castle, we'll see the only stone map of Florida in Florida."

Ed walked over to a 20-foot long table, carved in the exact shape and proportion of the state Florida, and he surrounded it with 12 one ton rocking chairs. Ed said: "I call this my Florida table for obvious reasons. You'll notice I put a little water filled bowl in the southeast corner here," he said, pointing, "to represent Florida's largest lake, Lake Okeechobee.

"Now Coral is very porous, so I lined the dug out lake bowl with cement, so it'll hold water; now it can be used as a fingerbowl, bird bath or punch bowl.

"I put twelve rocking chairs around the table, with one at the head of the table here," he said, putting his hand on it.

"Now the chair at the head here, is for the governor, and the rest of them are for the senators and representatives; now they can come down here, and sit around this table, and do a little rocking, and then, do what they do best—figure out how to raise your taxes.

"Well," he said, stepping on a chair to make it

rock, "let me see if I can get all these chairs rocking at the same time," and then he ran around the table, pushing the chairs until he had all twelve chairs rocking at the same time. Then he jumped up on the table, while the chairs were still rocking, and then, grinning broadly, he did a little tap dance routine and he jumped off the table, just as the chairs quit rocking.

Then Ed walked over and stood at the north wall. The huge, towering stone telescope stood out in the grass courtyard, about twenty feet behind the north wall. The telescope had a large, slanted, circular hole cut in it near the top, with two wires crisscrossing through it, like a rifle scope.

Ed made the eyepiece for the telescope with a pyramid-shaped stone, and he cut a slanted hole through it and put crossing wires in it, to match the one on his tall telescope. He mounted the eyepiece on the top of the north wall, so it matched up with the hole in the telescope that was twenty feet away in the courtyard.

"The north wall here," he said, "consists of about one hundred fifty tons of coral rock. Behind me, you see the Polaris telescope. It's twenty five feet tall, and weighs around thirty tons. Now at night," he said, pointing to the eyepiece, "you can look through the eyepiece here, and the North star falls exactly at the point of the crossing wires of my two-piece telescope.

"You see, Polaris, or the north star, is a fixed star with only a slight movement, so it will always be seen through my telescope—unless someone goes out there and moves my telescope, and I don't advise that unless you've got a good back."

Ed took a few steps, and then stopped at his moon fountain. Ed carved the moon fountain out of three separate pieces of coral. In the center, he put what looked liked a huge, round, stone washtub fountain, and he carved out the whole top to hold water, and this center piece represented the full moon.

On the left hand side of the full moon fountain, Ed carved out a curving replica of the quarter moon, to represent the first quarter of the moon. And he did the same thing on the right side, to show the last quarter of the moon.

The whole thing looked like a stone donut, laying on the ground, with two stone bananas, standing on their ends and curving outward, beside it. Ed carved out some stone seats in the bottom of the moon quarters, so people could sit inside the quarter moon and have their pictures taken. Ed explained all this to the crowd, then he said:

"The first and last moon quarters, each weigh around eighteen tons. The moon fountain weighs around twenty three tons, and I also had to line it with cement so it would hold water.

"The cement star you see in the middle of the moon fountain is the symbol of Latvia, my native country. Now after the tour, you can come back here and have your picture taken in the stone seats. Then, when you get home, you can show your friends the picture, and tell'em you've been to the moon."

Ed turned around and walked a few steps back to the north wall, and he stood in front of it. Behind him, the wall consisted of three separate blocks of coral. There was a long, 8 ft. tall, square center block, which had two, short fat blocks, like children's wooden building blocks; and resting on top of the fat building blocks, was a taller, inverted "V" shaped stone, with it's point, pointing skyward.

Ed said: "I call this my masterpiece stone because it's the largest stone that I cut and moved in the castle. The large center block stone you see here, weighs thirty tons, or sixty thousand pounds, and it's the king stone here, so I put a three stone crown on it, topped by the inverted "V" stone. I tell you, I had a heck of a time getting that thirty ton stone to fit in my wheel barrow; then, I had to push it over here and hope I didn't stumble with it."

And everyone laughed, knowing the stone wouldn't fit in the pathetic looking wheel barrow Ed had made out of scrap iron he picked up from Mr. Kilgore's junkyard.

Then, Ed took a few steps to his left, and stopped at what he called his "planet wall." Behind him, sitting on top of the east wall, were huge, stone replicas of the planet Mars, Saturn, (complete with a solid, coral stone ring around it) and a banana-curving Crescent Moon. Ed said:

"I've always been interested in astronomy, so I built myself a planet wall. The planet Mars there," he said, pointing, "weighs around eighteen tons.

"If you look closely, you'll notice the little palmetto air plant, growing out of the side of the planet Mars; I cut a hole in the stone and planted it there to indicate life, because I think at one time, there was life on Mars.

"Next to Mars," Ed said, "is Saturn, with it's rings, and it also weighs eighteen tons. Next to Saturn is the Crescent Moon; it's twenty feet tall and weighs around twenty three tons. Mr. Lucky Mizell and I moved this little stone from the original site in Florida City."

Directly behind him, there was a living-room-sized platform of smoothed, solid coral stones, sitting two feet off the ground. Ed called it his "throne room." The throne room sat directly below the planet wall and it had a coral stone stairway, with five steps, leading up to it. There were several varieties of coral rocking chairs sitting on top of the platform.

Ed said: "Well, every castle has a throne room, so this is mine," he explained, walking up the stone steps, and then he sat down in a high-backed, stone rocking chair and started rocking.

"This is the King's chair here," he said. "It weighs five thousand pounds and it's very comfortable."

He got up and went behind the King's chair and stood near a similar chair, sitting slightly behind and to the side of the King's chair. He put his hand on top of the chair and said:

"The Queen's chair here is for Agnes. It weighs three thousand pounds and it's very comfortable."

Then he moved over to his left and put his hand on another chair, directly behind the King's chair. He got a big grin on his face:

"This is my future mother-in-law's chair. It weighs three thousand pounds; I designed it to be the most uncomfortable chair in the castle.

"I did that, thinking that when she comes to visit, she'll take the hint and not stay too long."

To the left, facing away from his King's chair, Ed built something he called his "Mad Rocker" chair. Ed took one block of stone and built two chairs out of it; one seat faced north and the other faced south. He said:

"I call this my "mad rocker" chair. Now you notice I designed it so that two people can sit and rock in this chair without having to look at one another.

"You see, if Agnes, my Sweet Sixteen, and I get into a fight and get mad at each other, we can sit and rock in this chair without having to see each other; so we can rock until we make up or get hungry," he said, then he moved over and sat on a two-seater bench at a square stone picnic table. He looked out at the crowd and said:

"Then, we'll move over to this love seat and sit side by side and kiss and make up and then eat off this table. Well, now we'll go and look at my well," he said, and he got up from the table and walked down the steps of the throne room platform and over to his well.

He had carved out a stone stairway that went down six feet through a solid bed of coral; and at the bottom, you could see a pool of fresh clear water, Herman Harmless said. At the top of the well, Ed laid an old tree trunk down lengthwise across the top of the well, with a carved out, wood handle on one end.

He attached a rope at the center of the tree trunk with a wooden bucket attached at the end so he could drop the bucket and bring up his water.

"I dug out this well here," Ed told the crowd, "and this is where I get all my cooking and bathing water. The water stored down below is surrounded by a solid wall of coral stone and it stays cool year round, so I seal my food in jars and store it down there in the the water."

Everybody was gathered around the little coral stone wall Ed had built around the well to keep children from falling in. They were staring down at the water, and listening to Ed and they were all trying to figure out how one small man was able to dig six feet straight down, through that solid bed of coral stone.

Directly behind the well, and up against the east wall, next to the planet wall, Ed built his bathroom. Ed carved out a bathtub from a solid block of coral, just big enough for a five foot tall man.

He lined it with cement so it would hold water. He'd fill the tub from his well, and by mid-afternoon, the water would be warm enough from the tropical, south Florida sun, for him to take a bath.

Ed put a drain hole at the bottom of the tub and plugged it with a round plug of carved cypress that wouldn't rot; cypress trees grow in the tea-colored swamp water of the cypress ponds that are scattered all over Florida, Herman said.

Ed rigged it up so that the tub water didn't drain directly onto the ground, but it went through the coral stone, underneath the tub. He carved out a six-pointed star, the symbol of the Republic of Latvia, in the wall above the tub; and right next to it, overlooking the tub, he hung a picture of Agnes in a red dress.

At the end of the tub, Ed carved out a square, stone wash basin and mirror combined. He lined the basin with cement and he put a square piece of smooth black slate at the bottom of the coral basin, and then he filled it up with water.

Now, Ed told everyone on his first guided tour, "I can see my reflection well enough in the water to shave and comb my hair."

After Ed had described his bathroom to the crowd, he pointed at his wide, round sun couch, sitting on the ground a few feet in front of him; it looked like a stone merry-go-round without the hand rail. Ed said: "That's my three thousand pound sun couch there. It's eight feet in diameter.

"You'll notice I carved out three, raised, head-rest pillows on it. I mounted the sun couch on the brake drum of a Ford Model A truck, so I can spin it into any position I want to catch the most sunlight."

He stepped over to the huge stone, then he took one finger and pushed it, and the heavy stone spun around effortlessly.

"I got on my sun couch," he explained, "and sunbathed every day for a couple of hours; and that's how I cured myself of tuberculosis."

Then Ed walked over and stood in front of a large swinging gate that he'd carved from a single block of coral stone. He cleared his throat, then he said:

"Engineering this gate was the most difficult thing that I faced in building the Coral Castle. The gate weighs nine tons, and to get it properly balanced, I had to find the exact center of gravity of the stone. Then, I drilled a hole straight down through the stone and I ran a rod down it, and attached it at the bottom to a Ford automobile gear.

"Now what's amazing about this is, that the gate weighs eighteen thousand pounds, but it's balanced so perfectly, you can spin it around just by pushing it with your little finger.

"In fact, even a small child can spin it. Let's see," he said, scanning the crowd, "I need a brave volunteer to help me prove this; how about you honey?" he said, pointing to a little slim, blonde haired girl in a light blue dress.

"Sweetheart," he said, "would you like to come over here and help me?"

She eyed him shyly, and looked up at her father. Then her father urged her to go forward, and so she walked on up to Ed.

"At a girl," Ed said, encouraging her.

"What's your name honey?" Ed asked her.

"Allison," she answered.

"Okay Allison—are you ready to go to work?"

"Yes sir," she said, nodding her head.

"Allison, do you think you can push that big gate open?"

"No sir, I don't think so."

"Why not?"

"Because I'm too little," she said, shrugging her

shoulders. "Besides," she said, "I only weigh fifty pounds—I can barely push a lawnmower."

"Well, come on blondie," he told her, taking her hand and leading her over to the gate, "I'm gonna show you how easy it is."

Ed mounted the swinging gate to fit within a quarter of an inch of the walls on both sides of the east wall. The fit is so perfect, Herman Harmless said, that you can barely squeeze a little finger between the space on both sides of the gate.

"Now, here's what I want you to do," Ed told her. "I want you to put your pointing finger up against the gate, and when I tell you, I want you to push it open. Okay Allison, are you ready?"

She nodded her head. Ed said: "Okay Allison, give'er a good shove."

The little girl pushed hard with her finger, leaning into it with all her weight, thinking it would take all she had to do it. And she fell forward slightly, almost losing her balance because it was easier than she thought.

She was amazed when the stone spun around so quickly. Everybody smiled and looked at each other amazed, then they clapped. Ed tipped his hat to the crowd. Then he shook Allison's hand and thanked her.

Her father wanted a picture, so Ed and Allison posed in front of the gate. Dorothy Sue Skidmore, who was there covering the story for the newspaper, took their picture.

Then, Ed took a few steps and stood beside two, long, coral stone beds, with carved out, raised stone pillows, with enough space between them to walk through.

Ed called this his "bedroom suite." He explained to everybody that these two beds weighed three tons each and were for he and Agnes when she came over and married him. Next to Agnes' bed, he built a stone rocking cradle weighing 155 pounds.

Ed put the cradle next to Agnes' bed so she could be close to the baby if it cried in the night. And he put two small children's beds up against the wall next to his bathroom for their future children.

Then, Ed pointed to what he called his "Great Obelisk." Ed put it on the east wall next to his bathroom and directly behind the children's beds.

The Great Oblelisk is over 25 feet high and it weighs over 28 tons. Near the top, Ed carved out a six-pointed star of Latvia to show the origin of his birth. Ed said he buried the bottom of the huge stone in a six foot deep hole. He told the crowd that this obelisk is taller than the great upright stone at Stonehenge and he told them that he moved it by himself.

"I purposefully built The Great Obelisk stone, taller than the tallest stone at Stonehenge," he told them, "to prove that I understand the universal knowledge that is used at all of the great stone sites all over the world."

Ed walked a few feet over to his "repentance corner," that he planned to use when his children misbehaved. He built the corner out of four, tall square coral blocks, and placed them side by side to form a corner.

Then he cut out two openings in the coral that had just enough room for a person's head to stick through, and one of the openings was up higher than the other. There was a place cut out over the openings to wedge a block of wood so a person couldn't move once they got wedged in.

Ed put a little stone sitting bench at the base near the openings. Ed pointed to the shorter opening and said: "Now if my children ever misbehave, I'm going to wedge their heads in here, and then sit down on this bench and have a talk with'em. I think about an hour of this treatment should last at least a couple of months.

"The taller opening up here," he said, pointing, "is for Agnes, in case she ever gets sassy; when she does," he said, grinning, "I'll just stick her head in here and remind her who is the king around here."

Most everybody laughed at that, especially the men, and some of them even clapped. But one woman, dressed in a fancy, navy blue dress with white polka-dots and a wide-brimmed blue straw hat, spoke out.

Her name was Bernice Broadhurst and she was

a heavy-set woman, with wide, broad shoulders, and about fifty years old.

"And Ed, well, he was just playing around when he built the 'repentance corner' Herman said, "he didn't really mean to use it like he told people on the tour. Oh, he might've told Agnes he was gonna put her head in there—but he'd never do it, Ed was too tender hearted.

"But Ed loved to joke around and he knew he'd stir up the women when he built it."

Bernice Broadhurst said: "Wait a minute Ed—where's the hole to put your head in, in case you get sassy with Agnes?"

The women in the crowd loved it, even though they didn't particularly like Bernice because she was hard to get along with. And some of them clapped for a second and then quit, waiting on Ed's answer. Ed grinned:

"Now hold on Bernice—didn't I buy this land? And didn't I build this castle with my own sweat for my Sweet Sixteen Agnes? I think the king of the castle has the right to be sassy."

Sarcastic, Bernice said: "Well, with thinking like that, now we know why Agnes didn't marry you."

Her stinging words took Ed by surprise, and it hurt his feelings, Herman said. But Ed was always the diplomat, and he didn't like to cause trouble, so he said: "Well, Bernice, I reckon you do have a point there, and as the king, I promise to think about adding my own sassy hole too.

"Okay," Ed said, "let's go over here, and I'll show you my fancy bar-b-que cooker."

To build the cooker, Ed explained that he cut out an eight foot high block of coral; then he cut out the inside of the stone and put two, one foot wide windows on each side; and he cut out a coffee-can sized hole in the roof to vent the smoke. Ed built a pit in the stone's center for the fire and he embedded a pipe below the fire that exited out the bottom for a downdraft.

He built a cooking pot out of the rear end transmission housing gear box of a Model A Ford car. It was round and looks like two bells joined together at the mouths; then Ed put a spring where the two mouths joined so he could open it and put his food in it; then he'd close it back, and the spring held it tightly closed.

Then Ed built something like a trolley car rail, across the inside of the cut out stone, crossing up over the fire, and he mounted his cooking pot on the rail so he could slide it across until it stopped in midair over the fire. The food was now sealed inside the cooker, held tightly by the spring, and so it acted like a pressure cooker.

Ed said it would hold about a dozen hot dogs. Later on, after the castle had been open for awhile, he'd cook up hot dogs for his visitors and the school children, who liked to come by and play in the castle after school.

Then, Ed told everyone to follow him and he stopped at his "Valentine table." Ed carved the three ton table into a perfect heart-shape from a single coral block. It has five sitting chairs around it, shaped in square blocks of coral. There was a perfectly round, green Ixora bush with fingernail-sized leaves, growing in the center of the table.

Ed got a serious, far-off look on his face, Herman said, like he'd slipped into one of his trances, as he described the table.

Then, after a minute or so of silence, in a dreamy-like manner, Ed said: "I created this to be the world's largest Valentine's table. I made it heart-shaped, in case I forget to get Agnes a card on Valentine's day; now with this dinner table, she'll always have a Valentine's card.

"Agnes loves fresh flowers and I might not always remember to get them for her, so that's why I planted the Ixora bush in the middle of the table; that way, she'll always have fresh flowers on Valentine's day." Ed got silent again for a moment, staring down at the table. Then, he said: "I planned every detail of Coral Castle, to please Agnes. She's coming back to me one day; I know she's coming back, but I don't know when. I built the castle for her, so I'm just waiting for Agnes, and I'll wait until she gets here."

Then he turned and walked away from the table and the crowd followed him over to his two-story living quarters. It looked like a castle tower with a flat stone roof. Ed used the bottom story of his castle tower as a tool room and he put his perpetual motion holder in it too. Not everybody could fit into the small tool room so some of them stood outside and listened as he explained about his tools.

There were a bunch of old brown glass, long-necked beer bottles, wrapped with copper wire, hanging on the inside stone walls (these bottles are still hanging on the wall today, Herman said, exactly where Ed left them). Ed said the bottles were parts of a radio set he was experimenting with.

Ed pointed to some truck springs leaning against the wall that he had straightened out and sharpened into wedges.

"I used the truck springs you see there," Ed told them, "to break the coral loose once I'd cut it; now the only man-made marks you'll find on the stones in Coral Castle, are the wedge marks from those truck springs." (I think Ed said this to keep people guessing about how he actually cut and moved the stones, Herman said).

Ed pointed to a his home made wheel barrow; he used a car's brake drum for the front wheel, and it had no body; it only had the long wooden carrying poles mounted to the brake drum. Ed said:

"Now you'll notice the wheel barrow has no body; that's because after I cut the coral block out, I lifted it up onto the wheel barrow and then I could move it around in the castle."

A man in the crowd raised his hand and said, "Wait a minute Ed, didn't you say that "masterpiece stone," the heaviest stone you moved, weighed thirty tons?"

"Yes," Ed said, "oh, I might be off a pound or two—" "Are you saying," the man went on, "that you moved a thirty ton stone by yourself, on that flimsy wheel barrow?"

"Well, now I didn't ever say it was easy—no sir; why it must've taken me a good ten minutes to cut that stone, lift it up and then move it—"

"Ten minutes?" the man exclaimed, looking astonished.

"Well," Ed said, "I don't remember exactly—it might've been fifteen minutes."

"Why don't you give us a demonstration of how you did it?" the man asked him. Some people clapped and said, "Yeah, Ed, show us how you did it."

"Well, friends, I'd really like to," Ed said, "but I pulled a muscle after I moved that 'ol heavy stone—in fact, I'm just now getting over it—maybe when I get to feeling better.

"Now as you know," Ed continued, "coral stone is rough, and working with it can tear your skin up, so I made me some alligator gloves to protect my hands with," Ed said, holding the long brown gloves up for everyone to see.

Then Ed picked up a pair of leather shoes, with metal heels and soles, and as he showed them to the crowd, he fixed his eyes on a man in the crowd.

Ed said: "Well, I'll tell you, I got tired of wearing out so many pairs of shoes, walking around on all of this coral, so I went to David Friedrick, the shoemaker there;" Ed said, nodding at the man in the crowd, "and I said, 'Dave, how about making me some shoes with metal heels and soles, so I don't have to have'em re-soled so often.'"

"David laughed at me," Ed said, "until he realized I was serious—he couldn't believe anybody was that cheap—anyway, he told me to bring him the metal and he'd try it—he didn't think I'd be crazy enough to really do it, see.

"So I went down to Kilgore's and I took a bumper off a 1921 Ford Model A car; I used a bumper because the metal is thicker, and I took it in to David with my shoes, and I laid'em on the counter; I said: 'There you go Dave, let's see how good you are.'"

"And by golly," Ed said, "about two weeks later, Dave brought me these shoes. And well, Dave did a fine job. Now I just use these shoes when I'm working around my place here; but if anybody wants a pair, Dave is the man to see."

Then, Herman said, Ed showed the crowd his perpetual motion holder and explained how it worked off of magnetic power; and how it powered all his necessities in Coral Castle. He told them how he'd designed one to run his truck with.

"Friends," Ed said, standing by the machine, "one day, every household will be run by one of these magnetic machines; and when I get my patent on this machine, I'm going to sell it worldwide.

"I figure it'll cost about three thousand dollars for one of these machines; but you'll never have to buy electricity again. This machine will run forever—and with no service calls.

"Well," Ed said, "let's go upstairs and I'll show you my room." And as he was walking out of the tool room, he thought of something, and stopped outside and said, "I'll tell you what, everybody can't fit into my room at one time, so let's let the folks that had to wait outside the tool room go in first; then the other people can wander in later."

Ed walked over to a long staircase of wide coral steps that he'd carved out, leading up to his room; they ran along the inside of the front entrance wall. It was around two thirty in the afternoon now and it was getting hot.

Ed took off his hat and wiped the sweat off his forehead with his shirtsleeve and put his hat back on. Ed said: "Now if you noticed, most everything in Coral Castle has a purpose to it, and maybe somewhat of a mystery as to why I did it. Coral Castle answers some questions about how the pyramids were built, and I also used it as a place to display my love for Agnes."

Ed told them he built this two-story tower out of nine ton stones and the total of the tower stones weighed over 240 tons.

"When I designed these steps," Ed said, "I put a clue about Agnes in them. If you count the steps, there are sixteen of them; that's how old Agnes was when I met her, and that's the reason I call her my 'Sweet Sixteen.'"

The people were crowded into Ed's room now, and it was mighty small, Herman said, about the size of a large horse stall. A nice cool breeze came through the long, narrow, screened windows on both sides and the one on the back wall. Ed put a picture of Agnes on every wall and also pictures of the various pyramids his grandfather had visited and taken photographs of. Later, Ed also put up photos of his favorite movie stars all over the castle.

In one corner of the room, up about knee high on the wall, Herman said, Ed made some metal shelves out of the running boards off an old car; somehow Ed embedded them into the thick coral walls. He kept some books and empty food jars on them, and after he'd eaten the food in them, he'd wash them out and put the jars, with metal lids, on the shelves until he needed them again.

Ed took some old thick rusty car springs from Kilgore's, and straightened them out for more shelves. He mounted these up higher on the wall. Then, he embedded some square-shaped pipes into the walls, and he used the pipes as steps to reach the upper shelves. On the upper shelves, Herman said, you could see some light blue mason jars, with gray metal lids, full of string beans and little redskin potatoes floating in water. There were several jars of pickled okra up there too. Ed said he'd never heard of okra until he came down South; but Lamar McClung had brought him some one time, and once he tasted it, he started growing his own okra and putting it up himself.

Ed pointed up to the okra jars: "Now I can eat okra anyway you fix it—I don't care if it's fried or boiled, or stepped on—I love it; but the thing is," Ed told them, "Lamar didn't tell me that okra would eat you up, with it's little tiny nosehairs, when you go to pick it. Yeah, he left that part out. So," Ed said, looking at Lamar, "I get out there in that hot sun, in shorts, with no shirt on, and start picking that prickly green okra; and hey, in five minutes, all of sudden, I started turning red and itching all over—it felt like fourteen million mad ants were biting me all over.

"Boy, I'm tellin' you, I took off out of that okra patch, wondering, 'what in the world has got hold of me?—and how can I get rid of it?' So I ran over and climbed down into my well and soaked my body in that cold water and I got better. But I never picked any more okra without a shirt on."

Next, Herman said, Ed explained how he designed his bed. Ed made it 5 1/2 feet long and 4 feet wide, to fit his five foot frame. He took some boards and nailed them together and then he wrapped them in burlap sacking for a mattress effect. Ed mounted the bed on a pulley system, suspended from the ceiling by chains, so he could lift it up to sweep under it and keep it out of the way during the day. His dream weaver hung above the bed.

Near the bed, on the east wall near the window, Ed put up a hanging chair. He made the chair from scrap metal and bicycle parts; then he suspended it from the roof on two chains, and he attached them to the arms of the chair.

Ed had a kerosene stove in the corner of the east wall near the hanging chair. Above it, he built a screened in food box, suspended from the ceiling by a long iron rod he'd gotten off an old Ford truck. The rod passes through a funnel, attached just above the food box, and Ed filled the funnel up with kerosene. He sealed the crack where the funnel nozzle met the rod with tar, so it would hold the kerosene.

Ed pointed up at the funnel: "Now you see," he

said, "a bug might think all he's got to do, is crawl down that rod and pass on through the funnel and get himself an easy meal. But he's headed for trouble—there isn't a bug made yet that's kerosene-proof. A couple of laps in that stuff and his relatives can call the undertaker.

"I wasn't prepared for all the weird assortment of bugs you have down here—we don't have'em in Latvia. But I'm not complaining, I'll take the bugs over those cold Latvian winters any time."

It was getting along about four o'clock now, and Ed said:

"Well, that about does it for the tour. It's four o'clock, so let's quit working. I bought a bunch of hot dogs and stored them in my well. Come on folks, and we'll go down to the bar-b-que pit and roast up some dogs and listen to the Moonshiner's band and maybe do some dancing."

That made everybody happy and Ed went to his well and got the hot dogs and some baked beans that he'd cooked up the night before, and he headed over and started up a fire out of orange tree wood underneath his cooker.

Some of the women pitched in and helped cook the hot dogs while Ed and some of the men and boys started squeezing lemons, and they made up a bunch of lemonade and sweetened it with pure, brown cane sugar. And everybody got hungry smelling those hot dogs cooking; and in the baked beans, Ed put onions, mustard, ketchup, and dark cane syrup to sweeten them, and chopped bacon to give'em a meaty flavor.

Ed used orange tree limbs to do his smoking with because Lamar said that the smoke from orange tree wood had a natural sugar content to it, and it gave a wonderful sweet taste to meat. Ed said he reckoned it was because the tree sap must have natural sugar passing through it to feed the oranges and he said he thought any fruit tree would make good smoking wood.

Along about six thirty, Herman said, everybody

had eaten and was feeling well satisfied. The sun was going down now and it was getting cooler. The Moonshiner's had set up on the stone platform of Ed's throne room; some of them stood and others, mainly the fiddlers, sat in the big stone rocking chairs and tuned up their instruments.

Most of the crowd was sitting around in wooden folding chairs, just far enough back from the band so people could get up and dance if they wanted to.

When they were ready, Minnow Sutton walked up to the microphone and welcomed everybody, then he said: "Does anybody have anything special they'd like to hear?"

Alvin Truax's hand shot up first, and in a heavy nasal accent he said, "Minnow, I'd love to hear 'There's a time to wander.'"

Minnow Sutton pointed at Alvin and said, "Now there's a man with an ear for music—" then he turned around to the band and said, "Let's crank it up Moonshiners."

Lamar McClung was sitting next to Alvin, and he said: "Now Alvin, why'd you do that?—you know that song makes you sad."

"I know it," Alvin said, "ever time I hear it, it makes me think of my Jerry Fay Swilley; it was the first song we ever danced to when I first met her at the Sawdust Trail. She went home with me that night—I was staying at Lucky's garage, sleeping on a wood board bed, stretched across two sawhorses."

A chunky young blonde headed girl named Bernie Simpler sang lead for the band. She had on tight blue jeans, showing her bulging thighs; a red western shirt, embroidered with fancy, gold stitched wagon wheels on the front; and red cowboy boots with shiny gold tips on the toes and heels.

Bernie's voice, accompanied by soft banjo music, had a sweet haunting quality to it. She had a simple country face, not a pretty and not an ugly face, but a young face with a sorrowful droopy-eyed look. And she could put a real funeral tone into a sad song.

This song was about a young boy who leaves his mama and daddy's home, looking for adventure and happiness. It's about how, sometimes, we have to leave the place and the people we love to realize that we love'em. Bernie looked serious, she put her mouth close to the microphone and she sang out softly:

"There is a time, for us to wan-der, the grass is green-er over yon-der, the world is free—eee, the path is new." Alvin Truax sat there in his chair, frozen-looking, staring hard at Bernie, and softly, where nobody could hear, he sang along with her. Alvin's mind was far away now, he told Herman Harmless later: "I was thinking back to the night me and Jerry Fay were slow dancing to this song at the Sawdust Trail.

"I fell in love that night," Alvin said. "I remembered seeing the brown tobacco leaf stains on her fingers, from where she'd cropped tobacco in Arky Ogden's field. I vowed that night to earn enough money so Jerry Fay didn't have to break her back in the hot summer sun, picking that tobacco."

Thinking of this, Alvin said, reminded him that Arky Ogden still owed him ten dollars for a good coon dog puppy that Arky got and never paid him for. The dog died not long after Arky got him. Arky claimed he was wormy when Alvin sold him, and that the dog had died of worms.

But the truth was, Arky's wife Naomi had run over the puppy in the driveway one day, and Alvin had found out the truth from one of Arky's hired hands who'd let it slip.

Ten dollars shouldn't mean much to Arky, he was a rich man. But Arky acted like it was a thousand dollars, and he told Alvin he'd never pay it.

People had warned Alvin not to do business with Arky, but Arky had been so nice that day he came to buy a dog. Arky told Alvin that he was the best coon-dog trainer in Florida and he just had to have one of Alvin's dogs. Arky used his compliments to overpower Alvin.

Arky knew Alvin was a simple man who was good at two things: pulp woodin' and coon-dog training. Herman said most people in Homestead hated Arky Ogden for the way he did people. He'd charge things like gas and food and then take forever to pay his bills, if he paid them at all.

Sheriff Tommy Tramel said he was surprised that someone hadn't killed Arky; and he said he spent half his time trying to solve people's complaints about Arky.

Jerry Fay Swilley wasn't at Coral Castle today, Herman said, because she was in the tobacco field, but she told Alvin she'd try and meet him there when she got off. Alvin got sad now that Jerry Fay wasn't here to hear this good music and he decided to slip out and have himself a drink.

Alvin got up and walked through the aisle of chairs and walked through the 9-ton swinging gate in the east wall, and out into Ed's backyard where the outhouse was. Lamar McClung watched him walk out when he saw him get up. Lamar figured Alvin was slipping off to have him a snort of moonshine and he slipped out to join him.

And Herman said Lucky Mizell, the man who owned the tow truck, saw Alvin and Lamar heading outside and he slipped out to join them.

Lamar and Alvin were sitting on the ground sipping moonshine under an almond tree that Ed had planted when Lucky found them.

"I knowed you boys was up to no good when I seen you leaving," Lucky said, amongst the banjo picking sounds coming from the castle.

"Set down and have a snort," Alvin told him, handing Lucky the pint bottle of clear moonshine, fogged with peach bits floating around in it.

Alvin Truax was known, Herman said, to hide a

bottle or two in his bootlegs and maybe one in his back pocket. Lamar always said: "If a car ever hits Alvin, it'll bust every tire on it from the all the Moonshine bottles Alvin carries around."

They sat there awhile, drinking under that almond tree, Herman said. And when they got up to go in, Alvin muttered to himself, "I'm gonna whip Arky Ogden's ass."

Well, Herman said, while they were outside drinking, Jerry Fay Swilley had come in from the tobacco fields to Coral Castle and got to looking for Alvin. But while she was hunting through the crowd for him, she spotted her boss Arky Ogden.

Now as it happened, Herman said, Arky Ogden usually took him a good snort of whiskey after working in tobacco, and he was feeling good from the whiskey when he spotted Jerry Fay.

He'd eyed her before, bent over in the field "in them tight jeans," he told somebody, and he'd made up his mind to have her one day.

"Oh, Jerry Fay didn't have such a pretty face, with all them acne scars;" Lamar said, "them pimple pits was deep enough to drown a rat. But I reckon she does have a nice body. She's good enough for Alvin Truax—he shore ain't nothing to look at."

The band was playing a good dance number and a bunch of people were up dancing, Herman said, so Arky grabbed Jerry Fay by the arm, and breathing whiskey, he said, "Come on baby, let's dance."

Jerry Fay didn't really want to, but it put her in a bad spot, Arky being her boss and everything. And it happened so fast, they were out dancing before she knew what happened. But as Arky pulled her up close, Jerry Fay said: "Alvin will kill you, he sees you dancing with me—"

"What?—that little squirt? I just wished he'd try it," Arky declared.

Lucky and Lamar and Alvin came back in through the swinging gate. Alvin stopped a moment, watching the band, and the music got to him, and he put his hands behind his back and he started dancing a two-step number with his feet. All of a sudden, he spots Arky and Jerry Fay, dancing in the crowd. Alvin went off like a roman candle, Herman said, but he kept his cool, and he quickly looked down so Arky didn't see him. Alvin pulled down his sweat-stained, straw cowboy hat, and kept his head lowered, as he began dancing and easing into the crowd toward Arky.

When he got close enough, Arky had his back to him, and Alvin tapped him on the shoulder; when Arky turned around, Alvin punched him hard in the stomach, and Arky doubled over.

Alvin reared back and popped him in the face and Arky went over backward, like a bowling pin. Alvin landed on top of him, and he went to pounding away on Arky's face. Alvin would've hurt Arky badly if they hadn't pulled him off. Sheriff Tramel was there and he made Alvin leave for starting the fight. Tramel asked Lucky to take Alvin home. But before Alvin left, Tramel took him aside and said:

"Now Alvin, you done whipped his ass good, and got your ten dollars worth—now let it be, and quit talking about killing him."

Alvin got mad with Jerry Fay because she wouldn't go home with him, she said she wanted to stay and hear the band. And that put Alvin Truax in a bad mood when he left, Herman said.

So Lucky and Alvin loaded up in the old army tank and Alvin insisted he was driving, but Lucky said, "No, Alvin, you're too drunk."

But Alvin said, "I'm driving—it's half my tank," and Lucky didn't feel like arguing, so he gave in, and they took off for Lucky's place.

"Oh, I tell you," Herman said, "it was a mess that night. What happened, Herman said, was that Alvin was mad that Sheriff Tramel had broken up the fight, and Alvin knew that Arky's house wasn't far off the road on Key West Highway, near Coral Castle.

So, when Alvin got to Old Wire Road, where Arky lived, he whipped the tank off the main road and went a little ways and then he turned into Arky's driveway. It happened that Arky had just gone out and bought himself a brand new pulpwood truck; he hadn't even taken it in the woods yet, so it didn't have a scratch on it, which is rare for a pulpwood truck.

Anyway, Alvin spotted the truck, Lucky said later, and he cranked the tank throttle into high gear, and he slammed into Arky's pulpwood truck—the first blow knocked the truck on it's side and the tank crushed it down as it rolled over it.

And Alvin didn't quit until that truck was as flat as a sardine can. When Arky got home and saw it, his wife Pernina, she said he like to of had a heart attack. Pernina said, "I told you that Alvin Truax was crazy—you'd have been money ahead to have paid him for that puppy I ran over, and you said died of worms."

Well, right away, Arky knew who did it, I mean, there was tank tracks everywhere—Alvin had even bowled over a twenty year old mango tree that Arky was so proud of, on his way out. It had to be Alvin Truax, there wasn't too many people around here that owned a tank. (There was also yellow paint on Arky's truck, that got scraped off Alvin's tank when he smashed it up).

So, Herman said, Arky was looking for revenge, and two nights later, he got it. He'd been watching Alvin, and one night, Alvin had got drunk in town and he was staggering and singing along a back alley. Arky cranked his truck up (not the smashed one, he had to send it to Kilgore's junkyard; Kilgore gave him twenty dollars for a $1,000 truck).

Arky came roaring down the alley way, heading straight for Alvin. Alvin saw him just in time to dive headfirst into some trash cans and Arky just hit him a glancing blow (Alvin did get slightly cut up when his whiskey bottle busted in his britches as he hit the street). But Arky laughed like a hyena as he drove off because he thought he had really busted Alvin up worse than he did.

Alvin laid there in the trash cans, playing dead like a possum, until Arky had gone past him; then, when the coast was clear, Alvin got up, picked the glass out of his backside (he had the bottle in his back pocket) and he made his way back to his truck.

Alvin got to asking around and his cousin Aldine Feagle told him that he'd just seen Arky at Shorty's place, drinking beer and shooting pool and bragging about running over Alvin. So Alvin rode out to Shorty's place, and sure enough, he saw Arky's truck parked in front. Alvin hid his truck in some bushes so Arky wouldn't see it when he came out.

Alvin said later he waited over an hour, and then Arky came out; and when Arky opened the door to his truck, and had his back to him, Alvin said, "Arky!" And Alvin whipped Arky's ass again; and nobody in Shorty's place heard the commotion because the music was too loud. But Aldine Feagle was with Alvin and he kept him from killing him.

Aldine said, "Hey, Alvin, why don't you put Arky in your dog box (on the back of his truck) and ride him around town?"

Alvin liked that idea and so that's what they did. It was a bad night for Arky because Alvin hadn't cleaned that dog box out in about two years; it was about two inches deep in dog poop. (Alvin said he only cleaned it out on his garden spot in the spring; he didn't plant a garden last year, that's why it was such a mess).

Well, Herman said, somebody finally called Sheriff Tramel and told him that Alvin Truax had Arky Ogden locked in his dog box and he was riding him around town. Every now and then, Alvin would stop when he saw someone and he'd get out of his truck and point at the dog box and say, "Hey look, I got Arky Ogden in my dog box; and Alvin would look at Arky and say, 'Hey Arky, bark for the good people.'"

And later, Alvin got the idea to go home and get

"Moonshine" his old coon dog, and put him in the dog box with Arky. "Moon's" teeth were worn down, the one's he had left that is; and the old dog was bad tempered, he didn't like being in that dog box—Alvin said he'd been catastropic (he meant claustrophobic) since he was a puppy.

So "Moon" couldn't hurt Arky too bad with his worn out teeth; but every now and then, Alvin would stop downtown, and when a few people had gathered around the truck, Alvin would look at the dog and he'd point at Arky and he'd say "Sic'em Moon!" And "Moon" would turn around and snarl at Arky and nip him on the arms or legs or hands, when Arky put his hands up to protect his face.

And the people standing around laughed; and when Alvin Truax left, B.F. Bagley, who'd been standing there, said: "Now the moral to that story is, don't mess with Alvin Truax—he'll kick your ass and throw you in his dog box."

So Sheriff Tramel rode around until he spotted Alvin's truck and pulled him over. After he heard Alvin's side of the story, Sheriff Tramel didn't charge Alvin for having Arky in his dog box. And what Sheriff Tramel did was to pull Arky off to the side and he said:

"Arky, if you want to live to spend all that money you've got, I suggest you pay Alvin the ten dollars you owe him for that puppy—if you don't, next time, I'm gone be late getting there when they call me and tell me Alvin is after you."

Well, Herman said, riding around in that poopy dog box with "Moon" got Arky to thinking; he went over to Alvin and he apologized to him; he pulled out his wallet and handed him a twenty dollar bill. And, of course, that made Alvin happy; all he wanted was his money.

And later, when someone asked Alvin about Arky being in his dog box, Alvin grinned and he said, "Yeah, 'ol Arky, he didn't want anymore of my dog box—I reckon he was like the horny cat that was screwing the skunk—

after awhile, the cat got off the skunk, he shook his head and said, mournful like: 'Well, I ain't had all I wanted, but I've had all I can stand.'"

I went over to Ed's place for lunch one Sunday afternoon, Herman told Carl Swisher, as they sat inside the Coral Castle.

"We used to cook out a lot on Sundays on Ed's bar-b-que grill. It must've been around the year 1923—yeah, that was it; I remember now because that was the year Hitler got himself thrown in jail in Germany for trying to overthrow the government.

"Well, when I got over there that Sunday, Ed had the grill going and he was cutting the headlines out of the newspaper that told about Adolf Hitler being put in jail for treason. Ed was pasting the article onto some blank white paper in a journal he kept."

Ed let me look at the journal, Herman said, and one of the newspaper articles dated back to the first World War. It showed a young Adolf Hitler receiving the Iron Cross for bravery. Ed said Hitler got the medal for single-handedly capturing four French soldiers in a fierce battle near the small French town of Leeds.

That night, in 1923, after seeing the article on Hitler, Ed wrote in his diary that he had a dream about Atlantis, and Hitler was in the dream.

The things I saw in my dream, Ed wrote, came not in any sort of order, but they came in a variety of flashbacks, in the manner that dreams sometimes appear to us. And in the dream, my name was Rozano Sanz. I had the knowledge of the Atlantic time, like I knew the time of my present day life, as I lived it now, in Coral Castle. As this Atlantic dream sequence opened, I found myself inside a large, blue glass pyramid building, lighted on the inside by white lights.

I was a sculptor in this time, and I had many people of the various races working for me, including the alien race or "men from the sky," as the indians had named them. Dressed in a white lab coat, I was busy working on a group of life-sized elephants; they were to line one of the main streets of Atlantis. Hitler's name in this incarnation was Adolfo Hitler. He had heard of my project and he came by with an entourage of his people, all dressed in Nazi uniforms.

I recognized Hitler from having seen and read about him in the films and papers of the time, as he ran for political office, in the same way as he had in the year of our bodily existence in the year 1923. Hitler was introduced and he told me that he'd always admired my work, and that when he was elected president, he would appoint me his official sculptor of the First Reich.

I was flattered by his praises, but I didn't think much of his promises, because he was known as somewhat of a radical, in the same way he was known in the time of Germany.

But in this Atlantic incarnation of his eternal spirit, Hitler's hatred was aimed at the "men from the sky," people, or the Menon race as they were called in Atlantis.

Many of the other races in Atlantis shared Hitler's hatred of the Menons. People hated them because they were brilliant and things came easy to them so they were usually always successful in business. They were in charge of the government and most all of the important industries, from accounting firms to film production. They were a lot like the German Jews of our present time in this respect.

The Menon race kept a few humans in high places, so they could claim that Atlantis was a "people's government," but most people knew the humans worked for the Menons.

The scene (in my Atlantic dream) Ed wrote, changed now, and I found myself seated on a metal chair, on the front row, in front of a massive stone pyramid. There were hundreds of chairs there, separated down the center aisle by a red carpet. A stone podium, with a Nazi flag in the center, stood about fifteen steps up the pyramid's center.

Two huge brass blazing torches stood on both sides of the podium, and the flames were whipped around by a light breeze. Large floodlights, placed at intervals along the pyramid's front, lit up a wide pathway leading to the pyramid's wide flat top.

Then, I saw a large black, sting-ray shaped plane, making no sound, appear in the sky, and, it hovered above the pyramid's top and then lowered itself down onto the wide flat top.

There was a band, dressed in Nazi uniforms, off to the left side of the pyramid, and they started playing a lively military tune.

And the people in the audience seemed to know the tune and they sang along with it. When the crowd saw the black plane, with it's red Swastika, painted on the rear tail fin, they all stood and gave the Nazi salute. And from their throats came an enthusiastic: "Hail Hitler!" (They spoke a form of English, but I did notice that in Atlantis there were many different accents, like French, Spanish, Irish, and so forth, as if these languages had been blended into a form of English).

The side door of the plane slid back now and a shiny metal staircase emerged. Then Hitler came out, smiling and waving, as he walked down the stairs, then he stood on the top of the pyramid and returned the Nazi salute.

Some people stared up at Hitler with night binoculars and some of the women looked glassy-eyed as they were captivated at the sight of Hitler. Some of the women gasped out loud, and put their hands to their mouth, some clutching each other in the excitement of the moment.

Hitler, dressed in a white, double breasted dress jacket, with a red Swastika armband, black trousers, and a white military dress cap, walked slowly down the steps now; he seemed to be immersing himself in the adoring crowd. Nazi soldiers, dressed in white gloves and black uniforms, stood lined up along both sides of the lighted pathway.

As Hitler passed the soldiers, they turned, facing him, and snapped their right arm out into a stiff Nazi salute.

Flashbulbs went off everywhere, as photographers and news men filmed the scene of Hitler making his way to the pyramid's bottom. The pyramid height appeared to me to be about the length of four football fields, so it took awhile for Hitler to reach the bottom. He seemed to like making the crowd at the bottom wait for him, as he paused sometimes to acknowledge the crowd.

When Hitler got near the podium at the bottom, a tall slim man, dressed in a black Nazi uniform and slightly balding in the front, ran up the steps and stopped in front of Hitler. He gave Hitler the Nazi salute, and after Hitler returned it, the man stepped down to the podium and leaned into the shiny microphone and said:

"People of Atlantis, our glorious Fuhrer, Adolfo Hitler is Atlantis, and Atlantis is Hitler!" The crowd erupted in enthusiastic bursts of "Hail Hitler!"

Then the man backed away for Hitler to come to the podium, and he stood there, facing Hitler with a Nazi salute as Hitler came to the podium; then the man took his seat along the first row. And all the people (except for some of the Menon tribe, scattered about, who'd come to the rally out of curiosity) saluted Hitler, yelling out: "Hail Hitler!"

And Hitler acknowledged them and then motioned them to sit down and they did. Hitler put his notes on the podium, and stood with his hands clasped together in front of him. He put his hand to his mouth and cleared his throat. He looked down at his notes and then back up at the crowd. He spoke in a low tone and calm manner:
"Citizens of Atlantis, thank you for coming tonight. The news people from the Atlantic Press said I'd be lucky if a thousand people came tonight—it's seems as though I'm very lucky."

The crowd interrupted Hitler with a wild cheer. When it died down, Hitler said: "We'll try and get an accurate count for them—you know their reputation for accuracy when it comes to reporting on people who don't fit their mold—and didn't they say, 'They threw away the mold when they made Adolfo Hitler.'

"Because you're here—maybe you don't fit their mold either!"

Later, Hitler said, "I firmly believe the old saying that if you want to know the future, then study the past. And if you don't believe it, then you're doomed to repeat it. Today, in Atlantis, our laws are written by dishonest lawyers. That's why today, we have a crime problem."

As Hitler spoke, a middle-aged Menon man sitting next to me leaned over and whispered: "Get ready, Hitler has a habit of saying 'I must tell you—I have to tell you' in all of his speeches."

Then Hitler said: "I must tell you—I have to tell you;" Hitler paused and smiled, nodding his head, "I have to tell you, that I do overuse that phrase," and the crowd laughed and clapped.

Hitler ended his speech, saying: "Friends, I leave you with one last thought tonight. It comes from Alexander Heimer, a philosopher who lived over three hundred years ago. He said, 'God works wonders sometimes; behold, a lawyer, an honest man.'"

The crowd cheered wildly at this, and then a man in a Nazi uniform came up and put a white cape around Hitler's shoulders as he walked back up the pyramid to his plane.

Then, in my dream, Ed wrote, the scene quickly changed and I found myself dancing the jitter-bug with Agnes (she was in the same body and her name was Jami Portillo) in a pyramid-shaped night club in downtown Atlantis named "The Constellation Club." The roof top was done in clear glass so you could look up and see the bright stars in the night sky.

The scene changed again; it was night, and Jami and I were seated around the lighted pool at the Swiss-looking village; this place was near the park where Madame Drusa had seen us feeding the turtles in the vision she gave my mother in Latvia before I was born.

I saw a slim, lovely, blonde-haired woman; she had a distinctive, whiskey-gravel voice, and she stood under the open air patio singing a lovely song. And years later, when I first saw Marlene Dietrich, she reminded me of this woman in my dream, and I wondered if Marlene Dietrich had lived in Atlantis at this same time. This scene slowly faded and I woke up and looked at my clock, it was 3:30 A.M. I couldn't go back to sleep because I was so excited at having been with Agnes (Jami in Atlantis).

Later, as I remembered this dream, I thought of what Madame Drusa had said in her visions of me, that knowledge of past things would be revealed to me in dreams and visions.

I wondered if I had really known Agnes in a previous Atlantic life. Could I trust these visions to be real or were they merely a product of my active imagination?

I desperately needed an answer to why Agnes had jilted me the night before our wedding. And now, I wondered, maybe I did something bad to her in our former life in Atlantis that caused her to reject me in this time. But what, if anything, had I done?

And, if I did do something bad to her in that time, could I learn what I had done, and could I repent for it, and clear it up in this earthly time, so that she would come back and marry me in Coral Castle? Now, I thought, the only way I had of finding this out was through the information funnel of my dreams and visions of this former life.

I now undertook an even greater effort to concentrate on the dream time, and I developed a keen sense of the realm of the human unconscious mind; I found it to be a vast and mysterious realm. But it's my opinion that these former times are only revealed to those, like me, who believe in these things.

I like what the apostle Paul said, in 2 Corinthians 12: "Fourteen years ago, I was taken up to heaven for a visit. Don't ask me whether my body was there or just my spirit, for I don't know; only God can answer that. But anyway, there I was in paradise, and heard things so astounding that they are beyond a man's power to describe or put in words (and anyway, I am not allowed to tell them to others").

Like Paul, I have no proof of these things, but must admit that I took great pleasure in these dream times, because in them, I could hold Agnes in my arms and feel her body.

Agnes was the only person who made me love somebody more than myself; and Nick once told me that was how you could be sure you were in love; that you cared more about what happens to the other person in your life than you do your own fate. And using that as a barometer for love, I can only say that I'd gladly lay down my own life for Agnes.

One day, Herman Harmless said, Ed and I were walking out of the DeSoto drug store, around the first of March in 1925. I'd gotten some cold medicine for Opal and Ed had gotten some aspirin. It was lunch time and we were headed over to the Myna Bird when we turned the corner at Key West and Ervine street. Ed ran smack into a little boy named Tony Johnson, who was peddling newspapers, and the papers went flying everywhere.

"Whoa!" Ed said, grabbing little Tony to keep from falling on him. Ed apologized, Herman said, and we started helping Tony pick up his papers. And when we got done, Tony thanked us and he seemed to be in a hurry.

"Tony," Herman said, "you been staying out of trouble?"

"Oh, yes sir, Mr. Herman," Tony said. "I've been working real hard."

"You still saving your money for that Robin Hood outfit at McDuffie's?"

"Yes sir, I've got a long way to go, but I'll get there."

I dug in my pocket, Herman said, and pulled out two quarters and handed them to Tony: "Put them in your piggy bank Tony. I remember I wanted to be Robin Hood when I was a kid too."

Tony thanked him and hurried down the street.

"Herman, how old is Tony?"

"He's about twelve, I think."

"Shouldn't he be in school?"

"Yeah, well, his mama died of pneumonia when he was little, and his daddy, Ronnie Johnson, is trying to raise him; but he's a drunk and he beats the kid sometimes. Ronnie's a good house painter—when he's not drunk."

"That's a shame about Tony," Ed said.

"Yeah, Tony's been caught stealing chickens or anything that isn't nailed down."

"Poor kid," Ed said, "twelve years old and out hustling papers. Well, let's go eat, I'm starving. It's my treat today isn't it? I better see if I've got enough money," Ed said, reaching for his wallet, and finding it gone. "Hey, my wallet's gone!"

"You reckon you left it in the drug store?"

"I don't think so—I'm sure I put it back in my pocket—"

"Oh no!—Tony," Herman said, and he took off running after him, with Ed right behind him.

Tony hadn't gotten far, he was going by the Blanche Barber shop when Herman yells out, "Hey! Grab that kid!" And when Tony heard him yell, he took off running harder. A young policeman named Bobby Brewin was writing up a parking ticket to Harry Steedly for parking too close to a fire hydrant, next to the Blanche Barber shop.

And Bobby Brewin reached out and grabbed Tony as he went flying by him. Herman and Ed got up there, all out of breath, and while Bobby held Tony, Herman said:

"All right Tony, hand it over." Tony reached in his back pocket and handed Ed his wallet.

"I thought you said you were behaving Tony," Herman told him—"is that your idea of behaving—stealing people's wallets?"

Tony didn't say anything, he just hung his head down. Bobby Brewin said: "Okay, Tony, that's it. You were warned the next time you got caught, it's reform school for you—let's go," Bobby told him, and started marching him off.

"Wait a minute Bobby," Ed said, leaning down on one knee close to Tony's face: "Why did you take my wallet Tony?—were you hungry?" Tony got tears in his eyes and started sniffling but he didn't say anything, he just shook his head.

"Why'd you do it then?" Ed asked him.

But before Tony could answer, Bobby Brewin said, "Because he's a thief, that's why; come on boy," and jerked him away.

But Ed held him by the shoulder and said, "No, wait Bobby—let him tell me."

Tony's body shook and he was crying, he was scared about going to reform school, he told Ed later. Tony said:

"I'm sorry Mr. Ed, but Billy Hale, he's my best friend, and his daddy give him a Robin Hood outfit, with a bow and arrow set. And I wanted one too, but my daddy said no. He ain't never give me nothing but a whipping. I was gonna work for it, honest I was Mr. Ed—let me work for you—I'll pay you back—"

"That's enough whining Tony," officer Brewin said, "time to go."

And sobbing hard, Tony looked back at Ed and he said, "Please Mr. Ed—don't let them take me."

As I looked at Tony's frightened face, Ed wrote later, I was reminded of when I was a boy, and I had to quit sucking my thumb to get the bow and arrow set I wanted so badly. I knew I had to help this little boy.

"It's okay Bobby," I told the officer, "I'm not pressing charges."

"What?" Brewin said. "You're making a big mistake Ed."

"Tony," Ed said, "I'm going to let you work it out. You work a month for me, two hours a day, and we're even, okay?"

Tony agreed and they shook hands.

"But Tony," Ed told him, "if you miss one day, the deal's off, okay?"

"Yes sir, Mr. Ed, I'll be there every day at one o'clock, that way I can keep my paper route—is that okay—boss man?"

Ed agreed, and reluctantly, Officer Brewin took his hands off Tony and let him go.

The next day, Ed wrote, Tony rode his bicycle over

to Coral Castle, and, wearing his blue jean overalls, he got there right on time. First, Tony mowed the grass in the backyard—he mowed a little up front, but it was mainly filled with flowers and fruit trees. Then, Tony went to pulling out weeds from the flower beds and he picked up some fallen limbs and trash. Then he took it out back and burned it. Tony worked fast and went hard at it, like a beaver, Ed said. The hard work in the tropical sun didn't seem to bother him one bit.

"Now Tony," Ed said, "slow down some son, I don't expect you to kill yourself—you take a break when you feel like it."

"Oh, no, I'm fine Mr. Ed—I'm through picking up trash, what do you want done next?"

"Tell you what, we need to get the weeds out of the tomato bushes and the bell peppers; we'll work on that until it's time for you to go home."

While Tony was pulling out the weeds, Ed wrote, I went in and mixed up some fresh lemonade from the lemons that I'd picked off my tree. I still couldn't get over living in a place where you could grow your own fruit; a place where you didn't have to shovel snow.

I thought of how happy I was here, as I smelled the fresh cut lemons, and squeezed the juice into a pitcher of cool spring water. What a paradise it would be, if only Agnes were here to enjoy it with me—oh, well, maybe one day.

I reached into the pie safe and got out some fresh coconut cookies I'd made up last night, and put them into a linen-lined straw basket. I carried the cookies out back to where Tony was and stopped him in the tomato bushes.

We went over and sat on a stone bench under the almond tree, where Alvin had drank his moonshine on opening day. We sipped the cool lemonade and ate the cookies. When we were finished, Tony said:

"Mr. Ed, could I come visit you sometime, when I'm not working?"

"Well sure son, you can visit me anytime."

"Even if it's late at night?"

"Sure," Ed said, finishing off the last of his lemonade.

They were both silent for a moment, enjoying a passing breeze and listening to some gray African parrots, screeching overhead as they gathered up some palm berries with their long beaks.

"Tony, is that when your daddy beats on you—late in the night sometimes?"

"Yes sir, but he's not a bad man Mr. Ed, he's usually okay in the daytime; it's the nighttime that gets him—that's when he misses mama the most. But he always apologizes later Mr. Ed, he says he just goes out of his head with grief. When he's sober, he tells me to run next time, if I see him getting crazy, so I jump on my bike and take off."

Tony worked hard and was on time the whole month he worked for me, Ed wrote. Sometimes, late at night, Tony's daddy whipped him and Tony came over and stayed with me.

The month had passed now, Ed wrote, and Tony was working his last day, and I invited him to stay for supper. I cooked up Tony's favorite food—fat-back bacon, eggs and grits for supper. We sat down to eat at the Florida table at around six o'clock. It gets cooler there in Homestead at that time, Ed said, as the sun sets, about six thirty in the evening.

We finished up the eggs, and we took some big heavy biscuits and poked a hole in them with our finger, and then we filled the hole with whiskey-colored, cane syrup.

"Tony, Lamar McClung showed me how to eat these biscuits—that is some fine eating isn't it?"

"I don't care how I'm eatin' them Mr. Ed—as long as I'm eating them. I don't know what I like best—the rib bacon or the cane syrup—I reckon I'm thankful to have'em both at the same time."

"Yep, you're right about that. Well, son, today's your last day—the prisoner is freed. But you know what? I'm proud of you—you know that? You're a good little man—a hard worker, just like you said. And you know what? If you hadn't taken my wallet, I'd have never known you like I do now."

Tony got sad looking, and he wiped the cane syrup off his mouth with his napkin. Then he got up from the table and went over to where Ed was sitting. Tony said:

"Mr. Ed, please forgive me—I'm so sorry for what I done to you. Ain't nobody ever been this kind to me. Daddy says a lot of folks don't like him because he's a gypsy.

"But I'm only half gypsy—my mama was white. Daddy said folks looked down on her for marrying a gypsy—"

"Well, I wouldn't worry about that son—I like you just the way you are; you keep on smiling and working hard like you do, and somebody, somewhere, will respect that and you'll do fine.

"Oh, Tony, I almost forgot—I got you a little going away present," I said, and I reached around behind one of the stone rocking chairs, and pulled out a long gold box with a big red ribbon on it. Tony's eyes lit up as I set the box on the Florida table; Tony started opening it, and his little hands trembled as he tore off the paper.

"Now don't get too excited," I said, "you probably won't even like it—" and about that time, Tony got into it, and saw that it was the Robin Hood outfit he'd been looking at in McDuffie's window.

"Wow!—Robin Hood!" Tony said, and he turned and hugged me as hard as he could: "Wait'll Billy Hale sees this!" Tony said. "He's about the only boy that don't mind playing with me."

Tony put on his Robin Hood clothes and I took him to the backyard, Ed wrote. I set up a new target on some hay bales and I taught Tony how to shoot the bow and arrow.

"Now remember Tony," I said, "it's just like shooting a rifle: inhale, pull the arrow back quickly, let out a half-breath, aim, then let'er fly as you exhale."

Tony did it, and the arrow hit the target in the

upper right hand side. "Hey, you hit the target—that's a good start," I told him. After awhile, Tony got good at it; I even rigged up some lights in the backyard, and sometimes Tony would come over late at night, and we'd shoot arrows until the early morning.

Late one friday afternoon, Ed wrote, I was sitting at the counter in the DeSoto drug store, having a cup of coffee and talking to Novia Lilly. We were good friends now, and I enjoyed her company because she understood how I felt about Agnes; and we didn't have to worry about falling in love and hurting each other and that made things easier.

"Well," Novia said, sipping her coffee, "I sure do think it was a sweet thing for you to see about little Tony the way you have—he comes in here all the time, wearing that Robin Hood outfit. When he's done delivering papers, he'll hop up here on the stool, an' he'll say, 'Maid Marion, Sir Robin Hood will have a rootbeer float;' oh, it's the cutest thing, I tell you."

"Yeah, he's something all right—say, I'm taking Tony over to Gatorland tomorrow morning. I've never been—why don't you go with us?"

"Sure, I'd love to. I'm off tomorrow. I haven't been since I was a little girl. I can't believe you've never been—you'll love it."

"Great, I'll pick you up at 8:30."

We pulled into Gatorland the next morning, Ed said, about 8:45, and parked. To get through the front door, you had to walk through the head of a huge, turquoise-painted alligator. His open gaping jaws were filled with long, fierce-looking teeth, painted white, and the gator's jaws must've been opened up about fifteen feet high, from top to bottom.

The tourists loved this big gator's head, Ed said. They'd lean on the huge gator teeth, and have their picture taken.

When we got up to the jaws, Novia took a picture of Tony and I standing in the Gator's mouth. Then we bought a ticket inside the door and walked through the tourist shop. It was full of all kinds of gator teeth, hides, and gator feet key rings, and just about anything to do with a gator. We went through a glass door and stepped outside to a little wooden holding dock.

The whole place was like a long dock, covered with a tin roof, and it branched off to different places with deep and shallow water pools, where the gators swam around.

When the dock couldn't hold any more people, a man dressed in a safari hat, with a short-sleeve khaki shirt and shorts, came out from the front door. He turned around and roped off the entrance behind him with a thick piece of rope. He made his way through the crowd, and then stood out in front of us. He had on white sneakers and thin, army-green socks.

He looked about fifty years old, medium height, Ed wrote, with no gray hair, it was still a dark brown. He had a big beer gut on him that pressed his shirt buttons to their limit, trying to hold back his big stomach.

"Welcome to Gatorland folks;" the fat man said, "is everybody ready to feed the gators?" And everybody clapped and cheered.

Then, he said: "That's good. I'm glad so many of you showed up today—we may run short of meat so I may have to toss a few of you in today—the gators really like kids and dogs, and I don't see too many dogs here today—naw! Just kiddin' folks.

"My name is Bwana Bill and I'm your host today for our famous Gatorland Gator Jumparoo.

"Now parents, please watch your children closely today and don't let them lean too far over on the rails; unless they misbehave—then you might want to give them a little shove, and you can collect the insurance later!

"Okay folks, now some of the gators you'll see today are fifteen feet long and weigh over a thousand pounds. They're some of the largest in the world. Now, if you'll just follow me, we'll get started."

We walked a few feet forward to a large pool of

water, Ed said, surrounded by a round wooden corral on the outside. There were some huge gators swimming around in the pool and a wooden rail ran around the enclosure and people could lean their elbows on it and watch the show.

There was a wooden walkway with high rails leading out to a wooden island in the pool's center. A slim older man, with thin, wire-rimmed glasses, stood out on the island and he was opening up a big white bag of something.

Bwana Bill said: "Now folks, the man you see on the island is my friend Frank Fowler. Frank is a fearless gator handler. Why folks, sometimes I've seen Frank lean his head over that rail and dare a gator to jump up and bite him. Are you goin' to do that for the nice people today Frank?" Bwana Bill asked him.

Frank didn't say anything, he just shook his head.

"Okay, sorry folks, I shouldn't have said that—he's goin' to play chicken on us today—are we about ready Frank?"

Frank pulled out a dead chicken by the feet, feathers and all, from the bag, and held him up high. "We're ready Bwana," Frank said.

Then Bwana Bill called out in a loud voice, "Okay Frankie, make'em jump!"

Frank Fowler walked up to a high wood platform, holding the chicken, and when he reached the top, he leaned over the water and started jiggling the white chicken up and down. A bunch of gators started swimming around, nervous like, biting at each other as they tried to get a position under the chicken.

Then, all of sudden, one of those monsters—he must've been 12 foot long, Ed said, he came straight up out of that water like he was shot out of a cannon; he snatched that chicken out of Frank's hand, and he fell back in the water and swam off with it.

And, when the gator swam off with the chicken in his jaws, the other gators were waiting on him; they all grabbed at the chicken and tore off little pieces and there was feathers floating everywhere.

It didn't seem like the gator, who had worked so hard to out jump the other ones, Ed said, could have had enough chicken left over after his buddies got through grabbing it, to have made a good sandwich with. Well, Ed said, Frank Fowler fed about twelve chickens to the hungry gators, and every time a gator cleared the water and got the chicken, the crowd would gasp and clap their approval.

On the last chicken, Ed said, Frank jiggled him, and right as the gator jumped up and about had him, Frank moved the chicken and leaned his head out where the chicken was, and just as it looked like the gator was gonna bite his head off—'ol Frank timed it perfect and quickly moved his head away, making the gator miss. Everybody loved it and went crazy clapping and cheering. Bwana Bill pointed at Frank and said:

"Ladies and gentleman—fearless Frank Fowler!"

And the crowd chanted: "Frank, Frank, Frank," and he tipped his safari hat to them and took a bow. Then, Bwana Bill said:

"Thank you friends, that concludes the gator show. Now folks, just make yourselves at home and wander through and look at the snakes and the birds—and on the other side you'll see some native Florida panthers and little pygmy goats.

"Don't forget," Bwana Bill told them, "if you've never had gator tail, be sure and try it at our restaurant—it's real good," he says, patting his gut. "And if you don't believe that," Bwana Bill said, "just look at me."

As the crowd broke up and headed for the snake exhibit, I looked at Novia and said: "Novia, Bwana Bill was joking about gator tail wasn't he?—they don't really eat it—do they?"

"Oh yeah," she told me, and she explained that they sliced the hard tail open and took out the white meat and battered it and fried it up.

After awhile, it was around noon, when we heard the train whistle blow and we walked through the snake exhibit and boarded the little steam engine train.

Bwana Bill sat up in the engineer's place, wearing a faded blue railroad cap, and when everybody was on board, he pushed down the throttle and we headed back to the main entrance.

When we got off the train, and walked back to where the jumping gator show was, there was a man sitting in a bamboo building with a thatched roof. The man had a big boa constrictor snake, wrapped around his neck. The man also held a small gator, cradled in his arms, with a piece black rope tied around his mouth.

For twenty cents, Ed said, you could get your picture taken with the snake around your neck, and holding the gator in your arms. Tony wanted to do it and so I paid for it, and Tony was squeamish when they put that big snake around his neck: "He's cold," Tony whined.

But he stood it long enough for the picture and, later, Tony was mighty proud of that picture, Ed said.

Then, on the way out, there was a man selling bags of bait fish to feed the gators. I bought Tony a bag and we watched him throw the fish down into the water, where the gators had jumped for the chickens earlier.

Every now and then, a smaller gator would cruise by and snap up one of the bait fish. Tony took out a fish and reared his arm back to heave it. But just then, Ed said, a tall, white, egret bird, came running up behind Tony—he was as tall as Tony, and snatched that fish right out of his hand and he gulped it down in one quick swallow.

Then the bird just stood there staring at Tony, like he might try and eat Tony next. It happened so fast, Ed said, Tony didn't know what had hit his hand, and he screamed out and jumped back, as the bird started chasing him for the bag of fish in his hand.

Tony finally dropped his bag of fish and let the bird have it, as everybody was laughing at him. We watched the bird finish off the fish, Ed said, and then he started looking around for another victim. Then we turned and walked back to the entrance.

I put my arm around Tony as we walked along, and I said, "Well, Tony, did you have a good time today?"

"Yes sir," Tony said. "But if we come again, I'm gonna bring me a big stick for that fish-stealing bird."

When Ed finished moving Coral Castle from Florida City to Homestead, Herman said, he took pictures of the castle and he sent them to Agnes. He told her he built the castle for her, and that he was waiting for her to come to Florida and marry him.

And Ed was faithful in his writing to Agnes, Herman said. About every six months, he'd send her a letter, telling her he still loved her and that he'd wait all his life for her if necessary. But he never heard so much as a peep from her.

Ed kept himself busy giving tours of his castle and taking care of his flowers and vegetable garden. He loved to stick things in the dirt and watch them grow.

And Ed got to wondering why he'd never heard anything from the patent office about the patent on his perpetual motion machine, so he wrote them again.

And they sent him back a letter saying they had to study this thing, and make sure his machine was legitimate.

"I was kidding Ed at the time," Herman said, "and I told him the government wasn't interested in anything that would save people money—if they can't tax it, why should they bother with it?"

Ed's diary entry for Wednesday, April 10, 1927, read:

I got up early today, at 5 a.m., Herman came over at 6 and I cooked up some bacon and eggs for breakfast. We drank coffee and talked about how cool the weather was for April. Herman left for work at 8 and

I went to work in my garden.

Around two o'clock, I gave a tour of the castle to a family of tourists down from Ohio. They were nice people; they had a little three year girl with them and she had a good time rocking on all the rocking chairs.

Around 3:15, I put my hand in my bathtub and found the sun had warmed the water up good, and I was thinking about taking an early bath, instead of my usual time at four o'clock, when the front doorbell rang. So I walked over and opened the door.

There was a stocky built man standing there, in a gray suit with a gray, felt dress hat, turned down in the front. He looked about thirty years old.

"Good afternoon," I said, "would you like a tour of the castle?"

"Good afternoon," the man said, putting out his hand, "I'm Danny Duda."

I introduced myself, Ed wrote, and the man said: "Ed, I'm with the Meteor Motor company in Chicago. We heard about your perpetual motion machine and the company sent me here to examine it. You see, my company buys the patent rights to machines like yours, and then we produce and market the product.

"Sometimes it takes years to get a patent, and then, even if you do, it can take a great deal of money to get something off the ground—"

"You're telling me," I said. "I'm arguing with the patent office right now on this machine. But I can tell you now, it's not for sale—"

"Oh, don't be too hasty until you've heard my offer; if it works, we're prepared to pay a good sum of money. May I see the machine?"

"Sure, come on out back, it's in my truck. I've also got a generator in my tool room that runs all my house electricity."

When we got out back, Ed wrote, I opened the hood of the truck and explained how the machine worked, and how I had converted this one to fit inside the truck. Then I told him:

"Now look Danny, you could fit one of these machines into an airplane and fly out and have breakfast on Mars, do some shopping on Pluto, and then make it back home for dinner. You see, once those north and south pole magnets get to chasing each other, they never stop, until you interrupt the current. So, theoretically, you would never run out of energy. The farther you go the more it charges itself."

"That is amazing—Ed do you mind if I take it for a spin?"

"Sure go right ahead," I said. And Danny Duda climbed into the truck. I pointed over at my garden and said, "Just look out for my onions over there."

Danny Duda drove the truck around the yard several times; he'd come to a complete stop and then take off again, sometimes spinning the tires. Then he pulled back over to me and he got out grinning and shaking his head.

"I wouldn't have believed it if I hadn't seen it—that is a beautiful piece of work Ed," Danny said. "Ed, my company is prepared, right now, to give you one hundred thousand dollars for the rights to this machine and seven per cent of all sales. How does that sound?"

"Well, that sounds awful good Mr. Duda—"

"Wonderful," he said. "I'll get a contract out of my briefcase and we'll—"

"Whoa now, Mr. Duda—"

"Please call me Danny."

"Well, Danny, you didn't let me finish. I was going to say that sounds good, if I was going to sell it—but I already told you, it's not for sale."

"Boy, I tell you," Danny Duda said, pushing his hat back, "they told me you southerners were good traders and I guess I'm about to find out. Okay Ed, one hundred fifty thousand dollars and ten per cent—is that a deal?"

"Well sir, I'm not exactly from the south—I'm from Latvia, near Russia—but like I say, it's not for sale—"

"Okay Ed, I'll quit haggling with you. I was hoping to buy it cheaper and get a bonus for myself, but I can tell you're going to be too tough—okay? Now here it is—it's so much you might want to sit down; I'm authorized, without calling the company, to pay you two hundred and fifty thousand dollars.

"Now, I'll go get the contract—what a deal huh?"

Then, Ed wrote, Danny Duda quickly turned and headed for his car; it was a long, brand new, four door, shiny black cadillac convertible. But I stopped him: "Hold on, Danny—I told you my machine is not for sale."

"Oh come on Ed—that's a lot of money—I mean how many ten cent castle tours will you have to give to make that much money?"

"It's not a question of money Danny. I don't want to give up control of this machine. In a way, it's like my whole life is in it—it's like my baby, you know."

But Danny Duda just kept trying to talk me into selling, and finally, when he saw I was getting irritated, Danny Duda said, "Well, look Ed, I know you need some time to chew on this. I'll be staying over at the Blanche Hotel for a couple of days, so I'll get back in touch with you."

Well, Herman Harmless said, one night, little Tony Johnson was at his house (it was more like a shack, in the middle of a big orange grove) playing, Tony told me later. Tony said he was chopping the feet off a crow that he'd shot out of an orange tree near their shack. Sometimes at night, Tony said, the crows would roost in the orange trees, and I'd sneak up on them and shoot them with daddy's .22 caliber rifle.

Then, I'd chop their feet off and play with them. You could pull on the exposed ligament at the top of the leg and make the feet draw up tight on something. Sometimes I'd take the foot and sneak up behind a girl and I'd grab her ear with the foot and leave it there. She'd let out a good scream when she reached up and touched that 'ol cold crow's foot, hanging off her ear.

And as I was playing with the new foot, it was close to midnight; I heard my daddy pulling up in the old black Ford truck that he had cobbled together from Kilgore's junkyard. I started to run into the shack and get in bed and pretend I was asleep, thinking that daddy might not mess with me.

But then, I got a better idea, and I ran and hid behind some high palmetto bushes, near the shack where daddy's bedroom wall was. Then I heard daddy shut the truck off and start into the house. He'd been out drinking and I could tell he was really loaded, the way he was staggering towards the door.

And daddy was humming the phrase to a song he always sang when he got drunk: "Oh, I'm sorry I broke your heart, mother."

When daddy got in the house, he lit a lamp and I heard him calling out: "Where are you boy? You better get in here and fix me some breakfast—I'm hungry—boy, you hear me? Oh, I'm sorry I broke your heart, mother."

I knew the routine by heart, Tony said. Daddy would stumble around the kitchen and dig out some pork meat in the salt barrel; then he'd get a sweet potato and some cornbread out of the pie safe and he'd sit down and eat.

And every now and then, he'd cuss and say "Boy, I'm gone whup you good when I find you—you better get out here while you can."

So, when I saw the light go on in daddy's room, I leaned up against the shack wall. Just before daddy got in bed, he'd always pee through a big crack in one of the wall boards. Daddy was too drunk and too lazy to go out to the outhouse, so he just unbuttoned his pants and hung it out the hole. Daddy was right proud of his idea of having a private bathroom in his bedroom.

I was so close to the hole in the wall, that I could hear daddy undoing his pants, and he was still humming that song.

Then, in the bright moonlight, I saw daddy stick his peter out the hole, and that's when I pulled out that crow's foot, Tony told Herman later. I was so close, I was getting splashed from the urine when it hit the dirt; and I leaned over and took the crow's foot and got ready to put it on daddy's peter.

I slipped the wide open foot over daddy's peter, just behind the smooth, circumsized head, where that loose neck skin is all bunched up, like a scarf around your neck.

When I had it positioned just right, I tugged on the crow's foot ligament, just enough to let the little sharp foot claws get a slight grip on daddy's peter; but not too much to cause any pain; it was just enough to let daddy know something had him by the peter.

Daddy flinched a little and said, "Ouch!—Damn you cat!" when the claws bit into that delicate and tender neck-skin part of his peter. (We had a big, bob-tailed, yellow Tom cat named Frasier, and daddy thought Frasier had come along and was playing with his peter). Frasier was part Minx and he could be mean when he took a notion to.

I had to hold back a laugh when daddy said that, because I hadn't thought of daddy blaming the cat when he felt those crow-claws; but then I realized the crow's foot must feel just like a cat's sharp claws. And that was good, I was thinking, because now, no matter what, I can blame it on Frasier.

So, Tony said, to lay more blame on the cat, I let out a fierce cat growl, like cats do when they're mating or fighting. And when daddy heard it, he hollered out:

"Damn you Frasier—quit that!"

I was full of courage now, Tony said, so I tightened up on the ligament, and the claws dug in a little deeper into the neck skin, and it must've got to him, because daddy yells out:

"Oh, let me go! I'm gone git my shotgun and kill you!"

Well, I got scared when he said that. And I decided I better quit while I was ahead, but I wanted to give daddy one good last tug for all those times he'd beat me.

I got me a good grip on that ligament, and I reared back and I jerked that thing with all my might; and when I did, it buried those little razor sharp, crow's claws so deep into daddy's peter, that they just disappeared into the loose folds of all that bunched up neck skin.

And daddy, he let out a scream the neighbors down the road could hear: "Yee—oww!" he hollered out. But this time, after he yelled, he was silent for a moment.

Daddy knew now that Frasier was in control of this situation. Yes sir, Tony said, he knew that cat had hurt him bad. Then, I heard daddy say, real sweetly: "Frasier? It's daddy. Here kitty, kitty, kitty—please let your daddy go—you want some sardines boy? I'll fix you some, you let me go. Just ease up on them claws."

About that time, Tony said, from around the corner, here came 'ol Frasier himself, to see what all the commotion was about. He was meowing, which was authentic cat meowing, and came in mighty handy, and then he walked over and started purring and rubbing up against my leg.

I reached down with one hand and picked Frasier up and I rubbed his furry bob-tail on Daddy's peter, so he'd know for sure it was the cat. And I figured it was a good time to be leaving, so I let go of the foot ligament and eased it off daddy's peter, and I stuck it in my shirt pocket (I had on my Robin Hood outfit).

And with Frasier in my arms, I got my bow and arrows, and loaded it in the basket of my bicycle and I took off. I figured I better take Frasier with me until Daddy cooled off; I was afraid he'd get his shotgun and kill Frasier over something that was my doing.

My plan was to go over and spend the night with Mr. Ed, so with Frasier riding in the basket, I headed out for Mr. Ed's Coral Castle. And I reckon I about laughed my jaws off, thinking about what I'd done to daddy, and laid the blame on my cat. It was about the most perfect crime I'd ever done and I was proud of it.

While Tony was headed over to Ed's place, Herman

said, Ed was tired that night from working in his garden, Ed told me later, and he said he went to bed early, about eleven o'clock that night.

I was in a deep sleep, Ed said, when I felt a hand shaking me on the shoulder. And in the moonlight coming through the window, I saw Danny Duda standing in front of me. He was so close I could smell whiskey on his breath. I glanced over and saw the window screen had been cut, but before I could say anything, Danny Duda cocked his right arm back and hit me over my right eye.

The blow knocked me out of my suspended bed and I tumbled off and hit hard on the smooth coral floor. Then Danny jumped on top of me and slapped me in the face a couple of times.

"I'm going to ask you this last time to sell me that machine Ed," Danny said. "Don't take too long to think about it. I'll be over at the Blanche for a few days so let me know when you're ready. And don't think about going to the police—the deal's off then, and I just shoot you and save the money, okay?"

Then he got off of me, Ed said, and he left the door open as he walked down the sixteen steps and over to the iron front door.

But Danny was surprised, when he put out his hand to open the door, and as he did, there was little Tony, standing there with his hand out, about to push the door open. Startled, Danny Duda quickly reached in his back pocket and pulled his gun out.

I quickly raised my hands up, Tony said later, and I said:

"Don't shoot mister—I just came by to see Mr. Ed. Is he okay?"

And realizing it was a kid, Herman said, Danny put his gun away, and said, "Oh, sure kid. I just talked to him. Sorry I scared you—I work for a company and we carry cash sometimes so we have to be careful, you understand?"

"Yes sir—like in the movies huh?"

"That's right. Well, see you later son," Danny Duda said, and he walked over and got in his cadillac and pulled out. But I didn't believe him, Tony said later, and I wondered if maybe he was a gangster or something.

I was surprised, Ed said, when Tony came walking in. I was sitting in my suspended chair, holding a rag over my right eye to stop the bleeding. I figured Tony must've gotten in a fight with his daddy.

"Hi Tony. Did your daddy whip you?"

"No sir, I'm fine," he said, walking towards me. "What happened Mr. Ed?"

"Oh, I fell out of bed and hit my head on the floor. Tony, how about going down and drawing me some cold water—"

"That man beat you up didn't he? He pulled a gun on me at the front door. Why did he do it?"

I hesitated to answer, Ed said. I didn't want to lie to him after I'd preached to him about lying and stealing.

"I'm not sure Tony; he wants to buy my energy machine and I don't want to sell it and we got in a fight."

"Do you want me to call Sheriff Tramel for you?"

"No Tony, I'll handle this—"

"But Mr. Ed, he pulled a gun on me—"

"I'll handle it Tony—now please go get the water for me."

So I walked down the stairs, Tony said, heading for the well. And I passed by the tool room and I remembered there was a phone in there. I thought, Mr. Ed didn't say I couldn't call Mr. Herman. I went in and called him and told him what had happened.

When I got over there, Herman said, Ed was sitting up in the suspended chair, still holding a rag over his right eye. At first, Ed was irritated that Tony had called me, but he soon calmed down. I said, "Ed, do you want me to call Doc Spooner?"

"No, Herman, I'll be okay."

I begged Ed to let me call Sheriff Tramel, but he

refused. And after I'd done all I could, I went back home, Herman said.

But I was upset about Ed getting beat up, and Tony getting a gun pulled on him. So, the next day, I went by and told Sheriff Tramel what had happened, and he told me he'd run a tag check. So later, officer Bobby Brewin snuck over to the Blanche Hotel, where Danny Duda kept his car parked in front of the hotel, and Brewin got the tag number.

Well, meanwhile, Herman said, I met Freddie Mizell (Lucky) and Lamar McClung over at the Myna Bird for lunch, and I told them what had happened. I told them to help me keep an eye on this Danny Duda bird; I told them I believed that Ed was afraid to go to the police, and that Duda had pulled a gun on Tony.

That afternoon, Herman said, Lucky and Lamar went fishing with a wash tub full of iced down, illegal beer that Shorty had made up. And they drank a bunch of it, and got drunk and talked about how mean Danny Duda was. They didn't like the idea of a fella coming from Chicago and beating up one of their own.

When they ran out of beer, they quit fishing, and went by Shorty's place to get some more beer. Even though prohibition was the federal law in those days, Herman said, Sheriff Tramel never enforced it. Tramel knew most people were against the prohibition law and as long as people behaved themselves at Shorty's place, Sheriff Tramel let it go.

Two revenuers had shown up one time and tried to bust Shorty; and the rumor was that they ended up in the Everglades swamp, more than likely in some big gator's belly. And after that, the other revenuers reported that everything had been cleaned up around Homestead, Florida.

Well, anyway, Herman said, Lucky and Lamar got real drunk, and Lucky hatched a plot to get back at Danny Duda. Lucky drank down the last part of his beer, and he told Lamar, "Come on, let's go by the Blanche Hotel."

"What are you gonna do Lucky?" Shorty asked him.

Lucky grinned: "You'll find out later Short cakes—all I'll say is, it'll be a classic; then, you can tell everybody later that the plan was hatched out right here, in Shorty's place; and you can tell'em the exact stool I was sitting on when it came to me."

Shorty always said that Lucky had a flair for the dramatics of life, and that was the quality that everybody always admired Lucky for. Then Lucky said, "Shorty, bring me and Lamar one of them good Cuban cigars will you?"

"Sure," Shorty said, and he turned around and reached into the wooden cigar box and got out two, medium length cigars and handed them to Lamar and Lucky. Lucky paid him for the cigars and they lit them up and took a drag. Lucky said: "Well, Lamar, I reckon it's time to go—Shorty, be prepared to bail us out of jail."

It was around six o'clock, Lucky said, when Lamar and I stepped out onto the wooden porch at Shorty's.

"What are we gonna do now?" Lamar asked.

"We're going by the Blanche Hotel, Lamar, where Mr. Duda is staying; I need to see Cathy Driggers for a minute. I work on her car sometimes for nothing—she owes me a favor."

When we got over to the Blanche Hotel, Lucky said, I told Lamar to stay in the truck and I'd be right back. Cathy Driggers was a cute little thing, and she told me that Danny Duda had been asking her to go out with him, Lucky said. Danny Duda wasn't there when I talked with Cathy, and she agreed to help me, Lucky said.

"This Danny Duda keeps asking me to go for a ride in his convertible," Cathy told me.

"That's good," I said. "You might just do that tonight." And we went over my plan one more time, Lucky said, and she had it down perfect.

Then, Cathy told me that Danny Duda had dinner and started drinking whiskey in the Blanche every night about eight o'clock. It was just getting dark, around 6:30, when I got back in the truck and cranked it up, Lucky said.

"How'd Cathy look?" Lamar asked me.

"Like she always looks—fine," I told him. "She had her hair done up in a pony tail—"

"Is she still dating Oval Overstreet?—"

"Nope, not any more—Odean Cooks."

"Odean Cooks?—that skinny varmit. Man, I sure would like to have some of that—

"Yeah, in your dreams—better get your mind on business now. This Chicago boy is about to find out we play rough down here."

Lamar sipped his beer: "Where're we going Luck?"

"We are going to Gatorland—"

"Gatorland!—for what? They're closed now—why are we going to Gatorland?"

"Don't ask so many questions, you'll see when we get there. Hand me another beer will ya'?" And Lamar opened one and handed it to him.

"Lucky," Lamar asked, "how are we gonna get in there?—the place is locked."

"I've got a key—remember, I do their maintenance work."

When we got there, Lucky said, we went inside and walked over to a 10 ft. deep, cement holding pond, where they separate the juvenile-aged gators from the big ones. They do that, Lucky said, because sometimes at feeding time, the gators will go to fighting each other, and the smaller gators get all chewed up or killed, so they have to separate them.

"Now Lamar," Lucky said, "you be looking around in the cement pond there for about a four foot gator; I'm going over to the shed to get a catch pole."

When I got back, Lucky said, Lamar was shining the light down, still looking for a gator; he hadn't heard me, and I got me an idea. I laid the catch pole down, and I low-crawled on my belly through the grass, until I got close to Lamar, and he still hadn't heard me. And I reached out my hand, and I grabbed his leg, and I let out a loud growling sound.

And Lamar, he screamed out, and lost his balance and he about fell over into the gator pit. Now Lamar, he didn't think it was too funny, but I did. But anyway, Lucky said, we roped us a gator, about four feet long, and I taped his mouth up so he couldn't bite us.

We laid him in the back of the truck, and, oh, I guess it was around eight o'clock when we left Gatorland and headed for the Blanche Hotel. We got to the Blanche around eight thirty. I parked the truck at the street curb, in front of the Blanche, right behind Danny's Cadillac.

I got out and went to the hotel's front door and looked in. I saw Cathy Driggers talking to Danny and she saw me and she reached up and took the pencil from behind her ear, which signaled to me that everything was ready.

Ten minutes passed, Lucky said, and I went over the plan again with Lamar until he had it down good. Then, we saw Danny and Cathy come strolling out of the Blanche, arm in arm, talking and laughing. I could tell by the way Danny was walking that he was drunk. When they got near the car, and he was going to open the door for her, she stopped and said:

"Oh, darn! Danny, I left my purse in the hotel—I'll be right back. Now you just get in the car and I won't be a minute."

"Okay, baby," Danny slurred, as Cathy walked back into the hotel, "but hurry up."

Danny went around and got in the car and he turned on the ignition and went to hunting for a radio station. A snappy dance tune came on, Lucky said, and Danny went to tapping his fingers on the steering wheel and singing along with the song.

Well, while Danny Duda was singing, Lucky said, me and Lamar McClung grabbed that alligator out of the back of my truck and slipped the tape off his mouth.

"I put my hand over his mouth," Lucky said, "to keep him from biting me. We slipped up on Mr. Duda and throwed that unhappy alligator through the open window, and right in the middle of Danny's lap."

At first, Duda was so drunk, Lucky said, it took

him a minute to realize what had happened. When we pitched the gator in there on him, I yelled out:

"Hey, you Chicago bad man, let's see you whip his ass!"

I told Lamar to go around on the other side of the car so Danny couldn't slip out, Lucky said; and about that time, the gator flipped his powerful tail and caught Danny up side the head and about knocked him out. I leaned near the window and said, "Watch out Danny, he's got a wicked left tail!"

Well, that gator went wild in Danny's car, Lucky said. He was thrashing and flipping around, and he slapped his tail hard one time, and crashed out the front window of the car; and when he wasn't busy thrashing around, he'd bite Danny anywhere he could get hold of.

Then he'd start flipping and rolling around, like they do when they've got hold of something in the water, and they're trying to drown it. One time, the gator rolled over and flipped his tail so hard, he ripped out a huge chunk of the white convertible roof. And every now and then, we'd hear Danny Duda screaming, "Help! Get me out of here!"

"Well," Lucky said, "about that time, Marvin and Gladys Root come walking by, on the street next to where Lamar was standing. And just as they walked up, that gator slashed his tail through the roof, and they heard Danny screaming."

Marvin and Gladys stopped. Marvin said, "What's going on Lamar?"

"Hey Marvin, hey Gladys," Lamar said, "how y'all doing? We don't rightly know. We came by and seen this man wrestling this gator—"

And about that time, Lucky said, Danny screams out—"Help! He's killing me!"

And Gladys Root said, "Lucky, you better let that man out of there before that gator kills him."

"Oh, don't worry Gladys, he's just a young gator, with juvenile teeth—he can't hurt him too bad."

And then, Lucky said, Lamar goes and leans into

Gladys' face, breathing beer you know, and Lamar says, "You nice folks might want to move on, in case that gator gets loose."

And Gladys said, "Let's go Marvin—they're drunk!"

She grabbed Marvin's arm, Lucky said, to walk off. But Marvin, he resisted and says, "Wait a minute, ain't that the yankee's car from Chicago that whipped up on Ed?"

"That's it," Lamar told him, "and that's the yankee in it." And Gladys Root went to pulling Marvin away, Lucky said, and fussing at him all the time, but Marvin didn't want to go. He was saying, "But Gladys, honey, I want to stay and see what happens to the yankee."

After they left, Lucky said, Lamar lit up a cigar and he said, "Lucky, I believe Gladys might be right—we better get him out of there; I know that gator can't kill him, but he might bleed to death."

"Okay Lamar," Lucky said. "You get ready with the catch pole, and when I open the front driver's door, you put that noose around his mouth."

So we waited, Lucky said, and when the gator quit thrashing, I flung the driver's door open and Danny Duda came tumbling out onto the brick paved street, on his face.

While Lamar was busy catching the gator, Lucky said, I rolled Danny over onto his back and got on top of him and straddled him with one leg on each side of him, so he was pinned down. I grabbed his shirt and lifted his head up off the street, and I put my face down close to Danny's. I said:

"Okay, we're done playing now; I want some answers, and I better get'em. Why did you beat up on Ed?"

But Danny Duda didn't say anything, he just moaned and tried to sit up, but I told him he wasn't going nowhere until he answered the question. And then Danny noticed how badly his arms were bleeding and he screamed out: "Get me to a hospital, I'm gonna bleed to death!"

Just then, Lucky said, Bobby Brewin, the police officer, came pulling up in a brand new, black and white Ford squad car. Bobby pulled up close, so the bright car lights blinded me, and I put my arm up over my eyes until Bobby shut them off.

Bobby stepped slowly out of the squad car, and walked over to where I was sitting on Danny. Brewin was a stocky built man, about thirty years old, with a tire-gut around his waist. He always had his black boots spit-shined.

As Brewin walked up, Lucky said, I could hear his wide, black leather gun belt, spit-shined to match his boots, creaking under the weight of his tire-gut and the heavily oiled,.38 caliber Colt pistol, hanging low at his side. When Brewin got close, he pulled up his pants and gun belt at the same time.

Bobby Brewin squatted down until he was even with my face, Lucky said. Bobby said, "What you got there, Luck?" And Bobby took out a plug of Mule Kick chewing tobacco from his front shirt pocket; he peeled back the shiny red wrapper and offered me a chew, Lucky said.

I took me a good bite off of it and handed it back. "Thank you Bobby. This here is that yankee fella that beat up Ed. Me and Lamar had just pulled up when we saw the commotion—"

Just then, Lucky said, Lamar was struggling with the gator and he hollered for me to help him. "Excuse me a minute, Bobby," I said, and I went over and held the gator while Lamar taped his mouth up and we loaded him back into my truck. Then I walked back to where Bobby was still squatting down.

"Where'd the gator come from?" Brewin asked me.

"I don't know Bobby—I reckon he came from his mama, but I wasn't there. No, honestly, I don't know. Like I said, me and Lamar just pulled up and seen this guy with a gator in his car—he might've been trying to steal him."

"Well, I'll be darned," Bobby said. "I got a call from Gladys Root and she said y'all had a man locked in a car with a gator."

"That Gladys Root—she's a nosy bitch," Lamar muttered.

And then Danny Duda said, "They threw that gator in my car and tried to kill me! I want'em arrested."

"It ain't true, Bobby," Lamar said. "You can look inside—them doors ain't locked. He could've got out any time."

"I'll take your word for it Lamar," Brewin said.

"His word?" Danny Duda said. "Hey, what kind of law is this? I told you I want them arrested—"

"Now hold on there partner," Brewin said, and then he spit out a of stream of brown tobacco juice. "Kidnapping an endangered Florida native—this here gator, is a serious crime. Yes sir, and I reckon that with him being in your car, you was planning on carrying him across the state line—you having Chicago plates, you see. But seeing as how you didn't succeed, maybe you can pay a fine for gator transporting and we'll drop it at that."

"This is crazy!" Danny Duda protested. "If I was going to steal him, why would I have him in the front seat? Why wouldn't I have put him in the trunk?"

"I don't know;" Brewin said, "you're from Chicago—maybe it's your first gator heist. Save it for the judge."

Then, Lucky said, Brewin turned and said, "Boys, he's bleeding awful badly—I reckon we ought to carry him on over to the Lake Shore Hospital. Help him up and we'll put him in my car," Brewin said. "Oh, wait, damn, he's bleedin' like a stuck hog. I hate to get that blood all over my new car seats."

"Wait a minute," Lucky said, "we'll load him up and take him in his car—it's already got blood all over it."

Well, Lucky said, Bobby liked that idea, so Lamar and I loaded Danny up and took him to the hospital.

Bobby picked us up at the hospital and took us back to my truck at the Blanche Hotel. Before Bobby left, Lucky said, I started telling him the truth about what happened to Danny Duda, but Bobby said:

"Don't tell me Lucky, that way I can't testify against you."

Danny Duda spent about four days in the hospital, getting over his wounds, Herman said. He wasn't hurt that badly, just mainly some deep, juvenile-gator-teeth scratches on his arms, back, side and his legs.

He was bandaged up all over and his face was slightly swollen on the side where the gator's tail had slapped him up against the inside of the steel car door, but other than that, there was no serious damage done; except maybe to his yankee pride. When Danny Duda was finally able to walk out of the hospital on his own, Herman said, Sheriff Tramel came over and personally escorted him out to his shiny black Cadillac; with the ripped up, gator-bit, convertible roof and smashed out front window. Nobody had bothered to clean off any of the blood on the black leather seats.

And the bad thing was, Herman said, was that Danny's car sat in the lot at the Sheriff's office for four days in the blazing hot sun; and, well, it just cooked up an awful, disgusting smell of dried blood in that car you ever smelled.

Sheriff Tramel hadn't been able to find out much about Danny Duda, except that he'd spent some time in jail up north for loan sharking; and doing some odd jobs, like beating people up who owed money to a small time Chicago mob.

It was a hot, sweltering afternoon when Sheriff Tramel leaned over in the driver's window of Danny's car to say something to him before he ran him out of town; and the blood smell got to him and he had to back up and get his breath. And then, Sheriff Tramel told him to "git on the road to Chicago and don't even look back."

So Tramel watched Danny Duda drive out of Homestead, with the torn up pieces of his convertible top flapping in the breeze; and his hair blowing backwards from the wind coming through the smashed up front window.

Well, it had been about a month since Danny Duda had left town, Herman said. Wherever folks in Homestead gathered to talk, they still talked about what Lucky and Lamar had done to the yankee from Chicago.

One friday night, Ed wrote in his diary, Herman and I went to the Myna Bird diner to eat the friday night special, which was fried catfish, hush puppies, grits and cole slaw. Then we went over to Shorty's place and drank a few beers and shot some pool. It was about midnight when I came in.

And I wasn't drunk, but I guess I'd had just enough beer to throw off my sixth sense. I came through the back part of the castle, where the 9 ton swinging gate is, and as soon as I'd walked through it, I heard a man's voice, coming from the shadows near the gate: "Evening Ed," and then there was a flash of light and smoke from a match as the man lit up a cigar: "Hope you don't mind if I smoke," he said, and lit his cigar and threw the match on the ground.

In the half-moon light, I saw his face clearly and I recognized his voice at the same time, it was Danny Duda. He had a half-pint whiskey bottle in his hand and he took a drink, corked it and put it in his back pocket.

"What do you want?" I asked.

"Well, you look surprised to see me—I'm just paying a social visit; thought I'd come back for that castle tour you know."

"The sheriff told you not to come back—"

"Yeah, but the sheriff don't know I'm here. Don't worry, I'm gonna finish my business and then slip out of here before he knows it."

"Look, Mr. Duda, I had nothing to do with that alligator business—I didn't even know about it until afterwards."

At that point, Danny Duda looked angry and he pulled a gun out of his pants and pointed it at me. He said, "I don't believe you—turn around, put your hands up and start walking out that door."

We walked to the front door, and then I tried to turn around and say something to Danny Duda, but he told me to shut up and keep walking. So, I pushed open the iron door and went through, and just as I got outside, I stopped, and without turning around, I said, "Where are we going?"

"Oh, I thought we'd take a trip over to Gatorland, since you like gators so good—now move out."

Now that night, Herman Harmless said, little Tony Johnson and his daddy got in a bad fight, and Tony had headed over to Ed's place to stay with him.

I had just parked my bicycle on the wall, outside of Ed's castle, Tony said, near the corner of the front door. And just as I started around the corner, I seen Mr. Ed walk out, and that bad Chicago fella right behind him, and he was holding a gun on Mr. Ed.

I jumped back before they could see me, and I watched them walk through a pathway in some bushes that led out to a dirt road. I got my bow and arrows and I followed a safe distance behind them.

Mr. Duda had parked his Cadillac on this dirt road, Tony said, and when I got there, they were getting in the car; Mr. Duda made Ed get in on the driver's side and drive. I snuck up to the back of the car, and I noticed the trunk handle was half broke off, and the trunk was tied down with a piece of baling wire.

Well, I went to undoing that baling wire, and my hands were shaking—I was scared they'd hear me. But lucky for me, Mr. Duda was hunting a radio station (I could hear the radio stations go by as he turned the dial) and I was careful to be real quiet.

I got the baling wire undone, and I put my bow and arrows in the trunk—it was a Cadillac so it had a big wide trunk, and I crawled in, and closed the trunk down behind me; I held it down with my hand so it didn't fly up. And the car took off.

When we pulled into the parking lot at Gatorland, Ed said, it was deserted and quiet except for some crickets chirping. We got out of the car, and Danny made me open the back door and take out a big white sack of something that was fairly heavy.

"What's this for?" I asked him, trying to stall for time, hoping I could think of something.

"Don't worry," he told me, "you'll see—now get going."

I waited in the trunk, Tony said, until I heard them walking away, then I eased myself out. I made my way over to the wall of the building and climbed up an oak tree and stepped over on to the roof, so I could look down and see where they were.

When we got up to the front door, Ed said, Danny took out a small glass cutter and he cut a hole in the door, big enough to reach in and unlock the door. He had the gun on me and motioned me to move inside and I did.

There was just enough light, shining inside from some outside flood lights, to make our way through to the other side of the store. We passed by tables of stuffed leather baby alligators for sale, with their mouths open showing their tiny, sharp little teeth.

We came to another glass door that led outside to the long wooden walkway, surrounded by the pools of water, where the gators lived and they held the jumping gator shows. Duda unlocked the door and made me walk out first and then he followed close behind me. We walked to a place where another long wooden dock went off to the right. It led out to the round circular wooden platform where they held up the chickens for the gators to jump up out of the water.

We walked out on the platform, built over the water, and Duda told me to put the sack on the dock and I did. Then he untied the sack and said, "Well, let's see what we've got in here," and he reached his hand in the sack and pulled out a big white dead chicken by it's feet.

He held his gun on me with one hand and with

the other one, he handed me the chicken. He said:

"Here, chunk this chicken out there and see if anybody's home."

So, I took the chicken by his feet and slung him out into the calm, dark murky water. When the chicken hit the water with a big splash, the calmness disappeared as swarms of eager gators appeared, their large round eyes glowing luminous in the speckles of floodlight; their monstrous tails threw off huge swirls of dark water as they hurried to investigate the chicken.

"Oh, yeah!" Danny Duda cried out, "they're home!"

Then, he reached into the bag and pulled out another chicken and pitched it into the middle of the gator pack, as more gators arrived and tried to push their way through the crowded water. When Danny had pitched out six chickens, and watched the gators tear them up, he turned to me and said:

"Well, I guess that's a good enough appetizer for them—now it's time they had the main course," he said, taking a swig out of his whiskey bottle. Then he pointed his revolver at me:

"Go on and jump in," he ordered.

But I didn't move, I just stood there, gazing out at the feeding gators, like my feet were frozen to the dock. Then, he repeated his order, but I figured I'd rather be shot than eaten alive, so I said, "No, Mr. Duda, go ahead and shoot me—I'm not jumping."

"We'll see about that," he snarled, cocking back the pistol hammer with his thumb, and aiming it down towards my leg. "I'll just wing you and then shove you in;" he said, "that way, you can enjoy feeling their teeth, like I did."

I had found three, razor-sharp, hunting arrow tips at Kilgore's Tony said later. I put them on the arrows Mr. Ed give me, so I could hunt deer with them. I had a sharp arrow notched on my bow string, when I seen Mr. Duda raise his gun at Mr. Ed, and I pulled back hard on my bow.

I was nervous as a grasshopper in a chicken pen, but I remembered Mr. Ed's words on how to shoot; and I let out half a breath, aimed, and then released my fingers on the string. But I missed; my arrow fell short and stuck in the dock, right near Mr. Duda's foot—Ka-thud!

We were both surprised, Ed said, when Tony's arrow hit the dock.

"What in the hell?" Danny said, whirling around. Danny strained his eyes, looking behind him, Ed said. I could see a dark form, crouched up on the wood-shingled roof, built over the dock. Danny shielded his eyes from the glare of the floodlight with his left arm, and was trying to see what was on the roof. Then he spotted Tony and he raised his pistol to shoot.

And about that time, Ed said, here came another arrow, Zip! And this time, it got him in the left arm that he was shielding his eyes with. Well, Danny, he screams out, and he fell back some, and jerked his left arm down, but he recovered quickly and he fired a shot at Tony.

But little Tony flattened himself out down close, and he was hugging the roof as the bullet went high over his head and to the right.

Then Danny's left arm got to hurting him, and he quickly tried to pull the arrow out, and just as he did, Tony let fly another one, and this one caught him in the shoulder of his gun arm. When the arrow hit him, Danny whirled around and his gun went flying off into the water with the gators.

I took off and made a hard lunge at Danny, just as he was jerking the arrow out of his right arm. I put both arms around him and tackled him and we fell hard to the dock.

I figured his arms would be hurting him and I could handle him with no problem. But he was stronger than I thought, and he wrapped his powerful legs around me in a scissor-lock, and we started rolling around the dock.

Meanwhile, Tony saw us fighting, and he was trying to get down off the roof too fast, and his foot slipped on the shingle roof and he caught his hands on the roof edge; and for a minute he was dangling over the water, with gators swarming around underneath him; and then he swung his legs over and caught a support post, and he climbed down the post to the rail and stepped down to the dock.

And all of a sudden, Ed said, as we were rolling, I bit into one of Danny's legs and broke his grip on me.

And one of Danny's legs went out over the edge of the dock, and a big gator spotted it; he jumped up out of the water, just high enough to grab Danny's foot.

Danny screamed as the gator tried to drag him across the dock. Then, I got a quick glimpse of Danny Duda's face, and I saw the terror in his eyes; he realized he was about to be eaten alive. I only had a second to react; a moment where I could try and save him or let him be eaten.

I don't know why I'd want to save him, after what he'd tried to do to me. Maybe I needed him to answer some questions I had, but anyway, I yelled to little Tony to help me and he looked puzzled at me, but we grabbed Danny by the arms and started wrestling with the gator.

When the gator pulled his body away and twisted it, Danny's shoe came off in his mouth and well, I reckon, Ed said, the gator thought he had twisted off something he could eat, and he went under the water and disappeared.

And when little Tony yelled out, "He's gone Mr. Ed!" I grabbed Danny by the front of his shirt and dragged his body back, so that his feet weren't dangling over the edge anymore. And then I looked back at his foot, and his white sock was a bloody mess, but at least his foot was still there.

Danny went to screaming out loud in pain, and he was holding his foot, and he started rolling around from side to side. I looked over at Tony and yelled out,

"Quick, son, run inside and call for an ambulance," and he did it.

I went by the hospital the next day, Ed wrote later in his diary, to see how Danny Duda was doing. It was around lunch time and the doctor said his foot was badly mangled but he said in time his foot should fully recover.

I went into Danny Duda's room. He looked surprised when he saw me, and he got nervous acting and didn't know what to say. I walked over near his bed and grabbed a chair and pulled it up close to him. I said, "I want you to know that I didn't have anything to do with those men putting that gator on you. They just got drunk and did it and that's the truth."

"Why did you save me from the gators?" he asked me. "I don't understand."

"I'm not sure myself; maybe I wanted you to know I was innocent. Why did you want my machine? I'm sorry, but I never believed your story about working for that Meteor Motor company."

Danny looked away from me, he took a deep breath, and then he looked back at me, and said:

"Okay, I guess I owe you that much and more. I was hired by an oil company that's controlled by the most powerful men in the world. They've invested millions in the oil business. Well, you come along and invent a machine that can wipe out their entire business—do you think they're gonna let one little guy ruin their business?"

"But I don't understand; I applied to the U.S. Government Patent Office for a patent on my machine—what have they got to do with that?"

"Who do you think the head man of the patent office works for—the government?—only part time. Oh, sure, he gets a government paycheck, but he gets a lot bigger check from the oil company for alerting them to anyone who can hurt them."

I got a sick feeling in my stomach, Ed wrote, as Danny went on, and explained how the man at the patent office had simply picked up the phone and told the oil company man about my patent application; and that my machine could potentially be dangerous. When Danny finished his story, he said:

"Of course I'll deny this conversation ever took place, and I wouldn't bother telling anyone if I were you. Look Ed, I'm telling you this because you saved me—now I'm trying to save you—forget the patent on your machine.

"There's no way I would harm a hair on your head now, no matter how much they pay me; but if it isn't me, they'll send someone else, until the job is done. Oil men like the Rockefellers have got plenty of money and they intend on keeping it.

"Now I can fix it for you, if you want me too. I'll go back and report the whole thing was a hoax; I'll say it was a clever trick, and the machine was a fraud. That way, they'll leave you alone—it's not worth your life Ed."

I nodded my head in agreement: "You know Danny, I wanted to do something good for the world, but I guess people aren't ready for my ideas yet. Go ahead and do what you say—I won't be applying for any more patents. I thought this was a free country, but I guess it's not."

"It's free Ed," Danny told me, "but you've got to learn not to mess with the power system—they're in control I'm afraid."

I shook hands with Danny Duda, Ed wrote, and I told him I wasn't pressing charges. And as I turned to leave, Danny thanked me again for saving his life.

Today is Saturday, September 15, 1934, Ed wrote in his diary. It rained all day, so Herman and I went to the picture show to see King Kong. I'd read in the newspaper that King Kong was Adolf Hitler's favorite movie. President Von Hindenburg had died in Germany and Adolf Hitler had declared himself the Fuhrer. I couldn't help but think of Hitler as we sat in the movie, waiting for the film to start.

In those days, Herman Harmless said, before the main feature, they always showed a news film of the top stories from around the world. And before King Kong started, they showed a film of President Von Hindenburg laid out in his casket; and then they showed Hitler coming out through two french doors and onto the balcony of the president's headquarters.

Hitler was dressed in a formal tuxedo, with a long, black, split-tailed coat; a pleated white shirt, with black pearl buttons, black pearl cuff links and a shiny black, pure beaver top hat, like President Lincoln used to wear.

When Hitler reached the stone balcony railing, he took off his top hat and waved to the crowd. Hitler didn't smile, but instead, his face took on a look of strength and dignity.

I wasn't sure, Ed said, what kind of leader Hitler would be. I'd seen the news reports of how the Jews were being kicked around in Germany, and I was quite disturbed about it.

There, in the darkness of the theatre, Ed wrote later, when I saw Hitler come on the screen, I slipped into a deep trance, forgetting the present world I was in. I saw visions of a former life in Atlantis.

Suddenly, I was walking down the sidewalk (in my Atlantic vision) of a crowded street. I saw the same type vehicles moving down the street that we have, except these were all mainly wedge or bullet-shaped, and they were silent.

All the races existed here (including the Menons; men from the sky). It was tropical here, and hot most of the time. A lot of the women wore their hair pulled back tightly into a bun behind their head, because it was cooler that way.

There were all varieties of skin color here, but the most beautiful women here to me, were the ones with a bronze-colored skin; and their eyes were usually large, like the Spanish, but they had an Asian, almond-shape and they were coffee colored.

Across the street was a little park that was about as big as a city block. It was mainly filled with women cooking fried bananas, beans and rice, and all kinds of exotic fruits like pineapples. They cooked on a small glass stove, pyramid-shaped, with wood on the bottom to flavor the food.

Other vendors were selling music recordings and I could hear all types of music blaring out from the park. Some of the music was good and some of it was loud and terrible.

Just in front of me, was a big hotel named The Gran Sula, with a doorman out front, dressed in a fancy burgundy hotel suit with gold trim. Parked along the side of the curb were taxi cabs, there must've been at least twenty of them, lined up and waiting for customers.

Suddenly, I felt a terrible thumping headache pain in my forehead, and I reached up to rub it, and I felt a big gauze bandage on my head. I felt dizzy and hungry. I looked up at the Hotel Sula marquee and it read: "Filet Mignon by Chef Dumay. The finest steaks in Atlantis."

And I was thinking about going in and getting something to eat, when I noticed a cab driver, sitting in his cab just in front of me; he was reading a newspaper and he looked up and saw me. He stared hard at me, with a look of bewilderment, and then, keeping his eyes on me, he got out of his cab and came towards me. When he was a few feet in front of me, he stopped, and said: "Rozano! Where have you been?—I've been looking for you."

But I didn't answer him, I just looked at him. His manner was sincere and I wasn't afraid to talk to him, but my head felt foggy. Chino was short and powerfully built, with a round face and Mayan features. He had on a white dinner jacket, pleated white shirt, heavily starched, a black bow tie and black dress pants with black, freshly polished dress loafers.

"I'm sorry," I told him, "but I don't remember—who are you?"

"Oh, forgive me, I forgot that you don't remember. My name is Chino and I'm your best friend.

"You're a sculptor and you were in a bad car wreck and got amnesia. You were in the hospital a couple of days, and one night, you got up and walked out. How are you feeling?"

"Well, I've got a bad headache, and I'm hungry."

"Okay, I tell you what," Chino said, "let's go to the Gran Sula Hotel and get something to eat and we'll talk."

"What's wrong with eating in the park here? The food smells good."

"It is good Rozano, but it's too hot out here and too noisy. There's a breeze at the outside cafe in the Sula and it's quiet. Don't worry about how you're dressed."

I hadn't even noticed my clothes. But I looked now and saw that I had on a red, thick cotton hospital robe, with the words "Roatan Hospital," embroidered in white thread, and red cotton hospital slippers on my feet.

As Chino and I got to the steps in front of the hotel, three long, black, bullet-shaped convertible cars pulled up and parked in front. I looked at the first car and saw Hitler, dressed in a white military jacket with a swastika armband, stepping out of the car as a man held the door open.

Chino snapped to attention and raised his arm in the Nazi salute as Hitler came past us. Hitler recognized Chino and stopped and spoke to him and shook his hand. Then Hitler looked puzzled at me.

Hitler said: "Rozano? I heard about the wreck. I'm glad to see you're up and around. Call me when you feel better, I've got some work for you that I think you'll like." Then, Hitler looked at Chino: "Take good care of him Chino," Hitler said, "I can't afford to have the greatest sculptor in Atlantis sick." And Hitler walked off and into the hotel.

"You know him Chino?" I asked.

"Yes. I picked him up in my cab one night when he was campaigning and his car broke down. Later, he let me drive him down the street in a big political parade. It's strange; now he's the Fuhrer. You're in good with him, he likes your work. Come on, lets go eat."

The doorman knew me, and welcomed me back, Ed said, but I didn't remember his name. Then, as we walked through the lobby, Chino explained to me that I had an apartment here and that I drew a lot of the sketches here for my sculpting.

Then, (in my Atlantis vision) Chino and I were on the elevator; we got off on the sixth floor and went to room number 607. When we got in, Chino said, "This is your room and office."

The room was furnished in dark mahogany, and I saw a small drawing table near a window, overlooking the main street where the park was. On the bedroom dresser, I saw a framed photograph of a girl. I walked over and picked it up. It was Agnes (her name was Jami Portillo in this time). She was sitting on the beach, holding up a large conch shell in her hands.

Chino said, "That was your fiance, Jami Portillo. She liked to go to the beach and collect shells."

"What happened?" I asked him.

"Excuse me," he said. He took the photo out of my hands, and he pulled out a second photo that had been hidden behind the photo of Agnes (Jami). Chino handed me the picture of a beautiful girl, with long black hair. She looked a lot like Agnes (Jami).

"Her name is Elda Sanchez," Chino said.

"You met her here in the hotel. You and Elda had an affair, right on up until the time for your wedding. Two days before your wedding, you decided to have one more fling. You were driving along up in the mountains, at night, when your car came around a steep curve.

"There was a log truck in your lane—the driver had fallen asleep. You swerved to miss him and your car went down the mountain and hit a tree; Elda was killed."

Though my spirit was in another realm, Ed wrote, I had the capacity to understand what this meant. It was like being in a dream that you've had before, but you didn't understand it at the time, but this time, you understand it because you were in it again.

And suddenly, I remembered that in Madame Drusa's Atlantic vision before I was born, she described seeing me standing on the bridge near the lagoon of water; she said my head was bandaged, and the girl I was with (Agnes) was gone. This had to be what she was talking about. Evidently, Madame Drusa had been given the future knowledge that I would be in the wreck and lose Jami (Agnes). I was now revisiting the time shortly after the wreck as Chino was now my guide in this realm.

And later, after the vision, I felt like I was being told why Agnes had jilted me in my present life. I had been unfaithful to her. I remembered the prophet's words: "Be sure, your sins will find you out."

I felt sad now, knowing the truth, but I also felt a sense of relief; I understood for the first time what had gone wrong. With what I'd done to her, according to the Karmic laws, it was perfectly normal for her to have left me in Latvia, in the same manner that I'd left her in another realm of time.

Now I wanted desperately to find Jami (Agnes) in this time, and tell her how sorry I was. Maybe, if I could get her forgiveness in this time, she would remember it later, in the present time, where I found myself in Homestead, and come and marry me at the Valentine table I'd carved for her. But, would she talk to me now? She had every right not to. All I could do was hope.

Then, suddenly, the scene (in my Atlantis vision) changed. I was standing on a sandy road as the sun went down. Both sides of the road were lined with stone pyramid buildings. And in the distance, at the end of the road, I saw the Great Pyramid; and next to it was the Sphinx. A Menon man (men from the sky) stood beside me, and he asked me:

"What do you see?"

"I see The Great Pyramid," I answered.

"What does it mean?" he asked.

"I don't know sir. Please tell me."

"If you want knowledge you must work for it—I can't tell you what you can know by studying. The secret of the pyramid lies in the granite tomb—examine it carefully. The prophet said: 'Seek and ye shall find.'"

And the scene quickly changed again. I found myself alone in my room at the Sula Hotel. It was night, and I heard music coming from the park across the street.

I went over to the window and opened it so I could hear better. I sat on the inside window balcony, and looked down at the park. I saw a slim girl with long black hair, wearing a bright yellow silk dress. She turned away from the music and walked over to one of the taxis parked near the street. She opened the back door to get in, then she paused, and looked up at the window where I was staring down at her. It was Jami (Agnes).

It was as though she expected to see someone in the window, but she looked startled when our eyes met. She paused, staring intently at me, then she looked away and got in the taxi. At that moment, I returned to the consciousness of the present time, in the dark theatre in Homestead, and the movie King Kong.

Later, after the Atlantic vision in the theatre, I thought about seeing The Great Pyramid and the Sphinx in Atlantis. And I was trying to figure out the meaning of it. And, I don't know if this is right or not, but I wondered if maybe, the Menons (men from the sky) had built these same complexes in different places, like Egypt and Mexico, because they had advanced knowledge that Atlantis would be destroyed (like Edgar Cayce had said) and so, like a chain of hotels, they built these things to preserve their knowledge.

I told Dr. Alfred Feeny, Herman said, about Ed's latest Atlantic dream. Ed wrote in his diary about a session with Dr. Feeny, Herman said. Ed wrote:

Herman said Dr. Feeny, the retired psychiatrist from Atlanta, was having a fit to put me under hypnosis; he wanted to study my dream times through regressive hypnosis. I'd always been interested in dreams and visions so I agreed to it.

Dr. Feeny wanted to read the notes in my diary on my last Atlantic dream so I gave them to him. Herman and I went over to Dr. Feeny's house, on 302 north Leona street, at eight o'clock on a wednesday night. It was a clapboard, two-story house, painted white and built around 1885.

It was furnished with oak antiques, a big grandfather clock and hand woven rugs. A large rug in the parlor featured a fox hunting scene in England. Dr. Feeny said, "Well, let's go in the parlor and have some tea." Dr. Feeny, Ed said, had made up some special chamomile tea for me, while he and Herman drank regular tea. Dr. Feeny said chamomile tea was good for relaxing the nerves. After the tea, he had me take my shoes off and lie down on a green leather couch near the grandfather clock. Dr. Feeny said:

"Now Ed, I want you to just lie back and relax. You're already familiar with the psychic Edgar Cayce's work, and this session will be a lot like one of his famous readings.

"You know that under hypnosis, your unconscious mind will not reveal anything that you consciously would not want revealed.

"Okay, now in your last Atlantic dream, you found out that you had cheated on Agnes, or Jami in this time. Now what I'd like for you to do now, is try and program your conscious mind to go back to a time in Atlantis, any time that is before you cheated on Agnes."

Then, Ed wrote, Dr. Feeny got up and lit some candles and turned off the electric lights. He put a record on the victrola, of ocean waves crashing on the beach. Dr. Feeny said:

"I wanted the room darker to represent the mother's womb before you were born. I want you to listen to the ocean, this represents the water home where you lived in your mother's stomach. Listen to rhythmic ticking of the clock and think of time.

"Now, I want you to close your eyes and focus on the crashing waves; each time one crashes, I want you to think of going back to Atlantis.

"I'm asking your conscious spirit to agree with me, and go back to a time before you had the problem with Agnes. Listen to the soothing ticking of the grandfather clock—think of your own grandfather Nick, that you love so dearly—go back Ed, go back." He waited a moment, then said, "Are you back now Ed?"

I was impressed with Dr. Feeny's technique, Ed wrote later. I was taken back completely in the spirit, as I lay on the green leather couch. I know I went back in the spirit because my body stayed on the couch.

"Yes sir," Ed answered. "I'm back."

"Where are you Ed?"

"Atlantis," I answered.

I found myself walking down the main street in the capital city of Atlantis. I don't know why, but it came to me that the capital city's name was Germania (perhaps Hitler had changed it from Zolameta, the indian name). There were some buildings here that reminded me of the Berlin, Germany of my present time.

I remembered Adolf Hitler once told me, in World War I that he'd had a dream one time to build a great capital city called "Germania."

I don't know if this influenced me or not; I guess I'll never know for sure. Anyway, I was walking down the main street, when I saw Chino, standing outside his taxi cab. He was leaning on the fender reading a newspaper.

"Business must be slow again," I said.

"Hey boss—it's dead," he said. "You need a ride?"

"No thanks. I'm going over to see Jami's father about renting a building for my sculpting studio."

"Didn't she say he's a tightwad?"

"Yeah, but I've got to try. I want his building

because it's next to The Constellation Club. I like to be around music when I'm working—it helps inspire me."

"Oh, yeah. Well, maybe he'll give you a break since she's your fiance—"

"I don't think so. We don't get along. He doesn't like artists; he's strictly a bottom line business man—a cockroach knows more about art than he does. Well, I'll see you later."

I went into the empty building of Jami's father. He got right to the point.

"Rozano," he says, "I want two thousand limpiras a month for the place, take it or leave it, I'm busy."

"I'll take it," I told him.

"I need it up front," he said, coldly.

I pulled out the cash and counted it out to him. He looked surprised, and said, "I didn't think you had it. I'll be honest with you, I don't want my daughter marrying someone who can't support her—"

"Neither do I, sir. I won't ask her until I can. Fair enough?" It was all the money I had; but I had confidence that I could sell enough pieces in a month to make the rent.

Then, in my hypnotic state, the scene changed. I was in the studio I'd rented. Jami was standing beside me. We were watching a Menon man; he was working on a bust of Adolfo Hitler.

It was a bust with half of Hitler's body inlaid over a Swastika, with a wreath of leaves bordering the swastika. I told the Menon man, "That's good enough Lothar. Hitler is coming by shortly to look at it. I don't want him to know a Menon was working on it—he'd die."

"I don't like working on it either—if he's elected, we'll have to leave. Rozano, why does he hate us so much?"

"I think he resents your intelligence," Jami said. "It messes with his romantic notion of creating a master race—using only humans—"

"I don't like his politics either," I said, "but he pays cash."

"I'll see you tomorrow Rozano," Lothar said, and he left.

Jami said, "Rozano, do you think there's a chance Hitler could be elected?"

"I don't think so—he's too radical."

"Yes," she said, "but Atlantis is full of radicals just like him."

"Enough of politics—let's go to the Constellation Club and have a beer."

Jami and I got a booth at the club, and just as we'd ordered a beer, the band played "At last," so we got up and danced.

And it was strange, but as I listened to the words of the song, I was able to put in words what I'd always felt about Agnes. In Homestead, people were curious about what made Agnes so special that I would give up everything to wait for her. It was difficult for me to explain my love for her, but the words in the song came as close as I could to expressing it.

The words were: "I found a dream that I can speak to, a dream that I can call my own; I found a thrill to press my cheek to, a thrill, I've never known. You smiled, and then the spell was cast, and here we are in heaven, for you are mine at last."

Afterwards, when we sat at the table, I thought of something and I smiled; Jami asked me why. I said:

"Baby, do you remember when we went to the beach and we were going in the hotel room, and that lizard ran in the door when I opened it. And I didn't know you were afraid of lizards, because when you were a little girl, you woke up in your bed and that lizard was on your face, remember?"

"How could I forget?—when you caught him later and put him in our bed and scared me to death—remember, I had nightmares later about it?"

"I know, I felt so bad—how come you never told me about the lizard on your face when you were little, before that night?"

"Well, how could I have known a lizard would come in our room, and that you'd scare me with him? That's just one of those things that happens. What made you bring that up?"

"I don't know. I just remember how upset and mad you got. Sometimes I go too far with my jokes; I'm afraid, one day, I'll do something bad and you won't forgive me—"

"Oh, don't be silly. I can never stay mad at you for long."

"Okay, give me your hand," I said, and I took her small hand and put it in mine, and our fingers intertwined.

We put our elbows on the table, like we were going to arm wrestle. I said: "I want you to promise me, right now, that if I ever do something to make you mad, that you will forgive me."

"Oh, Rozano—are you serious?"

"Yes, now please promise me."

So she did. But then she added, "But that promise doesn't apply if you ever cheat on me—if you do that, it's over, and that I can promise you."

"Baby," I said, "that's one thing you'll never have to worry about with me. You're the only girl for me."

Later, after the hypnotic vision, at Dr. Feeny's house, Ed wrote, I thought about the vision and how strange it was that somehow I'd known that I was going to mess things up with Jami (Agnes) and that I was trying to provide a way of getting out of it before it even happened.

Dr. Feeny questioned Ed for over an hour that night, Herman Harmless said, and he took notes. Ed talked about Atlantis, Hitler, the Menons (men from the sky) and Jami (Agnes). Ed got tired and upset at seeing Agnes, and he quit talking. Dr. Feeny told him to rest for awhile. Then, Dr. Feeny and I went into the kitchen and got another cup of tea and talked.

Dr. Feeny spoke excitedly, as though he'd just

made a great discovery: "Herman, what an incredible mind he has—did you notice how quickly and deeply he went under?—he was all the way under I tell you! You can tell when somebody's faking it—this man believes everything he said. Herman, have you ever heard of Cryptoamnesia?"

"Cryptoamnesia? No—is it like amnesia?"

"Not really," Dr. Feeny replied. "It's very rare—I mean there's only been a few reported cases of it, so we haven't had the opportunity to study it. Cryptoamnesia is mainly a condition that affects people who read a lot and have strong imaginations.

"What happens, is that they're usually loners who get lost in their books, and over a period of time, from constant exposure to the stories, they begin to believe the stories are real. These people are especially vulnerable if something tragic happens to them.

"So, you see, Ed's system could've gone into shock when Agnes jilted him—that would've been a perfect environment for Cryptoamnesia.

"You see, with Cryptoamnesia, the unconscious mind is constantly bombarded with the world that the individual is familiar with from his books; and so, this fantasy world comes to life, it's acted out in dreams or visions, of what they've read.

"The mind is a wonderful creation; the unconscious mind will try to provide the conscious mind with all the necessary ingredients for happiness."

"In other words," Herman said, "if I'm not getting the necessary conditions that I need for my happiness in the conscious world, my unconscious mind may take over, and give me what I need in the only realm where it's possible—the world of visions and dreams. In Ed's case, it's giving him Agnes in another time because he lost her in this time and he wants her back."

"Yes," Dr. Feeny continued. "I mean, think about it, he's been exposed to this kind of information since he was a child, sitting in his grandfather's lap, hearing about all those stories of Atlantis, space men, The Great Pyramid, reincarnation."

"So, what you're saying," Herman said, "is that Ed read about all those things, and then his unconscious mind formulated all the facts together, and wove them into stories, played out in his dreams and visions."

"Yes, I mean it seems to fit Ed's case—"

"It sure does," Herman said, and thinking about it, something came to him, and he got excited and said: "Yes! I remember now, Ed told me that Hitler had told him in the first war that he believed that the German race was founded in Atlantis; Hitler believed the genius of German technology came from their Atlantic ancestors."

"Well, there you have it," Dr. Feeny said. "It's easy to see now, why he can put Hitler in this past existence in Atlantis. But, one of the most amazing things I learned from looking at some of Ed's books was the pictures of the swastikas on the Mayan pyramids.

"It makes you wonder, if you accepted the reincarnation theory, if Adolf Hitler could have existed in this Atlantic time, and then returned in our time to recreate his Third Reich. I had no idea that the Swastika was that ancient.

"You know Herman," Dr. Feeny said, "think about it, I noticed that in the photograph of Agnes, on the dresser that Ed described in his Atlantis vision, showed her at the beach collecting shells—the same thing that she loves in this time."

Dr. Feeny paused then said, "And you know, if you look at Ed's castle, what is it's most prominent feature?—walls, Herman, high, eight foot walls. I think that when Agnes Scuffs jilted Ed, on December 20, 1912, time stopped for Ed. He took flight from reality.

"Ed came here and surrounded himself with high coral walls. He can't control what goes on outside these walls, but inside them, he's the boss. He needed to feel a sense of control after the devastation of losing Agnes.

"Herman, most people don't realize how powerful a drug love can be for some people. I guess I came to respect it more because of my business. History if full of suicides over lost loves."

"So, Dr. Feeny, are you saying," Herman said, "that Ed's unconscious mind put Agnes Scuffs into his dreams, because he was unable to get her in reality—dreams are the only place where he can still have her?"

"Yes, that's the theory. Now, you see, if you or I got rejected like Ed did, we would probably get hurt of course, but we would get over it in time, and then begin looking for someone else. But everyone handles bad situations in their own way.

"I think Ed decided to ignore that Agnes rejected him, and he put up his high walls to live in the past. He then created this false sense of hope that Agnes is coming here to marry him.

"But," Dr. Feeny said, "maybe it's good that he did; it may be the thing that keeps him going. You know, Hitler must've deeply affected Ed's life in some way for him to carry him over in his dreams.

"We still don't understand how the mind assembles and processes information. Hitler is famous for having a hypnotic effect on people; it's always fascinated me how one uneducated man is blessed with such a powerful personality."

"Dr. Feeny, do you think Ed's got Cryptoamnesia?"

"Well, Herman, I never said that."

"What're you talking about?"

"All I did," Dr. Feeny said, "was to explain the theory of Cryptoamnesia to you, to give you another explanation for what can happen to someone who believes in reincarnation."

"Does that mean," Herman asked, "that you believe that these things Ed dreams about could've really happened to him?"

"Absolutely. I can't judge the information about what happens in someone else's life. It's not my job to validate it or cast doubts about it. I neither believe, nor disbelieve in Cryptoamnesia or reincarnation—in some cases, both of them could be true; one person could be affected by Cryptoamnesia while another is actually describing a former life.

"The important thing to remember here, is that there is no scientific proof for either, that's why they're referred to as "theories."

"As I said, in my opinion, after observing Ed and listening to him, I can tell you this—whether real or imagined, what he described, he genuinely believes that it did occur.

"And another thing," Dr. Feeny said, "think about this; remember how you told me Ed's favorite book was "The Time Machine," by H.G. Wells? Remember, the character travels forward in time and meets the girl. Ed's dream experiences are very similar to the character in that book. Did Ed's unconscious mind pick up the traits of the time traveler in "The Time Machine?" I don't know; as I said, all we have to explain these things are theories.

"Well," Dr. Feeny said, "it's getting late, I better go wake Ed up. I'll give you a copy of my notes tomorrow."

I went over to Ed's place the next day, to have lunch, Herman said. We ate on the Florida table and discussed what Dr. Feeny had told me. After I explained the Cryptoamnesia theory to Ed, he seemed interested in it. He asked me:

"Herman, do you think I've got Cryptoamnesia? I mean, it's okay if you think I do. It does seem to make a lot of sense."

"I don't know Ed. Not even Dr. Feeny knows—he said so himself. I got to thinking about this thing last night—what does it matter what you've got? Dr. Feeny said a lot of people commit suicide over lost loves.

"The way I see it, you took a tragedy and turned it into something positive—look at the miracle of Coral Castle. So don't worry about it, you've done a good thing."

What I said seemed to please Ed, Herman said,

and he thanked me for my long years of friendship. At night, Ed continued working on his magnetic experiments and reading his books.

Ed ordered a lot of material from the psychic Edgar Cayce's club "Association For Enlightened Research." And Ed spent a lot of time in the 1930's and '40's studying Edgar Cayce's writings on Atlantis.

Ed was particularly fascinated by the reading Dr. Cayce gave in November of 1940. In it, Edgar Cayce said that a man in a previous Atlantic experience:

"Had aided the priest in setting the records of Atlantis in the hall of records (Sphinx) that lies just beyond the mystery of mysteries (The Great Pyramid) in Egypt. Information is possible for those who seek to know what were the manners of thought of the ancients."

Ed told me, Herman said, that it was his dream one day to go to Egypt and explore the Sphinx.

One day, in the spring of 1935, Herman told Carl Swisher, the newspaper man, Ed and I were sitting on the porch of my fruit shop, drinking ice coffee and watching the traffic go by.

Roy Green, the mailman, came up the steps, delivering the mail. He handed me my mail and he had a letter for Ed from Latvia, so he gave it to him. Ed looked at the letter and said it was from Bruno, his friend who owned The Blue Moon bar.

I was busy going through my mail, Herman said, and I didn't pay much attention to Ed as he opened his letter and read it. But Ed got a painful, sickly-white look on his face; his hands dropped into his lap, and he closed his eyes momentarily, and as he did, he muttered softly: "Oh, God, no."

"Ed, what's wrong? What is it?" I asked him. But he didn't answer me. He looked like he was dazed. He looked at me and said, "Excuse me Herman, I've got to go home." And he got in his truck and drove to Coral Castle.

I wondered if something had happened to his

family, and later, I asked him what the letter was about but he wouldn't tell me. He said, "I'd rather not talk about it Herman; please don't ask me anymore about it." So, I never mentioned it again.

Ed's diary entry for March 4, 1935:

"Herman Harmless came by today and told me that Novia Lilly had gotten married to a navy pilot in Miami. She was working in a drug store there when she met him. I'm happy for her, she's a good woman."

Diary entry, June 6, 1935:

"From my experiments with magnets, I now understand that our eyes act like broadcasting cameras. They send out magnetic flashes and receive back the images from the objects we see. This may explain the "sixth sense" that I'm able to apply when people sneak up on me, trying to catch me at work.

"It's like when maybe you stare at somebody's back while the person doesn't know it, and the person gets restless and looks around. I've noticed, that sometimes, I can chase mosquitoes away from a wall by giving a sharp look at them.

"Sometimes, I can see tiny lightning bolts if I close my eyelids and give a side push to my eyeball from my nose outward, but I can't do it every day.

"When I keep eating more for sometime, then I can see the tiny lightning while my eyes are open. All I have to do is turn my head from one side to the other. This shows that we have, in our bodies, the same kind of magnets that are making the big lightning in the sky.

"When I connect my tongue and feet with a micro-ampere meter, the meter shows that I have magnets in my body. It's strange, but sometimes, I have more magnets in my body than at other times. I think it's according to what we eat.

"For instance, I've checked my body after eating only collard greens and pepper sauce and I've watched the needle on the ampmeter; it swings way up, so collard greens must be loaded with magnets—could be due to their high level of chlorophyll."

Ed's diary entry, December 10, 1941:

Three days after Pearl Harbor, I was sitting in the castle, in the spot where I put the stone chairs to read the Goldilocks story to the visiting children. It was around three thirty in the afternoon, and I was reading the Goldilocks story to some kids who'd just gotten out of school.

Coral Castle was filled with the playful noise of school children, climbing over the stone fixtures and some of the kids were having a tea party at the Florida table.

I heard the front door bell clanging over the noise, and I figured it was some more children arriving, so I sent one of the kids to open the iron front door.

But it wasn't more kids, it was Herman Harmless. He came walking over to me. He looked distressed.

"What's wrong Herman? Is Opal okay?" I asked. He nodded his head. "Could I talk with you, alone, Ed?" he asked, motioning with his head. I excused myself from the children and handed the book to an older girl, sitting to my left, and she picked up where I left off.

"Ed," Herman said, "it's Novia's husband—remember he was a pilot? They sent him to Pearl Harbor six months ago. When the Japs attacked, he tried to run out and get his plane off the ground so he could fight.

"He never made it. A Jap Zero came swooping down low and shot him on the runway. They just confirmed he was among the dead. I thought you might like to know."

"Oh no!" Ed groaned, "she had waited so long for the right guy."

"I'm heading over to Miami now to see her—do you want to go?"

"No. I'm not good at dealing with tragedy. Thanks for coming by. Herman, please tell her that I'm thinking of her."

"I'll tell her. I'll see you later," he said, and walked off.

A few days later, around four o'clock in the afternoon, Ed wrote, I hung up a "Closed for the day," sign on the front door of the castle. I couldn't quit thinking about poor Novia and how she was suffering.

I don't think that until I lost Agnes, I had ever suffered. I was always happy and rarely ever cried, unless my dog died or someone beat me up at school. I didn't understand how tragic life can be. For me, until Agnes, it had always been a thing of joy and laughter.

Right now, I didn't want to think about the war and people dying. It was my bath time, and there was something about sinking down into that warm water that relaxed me better than anything. I decided not to think about anything else until after my bath.

It was a nice sunny day. The sun had heated up the water in my bathtub to a perfect temperature. I put some rice, fresh pineapple, coconut, mango, and fresh-peeled shrimp into my outdoor smoker and built a fire under it. Then I went over and got in my tub.

I had just finished my bath and was toweling off when I heard the loud clanging of the front door bell, around 4:30. I figured it was some tourist and I didn't feel like giving a tour, so I called out: "I'm sorry the castle's closed."

Then I heard a woman's voice: "Ed, it's me, Novia. I need to talk to you."

"Be right there," I yelled, and told her I was getting out of the tub.

As I quickly put on my clothes and went to the front door, I tried to think of how I would console her on the loss of Roy Boyd, her husband. I opened the door and there she stood, in a long black dress with black high heels. Her face looked distressed and she had dark circles under her eyes.

She was still in shock. She shook her head and said, "Oh Ed, they shot him down! They shot him down!" and she burst into tears and flung her arms around me.

"Oh, God—I'm so sorry," I said.

After a moment, I said, "Come on in, and I'll make some coffee."

"Could I make it?" she asked. "I need to keep my hands busy."

"Well, sure. You know where I keep everything."

"Yes," she said softly. "I don't know anybody else who has their kitchen in their bedroom."

"Well, you know I like to keep things simple." She smiled and turned to walk off: "Oh," I said, "I just made some fresh pumpkin bread—it's in the pie safe," and she nodded her head and kept walking.

We sat at the Florida table and talked. Novia said she hadn't had any appetite, but we ate the pumpkin bread and the shrimp with the fruit, and it seemed to strengthen her. She said:

"Ed, I need to get away for a day; would you take me to Cypress Gardens tomorrow? There's lots of flowers there—I know how much you like flowers. You'd love it, it's so peaceful inside. Roy and I used to go there a lot. I've already got a picnic lunch made and we can take my car, if you don't mind driving. I just want to sit back and not have to think."

"Well, sure, I'll take you. What time do you want to go?"

"It's about a two and a half hour drive; how about if we left at seven o'clock in the morning? Then, we'll have time to see everything and not have to hurry through."

She put her hand on mine and said, "Thank you so much Ed. I'm sorry to burden you like this—but I knew you'd understand better than anyone."

We left at seven the next morning. She met me at the door, wearing a silky red, sleeveless shirt, with blue jeans and red, soft leather casual shoes with no socks. I noticed how lovely her tan exposed ankles looked, with the red leather pressed up tightly against her brown skin. Her hair was neatly fixed today, unlike yesterday when it looked uncombed, like she had slept on it.

There was an awkward silence for a moment, as we stared at each other, then she said, "I knew you'd like this outfit; Roy bought it for me. Red was his favorite color too."

We rode along, mainly in silence, except for some trivial talk about the peaceful scenery of pine trees and oaks, loaded with Spanish moss, that we passed along the roadside. We pulled into the sandy parking lot of Cypress Gardens around ten o'clock.

We got out and Novia carried the woven basket of picnic food. We walked along a wooden dock up to the entrance, bought our tickets and walked through a wooden, flower-covered archway, and emerged into the bright Florida sunshine.

With my left hand I shaded my eyes from the sunlight. I was surprised at the scene. Just in front of me, I saw an arched wooden bridge, crossing over a narrow canal of water.

Standing all around the opposite bank, at the edge of the canal, were lovely young girls, dressed in colorful gowns, and holding up lacy umbrellas to shield the sun.

And now, in the distance in front of me, I saw a small boat, loaded with people going down the canal. There was a guide in the back, dressed in a safari outfit and wearing a pith helmet.

Immediately, I remembered the reading Madame Drusa gave my mother, when she was pregnant with me, and she described being in the garden of Atlantis, with the boats going down the canal of water.

I knew this was the same place, in the Atlantic realm, where Agnes (Jami in Atlantis) and I had been together. The bridge in front of where the boat was now passing under, was where we'd seen the monkey catch the banana from the guide.

Knowing what I knew, this scene should not have surprised me. I had been in places that I'd been before, in another time, like when I visited Beaver Twist in the Chaco Canyon. And yet, I must admit, I always had a strange feeling to actually see something from a past existence.

For me, it was a confirmation of everything my grandfather and I had talked about since I was a child. I suddenly remembered Solomon's words: "There is nothing new under the sun. Everything that is, has been here before. Nothing new is ever discovered, only re-discovered."

And it occurred to me now, that here, this place, Cypress Gardens, had existed in a civilization that had been Atlantis.

According to the prophet Edgar Cayce, Atlantis had existed not far off the Florida coast, near Bimini. Why was I now in a place that was very near where Cayce said Atlantis had been? Did the powers that govern our world allow Agnes to jilt me, so that I would come here now and build Coral Castle?

Did I return in this time to prove, by building Coral Castle, that a secret science for moving large objects once existed, in another time and place? What am I to learn from this? Is it patience—as Madame Drusa suggested? If I wait, will Agnes come?

Standing here, looking at the things that Agnes and I had seen together in another time, gave me a sense of melancholy. But, for Novia's sake, I made up my mind to make it a happy time.

I convinced myself that I was fortunate to experience it. Most people would say I was hallucinating if I were to try and explain it. You have to believe in these things to know them. A lot of times, when God spoke in the Bible, he'd say, "For those who have eyes, let them see; and for those who have ears, let them hear."

"Is something wrong Ed?" Novia said, startling me from my thoughts. "You look like you're in a daze."

"No—it's just, so beautiful—all the flowers, just like you said."

"Oh, I knew you'd like it. Come on, we need to get in line for tickets to the boat ride."

The boat ride was the same, Ed wrote, except this time, they didn't scare the people with the fake gator like last time. The guide had the same nasal twang, as he talked about the philodendrons on the canal side. And later we passed the big seated golden Buddha that I remembered from before.

When the boat tour was over, we stepped off the dock and walked back over to where the wooden plank bridge (where the monkey sat last time) crossed over the canal. We walked over the bridge and then followed the winding concrete pathway ahead, lined on both sides by multi-colored mums.

As we walked along the flower path in silence, I could hear the distant sounds of music, coming from a pavilion where a live band played.

The winding pathway snaked into a long curve, and we came to a small pond; there was a big waterfall on the other side of the path. As I stood at the rail, looking over the pond, I recognized this spot as the place where Agnes (Jami in Atlantis) and I had fed the turtles in the Atlantic time. And then I remembered the waterfall too.

"Ed," Novia said, "let's have our picnic near the waterfall." There was a grassy spot next to the bottom of the waterfall. Novia spread out a large red and white checkered cloth and we put our food on it.

We had fried chicken, baked beans, and potato salad. It was good, and afterwards, I was full.

But Novia saw an ice cream cart pull up not too far from us. She said, "Oh, they have good vanilla ice cream, topped with fresh strawberries. I'll go get us some," and she walked off. As I watched her leave, I saw a long line of people lining up to buy ice cream.

I hadn't slept very well the night before, and now this good food and the lazy, sunny afternoon made me sleepy. I laid my head back against the soft folds of the picnic cloth and looked up into the sky at the billowy white cloud formations, drifting by slowly in the slight breeze.

I heard the band playing the Glenn Miller song "Moonlight Mood," and the words: "Although you're far away, we meet in my solitude, you are mine, when I'm in my moonlight mood."

As I thought on these words, time seemed to fly by and the next thing I knew, the day was over. We had just gotten back to Coral Castle and were sitting in Novia's car, parked outside the front gate. Novia had lost one of her earrings and she was looking for it in the car, when I heard music coming from inside the castle.

"Did I leave the radio on in the castle?" I asked her.

"I don't remember," she mumbled, occupied in her search for the missing earring.

"I'm going in to check it," I said, and got out of the car and walked to the front door.

The sun was low in the sky, my favorite time of day, when I pushed the door open and walked in. The golden sunlight made all the moss-grey, stone objects, look like a post card, and I stopped to stare at how lovely everything looked.

I saw a woman, with long black hair falling to her shoulders, sitting at the Valentine table. I wondered what she was doing here. She was looking into a make-up mirror on the table and combing her long hair. At first, I was puzzled and called out to her, as I thought she hadn't heard me come in because of the music.

She didn't hear me and I moved in closer and called out again. This time she heard me and turned to face me, it was Agnes Scuffs. She smiled and said:

"Oh, darling, where've you been? I've been waiting for you. Baby, please forgive me. I saved all your letters and photographs of the castle; I pulled them out, and looked at them, and I got so sad. That's when I decided to come. It's not too late for us, is it?"

She looked at me with those big brown eyes, framed in that oriental look, with long, curving eyebrows. My heart pounded wildly when she reached out with her small delicate hands and she put them in mine. I said:

"Aggie—don't you know this is all I ever wanted? Oh, God, I can't believe you're here, my dream came true."

She kissed me on the lips, and then she pulled back and put her arms around me and hugged me tightly. I could smell the fragrance of jasmine in her hair.

Then, I heard the creaking sound of the castle's thick iron door, and I turned to see Novia walking in. She stopped when she saw us embracing.

And suddenly, I felt my body shaking, and I heard Novia's voice: "Ed, Ed, I'm sorry to wake you, but your ice cream is melting."

I had fallen asleep waiting on her. I opened my eyes and flinched when I found myself on my back, and staring up at Novia as she leaned over me.

"I'm sorry it took so long," she said. "They ran out of strawberries and had to go get some."

During the war years, 1941 through 1945, Ed wrote, the tourist business slowed down considerably. Most of the people who came down to South Florida were people who were elderly, or too disabled to work for the war effort.

One saturday afternoon, in 1941, Herman Harmless and I went to the movies to see "The Seventh Sinners," with Marlene Dietrich and John Wayne. The newsreel, shown before the movie, showed scenes of Hitler touring Paris with his architect, Albert Speer.

It was a good movie. Marlene Dietrich looked good in it and she sang some good songs. I thought it was ironic to see Hitler on the screen before Marlene because she is German, and Hitler had begged her to return to Germany when the war began, but she refused, and stayed here in America. She didn't like the Nazis.

After the movie, I felt like going to the beach alone, so I said goodbye to Herman. I went back to the castle, put some firewood in my truck, got a couple of beers, and headed out on Key West Highway to Miami. It was only seventeen miles, and I liked the lonely stretch of road because there wasn't much traffic.

The sun was setting as I pulled onto a deserted stretch of beach facing Key Largo. I built a fire, opened a beer, and sat back; I looked out across the Atlantic Ocean, past Bimini, in the direction of England. I wondered if the British planes were somewhere right now, loading up with bombs for the nightly raids over Germany.

They were trying to destroy the man I had fought with in the trenches of France, so many years ago. Now, Hitler was a great warrior, the Fuhrer of Germany. Hitler gave the orders and German planes took off, loaded with bombs; tanks creaked along dusty roads, like iron tigers, looking for prey. Some guys leaving England tonight wouldn't be coming back to earth, no, they will die in the sky, never kissing their loved ones again.

All it took was one burst of machine gun fire from a German Messerschmidt, or a well placed flak pattern, and that big silver bird came tumbling down.

I watched the green ocean water, rising up and rolling down on the sand of the Atlantic. The word Atlantic made me think about how, 10,000 years ago, all that water out there was dry land. And there was a great war there too, when Cayce said Atlantis was destroyed by the death ray.

I thought of Hitler and the war he'd started. Why is it that one man comes back with hate and war in his heart, and another returns searching for a lost love? Who can understand it?

Edgar Cayce said Atlantis existed right out there, near Bimini, across that great expanse of water. I'd seen pictures of the area, near Bimini, showing roads and great temple columns, littering the ocean bottom.

Looking into the fire now, I thought of the fire Hitler had brought on the world. He and I had talked many times in the first war about how the only good thing about winter was the fire in the fireplace. And I noticed that later, in the films of the Nazi rallies for Hitler, the narrator said the Nazis used fire for a subtle cultic influence.

I laid my head back now on a piece of fat driftwood and listened to the crashing green waves against the sand. It relaxed me and I drifted off into a deep sleep. In a dream state, I had visions of Atlantis. This is what I saw:

The sun was setting (in my dream) as I found myself in a courtyard, surrounded by high walls. In front of me was a tall pyramid, with a staircase of stone steps leading up to a flat topped platform, like my King's throne room in Coral Castle. On the top of the platform was a beautifully carved throne chair of pink granite, adorned with red swastikas. On both sides of the chair were two grey granite sculptures of Hitler's head resting on a swastika.

On both sides of the chair, were two huge, intricately carved, crystal skulls, lit on the inside with a soft blue light. I heard beautiful music playing, that consisted of flutes, harps and violins.

Seated on the throne chair was a white man, dressed in a black Nazi uniform. And down below him, seated on stone benches were many people of the various races of Atlantis, but the majority of them were the Menon people (men from the sky).

The man in the throne chair stood and said something to the crowd and they all stood and began walking through a doorway leading to a ball court.

A Menon man stood beside me, and I asked him, "What is going on?"

"These are the people," he explained, "who took part in the street riots, and belonged to the outlawed political parties opposing Hitler. They are prisoners now. Once a month, there is a ball game and the winners get better food and clothing; the losers die. Come with me and I'll show you."

We fell in behind the crowd, walking about twenty yards to the ball court. We took a seat high up in the stone stands. It looked exactly like the pictures I'd seen of the ball court in the Copan ruins in Honduras.

The ball court was horseshoe shaped, with a grass infield, and it was lit on the sides with flaming torches. There were ten players on each side (the players were all Menons) and they wore white shorts and sleeveless shirts and white sneakers.

I didn't completely understand the game, but it seemed to be a combination of soccer and volleyball. The object was to keep the round soccer ball in play, without touching the ground. If it touched the ground in bounds, that team lost a point. Five men were up front, with five men behind them.

The five men in back wore a wide, horseshoe-shaped, piece of stone, tied at the waist with a leather string. When a ball came near them, they'd swing their hips and smack the ball up to the men up front. If a ball came in low to the ground, the men would dive at it with outstretched arms, like in volleyball, and keep the ball from touching the ground.

The Menon people were marvelous athletes, who could jump like a kangaroo and run like a gazelle. When the game was over, the losers were taken over to a tall stone pyramid, with short, steep, sharp-edged steps. The pyramid's top was a flat platform where the prisoners were assembled. With their hands tied behind their backs, the prisoners were taken to the edge of the pyramid and then pushed, where they tumbled down to their death.

Two large indian men, dressed in white robes, and leather sandals, came and loaded each body on a stretcher and carried them off. They took them and passed the bodies through a window, cut out of an altar wall, and two indians on the other side received the bodies and carried them away to be cremated.

Over the top of the window was a magnificently carved, winged angel, surrounded by stars and planets. In her right arm, the angel carried babies in swaddling clothes, and in her left, she carried adults; she seemed to be leaving the earth and ascending into the sky.

I didn't understand this ritual and I asked the Menon man standing beside me: "What does it mean?"

"It's an old indian belief," he explained. "That window is called 'The window of life.' It is meant to show that you are born here on earth and grow up and have a family. Then, when you die, your soul slips from it's clay vessel and your spirit is released from it's earthly confines; you are born again by passing through this window that represents your earthly house.

"So," he continued, "when a person dies, they bring them here and pass them through the window of life, and the angel comes to get them—you see her carrying adults and babies, that means that the adults begin new earthly lives, at the proper time of course, as babies."

Then, the scene in my dream changed, and I was standing beside the main street in the city. They were celebrating Hitler's 50th birthday; there were signs and banners everywhere proclaiming it. I saw a parade of men, dressed in medieval clothing, with swastikas on their chest, riding horses down the main street.

Then, Hitler appeared, wearing a shiny gold jacket with a Swastika armband. He was standing in a long black, convertible car; he balanced himself with his left hand on the front window, and with his right, he saluted the crowd, as the car passed by slowly.

Then, the scene changed again. I was in the Constellation Club, located on main street.

It must have been the time before I had the wreck, because Jami (Agnes) was with me. And I saw a woman who looked like Marlene Dietrich; she was dressed in a sailor's uniform and she was singing a song for Hitler's birthday.

She finished her song and came over, and Hitler

stood up from his table and kissed her hand. And as he kissed her hand, I woke up and found myself back on the beach of the Atlantic Ocean.

And later, as I thought about the dream, I wondered if, according to the Cryptoamnesia theory, I had put Marlene Dietrich and Hitler together in the Atlantic dream because I'd seen them in the movie theatre just hours before. But, if the dream was true, I wondered if, maybe, she had supported Hitler in this Atlantic experience.

It's possible, I thought, that stored in her unconscious memory was a past Atlantic memory of Hitler. Maybe, she instinctively distrusted him now, because of her previous life experience, and so she left Germany when he took control. I'm not sure, it's just my opinion.

Ed wrote in his diary: Two of the most important events in my time occurred in the 1940's. One was "The Philadelphia Experiment," conducted in October 1943. The other happened in Roswell, New Mexico in June 1947.

In 1943, under a veil of secrecy, the U.S. Navy conducted a series of tests, designed to make allied ships invisible to enemy radar. The German U-boats were sinking a lot of allied ships, and the Americans were desperate enough to try anything.

They never released the results of these tests to the public. The final test, resulting in a horrible nightmare, became known as "The Philadelphia Experiment." The navy took two ships out into the Philadelphia harbor, one was the test ship named The Eldridge. The Eldridge was equipped with a magnetic receiver, while the other ship received an extremely powerful, magnetic generator transmitter.

The plan was that, on command, the Eldridge would turn on her magnetic receiver and be blasted with a powerful cone of magnetic waves from the other ship's transmitter. The idea is based on the same principle, I believe, that everything is held together by magnets, so, in theory, it should be possible then, to make it disappear by the rearrangement of it's magnetic molecules.

But, if you were successful, could you make it reappear? The danger was, it had never been done with a force powerful enough to make a huge battleship disappear. And, the scientists had focused their attention on what would happen to the steel ship—they weren't thinking about the human bodies that were on the ship. What happens when you mix steel with flesh? The result, we now know is lead poisoning.

When the transmitter switch was flipped, the Eldridge was blasted with an incredible magnetic force. The unofficial report, given by the experiment's director, Dr. James Overstreet, stated that:

"Almost immediately, the Eldridge was covered in a thin, greenish fog, that gradually got thicker; we could see sailors running around in panic, their bodies took on the same greenish tint; appearing now as a pulsating current passing through their bodies.

"Slowly, the Eldridge began to fade from sight; five minutes passed.

"She has now completely vanished and even disappeared from the radar screen. We waited and watched. Ten minutes passed, and then suddenly, she reappeared at exactly the same spot where she had been. We heard the desperate cries from the sailors; some lying on the deck, unable to move. We sent out a small rescue boat.

"Thirteen men had died," Dr. Longstreet reported, "and many of the crew were badly burned. Some of the men who had been below, not exposed to the direct blast, seemed to be unharmed. They did, however, later report that their bodies had taken on the same greenish glow that everyone had seen covering the men on the upper deck.

"There were burnt bodies scattered across the deck. At one spot, all that was left of one man was his melted face, staring up lifelessly at the sky. We loaded up the living and took them to the hospital. Except for some occasional seizures, they seemed to be okay. So, they were assigned to other ships.

"Well," Dr. Longstreet continued, "later, they reported that one minute they were sitting on their bunks in the ship, drinking coffee, and suddenly, their bodies would take on that same greenish glow. Their body would shake violently, sometimes they'd sling the coffee cup wildly across the room—then, they disappeared; vanishing completely, as their horrified shipmates looked on.

"Ten minutes might pass, then, they'd reappear, just as the ship Eldridge had done, in the same spot, where minutes before, they'd been drinking coffee and talking to their buddy.

"I interviewed some of the sailors after this incident and asked them where they went during the ten minutes they were missing from sight. One sailor said that he found himself on a pirate ship that, from the ship's construction, and the pirate's clothes, he imagined, must've been from the 1600's.

"Another reported being on a ship so advanced that it hovered over the water when it traveled. I think what happened here is that the magnetic field between the two ships, maybe cross connected and created a vortex; which is a powerful whirlwind of air, like a tornado; it forms a vacuum in the center into which anything caught in the whirling motion is sucked into.

"This vortex could be a hole in the space time continuum, and those sailors fell into it. They may have suffered from a severe molecular transformation.

"If we had more time to figure out the correct measure of magnetic gauss, I think this experiment proves that it would be possible to transport a human body through time, and then reassemble it in the exact spot of departure."

This last statement made me think of H.G. Wells and "The Time Machine," Ed wrote. He didn't know how right he was when he wrote that book as fiction.

Not long after the war was over, Dr. Longstreet died in a mysterious car wreck. He had just spoken to an assistant who'd worked with him on the Philadelphia experiment; he had told the assistant that he had notes with him on the government cover up of the program, and that he was on his way to see him.

Dr. Longstreet also told the assistant that he believed government agents were watching him so he had to be careful.

Dr. Longstreet never made it to the assistant's house. The rumor was, that his phone was bugged and that government agents caused his car wreck. In the accident report there was no mention of his notes. The government later denied the assistant's claims of the missing notes.

For me, Ed wrote, this experiment proves my theory that the human body consists of, and can be controlled by magnets. If used properly, like I did when I cured myself of Tuberculosis, they can be of great benefit. If improperly used, they have great destructive power. But one thing that did surprise me about this, was the possibility of time travel by using a strong pulsating magnetic field—I hadn't thought of that.

After the Philadelphia Experiment, it didn't surprise me that the government also attempted to cover up the Roswell incident.

One night in June 1947, there was a bad electrical storm in the desert of Roswell, New Mexico. The next day, a rancher reported finding some strange looking debris scattered across his ranch.

The U.S. army came in and took control of the crash site, claiming it was only a weather balloon. Later, one of the soldiers who was there told someone that it was the remains of an alien crash. The soldier said that one of the aliens was still alive, wandering around in a daze near the crash site.

He described the alien as: "Small and frail looking; around four feet tall, with an enlarged head, large round eyes, small nose and mouth, and they had gray skin. They had hands with fingers and feet with toes, much like our own; but they were thin and delicate looking. The one alien who was alive, later died from his injuries. But before he died, he communicated telepathically, that: 'more of my people are coming.'"

The soldier said the army covers these things up because they want to study the ship's technology, with the hope of duplicating it, and they don't want the Russians to know about it. But I heard later, Ed wrote, that Joseph Stalin had heard about Roswell and was trying to get Soviet agents here to find out what they could about it.

After the Roswell incident, I felt better about the dreams I'd had where I encountered the aliens. I felt stronger than ever about their existence. Because of Roswell, people here had now seen in the flesh what I had been shown in my dreams.

I've often wondered, why would God create such a vast universe and only put one species of intelligent life on a tiny planet called earth?

From what I'd been shown in my dreams, the aliens had lived among us on the earth, in Atlantis. Something had either destroyed them or caused them to leave. Was it a plague, or had they simply left to avoid the persecution from humans, like Hitler had done to the Jews in Germany?

As I was thinking about the aliens, I remembered Nick's explanation for the aliens; the one he got from reading the Bible in Genesis 6, 1-3.

It said: "Now a population explosion took place on the earth. It was at this time that beings from the spirit world looked upon the beautiful earth women and took any they desired to be their wives."

I think God got mad about this because these spirit beings from "another world" were not supposed to do this. Well, to me, that explains that there was "another world" somewhere, inhabited by intelligent life forms.

Well, then I got out all the information that Dr. Edgar Cayce had given on Atlantis, and I found some fascinating things. I think he was the prophet that Madame Drusa said would come along with detailed information about Atlantis. Here are some excerpts from the Cayce readings for people who had past lives in Atlantis:

Reading #5056-1 (May, 1944): "in Atlantean land in those periods before Adam was in the earth. Among those who were then thought projections." (Possible aliens? Ed L.)

Reading #364-4: "the Sons of the Creative Force (Spirit Beings) looked upon the daughters of men; polluted themselves with those mixtures."

For me, the Edgar Cayce readings seemed to be saying that these spirit beings had projected themselves into flesh to indulge themselves with the beautiful earth women. But when they did this, their punishment for this, was that now they were entrapped in a material body, and now subject from birth to death to the laws of the physical universe.

They had gradually lost the ability to move in and out of these material bodies that they'd taken on to enjoy the sensual pleasures.

Cayce said that for awhile, the spirit beings were able to keep in touch with the realms from which they came before they took on flesh in Atlantis. Reading #5037 (April 19, 1944):

"in Atlantis, a priestess, a keeper of the white stone or that through which many of the peoples, (Spirit Beings) before the first destructions in Atlantis, kept their accord with the universal consciousness (the other world, Ed L.) through speaking to and through those activities."

There has always been a lively debate, Ed wrote, among those who believed in spaceships, that the vehicle described by Ezekiel 1:15-25, in the Bible, was a spaceship.

In reading #1859-1 (April 7, 1939) Cayce said that some people living in the lands of Yucatan and Egypt had been foretold of Atlantis' destruction. Cayce stated that the people fled in:

"the manners of transportation through airships of that period such as Ezekiel described at a much later date."

Reading #1177-1 Cayce said that one man: "was among those who journeyed from Atlantis to Egypt, entity young at the time, aided in development of mechanical appliances for cutting stone, etc." (maybe that was me, Ed L.)

When Edgar Cayce was in his hypnotic trance, he was asked how The Great Pyramid was built. He said: "By the cosmic forces of nature, that allow for iron to swim in water, stone also floats in the air."

In several readings given to different people, Cayce said that they had been involved in saving the historical records of Atlantis. Reading #378-16 (Oct. 29, 1933):

"records were preserved by entity in the hall of records (Sphinx). In position, this lies as the light falls between the Sphinx's paws.

Reading #2537-1 (July 17, 1941): "These records may be found, especially when the house or tomb of records (Sphinx) is opened, in a few years from now."

Reading #3575-2 (Jan. 20, 1944): "In Egypt, of the Atlanteans who set about to preserve records—(the entity) came with those groups who established the hall of records (Sphinx) and may directly or indirectly be among those who will yet bring these Atlantic records to light."

Dr. Cayce was asked: "Give in detail what the sealed room (Sphinx) contains."

Cayce answered: "A record of Atlantis from the beginning of those periods when the Spirit took form; together with the record of it's destruction and the record of the people's travels; together with whom, what, and where the opening of the records would come, that are copies from the sunken Atlantis."

I got excited, Ed wrote, when I read the part where Cayce said that the tomb of records (in Sphinx) would be opened in a few years. And that someone would be "directly or indirectly among those who will yet bring these to light."

In one of his readings, Cayce suggested: "that it would be natural for the person who discovers these things (records of Atlantis in the Sphinx); that it would not be mysterious to them, though they may not understand them, because the entity is seeking to understand the mind of the ancients."

Seek and ye shall find, I thought. I thought it strange, that here Cayce had labored to lay out all this information, and no one seemed to be interested in learning about it. Edgar Cayce had even explained where the entrance to the Sphinx was; I was determined to find it.

Ed's diary, July 10, 1951:

I saw an ad today in the Miami Herald newspaper, promoting a guided tour of Egypt's pyramids. I sent a money order to the tour guide, Famir Mamoud, and made arrangements for him to meet me at the airport in Cairo.

On July 22, I put a sign on Coral Castle's iron front door: "Closed, gone to Egypt for a week. Open when I get back. Ed L."

I made arrangements with Herman Harmless to look after the place while I was gone. I left on the 6:30 a.m. bus the next morning for Miami. I flew from Miami to New York and caught a direct flight from there to Cairo. I got into Cairo at six o'clock that evening. When I had gone through customs, and emerged into the airport lobby, I began looking for my guide, Famir Mamoud.

From the picture he'd sent me, I was looking for a fat man with a beard. The lobby was packed with people, but just then I spotted a tall thin man, holding up a sign with my name on it. I picked up my bags and made my way through the crowd to where he stood.

"I'm your man," I said, shaking hands. "Where's Famir?"

"Welcome to Egypt," he said. "I'm Raoul. Famir is waiting in the car, he's feeling a bit poorly—something he ate; he's always eating, you'll see. Come with me," he said, picking up my bags.

I didn't have much time to look around in the airport; I had to stay right on Raoul's tail, so as not to lose him in the crowd. Later, I would wish I'd seen a wanted poster of Famir Mamoud on the lobby wall. He was a thief, who specialized in fleecing unsuspecting tourists.

We stepped out into the heat and street noise of Cairo. The air was filled with the spicy aroma from the food being cooked over wood charcoal in the homemade stalls of the street vendors. This smell mingled with the strong scent of hash being smoked on a waterpipe. Groups of turban-clad men were sitting on the street side, drinking hot tea in a small clear glass and smoking hash. They were as casual about smoking it as people with cigarettes.

Famir's long black cadillac was parked on the other side of the street. Raoul opened the trunk, put my bags in and then opened the back door for me. I got in and introduced myself to Famir.

"I'm sorry I'm not feeling well," Famir said, "but I just took some bicarbonate soda, so I'll be better I'm sure."

Famir was short and fat, about 5 ft. 4 in. and over two hundred pounds. He was sweating in the heat and kept wiping his brow with a handkerchief. He was dressed in a black suit, white shirt with a black bow tie and shiny black dress shoes with thin black socks.

"Well," Famir said, "I have good news and bad news. I was able to secure the government's permission to spend the night near the Sphinx, but it cost me an extra fifty dollars—the bribe went up, you see."

"You had to bribe someone?" I asked.

"Oh, yes of course, that's the way it works here. You see, it's illegal to camp near the Sphinx. The Sphinx is still a sacred monument to many of the people here—it's greatly revered. It would be an insult—especially for a foreigner to be camped on the sacred grounds. That's where the bribe comes in, so I'll have to ask you to reimburse me for that."

I had no way of knowing if he was lying or not,

so I had to pay him. I was happy to be here and just figured that this was part of the culture, and I'd have to put up with it, so I decided to make the best of it.

I was supposed to be in Egypt for a week, but I didn't make it that long, thanks to Famir. What happened was this. We got a late start the next day, Famir was still complaining about his stomach. It wasn't until the late afternoon when we got to The Great Pyramid.

One good thing about the delay, was that I found a rare book in a little gift shop near The Great Pyramid. It was written by Alvarez Lopez, who had done extensive research on the granite coffin inside the King's Chamber. I didn't have time to read it now, but I bought a copy to take home with me.

When we got to The Great Pyramid, Famir declined to go in with me. He had worn the same black rumpled suit as yesterday, and he was already hot and tired; he said he was afraid of heights, so we left him behind.

Our guide, Ali Gabri, warned us before we climbed up the ladder to the entrance: "The descending passage is only 4 ft. wide and 4 ft. tall, and treacherously sloped at a steep angle. Then, we'll have to crawl on our hands and knees before we come to the Grand Gallery.

"The Gallery passage is steeply sloped upwards, and slippery from bat droppings. On either side of the Gallery walls, there are wide notches for your feet; be sure you've got a firm footing before you step upward. If you fall, there's nothing to catch you at the bottom but hard granite stones.

"You notice, there are no lawyers around here, passing out cards. I warn you now, The Great Pyramid is so revered that it is unlawful to sue for accidents.

"You know it's revered when the lawyers agreed to this, especially with so many tourists here, so please plan any accidents with LLoyds of London, they're the only ones who might insure you."

Then Gabri said: "Well, nobody left—that's unusual; at least one person always leaves after my speech. Okay, brave souls, let's begin. My valued assistant, Shamir, will follow us from behind to watch out for you, and remind you to be careful."

Equipped with four kerosene lanterns, we climbed up the creaky ladder to the entrance and made our way, bent over, through the descending passage. Being so small, I had no problem negotiating the cramped passage.

After passing up the slippery steps of the Grand Gallery—Gabri didn't tell us of the stench of the bat droppings—we ducked under a short hallway, and then, to our great delight, we entered the glory of the King's Chamber.

The kerosene lamps illuminated a beautiful room; the walls, floor and ceiling, were all made of finely polished red granite; perfectly squared and jointed, so they appeared almost seamless.

The lidless coffin was cut from a solid block of chocolate colored granite. Because of it's size, 6 ft. long, 2 ft. 3 in. wide, and 3 ft. deep, it could easily contain a human body, so it has been called a coffin.

I walked over and knelt down by the coffin and ran my hand along it's cool smooth sides. It was incredibly cool in here, while outside, the heat was almost unbearable.

As I touched the coffin, I thought of the Atlantic dream I'd had where the Menon man had told me the secret of The Great Pyramid lay in the coffin of the King's Chamber. But what could he mean by this? As I'd said earlier, I never believed that the coffin was meant to hold a body, because it had been proven that a lid had never existed for the coffin.

And in those days, no self-respecting Pharaoh would be buried in a lidless coffin. To the Egyptians, reincarnation was necessary for imperfect souls. The dead body was "preserved after death as a material basis for the living soul to re-enter the earth at the appointed time."

It was in the late afternoon when the tour was over. As I made my way back to our jeep, I found Famir Mamoud, sitting in the jeep's shade, drinking the strong tea and smoking a bowl of hash with some Great Pyramid groupies. They invited me to join them, but I declined, not wishing to bombard my brain with that toxic weed; I had seen how it made them act and I wanted no part of it.

Famir and I waited until dusk, when the tourists and tour guides had left. Then, we drove the jeep over in front of the Sphinx and parked it. We stretched a tent out from the jeep's roof and got ready for the night. My plan was to wait for Famir to go to sleep, and then I was going to sneak out and look for Cayce's secret doorway into the Sphinx.

I had gotten to the Sphinx in time to watch where the sun's setting rays had landed between the Sphinxs' paws (where Cayce had said the secret entrance existed).

Most of the Sphinx is composed of two layers of brick; but as I examined it as the sun went down, I found that the inner contours of the two forepaws had been filled in with large limestone blocks. The right hindpaw was built entirely of similar limestone blocks. There were also large limestone blocks at the rear of the body, where the tail begins.

I wondered why they would build the whole Sphinx of bricks except for these two areas. Later, as I thought of this, I remembered another of Cayce's readings, (#3575-2; Nov. 26, 1937):

"Entity among the first to set the records (in Sphinx) that are yet to be discovered of Atlantean time; and for the preservation of data that is yet to be found from the chambers of the way between the Sphinx and the The Great Pyramid."

Then it made sense to me. There must be a front entrance at the right paw, and also a back, underground entrance at the tail, leading to The Great Pyramid. The back of the Sphinx, where the tail is, would be the quickest route leading back to the Pyramid.

That could be the reason they used the huge limestone blocks because they would make for a perfect revolving doorway; much like the 9 ton revolving doorway I made on the east side of Coral Castle.

Famir made a small campfire near the jeep with some firewood he'd brought. At night, the intense heat of the day turned cool, so he brought blankets for us. We ate curried goat, rice and fig cakes for supper and drank hot tea. I was exhausted from the day's heat and the laborious climb into The Great Pyramid.

I told Famir I was going to bed and he said he was going to sit up for awhile and watch the stars come out. I could usually program my mind to wake up at a certain time and it rarely failed me, but tonight was different.

I guess I was more exhausted than I thought. But I remember, I was dreaming about The Great Pyramid, and I kept thinking that there must be a fire inside of it because I kept smelling a strong burning odor of smoke. Finally, it got so strong, I began coughing so hard it woke me up. I sat straight up in my bed roll, dazed, and saw the whole tent was filled with smoke.

In the smoky haze, I looked and saw Famir, sitting close to me, with a silly grin on his face. He was smoking hash on the water pipe. He took the pipe out of his mouth and said:

"Good morning, my friend. It's hash time—will you join me?"

My lungs felt queezy from breathing in all that hash smoke, and my head was dizzy. I noticed that when I spoke it seemed to take forever to get the words out:

"What time is it?" I asked.

Famir looked at his pocket watch: "It's three o'clock in the morning."

"Three o'clock?"

I don't know how long I had been inhaling the

hash smoke but it had a profound effect on me. Everything seemed to take place in slow motion. I was keenly aware of every movement my body made, and also sounds became crisp and clear; I heard the sound of a dog barking in the distance—he must be in the city of Cairo, I thought.

I wanted to move fast out of the tent, before I inhaled any more smoke, but as I went to move, I noticed that it seemed to take forever, and I found it difficult to get untangled from my bed roll; my difficulties at this seemed to delight Famir.

"I've got to get some fresh air," I mumbled, and made my way out of the tent. I did have the presence of mind to pick up my shaving kit, where I kept some matches and two small doughnut shaped magnets that I always traveled with. But, in my state of confusion, I left my wallet near my bed roll. I picked up a lantern and walked over to the Sphinx.

I was fortunate, there was a half-moon out tonight, so I had good light to see by. I stopped when I reached the area inside the two front paws.

I tried taking in some deep breaths to clear my head from the effects of the hash, but to no avail; everything still went in a slow motion time.

I looked up at the moon and it seemed brighter—I seemed to be able to make out the darker portion of the half-exposed face, but I later laid this to the narcotic effects of the strong hashish. No wonder people got hooked on smoking this stuff, I thought, everything looks different and deceivingly beautiful.

I held the lantern up to where the huge limestone blocks were, where I thought, from seeing the sun's shadow fall, the entrance door might be. The problem would be, how would I open it? I knew that, of course, it wouldn't be as easy as pushing it open, like I had designed my 9 ton castle gate.

And then I thought, how silly and pretentious of me to think I could come here and discover something that had been hidden for perhaps 10,000 years. But, encouraged by my success at Coral Castle, I had, perhaps, too much self-confidence. Well, this is my first trip, I'll do what I can and study it, and maybe later, I'll find a way.

I was aggravated that I had come all this way, solely for this purpose, and now I seemed to be handicapped by the effects of the hash. At first, I got mad with Famir, but then I thought, well, if he hadn't been smoking it, I might not have awakened and had this opportunity. Like I do everything else in my life, I thought, well, I'm here, I must not complain, but make the best of it.

Well, I thought, I'll sit down a minute and think about this thing. I went to take one of the little magnets out of my shaving kit and I dropped one of them.

I heard it hit on the limestone floor and I shined my lantern down to look for it. But it hadn't landed on the floor—as I shined the light down to look for it—there it was, stuck against the inner limestone wall, near the right front paw.

This made me curious. I knew, and it has been proven that the shape and the alignment of The Great Pyramid causes a magnetic field inside it, but was it powerful enough to go as far as the Sphinx? Or, was there something else behind the wall (some kind of metal perhaps) that caused the magnet to be attracted to it?

I bent down and pulled the magnet away from the wall. Then, I began to run the magnet slowly across the face of the stone. As the magnet went across the stone's middle, I felt a stronger magnetic pull; and I heard a faint clicking sound, a metal against metal sound.

I pulled the magnet across this area repeatedly, until I had heard seven distinct clicks. On the seventh click, to my great surprise, a four foot bottom section of the stone swung slowly open. I squeezed through the small opening. On the other side of the doorway, I saw a window-sized, metal panel control box. I didn't spend much time thinking about it's engineering.

I figured that it had a simple plan of opening at seven clicks from an outside magnet; perhaps in it's simplicity was it's genius. I never would've thought to run a magnet over the stone. Like a lot of discoveries, this one too was made by accident.

I ran the magnet back over the center of the metal box and on the seventh click, the stone door slowly swung back into place. I now found myself in a small 8 by 10 room of white limestone. Painted in vivid colors on the wall, were scenes that I recognized from one of my Atlantic dreams. One scene showed the Mayans putting the body of a Menon man (men from the sky) through the "Window of Life" and the angel was seen above this, carrying a human baby and a baby Menon in it's arms.

Below this scene on the wall was a descending stone staircase. As I looked at the staircase, I could barely contain my excitement. One minute, I felt like Howard Carter must've felt when he discovered the entrance to Tut's tomb. And the next minute, I felt like this couldn't be happening; my mind must be under the hallucinations of the narcotic hash.

I reached out and touched the wall where the painting was. The limestone was cool to my touch. I can feel it, this has to be real, I thought. Taking up my lantern, I walked slowly and carefully down the smooth stone steps. The steps ended and I emerged into a limestone tunnel, with what seemed to be about a twelve foot high, smoothly finished, limestone ceiling.

On both sides of the tunnel, there were doorways cut into the stone sides, appearing to be about 4 ft. wide and 10 ft. high. On left side, it appeared to be a place for storing records, artwork and documents; there were tall, aluminum-looking filing cabinets up against the wall. And the right side seemed to be for storing equipment and furniture.

On the right side, I saw futuristic looking planes,

shaped like stingrays; they resembled the same ones I'd seen in my Atlantic dreams. There were cars, trucks and tanks, with the curved-blade swastikas painted on them; it was the same swastika I'd seen in pictures of the Mayan Pyramids.

On the left side, there were photos, made of what appeared to be a thin metal, scattered everywhere. I saw black military uniforms, with sewn Swastikas on the arms, that were left in piles; various forms of odd looking, black metal rifles. It all seemed to be thrown in here with no attempt at any form of organization.

There seemed to be one section of photos that was fairly well organized. In it, I found nothing but photos of singing and motion picture stars from the present time realm. At first, I was puzzled at why finding this should surprise me. Solomon had said, "There is nothing new under the sun. Whatever is, has been and will be again."

I remembered Edgar Cayce said, "Each soul chooses the time, place and the people for it's return." And so, maybe, this had been like a fraternity of Atlantic souls that had existed in Atlantis, and had all chosen to come back in my present time.

And yet, knowing this, I still found it astonishing to behold. Later, I remembered that Napoleon had visited The Great Pyramid, as Alexander the Great had before him. Napoleon had gone into the King's Chamber alone. They said he came out pale looking. When they asked him what he'd seen, he mentioned that he had received a vision of his destiny.

Then, he said, he: "never wanted it mentioned again." He almost revealed it, right before he died in St. Helena, but they said he shook his said, saying, "No. What's the use? You'd never believe me." I did take some comfort in Napoleon's words as I looked at these photographs.

I saw a photograph of Humphrey Bogart and Lauren Bacall; her hand was holding his arm as he held a gun in his right hand. They had a concerned look on their face, as though they were expecting some sinister character. There was a picture of W.C. Fields, with his head resting on Mae West's shoulder.

But my favorite was a photograph of the Three Stooges, dressed in Nazi uniforms; Moe had a cropped mustache and was portraying Hitler; Larry was Josef Goebbels, and Curly was Herman Goering. A caption under the photo read: The Three Stooges in "I'll never Heil Again!" Released by Atlantic Motion Pictures. Ironically, Herman and I had seen this film, around 1940, I think it was.

I kept this Stooge photo to have some later proof of what I'd seen here. In another room, I saw the bodies of several different species of alien-like people. Some of them were encased in glass tombs. As I viewed the gray skinned bodies, I thought of the passage in Genesis, about the spirit beings taking earth women for their wives. I wondered if these bodies were perhaps the result of that experiment.

I decided to leave this room, and follow the tunnel and see where it ended. The tunnel made a gentle curve in the general direction of where I thought The Great Pyramid was.

I walked for what seemed to be the length of a football field, until the tunnel emerged in a large room that reminded me of a movie theatre, with a down sloping floor. The soft theatre chairs were covered in a deep purple velvet cloth. I climbed up some stone steps leading into the projection room. I pushed open a metal door and went inside.

In front of me, I saw the metal projector, pointed at a large white screen below, surrounded by a panel box of buttons and levers beneath it. There were six metal easy chairs in front of the panel, with tattered purple cloth coverings. I laid the Stooge picture down on the panel box, wiped the dust off a chair, and I sat down. I began to study the various buttons and levers.

I saw an ivory colored cue ball, imbedded halfway into the panel; it had a small emblem of a positive sign above it and below it was a negative sign. With my index finger, I rolled the ball upwards, in the direction of the positive sign.

Immediately, a cone of light beamed out of the projector and the screen down below was hit with a grainy, black and white picture, accompanied by the sound of static, as though there had been a sudden power failure. As I busied myself looking over the panel board, to see if I could get a clear picture to come on, the static abruptly stopped and emerged into a nice color picture.

But the sound was very loud. I looked and saw the symbol of a pair of open lips, and down below it was a pair of closed lips. In between the lips was another cue ball. I rolled the ball in the direction of the closed lips and found that I could control the volume, so I adjusted it to a comfortable level.

On the screen down below me, I saw a black plane, formed like a stingray, flying through a dark sky. The plane hovered and then landed on a huge, flat-top pyramid. A door opened and Adolf Hitler stepped from the plane and onto the pyramid. He smiled and saluted a frenzied adoring crowd down below. It appeared to be the same type scene that I'd seen in my Atlantic dreams.

Hitler walked slowly down the pyramid steps, pausing for effect now and then, as he saluted the cheering crowd. The scene changed to nighttime; I saw a man standing on top of a pyramid, lit up with torches around him. He had on a dark suit, with a black and white bow tie and he was smoking a pipe.

The man said, "Welcome to Past Times. I'm Munroe R. Murrow. This pyramid I'm standing on is very similar to the one Adolfo Hitler made a lot of his early speeches from in Atlantis. From where I'm standing, Atlantis would've been in that direction, where the sea is," he said, pointing.

"It has now been fifty years since Adolfo Hitler was assassinated and Atlantis was destroyed by the death ray. Join me tonight, as we look at, Atlantis: "The Final Destruction."

Then, the scene changed to people of all races fighting in the streets, with policemen trying to break them up. Some of the pyramid buildings in the background were on fire.

Munroe Murrow's voice was heard narrating the film: "When Adolfo Hitler came to power, Atlantis was in great turmoil. Hitler's Nazis won the street battles and his promise to restore order put him in office.

"Things got better, for most people. People went back to work, and to the movies." (The scene changed to a varying collage of popular movies. I saw scenes of movies I knew, such as "Seventh Sinners," with Marlene Dietrich; "Destry," with James Stewart; W.C. Fields and Mae West; The Marx Brothers, and The Three Stooges. Ed L.)

"Things stayed good for seven years," Murrow said, "until Adolfo Hitler invaded a sect of rebels in the Cusancho mountains who had refused to pay taxes. They were better armed and in greater strength than Hitler had realized. Hitler's forces were slaughtered when they got into the mountains." The film switched, showing dead soldiers scattered on a mountain side. And then it switched to a camp of rebel soldiers, firing their guns in the air, celebrating victory.

"The rebels began taking cities, on their way to the capital city of Germania. In a desperate attempt to rally his people, Hitler came to the Pyramid of the Sun to speak, and he was assassinated by a traitor."

The film switched to Hitler speaking from the pyramid top on a bright sunny day. As Hitler ended his speech, he stepped from behind a podium and saluted the crowd. He had taken one step down the pyramid, when a rifle shot rang out; Hitler was hit in the chest and tumbled down to his death.

"The killer was caught," Murrow said, "and brought to the same pyramid where Hitler died. He was pushed to his death."

The scene switched to a man standing at the top of the pyramid with his hands tied behind his back. A man in a Nazi uniform kicked the man in his back, and he tumbled down the stone steps.

"In an effort to stop the rebels from taking the city of Germania," Murrow said, "some of Hitler's radical followers unleashed the untested death ray. They set it up on a tall pyramid, and aimed it at the mountains of the rebel stronghold. When it was switched on, the blast from a cone of red light, set off a chain of volcanic eruptions and earthquakes.

"These last scenes of Atlantis," Murrow said, "were filmed by those who narrowly escaped in air ships."

The film showed people running for their lives in bombed out ruins. There were traffic jams and the sea was crowded with ships, large and small, fleeing the coming devastation, as the sky became dark with smoke and volcanic ash.

As I watched a dying Atlantis, Ed wrote later, the film got wobbly, as though someone was losing control of the camera. Then, there was a loud crashing sound, as though the camera had been dropped, and suddenly the film went back to a black and white static.

I looked for a button to try and bring the picture back, when I saw a red button start flashing. I wasn't sure what to do, but I thought the button might be something like a breaker switch that would bring back the picture, so I pushed it.

When I did, to my surprise, a thick green smoke blasted out of the wall below my feet, engulfing the entire room. That was the last recollection that I had of being in the Sphinx. I don't know how I went out. Later, when I thought about it, I wondered if the green gas had been some sort of protection device, cleverly inserted to go off as the historical film was over.

Had someone planned that a person like me would come along, and follow the prophet Edgar Cayce's visions, to the secret doorway of the Sphinx? And then, after seeing these things, the green gas was used to make the person question the things they'd seen? I'll never know.

It was several days before my mind was completely clear, and then these things of the Sphinx came back slowly to me. I thought of the men in the Philadelphia experiment, whose bodies had given off a greenish glow when they were exposed to the intense blast of magnetic energy. And then, their bodies and the ship vanished from sight.

I wondered if, somehow, there had been a pulsating magnetic field created inside the blast of greenish gas in the Sphinx that caused a similar molecular transformation; like the men of the Philadelphia experiment, and my body was transported to the area near the Sphinx. I wondered if the things I saw in the Sphinx were real, or the product of the things I'd seen in my dreams and visions; and if I do have Cryptoamnesia, perhaps these things came from my unconscious memories of things I'd read and movies I'd seen.

I don't know, it's just my opinion, as I stated in the beginning of this diary.

Later, I wondered if I'd even gone into the Sphinx; I wondered if my mind had conjured up the whole thing from the narcotic effects of the strong hashish. I thought, maybe I just wandered outside the tent and collapsed in the sand.

It was sort of like the feeling I had that time when I'd snorted the tobacco with the indians in Chaco Canyon, only this hash stuff was a lot more powerful. I don't know how they keep smoking so much of it. Maybe it makes camel riding more comfortable, I don't know. I sure wished I knew the truth of what happened that night.

I had waited so long for the trip to Egypt, and then, to have it ruined by some sweaty, hash smoking thief of a guide. With my luck, if it was raining soup, I'd have a fork. Oh well, that's life I guess. Gotta move on. But I'd have given anything to have been able to retrieve that Three Stooges photo, if it was ever there, that is.

Anyway, the next thing I knew, after the green gas hit me, I woke up with my face in the hot sand of the desert, not far from the Sphinx. I was weak and dizzy; as I tried to lift my head out of the sand, in the distance, I saw some men coming towards me, but I was too weak to keep my head up, and I fell back to the sand.

Then, I felt something poking me in the back, and I heard a voice in broken English saying, "Get up! Get up!" I rolled over and sat up, and brushed the sand off my face. Shielding my eyes from the sun with my hand, I saw four men in police uniforms standing around me. A big fat man, with an acne scarred face, and dressed in an officer's uniform, said in broken English:

"What you doing here?"

"What's the problem officer? My guide Famir said he had the proper paperwork to spend the night out here—"

"Proper paperwork? To camp on sacred grounds? You Americans! You don't "camp" on holy sites! Some passing Bedouins reported your "camp," you're lucky they didn't slit your throat."

"Sir," I said, standing up, "I'm sorry, but Famir, my guide said—"

"Famir? Can't you read? Didn't you see his wanted poster in the airport, warning tourists not to use him? He's a thief."

I looked in the direction of where our tent was, and saw that it was gone. Famir had packed up and taken everything. After a sincere apology, the captain let me go, on the condition that I leave Egypt immediately. I agreed and left on a four o'clock flight (Famir had kindly left my airline tickets behind).

I wished that I'd had more time to go back to the Sphinx, look for the hidden door, and confirm what I thought I'd seen. Oh well, maybe next time. When I got back to Homestead, Ed wrote, I was exhausted and I slept for almost a whole day. I called Herman up and he came over and we ate lunch at the Florida table.

I told him about leaving the tent to get away from the hash smoke and what had happened to me inside the Sphinx. I explained that I was surprised at what the hash had done to me.

"Oh, that doesn't surprise me," Herman said. "I read where that Middle East hash is powerful stuff.

"Wouldn't you know it?—you go all the way over there, and then get hooked up with a crooked, hash smoking guide."

"Yeah, my luck. But you know, the strange thing is, Edgar Cayce said the history of Atlantis was stored in the Sphinx; and what I saw was a lot like the Atlantic dreams I'd had. If I could only be sure if I've got Cryptoamnesia, or if those things really happened.

"You know Herman, sometimes I feel like my life's been a failure. I mean, I worked so hard to put this castle together, hoping Agnes would come and marry me. Maybe I look like a fool now."

"Oh, that's not important."

"What do you mean?"

"Look, you've always followed your dreams. A lot of people say they are gonna do things and never do them. One thing I've noticed about you, if you say it, you do it. I admire that. Oh, I admit, I used to think you were crazy, waiting for her, but not anymore."

"Why's that?"

"Well, you made up your mind to wait. I think what triggered that was when Madame Drusa had said, before you were born prematurely, that you'd never be able to wait for anything. So, in your patient waiting, you proved her wrong. The thing that kept you alive, see, was the hope that she'd come."

"You don't think that people think I'm a fool for what I did?"

"Oh, sure, some do—I've heard them say so. But I don't argue with them, they have no heart; they don't understand the kind of love you have for Agnes. She was the only girl who could have touched something in you, that made you create this castle monument to her."

One afternoon at four o'clock, Ed wrote, after I'd

closed the castle for the day, I sat down in my stone easy chair and began reading the book on The Great Pyramid; the one I'd picked up in Egypt by Alvarez Lopez.

Like me, Lopez was convinced that the coffin in the Pyramid had never been built to hold a body. He measured the granite coffin and then he converted the measurements from inches into miles. He discovered that these mathematical figures gave the distance from the earth to the sun and the weight of the earth, moon and sun. Lopez believed that an advanced race of people had secreted their knowledge of higher mathematics into the dimensions of the Pyramid's coffin. I remembered the Atlantic dream I had where the Menon man had told me the secret of the Pyramid lay in the coffin. I was now convinced that this was the secret they had left behind. The coffin had been designed to hold not a physical body, but a body of advanced astronomical knowledge.

Ed started complaining of stomach pain in late November of 1951, Herman said. I tried to get him to go to a doctor but he refused. He said it may just be an ulcer and that it would pass. On the morning of December 17, 1951, Herman said, Ed got up with terrible stomach pains. In agonizing pain, Ed decorated the Valentine table, where he had hoped to marry Agnes, with a red table cloth.

He set out red dishes and drinking glasses, with his best silverware and red cloth napkins.

Then he set a framed picture of Agnes in the red plate where she would have sat and ate with him. Ed was so sick, he thought he was going to die, and he decided to go to the hospital. He sat down to write his last letter to Agnes. But for some unknown reason, he never mailed it, but left it behind in a box in his room. Ed wrote:

To Agnes, my Sweet Sixteen,

Hi darling, I hope this letter finds you happy and healthy. I don't feel so good today—bad stomach pains; I'm going to the hospital. I have a feeling I won't be coming back, so this may be my last letter.

I wanted you to know that my love is as fresh and strong as it was on the day I first saw you, when you walked into my shop in Latvia. After I saw you, I never looked at another woman. I'm taking one last look at the castle I built for you; I wish you'd come and see it after I'm gone, I think you'd like it, especially the Valentine table. Aggie, I have to go now, the pain is getting bad. I only wanted you to know that I'll wait for you still, as long as I have a body here. I wonder now where we go when it's over; I think there's another dimension we step into.

With all my love,

Ed L.

Ed put on the record "At Last" Herman Harmless said, and sat down at the Valentine's table and listened to it. When it was over, he got up and walked out the front door. He put up a sign on the front door saying: "Going to the hospital."

I was down in Key West, on a fishing trip, Herman said. Ed had called my wife Opal and told her where he was going. Ed took a cigar box of photos, his diary, and then he took a bus to Jackson Memorial Hospital, in Miami.

Shortly after Ed checked into the hospital, he slipped into a coma. I got there on the morning of the second day that Ed was in the hospital, Herman said. The doctor told me that Ed had stomach cancer: "Herman, I don't think he'll come out of this coma," the doctor said.

"Don't count this man out yet Doc," Herman said. Then I told him about how Ed had cured himself of Tuberculosis and the doctor was surprised to hear it.

I pulled up a chair, right next to Ed's head, Herman said, and I began to talk to him. I said: "Ed, don't you leave without coming back and telling me where you are. Knowing you, you're somewhere, doing something and I want to know about it."

Ed was silent as I talked to him. Then, I thought, maybe I should say something more drastic, something that might shock him into waking up. So, I said, "Ed, I bumped into Agnes when I went by the castle. I told her you were in the hospital, sick, and that when you got better you'd come and see her. Yeah, I guess she's sitting right there in the castle, waiting for you to get out. If you don't hurry up and get well, she might get bored and go back home. Don't you want to see her?"

But not even telling him that, brought him out of the coma, Herman said. It was lunch time now. I told Ed I was going across the street and eat some smoked sausage and rice for lunch (I was still trying to lure him out of the coma, knowing he loved smoked sausage like I did). I got up out of my chair and left the room.

I had gotten down the hallway, and was about to walk out the front door, when a nurse came running up to me, out of breath. She said, "Mr. Harmless, he woke up! He said to bring him a plate of sausage and rice—he must've heard you." So I did, and Ed and I ate our lunch. He looked tired and weak, but after he ate, he seemed to get stronger.

Ed asked me what was wrong with him. I wasn't sure what to say, and noticing my hesitation, he asked me to tell him the truth. I said, "Ed, you've got stomach cancer. Look, why don't I go back to the castle and get your magnet machine, the one you used to help you beat tuberculosis. I remember you saying you thought cancer couldn't live in a magnetic field."

But Ed refused. He said, "No, don't bother Herman—I'm just too tired. I had the will to live in those days; I wanted to finish the castle for Agnes. But my work here is over, I'm ready for the next dimension."

Ed was too weak to write now, Herman said, and he pointed to his diary, "Herman," he said weakly, "I want you to write down a vision of Atlantis I had." So

I wrote it down as he spoke.

Ed said that right before he slipped into the coma, he had been looking at Agnes' photo.

When I slipped into the coma, Ed said, my spirit rose above the bed, and I looked down on my body. Then, I heard something like a rushing wind, and the room became a dark misty fog. I was carried away in the spirit; I knew it was a spiritual journey because my body was still on the bed, in room 202, at Jackson Memorial Hospital.

Suddenly, I found myself floating above the hospital, and then, I drifted away, like an untethered balloon. I must've drifted in a southwest direction from Miami, because I looked down below me, and saw that I was over the Coral Castle. It was a strange feeling, to see the gray stone castle I'd built; it seemed even grayer now, with no life in it.

Then, I drifted back towards Miami and out over the sea. The wind was whipping the waves up into large whitecaps. As I neared the island of Bimini, where Edgar Cayce said Atlantis existed, the water was a clear, blue-green color; in the water below me, I saw a swirling funnel of water (perhaps creating a vortex, like Dr. Longstreet in the Philadelphia Experiment mentioned) with a six foot wide mouth.

As I drifted over the tunnel of water, I felt a strong, vacuum-like pull and I was sucked into the tunnel. My spiritual journey, Ed said, took me back to Atlantis. I felt peace and calm—there was no urgency of drowning, only a slightly dizzy feeling, like I'd felt before, in some of my Atlantic visions.

When I emerged, it was dry land again, like it was 10,000 years ago. I was near the front of the Constellation Club, where Agnes (Jami) and I used to go dancing.

There was a Menon man, (men from the sky) dressed in a red silk robe, sitting on a stone bench. He was writing something on a tablet of paper. He looked at me and smiled.

"Congratulations," he said, "you have finished the work you were given to do. You developed patience and were loyal to the end; you will receive your reward. Now, go inside, your friends are waiting for you."

"What's going on? I don't understand," I said.

But he waved me on, saying, "Don't worry, you'll be protected. Your name is in the Book of Life; but don't stay here, flee to the mainland, Atlantis will be destroyed. Please hurry, there's not much time."

"What are you writing?" I asked him.

"I'm a historian," he replied. "I'm writing of Atlantis' destruction. The idea is that maybe one day, man will discover these records, near the end times, and rebuke his spirit of murder before Armageddon. But we haven't much faith in man, so we're leaving earth."

"But where will you go?"

"I don't know. But there must be another place like earth, somewhere—maybe we'll find it. Alpha and Omega warned us to never come to earth, but lust overcame our sense of duty. The earth was intended for humans—this is not our home.

"Now hurry," he urged me, "for the time of destruction is near. Atlantis won't be destroyed until you've left it."

I walked into the club and saw Chino, the man who was my taxi driver. He was sitting at the bar. When he saw me come in, he got up and came to where I was standing.

"You couldn't find her? She's probably already gone."

"Who?" I asked him.

"Who? What's wrong with you? Oh, I keep forgetting, your memory is bad—Jami, you went to look for her. Come on, the last I heard the rebel forces are only twenty miles from the city. I've got a boat waiting for us."

Chino and I walked out the door. The Menon man was still sitting on the bench, writing. I looked at him and started to ask a question, but he said, "It's okay, go with him; don't worry, you'll find her."

The scene (in my vision) quickly changed: Chino and I were in the boat and had traveled halfway in the water to the mainland. For some reason, even though I was in another time realm, I seemed to think that we were nearing what was the coast of Mexico, in the present era. From the boat, I could look on the shore and see a large complex of tall pyramids near what I assumed was the Mexican coast.

On the island of Atlantis, on the distant mountain tops, I saw tall, glass pyramid structures, with their tips pointed toward the rebel stronghold in the Cusancho mountains. I figured these were the death ray machines that Dr. Cayce had seen in his visions of Atlantis.

The scene changed again: Chino and I had reached shore and stood at the top of a tall pyramid, on the mainland, as the sun went down. I saw rebel planes in the air; they were trying to attack the death ray machines, but they were being shot down. Suddenly, a brilliant red beam of light flashed out of a death ray machine.

The red cone of light struck a distant mountain top of Cusancho and blew the top of the mountain completely off; the mouth of the sheared off mountain then exploded into a volcanic mushroom of dark gray smoke and flying bits of rock and ash. Other surrounding mountains now exploded in the same fashion.

Chino and I watched in amazement as devastating earthquakes shook Atlantis. In less than an hour, it was over, Atlantis sank into the sea.

The scene changed again (in my vision of Atlantis). Chino and I stood at the base of a tall stone pyramid, amongst a vast crowd of people, who had escaped the final destruction of Atlantis. On top of the flat-topped pyramid, stood a shiny metallic air ship, shaped like a stingray.

At the bottom of the pyramid, there was a procession of the Menon people, walking through a cleared pathway, amongst the crowd of all races. The Menon people, dressed in colored silk robes were walking up the pyramid steps and entering the airship. These air ships were everywhere, scattered across a great flat valley, filled with pyramids.

I knew the humans had come to say goodbye. There was a band of Menons, at the pyramid's base, playing music. In front of the band, a black man in a tuxedo was singing a beautiful song. Then, in the crowd, I spotted Lothar, the man who had been my assistant in the sculpting shop. He was carrying a small black and white dog in his arms.

"Lothar!" I said, and, seeing me, he handed the dog to someone else and he hugged my neck. Then he took the dog back and he handed him to me. He said:

"Rozano, will you take care of Juvy for me? I don't know where we'll end up."

"But Lothar, he's your baby—he'll be lost without you."

"I know," he replied, "but the earth is his home. He may not be able to adapt elsewhere."

"No, you're wrong—his home is wherever you are."

"Please take him Rozano, I don't want to see him die," Lothar insisted.

"Okay, if that's the way you want it. Will you ever come back?"

"I don't know—maybe we can visit one day."

"I'm sorry for what we did to you," I told him.

"No, don't blame yourself, it's our fault. Maybe one day, when the Prince of Peace comes, and there's peace, we'll have knowledge of our earthly mother, and we can come back and visit our half-brothers and sisters here on earth."

"Good bye Lothar," I said. We shook hands and Lothar turned and began walking up the steps of the pyramid. When he reached the top, before he entered the air ship's door, he turned and waved. His dog Juvy began strongly squirming in my hands, and he broke free of my grip.

He landed on the ground and took off like a rabbit, running up the steps toward Lothar. Lothar saw him, and stopped and he waited for him. When the little dog reached him, Lothar reached down, picked him up and he hugged him tightly to his face. Then, Lothar looked down at us and he smiled and shrugged his shoulders. He took the dog's paw and he waved goodbye to us with it, then he turned and entered the air ship.

Then the scene (in my vision) quickly changed to a sunny day. Chino and I sat inside an outdoor, open-air restaurant, made of bamboo with a thatched roof, overlooking the ocean. We sipped a fruit drink and listened to music as we watched the ocean waves falling on the white sand.

I spotted a petite girl, with long black hair, walking down the beach. She was barefoot, and dressed in a brightly colored dress.

"Chino, look!" I said, pointing, "there's Jami!" (Agnes).

"It sure is," he said.

I sat there frozen, unable to move, as we watched her walking down the beach.

"You better go catch her before she gets too far," Chino said.

"But what if she won't talk to me?"

"Well, you'll never know by sitting here."

"Yeah, I guess you're right. I'll finish this drink and go."

"No, you'll go now. Go on and face her and get it over with."

"You're right, I'll go now," I said, and I got up and walked quickly towards the beach.

I was out of breath when I caught up to her, and walked alongside her. She was startled at my approach as she turned and looked at me.

"Mind if I join you?" I asked her. But she didn't reply. She looked coldly at me and kept walking. I started apologizing and she suddenly stopped and said:

"Do you have any idea how I felt? Looking at my wedding dress one night, thinking of how happy I was? And then, hearing the next day, that you, right before our wedding, are heading up into the mountains, with your lover. Do you understand what that did to me?"

"Jami, I can't take back the past and what I did. If you'll only forgive me—"

"I can't Rozano. It's too late for us. You need to start over with someone else."

"I understand. But I feel better now, being able to face you and confess—it's as hard to do as to forgive. I'm sorry I bothered you. But if you ever think of me in the future, try and remember the good times we had. Goodbye Jami," I said, and I walked away.

But I hadn't gone far when she called out to me: "Rozano, wait," she said. I walked back up to her.

"You don't have to give up so quickly," she said. "You could walk along with me, and let me think about it."

"Do you remember," I asked her, "after my accident, when I was looking down at you from the Hotel Sula? You were in the park, listening to the music. And you went to get in the taxi and you looked up and saw me looking at you. What made you look up at me?"

"You don't remember now, but we used to meet and dance in the park, but you were always late. So, I'd wait by the sidewalk and you'd raise the window, and call out and say you were on your way down."

"Were you surprised to see me in the window that night?"

"Yes. I told myself I wouldn't look up there—too many memories, but I couldn't help but look. I wanted to hate you, but I couldn't."

I stopped walking and said, "I promise you, I'll never hurt you again." She looked at me now, her coldness had melted. I kissed her and she put her arms around me and kissed me. And so ended my vision. My spirit returned to my present bodily condition in Miami, at

Jackson Memorial Hospital.

We talked briefly, Herman said, about Ed's spiritual trip. We both wondered if Ed's unconscious mind had taken over during the coma, and given him what he had waited for so long in the conscious realm.

But we didn't get to talk for long, Herman said, Ed was exhausted after dictating the story to me. Ed asked me to hand him the cigar box of photos on the night table, and I did.

Ed picked through the photos until he came to the one of Agnes, she was dressed in a red dress with red high heels. Ed laid his head back on the pillow and studied the photo for a minute. Then he smiled weakly, and laid his hands on the bed. His hands were so weak he couldn't hold the photograph of Agnes, and it slipped from his hand to the floor.

As it slipped, he mumbled, "I always wanted a girl, but I never had one."

I picked up the photograph off the floor, Herman said, and I put it back in the cigar box. I looked and Ed had his eyes closed. I spoke to Ed, and he said he was okay, he just needed to sleep some. I told him I was going to get a cup of coffee, and he said, "Okay, I'll see you in awhile."

I left the room and went over to the restaurant across the street, to get away from the hospital smells.

When I came back to the hospital at five o'clock, the nurse said Ed fell back into a coma thirty minutes earlier. I sat in the chair at his bedside, occasionally reading, as I kept an eye on him. I had a feeling he wasn't coming back; he didn't respond to anything I said, trying to bring him out of the coma.

At 11:45 P.M., on December 20, 1951, with his eyes closed, Ed called out softly, he said: "I'm going."

I leaned over, and put my mouth close to his ear. I said, "Ed, it's Herman; hold on, don't go!"

Ed, with his eyes closed, mumbled, "Watch—Bimini, I'm going, I'm going."

His eyes fluttered open, he was gone. Ed died fifteen minutes before midnight, December 20, 1951, on what would have been his anniversary with Agnes Scuffs. It was also the exact time that he had entered the earth, on March 26, 1887, in Latvia. He was 64 years old.

Carl Swisher, the reporter for the Homestead Enterprise, asked Herman: "What do you think Ed meant by, 'Watch Bimini?'"

"Well, Carl, I didn't know for a lot of years," Herman said, looking through his worn leather travel bag. He pulled out a 3 X 6, faded yellow newspaper clipping, and handed it to Carl. Carl took it and began reading it. The headline read:

Pyramid claimed found in ocean

BIMINI (AP): One archaeologist insists an underwater pyramid lurking off the Bimini coast, somewhere between Bimini and the Florida coast, may be the most significant discovery since Tut's tomb in 1922. Another politely calls the idea unbelievable. The first archaeologist works for a Vero Beach treasure hunter claiming the pyramid find. The second archaeologist works for the state.

Thomas Chisholm, an Orlando Florida man, who is Underwater Salvage's archaeological consultant, said: "This discovery represents the 20th century's greatest treasure, because it demonstrates a pyramid culture predating the Near East and the New World."

Culvin Jones, the state's archaeologist, said: "It doesn't sound real to me. The idea of a mound made of rocks under more than 100 feet of water—the chances are about one in a million."

Alfred Conway, owner of Underwater Salvage, claims he and another pilot, flying over an area, whose location he refused to give, saw a stair-stepped pyramid, at least 30 feet tall, with a base of about 80 feet long, on each of it's four sides.

Conway refused to even give a good hint about the exact location of the pyramid, saying only that: "It's in an area of about 100 feet of water." Conway added: "It's hard for me to believe it's out there too, but I saw it with my own eyes."

Conway noticed something odd on the sea bottom in 1980, when he was taking a depth reading on a cruise in the Bimini area. He got readouts showing an intriguing, stair-step structure, but it wasn't metallic, and didn't seem to have any salvage value.

Conway has tried twice in the last two years to drop buoys on the spot since spotting the pyramid from a plane. Once, in 1985, the buoy mysteriously disappeared the next day. Last summer, the buoy line got tangled in the plane's stabilizer.

"It's like something out there doesn't want us to find it," Conway said, smiling. "Maybe it's because it's in the Bermuda Triangle. But I don't care—I'll keep looking until I find it."

Archaeology consultant Thomas Chisholm said: "The pyramid would've had to have been built between 10,000 and 6,000 B.C., when the continental shelf was not covered by water."

"Herman," Carl Swisher asked, "do you think that's what Ed was talking about—the existence of a pyramid near Bimini?"

"I'll never know for sure, Carl, but that's the closest thing yet that I've seen relating to Bimini. And the interesting thing is the time frame of 10,000 B.C., that's the same time when Edgar Cayce said Atlantis existed. That area would've been dry land then."

Herman looked at his watch: "Whew, it's almost five o'clock, I reckon I better be getting home."

"Oh, wait, Herman," Carl said, "you said to remind you about the strange configuration of stones Ed put over his 30 ton stone."

"Oh, I'm sorry son, I forgot—it's hell to get old I tell you." Herman picked up his leather travel bag and they walked over to the heavy stone.

Herman reached into the leather bag and he pulled out an old worn looking book on The Great Pyramid. "Ed had told me he wasn't going to tell me about this configuration of stones," Herman said, "but he said he would give me a hint, like the Menon man had given him, about the secret of The Great Pyramid being in the King's Chamber of the Pyramid."

Ed said: "Herman, the secret of these "crowning" stones here, also lies in The King's Chamber."

"Well, I didn't think too much about it as the years went by, but one night, I got to studying a picture of the King's Chamber; and I saw something so plain, if it'd been a snake, it'd of bit me."

Herman opened the book to a book marker, to a picture of the King's Chamber in the pyramid, and said: "Now look at this picture of the Chamber Carl—do you see anything familiar in there?"

Carl studied the picture a minute, then shook his head. Herman reached over and put his forefinger on a section of wall, located high up in the northern wall of the gabled roof. Herman said:

"Look at that configuration of three stones." Carl looked and saw that it was identical to the three stones Ed had placed on top of the thirty ton stone.

"I'll be darn," Carl said. "But what does it mean? Why did he put it there?"

"I'll never know for sure," Herman said, "but I think the message Ed was trying to leave behind with these stones, was that he understood the secret of The Great Pyramid."

"Did Ed ever say anything to you about how he cut and moved the heavy stones here?"

"No, but he did give me a hint. Let's go over to the moon fountain and I'll show you." Herman picked up his leather bag and they went over to Ed's fountain, flanked by the curving moon quarters, where everybody liked to have their photo taken.

Herman reached into his leather bag and he pulled out the magnets that Ed used to play with. One of the magnets was the small doughnut shaped one, about the size of a quarter, with a hole in the middle; and the other one was cut in half and about the size of a grapefruit split in half.

"About a month before he died," Herman said, "I had lunch with Ed here in the castle one Sunday. After lunch, Ed took me over here to the moon fountain and he pulled out these two magnets. I think Ed knew he was going to die soon and he wanted to tell me some things because he trusted me."

Ed reminded me of what Edgar Cayce had said about how The Great Pyramid was built. Dr. Cayce said: "By manipulation of the cosmic forces of nature, that allow for iron to swim in water, stone also floats in the air."

"Now think about it Herman," Ed said, "what force of nature was Cayce talking about? The only force I know of, is the one I've always said controls everything—magnets; that is what gravity is.

"Now look at this," Ed said. He took the two magnets out, and he put the small one in the fountain of water in the moon fountain. Then, he took the bigger, half grapefruit-sized magnet, in his hand. He held it over the water where the small magnet was. He kept lowering the bigger magnet down, until it's more powerful magnetic force drew up the smaller magnet.

The smaller magnet came flying up out of the water and slammed up against the side of the bigger magnet. Then, Ed removed the smaller magnet from the big one. He reached down to the ground and he picked up a small pebble and put it over the hole of the smaller magnet.

"Now," Ed told me, "let's suppose we want to move an object from one place to another—in space time, a stone for example, we could do it like this."

Ed put the small magnet, with the pebble in it's hole, in the moon fountain. Then, he took the big magnet and held it over the water where the small magnet was, until the magnetic force drew it up out of the water, bringing the magnet and the pebble with it.

"Now of course this is a small stone," Ed said, "so to move the big ones, you need a more powerful magnetic force. This force exists in the earth if you know where to find it."

Then, Herman said, Ed explained the earth's "harmonic grid." Ed said this harmonic grid exists in certain spots all over the world. It produces "etheric energy" from the pull of the earth's north and south pole magnets.

David Zink, Herman said, came out with a book in 1978 named "The Stones of Atlantis." In his book, he talked about this etheric energy. He said: "The earth is seen as a crystalline structure reflected up through power points. These power points cover the earth and have significant intersections in:

"The Bermuda Triangle (including Bimini), at Giza, where The Great Pyramid sits, and in Peru. These and other intersection areas, serve as energy accumulators or switching stations in a world wide power grid."

"It seems," Herman said, "that water acts as a storage battery for this magnetic energy. That's why Ed used his witching rod and looked for water on the land in Florida City, where he first built Coral Castle."

"Why did he move the castle from Florida City?" Carl Swisher asked.

"Ed told me that he didn't completely understand how this energy grid worked. But he said when he was moving the last stones of the castle in Florida City, he noticed that the magnetic force of this harmonic grid seemed to be fading. From this, Ed thought that perhaps, for some unexplained reason, after a long time of existence, this magnetic force or "harmonic grid" could weaken and disappear.

"So Ed went over to Homestead and found a place, on Key West Highway, where the castle is now, where the etheric energy, "harmonic grid" was much stronger. Ed bought the land and then he moved the castle to Homestead. Let's go sit down at the Florida table,

I want to show you something."

When they got to the Florida table and sat down, Herman dug around in his travel bag until he found some paper work and he handed it to Carl Swisher.

"I'd forgotten about this," Herman said, "it's a summary of a book written about Coral Castle by Ray Stoner."

The paper read: Only recently has the mathematical truths of sites like The Great Pyramid, Stonehenge, and now Coral Castle been understood. How then was Coral Castle built, using all this forgotten knowledge, when this mathematical information was not published until 14 years after Ed's death? There are three possibilities:

1) This knowledge has not been completely lost.
2) Ed was a time traveler or an interdimentional being.
3) Ed was an extra-terrestrial.

Ed's story of building the castle for his "Sweet Sixteen" love is okay, but Ed forgets to tell the other story of Coral Castle:

Why did he design it to be a polaris, star-aligned astronomical observatory, out of 1100 tons of coral; completely furnished with a sundial, twenty-five one-ton rocking chairs, and a 9 ton swinging gate in the middle of the Florida Everglades?

It makes you wonder if he had some other reason for all these chairs and room layouts. Was Coral Castle also designed as a future conference site?

Maybe Ed simply told people what they wanted to hear. They may not have believed the truth. While the spurned lover (Agnes) is the "story," some of Ed's visitors have doubted that he revealed the whole truth. Noted researcher Fred Graham said:

"B.J. Cathie, author of "Harmonic 695, the UFO and Anti-Gravity" gives a different story of Coral Castle that Ed might smile and agree with if he were alive today.

"Cathie's well researched theory, is that a vast power grid that governs a whole array of extra-ordinary, and unrelated world phenomena, has been set up between some groups on this planet and the UFO's.

"Cathie explains the existence, on our globe, of a worldly power grid, the interlocking lines of which correspond to the lines of flight of verified UFO appearances.

"Cathie stated: 'All major changes of the physical state, anywhere in the world, are caused by the harmonic interactions of what we refer to as: gravity, light, mass, electrical and magnetic forces. The controlled manipulation of these resonant forces would, in hypothesis, make it possible to move mass from one point to another in space time—instantaneously.'

"The final check," Cathie said, "of the distance between Coral Castle and the grid pole in the north, dispel any doubt about the site (Coral Castle) being in an ideal position to allow Ed to have erected the huge blocks of coral with relative ease.

"Due to it's location, Coral Castle possesses the geometric harmonics, necessary for the manipulation of the anti-gravity forces."

"It seems," Fred Graham concluded, "that Ed knew exactly what he was doing when he carefully selected the two sites (Florida City and Homestead) where he built his famed Coral Castle."

"Isn't that something?" Carl Swisher said, handing the paper back to Herman. "What do you think ever happened to Agnes Scuffs?"

"I can tell you," Herman said, digging through his leather bag again. He found a letter, turned yellow with age, and he handed it to Carl.

"I found this letter in a box, with my name on it, that Ed left behind in his room. The original was written in Latvian. I sent it off to the University of Florida and had it translated. It was written in 1935. This was the letter that Ed got when we were sitting on the porch of my shop; he got upset and left when he read it. It's from his bartender friend Bruno.

"In the letter, Bruno told Ed that Agnes' cousin Eldar, the boy who was a jockey and got kicked in the head by a horse, came by Bruno's bar one night and he'd been drinking. Bruno kept feeding him drinks and he got Eldar to tell him what had happened with Agnes. Eldar had taken a vow not to tell, but Bruno said that liquor had loosened his tongue.

"Bruno said that what happened on the night before Ed's wedding in Latvia, was that Agnes had run off to Ireland with the boy she'd been in love with before Ed. It seems that Agnes had written the boy a few weeks before she was marrying Ed, and she told this boy she was marrying Ed.

"I guess this boy suddenly decided he wanted Agnes, and he came over from Ireland, and surprised her on the night before her wedding to Ed. That's why she called Ed that night, and broke off the wedding—she was confused; she knew she still loved this boy, she'd never really gotten over him. She met him on a summer trip to Ireland with her father. Her father was over there to train a race horse and he took Agnes with him.

"The boy broke up with her before she went back to Latvia with her father at the end of the summer. She tried to forget him, but she couldn't, Eldar had told Bruno.

"Agnes was ashamed of hurting Ed, and she didn't want him to find out that she left him for another man." Eldar said: "So she made me take a vow not to tell. But I reckon it's been long enough not to matter now. Besides, I don't think Ed is ever coming back to Latvia."

"That's incredible," Carl said. "So Ed knew, in 1935, what had happened, and yet he kept saying he was waiting for Agnes to come over here and marry him. How do you figure that Herman?"

"I can't, that's just one of Ed's quirks I guess. I've

thought about it a lot and I think that Ed simply decided to ignore the reality of the situation—I mean, when you think of it, Ed was an expert at denial. I'm not criticizing him, you only have to look at what he's done here at Coral Castle to realize he was no ordinary man.

"But his love for Agnes was both his strength and his weakness. I think that he had lived with the invention of his story of waiting for her for so long, that it became his last link to the conscious realm. Take that away from him, and I don't think he'd have wanted to live.

"Knowing Ed, if you could question him now about this letter, he'd tell you that he was hoping she'd get a divorce one day and remember his love and come back to him. The ability to stay positive in a negative environment is what kept him going."

"Do you have any recent information on Agnes Scuffs?" Carl asked.

"In 1980," Herman said, "one of the staff members of Coral Castle started looking for information on Agnes, and somehow he got her phone number. She was widowed now, and back in Latvia. The staff member called her and told her he was calling her from Coral Castle.

"He started asking her some questions about Ed, and about whether she would consider coming to Florida as Coral Castle's guest. They were going to pay for everything; it would've been a great publicity stunt. Can you imagine the headlines? 'Agnes arrives at Coral Castle—68 years after jilting Ed.'

"But in the middle of the conversation, Agnes got irritated. She told the castle staffer, 'I didn't want to see the castle when he built it, and I have no intention of coming over there to see it now—I never loved him' she said, and she hung up."

"I don't think it was true that she never loved him," Herman said. "I think it was like her cousin Eldar had told Bruno, I think she was embarrassed by it. I mean, think about it, she had no idea that Ed was going to build this incredible monument to her—look, there are people from all over Europe who come over here to see Coral Castle.

"You see, Coral Castle is actually better known in Europe than it is here because Ed was European—I mean they can point to the glory of Coral Castle and say, 'Hey, that guy is one of us, he's from Latvia.' Now you ask somebody from Florida where Coral Castle is, and they'll look puzzled, and say 'I don't know, Disney World?' It's sad I tell you.

"But anyway, you see, I think when the man from Coral Castle called Agnes, it put her on the spot, you see. I mean, if she came over here, she'd have to explain about jilting Ed the night before the wedding. And you've got to remember, in defense of Agnes, she was a kid—"Sweet Sixteen" as Ed called her. But people tend to forget that, and they only remember what she did.

"I think what had happened was that Agnes was on the rebound from this Irish boy when she met Ed. I think Agnes loved Ed, but it was a weaker love than she had for the Irish boy.

"I think Agnes hoped, that by writing the Irish boy, and telling him of her marriage to Ed, she gambled that she could shock him, and shake out any love that he might still have for her, and her gamble paid off."

"That makes sense," Carl said. "Herman, what about the altar with the alien face embedded in it?"

"Oh yeah, let's go over and take a look at it," Herman said, and they walked over to the altar, located near Ed's tool room.

Herman said, "Ed found this natural chunk of coral here when he was building the second Coral Castle, here in Homestead. He liked the formation of it, he told me later, because it's sort of shaped like a mountain. Ed got the idea to make this a shrine to Atlantis and Agnes."

Herman pointed to the top of the altar, where there was a row of four small, cone shaped pieces of coral, and explained that these cones were shaped by Ed, to resemble the smaller mountains in Atlantis. Below these cones, Ed shaped a volcanic mountain, with smooth, steep sides, to represent the eruptions that caused the earthquakes, and, as Edgar Cayce had said, brought on Atlantis' final destruction.

"Now you notice," Herman explained, "all these large conch shells, and the smaller ones embedded in the altar. Ed put these in the altar in remembrance of Agnes' love for sea shells."

Then, Herman kneeled down on one knee, near where the alien's face was, at the altar's bottom, surrounded by large conch shells.

"Ed told me that he put this alien face here, in honor of his Grandfather Nick's belief that these 'men from the sky,' as the Mayans had called them, had given the world the science required for pyramid building.

"You see Carl, Ed believed that the Menons had known Atlantis was going to be destroyed—remember, Cayce had said that many would be forewarned, and flee Atlantis before it's destruction? And the best way to leave behind information, is to leave it in stone. Ed believed The Great Pyramid was built in pre-Egyptian times.

"Ed believed that the Menons created it for someone, one day, to uncover their secret science. I think that's what Ed's life was about—he rediscovered the science and showed it to us in Coral Castle."

"Oh, that reminds me," Carl said, "I understand about the magnetic force or "harmonic grid" underground here, that Ed possibly used to levitate the huge blocks of coral with, but how did he cut them so perfectly smooth?"

"I can't be sure about this, but if you remember, in one of Cayce's readings for a person who had a previous life in Atlantis, Cayce told him that he 'had invented a machine for the cutting of stone.' Not long ago, I saw where someone had invented a machine that used water to cut metal. The machine used a pump to put the water under great pressure, and it pushed the water out of a small nozzle.

"I think what Ed did was to build a similar machine to cut his stone with at Coral Castle. I mean, if water will cut metal, it'll cut stone. And using water to cut the stone would also explain the smoothness of the jagged coral. When he finished cutting the stone, I think he dismantled the machine so no one would find it. He probably got the parts for the machine at Kilgore's junkyard.

"Oh, there's one other thing about the 9 ton swinging gate that might interest you," Herman said, and they walked over to it.

"Not long after Ed died," Herman said, "the swinging gate quit swinging. After all those years, the weight of the stone, sitting on the wheel bearings of that 1920 Ford truck wheel finally crushed them. The castle staff didn't know what to do about it. Somebody suggested they call the University of Florida engineering department, so they did.

"They explained the problem, and asked them if they could come down and fix it. The department head said, 'Sure, no problem. I'll send a team of our best professors down there.'

"But see, they didn't know what they were getting into. They came down here, and got to studying that 9 ton gate, and it made them scratch their heads.

"What baffled them so much, was the 9 ton stone Ed used, is extremely uneven, and to make it balance on the Ford wheel, Ed had to find the center of gravity so he could bore the hole to put the connecting rod to the wheel at the bottom. If he was off a frog hair when he drilled that hole down the center, the stone wouldn't balance.

"The engineers said the hole that Ed drilled to insert the rod was done with such precision, that today, to duplicate what Ed did, would require the use of a laser beam.

"They spent about six weeks down here, probing and measuring; they even brought a machine and X-rayed the stone. They couldn't fix it and they got disgusted and left. It embarrassed them that they couldn't figure it out.

"I was over here one day when they were working on it, and I heard one of the frustrated professors say: 'Oh, what does it matter? This is just a pile of rocks—the answer to this is so simple we just haven't found it yet.'

"Oh, it made me mad when he said that," Herman said. "See, it was tearing their ego up, that here some little Latvian guy, with a fourth grade education, had built something that they couldn't even begin to understand.

"I told that professor, 'Well, if you look at it like that, I guess Stonehenge is just a pile of rocks too—sure makes you wonder how they piled them up though, doesn't it?'"

"What did he say?" Carl asked.

"He didn't say anything, he just gave me a dirty look and walked off—he was not a happy man."

"What happened to the Castle after Ed died?"

"Ed only had one relative here, a nephew, he lived in Michigan and Ed left it to him. But his nephew was in bad health, and right before he died in 1953, he sold it to a family from Chicago."

"Where did they bury Ed?"

"They buried him in Miami. Ed wanted to be buried here, on the grounds of Coral Castle. I had promised him I'd take care of it, but it was a mess. I was trying to get a permit from the city of Homestead to bury him here, and Ed's body was in Miami and they kept hollering for me to do something, so I had to bury him in Miami.

"It's a shame too, Ed had already built his tombstone out back there," Herman said, pointing to the backyard. "You want to see it?"

"Sure," Carl said, and they walked through the 9 ton swinging gate and into the backyard. The tomb was located at the end of the property, at the edge of a wooded area.

The tombstone Ed had carved for himself was shaped in the form of a huge heart, identical to the Valentine table he had created for Agnes. In the center of the heart-shaped tombstone, Ed had put a smaller heart, made of concrete. He wrote in the concrete:

"Still waiting for Agnes. Ed L."

Carl Swisher read it and said, "Amazing. He was totally obsessed with her wasn't he?"

"Oh yeah, that was his style," Herman Harmless said. "When he got on something, he never got off—he rode it hard and put it up wet."

"Herman, when Ed was in that coma, he said he was back in Atlantis with Agnes. You think it's possible when we die, it could be like that?—do you think he was going to Atlantis when he said, 'I'm going?'"

"I don't know Carl; like Ed and I always said, that is beyond the grave stuff, but if anybody could will himself there, to find her, Ed's there now. Well, I'm usually at the Myna Bird for breakfast every morning, around eight o'clock, come by some time and I'll buy you breakfast."

"Thanks Herman. Ed was something else wasn't he? He did all this out of love for one girl."

"Oh, yeah, and he's the only man in history to find the secret science of The Great Pyramid and he's been virtually forgotten. People know about Stonehenge, but not Coral Castle. And think about this, as high as oil prices are, why doesn't an engineering company come down here and copy Ed's energy machine?"

"I know," Carl answered. "Here it is, still sitting in his tool room, collecting dust."

"You gonna go home now and write an article on the castle for the paper?" Herman asked.

"I don't know Herman; I was just thinking, with all this material, I should write a book."

"I wish you would for Ed's sake. I'd like to see it before I die; you know, at one time, there was talk of making Ed's Coral Castle the eighth wonder of the world, but I never heard any more about it.

"Carl, I hope you do write a book; I never figured out why somebody hasn't done it. Maybe you're the man, maybe it's been waiting for you. And just think, if it hadn't been for Andrew, we'd have probably never met. Hey, Carl, you aren't Ed, in a different body are you? You came back to check up on me?"

"I don't think so Herman. But I was just thinking about it; I was born in November of 1951. Ed was going out and I was coming in."

"I'll be dogged. Good luck on the book son. Hurry up with it, I'm getting old. Call me if you need me. Well, I'll see ya' at the Myna Bird."

Final Notes

When Ed died, he carried his secret knowledge of the lost science of moving heavy stones to the grave. Many people have asked me: "Why didn't Ed tell someone how he cut and moved the stones at Coral Castle before he died?" I think Ed answered this question in the last paragraph of his little book "A book in every home."

Ed said: "People are individuals. For instance, if you want an excitement, you will have to test the thrill yourself, or if you have a pain, you will have to bear it yourself; if you want to eat, you will have to eat for yourself.

"Nobody can eat for you and so it is that if you want the things to eat you will have to produce them yourself; if you are too weak, too lazy, lack machinery and good management to produce them, you should perish and that is all there is to it."

Apparently, Ed didn't believe in giving anything away. When a person once asked Ed why he wouldn't reveal the lost science, Ed said, "If you want to know how I did what I did, then you should go to the library and read the same books I read; if you want to know what I know, then, you must be willing to work at it like I did. Knowledge in the hands of irresponsible people who want answers without working is dangerous."

I think Ed enjoyed having the power of knowing something mysterious that fascinated people. If he'd told how he did it, he would've lost his power. And after Ed lost Agnes, he needed to have the feeling of power over something. Ed enjoyed taking people through Coral Castle and telling them his lost love story.

Ed made the uncomfortable "mother-in-law" chair, for a mother-in-law he never had; he made the furniture for Agnes and the children he never had. Ed had a wonderful imagination and I think that by talking about these things as if he had them, helped him deal with not having them.

Ed could've given up when the doctor gave him six months to live, but his desire to finish the castle for Agnes made him go to the library and check out books on cancer and tuberculosis. Ed died without a trace of it in his body. Ed is the only known person in history, in his time, to have survived tuberculosis in it's terminal stage when it was discovered.

For more information on Coral Castle, you may reach them at:

CORAL CASTLE
28655 South Federal Highway
Homestead, Fl. 33030
Ph. 305-248-6344

I'll be happy to hear your comments or answer any questions you might have. Thank you for taking this trip with me through Ed's life.

Joe Bullard Jr.
Rt.10 Box 862
Lake City, Fl. 32025
Ph. 904-752-1059